THE
GIRL
& THE
SWORD

GERALD WEAVER

Gerald Weaver is the author of *Gospel Prism* and *The First First Gentleman*. He has a bachelor's degree from Yale University and a Juris Doctor from Catholic University. He has been a Capitol Hill chief of staff, a campaign manager, a lobbyist, a stay-at-home dad, a teacher of English and Latin, and a collector and seller of Chinese antiquities. He has contributed to *The Sunday Times*, the *Guardian*, and *The Times*, as well as many other publications, and has been interviewed on British and American radio and television. He holds dual citizenship in Italy and the United States, and lives in the suburbs of Washington, DC, with his wife, Lily Chu.

Also by Gerald Weaver

Gospel Prism
The First First Gentleman

THE
GIRL
& THE
SWORD

GERALD WEAVER

First published in 2023 by whitefox

Copyright © Gerald Weaver, 2023

www.wearewhitefox.com

ISBN 978-1-915036-88-9
Also available as an ebook
ISBN 978-1-915036-89-6

Designed and typeset by Typo•glyphix
Cover design by Dominic Forbes
Project management by whitefox
Printed and bound by 4edge Ltd

For my mother,
Angelina Blandino Weaver

HISTORICALLY, women have been fording a stream in a gale. They have struggled against the current of male control over the means to change history, while also being buffeted by the gusts of history as written by men. Occasionally, women have overcome the current, to command important events. But then they and their deeds have mostly been concealed by the squall of a history women did not write. The weave of any fiction that seeks to address these injustices contains the warp and woof of fact and truth. How many momentous historical accounts by and of a woman have we lost?

This is her story.

Cast of Characters

Pauline de Pamiers, a Cathar Christian girl of Occitania

Simon de Montfort, a knight of northern France, later 6th Earl of Leicester

Gauseran de Saint-Leidier, a troubadour of Occitania

Rocco Tzu, the troubadour's exotic companion

Guy Alain, a priest

Amaury, le Comte de Montfort, elder brother of Simon, leader of crusade against the Cathars

Esclarmonde de Foix, deceased Perfect of the Cathars

Simon de Montfort the Elder, deceased leader of the crusade against the Cathars, 5th Earl of Leicester

Louis IX, King of France

Blanche of Castile, Queen Regent of France, mother of Louis

Henry III, King of England

John, late King of England, Henry's father

Isabella of Angoulême, John's wife, Queen Dowager of England, mother of Henry III

Rachel, a girl of Leicester

Ranulf de Blondeville, 6th Earl of Chester

Robert Grosseteste, Bishop of Lincoln

Adam Marsh, a priest who serves the Bishop of Lincoln

William Marshal, late 1st Earl of Pembroke, Regent of England during King Henry's youth

Hubert de Burgh, 1st Earl of Kent, Regent of England during King Henry's youth

Eleanor of Provence, Henry's wife, Queen of England

Cardinal Sinibaldo Fieschi, papal legate

Eleanor of Pembroke, widow of William Marshal, sister of King Henry, wife of Simon de Montfort

Richard, 1st Earl of Cornwall, King Henry's brother, later King of Germany

Hugh de Lusignan, Comte de la Marche, second husband of Isabella of Angoulême

Emily, a widow of Leicester

Richard de Havering, steward of Leicestershire

William de Valence (Guillaume de Lusignan), King Henry's half-brother

Roger Bigod, 4th Earl of Norfolk

William Longespée, son of the Countess of Salisbury, illegitimate half-brother of King John

Richard de Clare, 6th Earl of Gloucester

Gilbert de Clare, 7th Earl of Gloucester, son of Richard

Prince Edward, elder son of Henry III

Alphonse, King Louis' brother

Roger Bacon, scholar and priest in service of the Bishop of Lincoln

Henry de Montfort, eldest son of Simon

Simon de Montfort the Younger, son of Simon

Guy de Montfort, son of Simon

Amaury de Montfort, a priest and son of Simon

Roger de Mortimer, marcher lord of Welsh borderlands

Roger de Leybourne, marcher lord of Welsh borderlands

Llewellyn of Griffith, Welsh chieftain

King Henry III of England

(Parents: King John of England 1167–1216 and
Isabella of Angoulême 1187–1246)

Married:
January 14 1236, Canterbury Cathedral, Kent, to Eleanor of
Provence 1223–1291 (Parents: Count Ramon Berenguer IV of
Provence 1195–1245 and Beatrice of Savoy 1200–1266)

Children:
King Edward I of England 1239–1307
Princess Margaret of England 1240–1275
Princess Beatrice of England 1242–1277 married to
Duke Jean II of Brittany 1239–1305
Edmund Crouchback 1245–1296 married to
Aveline de Forz 1259–1274 and Blanche of Artois 1248–1300
Princess Katherine of England 1253–1257

Siblings:
Richard, 1st Earl of Cornwall, King of Germany 1209–1272
Princess Joan of England 1210–1238
Princess Isabella of England 1214–1241
Princess Eleanor of England 1215–1275 married to
Simon de Montfort 1208–1265

Half-siblings:
From Isabella of Angoulême 1187–1246 with Count Hugh X
Lusignan of Marche 1195–1249
Guy de Lusignan-Marche †1264
Count Hugh XI Lusignan of Marche 1220–1260
William de Valence 1230–1296 (Guillaume de Lusignan)

King Louis IX of France

(Parents: King Louis VIII of France 1187–1226 and
Princess Blanche of Castile 1188–1252)

Married:
Marguerite of Provence 1221–1295 (Parents: Count Ramon
Berenguer IV of Provence 1195–1245 and
Beatrice of Savoy 1200–1266)

Children:
Princess Blanche of France 1240–1243
Princess Isabelle of France 1241–1271
Prince Louis of France 1244–1260
King Philip III of France 1245–1285
married May 28 1262 to Princess Isabella of Aragon 1247–1271,
married August 21 1274 to Maria of Brabant 1256–1321
Princess Jean of France 1248–1248
Princess Jean Tristan of France 1250–1270
Prince Pierre of France 1251–1284
Princess Blanche of France 1253–1320 married to
Prince Fernando of Castile 1255–1275
Princess Marguerite of France 1254–1271
Prince Robert of France 1256–1317 married to
Beatrix of Bourbon 1257–1310
Princess Agnes of France 1260–1327 married to
Duke Robert II of Burgundy 1248–1306

LONDON

ENGLAND

DOVER

BRUGES

CALAIS

LILLE

English Channel

LE HAVRE

ROUEN

BEAUVAIS

REIMS

Seine

Normandy

PARIS

BREST

Brittany

CHARTRES

TROYES

RENNES

Maine

ORLÉANS

VANNES

Anjou

ANGERS

BLOIS

Loire

NANTES

TOURS

FRANCE

Saône

POITIERS

Poitou

VAREILLES

LIMOGES

LYONS

ANGOULÊME

Limousin

Rhône

PÉRIGUEUX

BORDEAUX

BERGERAC

Bay of Biscay

Auvergne

BAZAS

Occitania

AVIGNON

Garonne

SAINT-SEVER

MAILLANE

Gascony

TOULOUSE

LABÉCÈDE

BÉZIERS

CARCASSONNE

NARBONNE

Castile

Pyrenees

Navarre

SPAIN

Aragon

Ebro

N

0   kilometres   100

0   miles   100

*Mediterranean
Sea*

N

SCOTLAND

INVERNESS

STIRLING

EDINBURGH

North Sea

E
N
G
L
A
N
D

NEWCASTLE

Tyne

CARLISLE

LANCASTER

YORK

Irish Sea

I
R
E
L
A
N
D

LINCOLN

Trent

CHESTER

NOTTINGHAM

Norfolk

LEICESTER

W
A
L
E
S

Severn

WORCESTER

NORTHAMPTON

EVESHAM

Watling Street

GLOUCESTER

PEMBROKE

NEWPORT

ST. ALBANS

PICCOTTS END

Fosse Way

Thames

LONDON

BATH

Kent

SALISBURY

WINCHESTER

LEWES

DOVER

EXETER

Cornwall

English Channel

PROLOGUE

April 18, 1225

They did not see it coming and if they had it would not have made a difference. They heard the horses only when the men were already upon them.

A dozen girls and their teacher had traveled two hundred miles to the east from their school in Foix to shelter in a smaller school concealed in a forest. They had fled before the knight crusaders from the north, from France, who had made war against the towns, nobles, and people of their home region to the south. They had been born in the various towns of the Occitania but the school in Foix had been their home for most of their lives. Here in the Alpilles Forest, the girls were a good distance from the frightening heart of that conflict. They felt safe in the much smaller and more rustic school, hidden from the eyes of the local townspeople.

These several men on horses were knights but some half of the two dozen men with them were not part of any crusade. There was nothing about them that was that upright. Nor were they soldiers from the north. They were local men. A Catholic priest commanded

1

the entire group, these locals, and the knights and other soldiers on foot from France. He ordered the men to corral the girls in a clearing in the middle of the compound of huts. The girls stood in a small circle. They were aged from six to sixteen years and their teacher was a woman of twenty-five years. She was compact and dark and youthful, with short hair, and could easily be mistaken for one of her students.

"What right have you to accost us? We are free women, and we are on this land with the permission and protection of its lord," she said.

"Good," said the priest, "then you are free to kiss this cross and swear your allegiance to Christ."

He dismounted and held a wooden cross before him.

"We have Christ in our hearts and in our souls and there is no need for us to swear any oath or worship an icon."

The priest merely looked aside and one of the men struck her quickly on the shoulder with his sword. She gasped and clutched it with her other hand as blood seeped out through the cut linen of her smock and between her fingers.

"One more time," he said. "Do you recognize the Holy Christian Church of Rome?"

The teacher reached forward with her bloody hand and grabbed the cross. The priest yanked it away from her and stepped back. This time he nodded and two of the men seized the young woman by her arms and swiftly walked her off into the woods. She made no sound. The girls knew they would never see her again. They huddled more closely together and held on to one another. They had come from different towns just north of the Pyrenees mountains—Toulouse, Narbonne, Pamiers, Castres—and they reflected their region's diverse Mediterranean history. They had long since descended from Romans, Jews, Franks, Moors, and Catalonians and were united by their affection for one another and by their distinct Christian faith.

They were Cathars, the separate Christian sect that the Church in Rome was determined to exterminate. They were stricken now, without their teacher. One of the other girls stood forward.

It was Ermengarde, an older girl of a minor noble family. She was tall for a fifteen-year-old and of erect bearing. She was lighter in complexion than the other girls, with sandy blonde hair.

"That blood on your cross is the blood of your sins against God," she said. "And no amount of praying in your opulent churches will remove that stain from your souls."

The younger girls began to cry. Several of them shouted that they would kiss the cross. Several more fell to their knees and silently prayed. One of the older ones broke out of the group and tried to run away. She was quickly struck down by a sword. They all became quiet. They held each other tightly and they cried low, plangent sobs.

"I like this one," said the priest, pointing at the tall blonde. "I will question her more later. Bind her hands and gag her. Throw a sack over her head and send her ahead." He ordered one of the knights to carry her north on his horse. The rest of the men stood around the girls and pointed at them and made lurid comments. They laughed and sneered. The girls cowered.

The priest left them and he and some of his own soldiers searched the huts. They found some food, which they ate. They built a fire and warmed themselves. They watered their horses and prepared for their journey to return to their posts, ten miles to the north. The girls were hushed and had drawn even more closely together. The priest and a few of the men mounted their horses. The soldiers moved to stand beside the horses. The rest of the men, roughly a dozen, the local men, remained watching the girls. The priest spoke.

"My men and I will leave here now. You others have been paid and you have done what was asked of you. Now you may do what you would choose. These heretics are outside the law and the Church.

I only ask that you leave no trace of what was here. Set fire to all these huts."

He turned with the knights and the soldiers and left the girls and the brigands behind. The priest smiled. As they rode north, the sounds of men shouting and girls screaming receded behind them. The men were roughly rounding up the girls. They would later carry them off, to be raped and to meet their deaths somewhere far from this place.

BOOK ONE

ONE

It was the seventeenth of April in the year 1225, and Simon de Montfort was eighteen.

The girl was fifteen and she had approached the knight in the late evening while he was on his watch outside the town of Avignon. Because of her relatively young age and her attractiveness, the advance patrols had not stopped her. Simon was struck by her appearance. She was tall for a girl. She had a Mediterranean beauty, with deep-set, dark eyes, olive-toned skin, and black hair that shined in the moonlight. She spoke quite directly to him, and in French but with an accent that seemed Spanish but was really because her first language was that of the Occitania, also known as Languedoc. Her voice was dusky and a bit deep for a girl. He was surprised and only a bit put off by her approach. She had boldly begun to question him about his religion a few minutes earlier, and had not ceased speaking to him in her blunt manner on the topic of his faith, something he had always felt was beyond discussion.

He finally bid to stop her.

"Who are you?" he asked.

"I am one of the girls whose life you are going to save."

He had no idea why she had said such a thing to him, but its urgency touched him and made him wonder. He looked at her and felt his feelings soften. She noticed his eyes.

Pauline had a sudden flash of insight about this soldier, and it changed her mind about what she had been sent to do. He was a striking example of northern knighthood, but she was immediately aware of something about him that was deeper. Her instinct told her something more profound about the heart of this knight. And that changed what she thought she should do. She felt this young soldier had the spirit of a protector. It seemed like this was quite a major determination to reach in just a few minutes of observation and conversation. But she knew she felt that decision more deeply than she had felt anything before.

She had reluctantly agreed to come to Avignon on an errand to barter some sewn goods for bread and fruit for her group. Among her schoolmates, it had simply been her turn to make that customary trip. But she had left for town with a feeling of foreboding. She did not really have her heart in the matter of mere barter. It was troubled by a sense that the war she and her friends had fled was still not all that far behind them. Seeing what she discerned was the compassion of this young knight more than reminded her that she had always been far more worried than her friends about their safety. They had fled from town to town, eastward, away from the advance of the conflict. They had only escaped as far as the edge of the fighting, and she feared there was nowhere more they could go on their own. At this moment, she instinctively decided that this French knight might be their savior. She had not been able to act on her fears before, because no course of action had ever presented itself. One of the reasons she had not wanted to run this errand was that she felt she should stay with her friends to perhaps protect them. But her insight about this man suddenly made her feel relieved she had been the one to come to town because she felt he presented her for the first time with a way to act on her concerns. The plan to act on them fell into her mind immediately. She would seek his protection and she believed he would give it. And she felt it was now more necessary than it had seemed before.

Pauline had always relied on her instincts, and she was observant and kept her own counsel. These traits may have been in her blood, but her land and people had also known nothing but war since a few years before her birth. She had learned to think first and act second, to observe, and to trust herself rather than authority. The dangers that surrounded her had forced her passions into a deep and strong current. It was not normal for her to act precipitously on a mere feeling, but this knight had touched her at that same profound level as her passions. She applied her intellect to the matter of what she began to feel was in this man's heart.

Pauline had little understanding of the devout belief of the knight standing in front of her, a man of the Roman Church. She had always been the brightest, most inquisitive girl in her town and school. She read every book she could ever find. She played and ran with the boys. Her teachers had always taken a special interest in her. She had an inherent confidence in her intellect and in her instinct. This knight of the Roman faith was a new subject for her to study. But what she had seen in his eyes and in his heart added to her innate confidence. She felt she could talk to him and that he would really listen.

She had initially approached him moments earlier with a question along the lines of his faith. She wanted to immediately break down the barrier between them.

"Do you believe in Christ?" she had asked him.

Outside of the rote litany of a Church ritual, such a question had never been posed to the devout Simon. He never contemplated its sincerity or the reason that any lay person might ask it. He was stunned by her directness. It was impertinent, but she also struck him with her candor and intelligence. He almost had the sense that she was speaking to him from some future that they might share. He felt something oddly comfortable in what was so surprising about her. He was too charmed by her to simply reject the premise of her question. He responded that he did believe that Jesus Christ had died for our sins, as everyone believed.

"We believe in Jesus, too," she said.

There was plaintive warmth to her tone and an openness and intellect behind it. He knew instantly what he should have suspected when he had first seen her approaching, that this girl was one of the heretics, one of the Cathars. He knew little of their faith, only that it was a perversion of his own, the Roman Catholic faith of all his countrymen, of all of Europe. He could have ordered his men to seize the girl and to take her to one of the churches, taverns, or castles where her fellow heretics would be questioned by the Catholic clergy and be offered the opportunity to choose the one true faith and to save themselves. But something stopped him. Perhaps it was because he knew that the Cathars were often tortured into forced conversions in those places, and he could never subject this uniquely remarkable girl to any such thing. She had already riveted his attention and had begun to gain his affection.

Something about this tall, slender girl spoke to a deeper part of him, perhaps to his heart or to some sense he had that she was linked to his own destiny, something he simply would never be able to explain. He only knew that he wanted to talk to her, that he needed to get to know her better. And in that realization, he also understood that such a conversation and that journey of discovery would take a great deal of time, certainly more than he had this evening. The one thing of which he was certain in this unexpected and puzzling scene was simply that he liked this girl. She then commented on his attractiveness in a way that no one ever had.

"You are handsome," she said.

She said it as if it cast a shadow upon his character, as if it meant he might be thoughtless or shallow. It was one of the many things about her that was at once surprising and unique, both challenging and alluring, attractive in the same way that he found it irritating.

The girl knew she was not flattering him. His appearance had been the first thing she had noticed about him, the quality that had singled him out for her and made her pay special attention to him, to begin to watch for him, and observe him. He was tall and had a military bearing with strong straight features, a high and intelligent forehead, an aristocratic nose, a dramatic jawline, and deep-set brown eyes that carried a hint of hazel. The depth and sparkle of those eyes had been the second item that had struck her and that made him seem different, that had given her the idea she might be able to approach him at some point. The light that lay within those eyes was not bare ambition or blind faith or masculine rapacity. It was nothing less to her than the echo of thoughtfulness or an innate irony that might lead to compassion. She felt drawn to a certain masculine element of his person, one that surprised her, given his youth. There was something about him that was fatherly. He was the only one of the invaders who made her feel like she might be safe with him. He was as surprising to her as she was to him. She had never expected this depth of humanity in one of the region's armed intruders. On his part, he had simply never known anyone like her.

When she answered his question about her identity and told him that she was one of the girls whose life he was going to save, she added, "Because it is the Christian thing to do."

"You can know nothing about Christ because you live in darkness without the guidance of a priest and without knowledge of Latin," he challenged her. And now, it was as if he was overhearing himself for the first time, as if it were another's voice because he detected in his tone a hint of playfulness.

"Then you must know what you are talking about because you do have the guidance of a priest and know Latin?" she asked. If she had detected any of his irony, she ignored it and spoke seriously.

"That is certainly the case," he said to this enigmatic fifteen-year-old girl.

"Then you will know that Christ has said we must love our enemies, and that there is never a cause for violence and killing. And yet you kill."

She watched his eyes very closely. And in them she saw what she had hoped to see. There was a flicker of hesitation, a reflection of deeper thought, and perhaps a flash of shame.

"The Gospels are truly known by the Church and only the Church, and we faithful must do what is the will of God as it is conveyed to the Church. I am not competent to know the will of God." He recognized that he said this with less conviction than he had ever expressed this doctrine before.

"But you do believe that you are competent to make that initial decision, to surrender your soul and fate to the Church and its priests," she said, remembering the teachings of her own Cathar Christian faith. "If you are competent to make that most important spiritual decision, then you can surely make all other spiritual decisions and make them based on what you know of the teachings of Christ."

Simon had never had a girl or woman speak this way to him, nor had he ever heard any person say such things. His first instinct was wonder. His second was a curiosity that was colored with affection. There was something he admired about this impertinent girl. He knew at that moment that he would never send her off as another Cathar heretic. He wanted to keep her around a while longer, perhaps a lot longer. He was deeply and affectionately curious about her, about what she said and how she acted, about what made her different. Mostly, he was curious about the way she made him feel differently, made him seem different to himself.

He had been enrolled in this war since he was a child and as a family matter. His father had been the crusade's commander and his remarkably independent mother had joined his father on his campaigns. He had known little else other than the conduct of the war, until this moment when just a few pointed words and the shining presence of one singular girl would change him and cause him to reflect upon the dire consequences of his role and that of his family in this conflict, and to think for the first time in another manner. Before this, he had been gratified and even honored to be fighting in what was a holy war, initiated by the pope against enemies of the Church. He had not considered what worldly motivations really might have been behind the holy pronouncements. He and his family had also been serving the French crown, which was acting in response to and on behalf of the Pope. It was a crusade, the Albigensian Crusade, the only one ever conducted solely on European soil and against a Christian sect. There was also the promise of additional land and titles. Simon's family, the de Montforts, could be given the land and titles of some of the local lords who had sided with Barcelona and Aragon and who encouraged the heretical faith of the Cathars of the region. The new consideration of that prospect for gain stung him. Now, that all seemed a bit less than honorable.

Young Simon had also long had his own deeply personal motivation. He had been a young boy of eleven in the service of his father's troops when his father had been killed in that war, in 1218, in the Siege of Toulouse. From then he served his elder brother, Amaury, who had taken over his father's command. His mother, the formidable Alix de Montmorency, stayed on with the campaign after the death of her husband. He had known nothing else, nothing more than this fighting, until this moment of being boldly confronted by this earnest, direct, and intelligent girl. And it was a moment unlike any other in his life, one that he began to feel would change his life forever.

"You are a curious girl," he told her. "You speak directly as a man might speak, and as an educated one at that."

"I think you may not have known very many women," she said, smiling. "And I doubt you have known any outside of your faith. That may be why you and your comrades are here, destroying my people."

She had seen that this crusade had been against all that made her region different, its tolerance, its diversity, its urbanity, its freedom, the equality of its women, and the different faiths of its diverse peoples. She was also a product of her faith and particularly of the tenets that held that a woman could know the divine truth as equally as any man. Cathar women and men were equals before God and therefore in all other ways. This was a circumstance that had not escaped the notice of the leaders of the Roman Catholic Church, which was as threatened by this freedom for women as it was by the fact the Christian Cathar faith was not under the control of Rome.

For Pauline, the concept of family was also a rather fluid one, since Cathar marriage was unusual and the relations between men and women were not in any way within the traditions of the Catholic Church. The Cathars were first a spiritual community of Christians. Parents gave up their infant children to communal schools that raised them in the faith. Children of three years or four years of age could no longer remember their parents. They were raised to be part of a civic society of deeply religious Christians. Pauline did not know her parents. Like other girls of her faith, Pauline had been raised by women in a group house for girls. It was as much a school as anything. She had been taught by the equivalent of very learned aunts from noble families. She had read many books and chronicles. Pauline's life experience was beyond the imagination of young Simon de Montfort, and she was in fact more learned than he.

Her comment about the forced conversion of her heretical sect struck a part of him too, a part he had kept submerged. It resurfaced the suppressed memory of the stories of persecution he had heard. This made him very uncomfortable. He had heard of the steadfast and stoical devotion of the Cathars under torture. They were humble in their devotion to their heretical Christian faith. And he had heard the rumors of their massacre at Béziers, sixteen years earlier, in 1209. Raymond, the Viscount of Béziers, had promised protection within the town's walls to the local Cathars and Jews. Some crusader soldiers in the siege outside the town broke discipline and stormed into the town. Rather than restrain them, the crusade commander let his regular forces join them and the town was pillaged and burned. Even those who had sought refuge in the churches were massacred. This commander, the Abbot of Cîteaux, had said to "kill them all and let God sort them out."

Simon had long felt compelled to do his duty, but he had never had the absolute devotion to it that his father once had, and that his elder brother now had. In the soil of his growing affection for this girl, there began to sprout a strong sense of shame for what the crusaders had done, for what his own family had done. It was a new sensation to him, and it was profound.

"So, what would you have me do?" he asked her. This time his tone was plaintive and sad.

"Meet me here at this time tomorrow, and I will let you know. I need to persuade my friends to come here with me to meet you." And then she paused, looked at him closely, and changed her topic. "Perhaps I may be of some help to you as well. As you are clearly of a noble family but are not a first son, your future is less defined for you. You will have to learn some more about how to think for yourself."

"How do you know that about me?" he asked, at first a bit annoyed at her impertinence. But then he waved her off on any answer, thinking almost fondly to himself, "*Who is this girl?*"

"Tomorrow then, I will see you," she said. "We will see you."

"I will be here. I give you my solemn promise that I will meet you here."

"You have a true soul," she said. "A true soul will disdain to be moved except by what it inherently senses are God's commands." Then she left.

Pauline had decided to act on what her instinct had told her about this man, what it had told her about his own heart, which was that he could help. She began to see that her decision was part of a larger and partly hidden realization, that this meeting would change her life. Now, she also had a specific plan to present to her friends. She would not just be telling them that she did not think they were safe any longer. She would be able to present them with a possible way out of the trouble that she alone thought was still pursuing them. She felt renewed and she was relieved to be able to offer them a practical way to act on her dark premonitions. She would convince her friends to return here with her and seek the assistance of this knight. She believed he would help them, and something about that belief placed a new urgency on her earlier foreboding. She was more worried about her friends now that she felt she had a way to help them.

The soldier, Simon de Montfort, stared at her for a long time as she walked away. His army had come to Avignon because it was one of the last towns that still harbored and protected the Cathars. The crusade had driven to this spot from the west, in just the same way that Pauline and her friends had moved east to try to escape the conflict. He felt that a strange thread of fate had brought her into town. She felt the same way. Meeting him had awakened in her a new sense of hope, and that had also cast light on her apprehension that trouble had been brewing for her and her friends.

In a way, Simon had always known what he was going to do in this situation. He had known it in a sense even before he had been confronted by it, before he had ever seen this girl. He simply would do what he alone thought was right. It went against his faith and his

Church and the dictates of his family and his friends and his entire world. He had doubts about all those for the first time. This girl had touched him in a way that made him feel as if he were suddenly confronting how he would conduct the remainder of his life. He too felt a sense of relief, but it was a surprise to him. He did not know now for certain if what he had decided was the Christian thing to do. But he did know one thing. He would save this girl and her friends.

TWO

Early the next morning, Pauline was on the road to Maillane, called Malhana in the Occitan language, a path she had traveled several times. It had not occurred to her at any of those times that the road usually contained an occasional fellow traveler, that she had often seen people walking, or on horseback, or on a cart. It was only now, when she had trod half of the three-hour walk and had seen not one soul, that those other journeys came back to her mind for the fact that they had never been as lonely as this one. She had thought herself to be on an encouraging errand, to return to her friends and convince them that they needed greater safety and that she had found a possible way to provide it. But the empty road was ominous.

She knew her fair share of roads. Her home in Pamiers and the rest of the places where most of her people had lived were well to the west of here, closer to Catalonian Spain and the Pyrenees. Those domains had been the most ravaged by the sixteen years of war. Not only had the environs of Avignon been one of the last stands of the Cathars, but it was also a current location of the crusaders. The Cathar communities had always been protected by the Occitan nobles, and the landowners and burghers of Languedoc, who often had friends and relatives among their ranks and who felt a sympathetic cultural bond with the faith. These benefactors often funded their schools and provided them with buildings and land. The elders of Pauline's particular community had dispatched her school and its teacher to the protection of a landowner in the east near Avignon, while they had made the fateful decision to remain in their land and try to withstand the crusaders.

Pauline had been concerned about the safety of her friends, but she had known there was little she could do about it without some outside help. Oddly, or perhaps typically of her, she had decided to now find that assistance where no one else would have looked, in the person of a knight from the north.

She had traveled longer distances than the one she was to cover today. Maillane had been her most recent stop before Avignon. Now, she was returning there on a mission. The good road from Avignon to Maillane, which the Romans had once called the Via Agrippa, was just like the roads she had taken from her homeland, the Via Aquitania and the Via Domitia.

These solidly paved surfaces had stood almost unchanged for over a thousand years, and the compacted stone road she was on was therefore normally heavily traveled. The absence of traffic was all that much more noteworthy and melancholy. A new apprehension began to dawn on her, the notion that she was being followed. And yet, each time she turned around, she saw only the same thing that was also in front of her, a long, flat ribbon of stone. She thought she heard a sound here and there but could never be certain. At one point, she was half convinced she had heard someone singing.

At length, only a couple of miles before Maillane, did she see something. It was in front of her and moving in her direction. It was an armed entourage of men on horses, followed by men on foot. She stopped. Only then did she realize that her instincts had been correct. She had been followed. There were suddenly two men behind her, one taller and older than most men, aged fifty, and the other shorter and younger, in his mid-twenties. This second man was unlike any man she had ever seen. She could tell by his clothes that the taller, older man was a traveling troubadour, of the tradition that had begun in the Languedoc.

The older man was dressed in a long, well-made, well-appointed blue tunic, suiting the fact that most troubadours had been of noble families such as the Duke of Aquitaine, who had been the first famous one. But it was the other man, the smaller, younger one, whose appearance captured Pauline's attention. He was dressed in a short tunic embroidered in the Byzantine mode, not a colorful hemp cote-hardie that a local man would wear. His trousers had the blousy cut and rich, dark maroon color of those of a man from Venice. His medium-length hair was exceptionally straight and equally as remarkably black. His complexion was sallow, but with a bloom, and his nose was a bit shallow on his wide face. His eyes garnered most of her attention. They had an unusual angle and slenderness to them. His beard seemed to be very light, or perhaps he was particularly close-shaven, as few men she had ever seen were. He had the look of gentle strength. He stood by, utterly silent, and largely unmoving, as if he were the older man's servant.

"Please join us, miss, as we break our fast here by the side of the road," the troubadour said.

Pauline hesitated. The older man glanced forward down the road, then looked at her and opened his arm and hand to the side of the road, to gesture toward the spot where he intended that they sit. It was shaded in a low place behind some bushes and could not be seen readily from the road. Pauline had not survived so well by accepting offers from strangers, but this gentle older man had gained her confidence. Something about his glance at the approaching men also persuaded her. And the unusual servant had suddenly and quietly appeared at her side as if to escort her off the road. She walked with them behind the shrubs and into the hollow under the trees. It was only after she sat down that she wondered if maybe her escort may have become a little bit forceful if she had refused. This realization did not frighten her, but in fact gave her the opposite feeling as she watched the troupe of armed men begin to pass.

They were French knights, dressed for battle, tall in their saddles. There was a small retinue of foot soldiers behind them. All these men were noisy, confident, and inattentive. They could not see the girl and her companions though she could see them through the undergrowth. They looked much as Simon did, but they lacked his benevolent eyes. And they appeared to be led by a Catholic clergyman of relatively high rank. She could see that his bearing, his dress, and his aristocratic face were nothing like she had seen among the common Catholic clergy of the area. He was exceptionally tall and thin, with dark brown hair and an aquiline nose. And perhaps most noticeably, he had a thin, straight scar that ran from his left cheekbone to his chin as if he were a warrior and not a priest.

When they had passed, the strange servant took a cloth out of the sack he had been carrying and spread it on the ground. He ladled some cold oat porridge from a pot into a small bowl for Pauline and poured her an iron cupful of water mixed with a bit of wine to give it more health, flavor, and some protection from impurities. He brought out some bread and fruit. The troubadour watched her closely and kindly.

"We did not want to be in their way," he said.

Pauline looked at him and slowly let her eyes show some agreement and understanding.

"You're a rather young sprig to be found so far from home," he added.

"Yes, sir," she said, "and you are a bit old and dignified to be sneaking up on people."

He laughed a gentle laugh and for the first time glanced at his sallow companion, who also for the first time had relaxed and allowed the shadow of a smile to cross his face.

"Your tongue is every bit as singular as are your circumstances," the older man said.

"Forgive me, please. It has a way of running ahead of my thoughts sometimes. I realize that you had good reason to lead me off the road at that time. And now I understand that you knew that had you announced your presence earlier, I might have changed my course or otherwise tried to avoid your company."

"I see that your tongue is not the only extraordinary thing you have in your head."

"Who was that priest? I have not seen him before, though I have seen many soldiers."

"You are correct to note him. He means no good to the people of our land."

"And you, excuse me, sir, are?"

"You and I have little need for names. I am on the road to Spain, never to find my way back. And it may be better if I cannot ever say who you are or that you cannot say who I am."

This remark struck her as abrupt and ominous, and then it occurred to her that there was no meat offered in the meal and, in fact, the older man was not eating at all. His grace and presence and demeanor were nothing if not beatific. She recognized that she had seen this all before, many times. She ventured to say what had long been the custom of her faith in such circumstances, the custom of her people when in the presence of such a holy man or woman.

"Bless me, Good Man," she said. "Pray to God for me."

"God be prayed that God will make you a good Christian and lead you to a good end," was his answer.

She knew then that he was a Perfect, what in her faith might correspond to a priest but entailed a great deal more withdrawing

al world. A Perfect was not part of an institution.
ling more along the lines of an ascetic monk. And
d also be a Perfect. The founder of Pauline's school
for w—   sclarmonde de Foix, had been a Perfect. Pauline had
seen others, women and men. The one unifying aspect they shared
was that they had all seemed more peacefully removed from worldly
concerns than others of the faith.

"The identity of interest," he said, "is that of the priest you just
saw, the one you noted. He is Guy Alain, and he is a special envoy
from the Vatican. He is known as the Hound of God. It has long been
his determined cause to begin an inquisition into the true beliefs of
those who have been forced to convert to his Catholic Christian faith,
not only from our faith, but from others. Now that their crusade is
successfully concluding, and the physical establishments of our faith
have mostly been removed, he wants to focus on those who have
been made to wear the yellow cross, those former Good Men and
Good Women who now only profess to belong to the Church of
Rome. He is already a dangerous man and will only become worse.
When this war is over, he will get his inquisition."

They later packed up and resumed their journey. Pauline could
not keep herself from glancing inquiringly in the direction of the
silent assistant. He did not return her looks but remained quietly by
the older man's side. She contemplated all that the troubadour had
told her during lunch about his quiet young associate from the east.

She would separate from them at Maillane and they would
continue. On her original journey east, she and her schoolmates had
been directed to travel to the landowner in Maillane, which was
supposed to have been their last stop. He had felt that the clandestine
school he had set up for the Cathar girls in the Alpilles Forest would
be safe. It seemed that way to almost all the girls. They had been
undisturbed for several months. They took turns traveling to Avignon
for supplies and they received some support from the landowner. On

Pauline's trips to the town, she would closely and discreetly watch the French knights. Simon de Montfort had immediately caught her attention, as he would stand out to anyone. She had acted on intuition when she approached him and confronted him. When their surprising conversation led to his promise of assistance, she knew that her next task was to get back to her friends and again try to convince them that they may not have been as safe as they seemed. She knew that would take some effort, but it would be even more difficult for them to believe and to trust her that this invader from the north would be of assistance to them. Then she would have to bring them to Avignon. She felt confident she could do all these things, but she felt a new urgency about it. The empty road increased her resolve, and also her fear.

For many reasons, she became less anxious about the trip while these two men accompanied her. When they parted at an intersection and the men moved down the road, she was not too preoccupied to notice that they stopped and looked back at her. And the older man seemed to be talking to the younger one about her. The troubadour gestured back in her direction, while the younger one looked at her. Then they gave each other a small nod in agreement, turned, and continued their journey. After this, she again found herself worrying.

The school where she had stayed was a little south of the town, well off the road, in the Alpilles Forest. A handful of huts had been made available by the sympathetic lord of the land, and the school itself was slightly more than a dozen young women and girls. As Pauline moved on through the woods, she was alarmed as she came upon the tracks of horses and men. The disturbed brush and shrubs disconcerted her. It was not long before she began to smell the scent of burnt wood and stale smoke. She was stricken with dread. She could hardly walk but she propelled herself forward. Reaching the huts, she found each of them burned to the ground. The girls were nowhere to be seen, but there were signs of struggle everywhere.

She found a knife in the grass, with blood on it. There were pieces of torn clothing, also with some blood. There were broken pots and furniture. When she began to find items that she recognized as belonging to individual girls that she knew, a hairbrush, a hat, an amulet, a book, and worst of all, a torn smock, a dark horror began to settle in her stomach.

She knew that they had all either been taken, or worse. Her anguish was tremendous. She had not been there to protect them. She had not been there to sense the danger and to warn them. She had not been there. She was in shock. The pain and loss were too overwhelming for her to process at that moment. She only knew she had to struggle back to Avignon and to her appointment. She had not really thought about it. It was more of an automatic action, doing the next thing she had intended. She would have to take the same road back. Her shock would later give way to deep sorrow and then guilt. She felt responsible for not having devised a plan earlier. Mostly, she felt she should have been there. Every absence of every one of her friends spoke to her and made her feel an unmoored guilt. Those absent voices and the scenes of violence told her she would never see them again.

She found that the road was just as deserted as before, and this increased her fear and her disengagement. She stepped quietly and looked ahead and behind periodically. She moved very quickly for the first hour, unable to think clearly of what she had seen. At a certain point, it began to take hold of her. She began to become preoccupied with it. She stopped looking around. She blamed herself for the loss of her friends, for what most likely was their death. If only she had acted on her premonition earlier, they would have been saved. She could not forgive herself for not having seen it all more clearly sooner, and for not having acted earlier. But her pain was also deeper and more blunt than that. She was alive and well. Most likely, they were not.

By the time she came to the bridge over the river that led into Avignon, she was crying tears of remorse and was walking in a state of shock. Pauline then learned the way in which a crisis can compound itself. She was too preoccupied to notice that she was about to be apprehended by the Hound of God.

THREE

Pauline had never known pain such as this, or perhaps she had. There was no way to measure. This was simply the worst pain she could possibly remember or even imagine. She had been strapped into a chair; her wrists, ankles, and waist were secured. She was in a windowless room with stone walls, perhaps in a castle or a crypt. She had been gagged and her head had been covered. A plank with short spikes had been strapped loosely to each arm. Those straps would occasionally be tightened, driving the spikes into her skin at first, and now beginning to push into her flesh. The intervals were occupied with questioning. The man seeking the answers, the only other person in that dark room, was an exceptionally tall and thin man with dark brown hair and an aquiline nose. He had a thin, straight scar that ran from his left cheekbone to his chin.

Father Guy Alain had taken the opportunity to show her how her ordeal would proceed. He had forced her to watch him torture the young woman he had sent ahead of his patrol from the school in the Alpilles Forest. Pauline knew her as one of her friends from the school, a strong girl her age. Pauline had watched those spikes be driven into her friend's arms, as far as her bones and more, until she had either passed out or bled to death. As soon as the spikes were pulled out of her arms, she bled so freely that she would soon be dead, if she were not already. This had its intended effect. Pauline answered all the priest had asked. She told him about the troubadour and his servant, and how they had helped her to avoid the priest's party on the road. Since she did not know it, she could not tell him the name of the troubadour, and her description of his companion was lacking clarity. That is why the priest had begun to tighten the straps. He thought she was lying.

Simon had to allow his eyes to adjust to the light once he had quietly entered that room. He stood in the dark shadows as his vision began to correct and to admit the scene before him. He saw the tall, handsome girl who had so moved him only yesterday. She was strapped into a torture chair. Spikes were beginning to dig into her forearms. She was bleeding, but not heavily. His first instinct was to draw his sword and plunge it into the heart of her torturer. But that man was a priest. To Simon, as well as to every person he knew, a priest was not merely a man of God. He was God's representative and conveyed the word and will of God. There was never any question about it. Simon could only see it one way; God had deigned that this should happen. Anyone else he knew would see it that way, except for the girl in that chair. This remarkable girl had germinated something in him that allowed him to apply some doubt to all that he had once thought inviolable. That doubt caused him to look at the scene and see the injustice and horror of it. These second thoughts now combined with his first instinct and tempered it. He silently drew his sword and held it at his side. He had only to consider from there what to do.

He had been part of his father's and elder brother's army since he was a child, when he had served as a page. He had watched them fight and had himself fought against the men of the Occitania. He knew these people of Languedoc retained the remnants of old

Roman law and were relatively free of the control of their lords. The nobles allowed women to own property and to inherit. They were tolerant of other religions. Unlike the Catholics, they owned Bibles. They believed an individual could find his or her own way to Christ, without the Church. They were clearly a danger to all that Simon, his family, friends, king, and kingdom represented.

And here, before him, was an officer of the Vatican, a man of great importance to God. He was questioning the heretic.

"I do not believe that you don't know the troubadour's name, or that you cannot adequately describe his servant. But I am interested in your vile heresy. Tell me. Do you believe that God created the world?"

"I believe in the spirit of Christ, our Lord," she said.

"Answer the question."

"God is perfect and good and permanent. Is the world? Are you?"

He gave a turn to the knob that tightened the straps. She cried out in agony as the spikes drove just a bit deeper.

"Please," she cried.

"Will you swear your faithfulness to this cross?" He held it in front of her.

"That is just a symbol. You may worship an icon if you like. My spirit is with Christ's. An oath is spoken, and any speech may be a lie. My heart is all that matters. It is true."

"Those are heresies; you must know."

"You and your kind," she said, "are part of the corruption and chaos of this impermanent world. God is permanent and perfect and good. You can be no part of Him."

"I see you have no interest in life and that you feel free to speak your lies now. Your friends from your school in Maillane were not so bold when they were about to be sent from this world. They cried and some tried to plead their allegiance to the Church and the cross, and they begged for forgiveness. You will too."

Pauline's pain was now supplanted by the certainty that her friends had suffered all that she had feared. She had assumed they had been sent to their deaths, but hearing it made her blind with remorse.

"But I am interested in your sacrilege," the priest continued. "Tell me more. Is there a Hell?"

"You know there is not, or else you would live in terror that your actions would send you there."

"Then what will happen to your soul when you leave this world?"

"It will migrate to another being and will continue to do that until I have the strength to learn to live entirely in my spirit, to become perfected. Then my body may pass, and my soul will go to Christ."

"Will you eat meat?"

"No."

"Why? Because an animal might hold the soul of one of your departed friends?"

"No. It is simply a sin to kill any living creature on purpose," Pauline said. "Her name was Ermengarde, by the way," she added, "that girl you made me watch you kill. She was fifteen. She was gentle and good and walked in the ways of Christ, with humility and generosity toward all."

"Do you believe in the holy sacrament of marriage?"

"A sacrament is an illusion, a ritual, a trick of your craft. There is only the spirit. Spirits may not join in marriage, which is a worldly state and not a spiritual one."

Simon was appalled by the girl's statements. He particularly and personally lived by the cross. He wore one around his neck. One was embroidered on his tunic. He had several among his belongings. He prayed to it. It gave him comfort. The idea that a man or woman may be brought back in another body, be reincarnated, was appalling and a vile heresy. Why did these Cathars not eat meat? And how can the world exist if God had not created it? He created everything. This girl sought to cast doubt upon certainties, upon realities. God would not and should not permit it. He had never heard such sacrileges spoken before, nor had he seen such an infidel tortured or so confess her heresies.

"You may say your prayers now," the priest said, "although I know your kind only say one prayer, and do not believe in the rest of the liturgy."

She began to pray. At first, Simon did not recognize the prayer, because she spoke it in her own language, and not in Latin. This alone was a profanation of Christianity. It deeply disturbed him on an elemental basis. Then the priest tightened the straps and began to drive the spikes further. She screamed in pain and then did something remarkable.

In this darkest moment, when she should have been purified of her sins and could have been confessing them, when she should have pledged her life to the holy Church, she instead did something to spite this great cleric who had been sent from Rome as an envoy of the Vicar of Christ. She was in pain and the certainty of her friends' deaths filled her with rage. She stopped praying in the Occitan language.

She began to say her prayer in French so the priest would know exactly what she was doing, which prayer it was that she was praying. Simon then recognized her prayer as the common version of the Pater Noster, the Lord's Prayer, but this was clearly not in Latin. The Pater Noster, like all formal elements of the Catholic faith, was always in Latin. It had to be. It was like a sacred relic of the Church. He had never heard it in French. The idea of removing it from the realm of the priests and the Catholic liturgy was outrageous. The priest was angered and moved toward the spikes and straps.

Simon had finally been convinced of what to do.

He raised his sword arm high, turned the sword to the side, and swung it with almost all his strength, striking the cleric on the back of the head and knocking him, flying, to a heap on the floor, unconscious. He quickly cut off two strips from the man's vestment, cut all the straps on the girl, gently pulled out the spiked boards, and tightly wrapped her arms in the cloths and tied them off. He took time to examine the wounds first and determined they were not too deep. Then he reached under her and picked her up and began to carry her out of the room. She was losing consciousness, but she turned to whisper in his ear.

"What took you so long?" she asked, and then passed out.

The next morning, he went to her bedside. As the commander's younger brother, he was entitled to one of the better local estates that the crusaders had commandeered. He had taken her there immediately the night before and had her wounds cleaned. He had put her in his own room before he slept in the hall outside. He had sent a squire to the town to find a local healer, who had cleaned the wounds and wrapped them again in new bandages. Pauline looked at him and said nothing. Her eyes seemed to speak a gratitude that he could understand. He finally spoke.

"You're welcome," he said.

"And you are a good Christian," she answered.

"I see you are feeling better."

"I will be fine, so long as these wounds do not fester." Pauline could not give words to the unspeakable despair she felt at the murder of her friends, nor did she wish to share it.

"I think you will be all right. The woman who attended to you seemed to know what she was doing."

"You seem to be getting familiar now with women of that type."

He smiled and said, "I was told where to find you by the most peculiar-looking man. He was some manner of Byzantine, but with a very strange appearance. And even more strangely, he spoke French to me with a Venetian accent."

"He spoke to you? I never had that honor."

"Oh, he was quite clear, and made it known that it was his duty to watch over you."

"I see. He is from a place the Romans called Serenica, or the land from which silk comes. It is east of Byzantium. There is more to it, but I do not have the energy now to tell the tale."

"Please rest. You will be all right here. I will see to that. And one more thing, may I ask?"

"Yes."

"What shall I call you?"

"My name is Pauline."

Simon went to sit in the great hall of the estate. It was a large, open room, with a high ceiling, all made of wood, some colorful rudimentary tapestries to cover the walls, a large candle wheel to light it, and a good-size fireplace at one end that seemed to be little used. There were other traces of warmth and color, some rugs from Genoa, a bowl of fruit that was as much decorative as it was sustenance, large windows on the southern exposure. The wooden furniture was light and carved for ornament. Simon had sat in this room dozens of times but for this once he finally noticed it, particularly in its contrast to the great rooms in the stone buildings of the estates of the north, with their small windows, great fireplaces, heavy furniture, and lack of color. Curiously as well, he noticed something that should have been apparent to him from the start. There were no crosses other than the ones he had brought. Perhaps he had noticed that before, but had given it only passing attention, assuming the owners had taken them when they had left. Meeting Pauline had made him more attentive. Saving her had made him more contemplative.

More than anything, he also wondered about himself. As this strange girl had presumed, the duties that traditionally rest on the shoulders of a firstborn son were not his and did not put him on a distinct path. His brother Amaury had inherited his father's rights, titles, and estates. Still, Simon would always have some small choice of what to do. The custom would have been for him to become a priest or remain a knight. For the first time, he began to confront the more general question of choice. He realized it meant that there were many other things he might choose to do or to be. But first, he had to decide what to do with this girl.

He sat there for a good period of time. A cook brought him a meal and some wine, and that also helped him to think. At length he became tired. Much had happened in the last two days and he had been worn out not only by the events, but by the inward changes that had occurred and were still happening. He realized that he had already begun to take a path and to make certain choices, though he had never given that much thought. He had just reacted. That had all changed. He would spend much more than just this evening thinking about it.

FOUR

Pauline passed the following year occasionally and vainly looking for what she had lost. She had not been raised by her parents, so the girls in her school had been the only family she knew. They had been taken from her in the most terrible fashion and she felt responsible for not preventing their deaths, and guilty for having been the only one to have survived. She had also lost a good number of intangible things at the hands of her torturer. And yet, she still breathed. Great loss takes a while to be fully and deeply realized. When our home burns down we only feel loss. It is not until we begin to miss the individual items within the house that full inventory of the loss begins to be known.

Simon felt his own remorse. He listened quietly and painfully over the days and weeks it took her to relate what she had found and had seen in the forest. He had also looked into the matter of the landowner who had sponsored the school and found he had been detained. Pauline had no place to turn, no place to go. Simon began to see the mechanism of the crusade for what it was, a campaign to conquer a free people, and worse, to eradicate another faith. He knew that he had saved Pauline, but he felt as if it had not been enough. He needed to help her recover, for his own sake as much as hers. If he could help her heal it would make him feel less responsible for his role in the crusade.

So, he spent many silent hours listening to her quietly tell him about each girl who had been killed, about their lives together and in the Cathar faith, and of her overwhelming feeling of responsibility for their passing. For most of that time his heart told him just to listen and to understand. But he also came to know of the tenets of this gentle Christian sect. They believed that God created their souls but not their bodies, that the world was imperfect and not of God's making. They did not eat animal flesh and they elevated spiritual love and scorned romantic love. And above all, they treated each other and humanity with a very Christian gentility and respect. They eschewed the way of the earthly world, and it was not uncommon for one of their leaders, their Perfects, to simply fast to death as a way to pass into the spiritual world.

As months passed, he began to do more than just listen. He would try to assure her that there had been nothing she could have done. He might have helped her to help them, but they had met too late. And before that, the girls could not have escaped the Hound of God once he had learned of them. Sometimes, she would listen, and he would feel he was making her feel better. Other times, she would simply cry, and he knew that her tears were the tears of a survivor. He had known the feeling himself, whenever he had lost a companion in the war. The trauma had put Pauline in a walking trance from which she only slowly began to emerge. At first, Simon was merely just there for her. She would look at him blankly. At length she began to see him and to appreciate his way with her. After many months, he began to feel that she was coming to rely on him.

Simon had given Pauline a position in his retinue as a cook. She kept herself occupied in this position, and it allowed her some distraction from the memory of the killing of her friends. She had also found a small library in the chapel of the manor and had gained permission to borrow the books at the local parish church. She buried her thoughts in these books whenever she was not working on her cooking. Sometimes Simon would quietly read in the room with her.

She had previously learned how to prepare food in the manner of the common people of her region. She quickly had to learn the skills needed to work in the kitchen of not just a Catholic nobleman, but one from the north. She had known how to make porridge and coarse bread from oats, barley, or rye. Now she learned how to make a better bread from wheat. Olive oil, pomegranates, garlic, grapes, olives, citrus fruits, wine, and nuts had long been part of the local cuisine to which she had been accustomed. She now began to incorporate apples, lard, mustard, pears, sausage, and beer brought in from the north. She also had to learn to prepare other dishes of the upper classes, using almonds and almond milk, spices, and, most notably, meat, which tended to be chicken or pork. Beef was quite costly, even for the wealthy.

The religious component of the dining customs was something else Pauline had to learn. These Roman Christians fasted more generally, and all day Saturday, the day before receiving the Eucharist. She accustomed herself to feeding and dining with the entire household, masters and servants, gathered in the great hall as part of the continuity of their community. Eating alone was considered egoism. Servants served nobles, but all dined together. For Pauline, this also meant that eating with a spoon off a dish became the norm. Commoners ate food right off the table with their hands and perhaps a shared knife. Noble house residents sometimes ate their food off a large slice of bread, a plate of wood, or, as in Simon's household, a plate of pewter. On certain occasions Simon would dine in his quarters with favored guests, in which case Pauline was always the cook and server.

To preserve the hierarchy of the estate while its disparate members kept such close quarters, the divisions between lord and servant were all that much more enforced. The formalities, such as always referring to the master as "milord," grew as a necessity from this closeness. The master knew everyone in his house, and they were all on speaking terms with him, none more than Pauline.

Simon made a point to speak with her every day, and she was always honest with him. His gentle and attentive manner began to encourage her to again be more forthright, to speak more of her mind. That endeared her to him as much as he often found it surprising. Most often they would speak briefly in the morning, and again well into the evening, when he would always retire to his quarters and she would bring him spiced wine and a dessert. He made it a point that they would sit and talk. They had also developed a habit of playing chess together. The game had been brought from the Middle East through Spain and had begun to become popular in France only a couple of generations before this. It was almost a metaphor for their conversations. He was carefully making moves in order to bring her back.

Simon found himself in the incredibly strange position of speaking to Pauline not as if she were a woman, not as if she were a commoner, not as if she were a youth, and not as if she were a heretic. He often found himself speaking openly to this girl as if he were speaking to his brother, only he was more forthcoming with her and more accepting of her commentary. And she was more challenging. Perhaps nothing was more illustrative of all of this than the fact that he allowed her to speak to him privately, using his first name. She often called him "milord" as did the other household staff when she was among them. She had not yet learned to call him "my lord," as another noble would. When she had dared to call him "Simon" one of the first times she was alone with him, he did not correct her. He merely smiled.

To the proud, brave, and gifted knight, her growing candor was at once completely comfortable and as strange and surprising as any of his oddest dreams. This young woman whose life he had saved was somehow something more to him now. There is a gradual process that we lose sight of with familiarity. If we live with a person, we do not abruptly notice one day that their hair is longer than it had been a month earlier. We only notice when it is cut. Pauline had grown into a person of some importance to him, and he had not really noticed it. Part of the matter for him was that her heart had been deeply wounded. He had lost his father so he was sympathetic to the suffering she felt from the loss of her friends, and he understood why she would take responsibility for it. He had patiently listened to her story many times. As she recovered her bearings, he had not noted the change by which his sympathy had grown into fondness and his attention had generated a frank and open friendship. It was a friendship that had begun on the most compassionate terms.

He had also not closely noticed the other changes in her over the year. She had begun in his household as a wounded, traumatized fifteen-year-old girl who had lost all that she had ever had. With his gentle manner and his careful listening and comforting, she had slowly grown more assured, less inward, and more relaxed. She had also grown healthier, slightly taller, and stronger. Her natural independence began to return and strengthen. It became more refined and controlled, and on occasion more evident. In her sixteenth year, she had become quite remarkable, and a woman. This unnoticed gradual process had also marked her permanence in the household. Simon had merely taken her in and they both came to assume that would remain the state of events. She had lost her home, family, school, and friends. This household was the only place where she felt she had begun to recover some of those things.

Simon had altered over the year, too. The king of France now managed the crusade, and he had his own staff and counsel. Simon had been an instrumental lieutenant to his brother when Amaury had been commander. Simon was merely another of the king's knights now. His brother had gone back to the north. Even though Simon was a knight in the French force, he no longer felt at one with his life. He was certainly more contemplative, or perhaps was so for the first time in his nineteen years. His deeds had always been the firstlings of his heart. Now his thoughts were. And this day he had been thinking about something that he must tell Pauline. It was news, information that was important to her. He waited until the communal supper was finished and she brought him his spiced wine and a sugared apple in his room. She sat in the chair at a perpendicular angle to his, so they could see each other and the fire. They played a game of chess that was on the table in front of the fire.

"Pauline—" he said.

"You have news for me," she interrupted. "Forgive me. What is your news?"

"No. Please, you go first, young lady."

"I could not think of doing that, milord. I apologize for interrupting you."

"I cannot think which is more curious, that you would call me 'milord' or that you would pretend to apologize. But I will tell you that I spoke today with your friend, that strange Byzantine or Venetian fellow. He is back from whatever may have been his travels, and he has asked if he may be of some service to me. I favor him because he speaks with an economy of words and has an honorable bearing. I should like to find a way to put him in my employ, but I fear he might be a bit too noticeable."

"That is so, but for someone who does appear unusual, he has a way of making himself less remarkable."

"You are correct. His demeanor is very quiet."

She was silent for a moment. By this point in their game, they each had moved several pieces.

42

"Perhaps you might make him one of your guards. I have never seen him fight, but he has the presence of a warrior," she added.

"Again, I see what you mean, and I agree. What was your news?"

"He came to see me today too. He brought some disturbing news for you, for both of us."

"What did he say?"

"He said that Guy Alain, the Hound of God, has been asking about you. The priest was bedridden for several weeks after that night. And his memory of what happened is gone. But over the last several months he has methodically questioned all the soldiers, clerics, and servants who were around then. He began to put together a mental picture of who might have rescued me. He has done the same with piecing together a description of me, since he does not remember what I look like. Our friend cannot say whether Alain has made you a target, but it seems that you are one of the people on his list."

"I have little to fear from him."

"I know that I have personally benefitted from your tendency to ride into the stream without testing the water's depth first, so I hesitate to mention that it can be dangerous."

"I suppose that is all the more reason to bring our nameless friend on board. He seems to be well informed, unusually so. And his own propensity seems to be that he shows up at just the correct moment."

"You have made a pertinent observation. That seems to be becoming a new habit."

"What is his history? You once said you would tell me."

"The troubadour told me this much: there is a land to the east beyond Byzantium where all silk originally was made. This land was called Serenica by the Romans, the Middle Kingdom by its own people, who are known as the Chin."

"Your friend is a Chin-man, a man of the Middle Kingdom, then. By his appearance, it seems an exotic land. What is his name?"

"His Venetian name is Rocco. He is from the land called Tzu, in his home kingdom."

"Rocco Tzu will be one of my guards then, one that works inside the estate and not at the gate. I am sure that will make you feel safer, and I know I will feel better. You are right about Father Alain. My assistance to you has placed us all in some jeopardy."

Here, Pauline said nothing, and only looked into Simon's eyes, the same eyes she had studied a year ago. At that time, she had seen some flicker of thoughtfulness. She was looking for something different now, something more solid, something definitive. The two of them had passed along a journey together. He had gently walked her back from the fog of shock and guilt. She was comfortable with him now and felt she could read him well. But at this moment, she did not feel like she could put her question for him into words. She merely felt what she wanted to ask as she looked at him.

He looked back at her for a long time. Nothing was said between these two for some long seconds, perhaps minutes. Time had slowed. At first, she could see in his eyes that he did not know what she was seeking in his. She could see that he was thinking and that he knew her gaze contained some significance.

At first, he was puzzled. Then he concluded that she was seeking something from him. So, he had to consider what it might be. He had an innate sense that she would not speak to him about it and he would not break the silence. He considered what they had just discussed, bringing on as a guard the one other person who had protected her. And he reflected on the past he and she had shared this last year. Then he thought she knew what she wanted to know. But he again wondered why she might not simply ask.

He believed he had made it clear earlier, with his words. He felt he had already told her what she was now seeking. Then he remembered. And he was sorry he had not understood it more quickly. It was something she had said she believed when she had been in the torture chair. She had said that oaths may be lies, and only hearts mattered. She was looking to see what his heart said. She did not want to hear it. She wanted to see it. And before he could think to show her, he felt his eyes well up. He had once saved her. And he had protected her and nurtured her. The reason he had done that was now all that he was feeling, all that he could feel. He stayed silent about it and realized that to speak of it might somehow diminish it. He was emptied of all guile, of all words. He looked at her with unadorned emotion.

She saw it when his eyes told her. She had watched him go through that progression. First, his eyes had shown that he knew she wanted to know something from him. Then she had seen him thinking. At this final point, she only saw his feelings. It was much like that original meeting, where she had an insight, but this time it was all right there in his look. He was bound to her, deeply and in ways that no words could express. And she also saw his steel. She saw the noble knight who had made his stand for her. She saw it as clearly as she saw him, sitting there. He would never betray her, not even to his Roman Catholic Church. He would die before he would let anything happen to her. His eyes showed her his heart.

FIVE

❧❧❧

The sun was shedding its first light in the spring of 1228. Anyone was able to see the beauty of this day, a gift to all living creatures. Some could never see it because they only worshipped their own inventions for imposing their will on others.

There had been such a holy man at work in Languedoc. His goal was to purge the region of its last heretics, the secret ones, the ones who had pretended to convert to the Catholic Church, or who had simply ceased the open practice of their Cathar Christian faith. The king's army was eliminating the last pockets of armed resistance. Avignon surrendered in 1226. But thousands still practiced the local faith in secret. Guy Alain had long argued that the only method to ferret out those individuals would be a large-scale inquisition. The Vatican had yet to agree, but the signs were likely that such a program would be officially mounted. In the meantime, Father Alain conducted his own campaign of inquiries with the full support of the Catholic Church. He was testing methods that later would become general practices.

Upon entering a village, he would assemble all the adults and ask them to speak an oath of faithfulness to the Church. By this time, nineteen years after the beginning of the crusade, the most defiant Cathars had been killed or driven into exile, and those who remained had learned to speak that oath. But then Father Alain would offer all the villagers a chance to confess their secret heresy and receive lenient treatment only if they would inform on others. Many times, a village might have entered a conspiracy of silence, but it would only take one informer to begin a cascade of recriminations. Sometimes the priest would tell the lie that such an informant had already come forward. Other times a Catholic villager would implicate his neighbors. Yet other times, the process would be used by the locals to exercise some other feud against a fellow citizen. These conspiracies of silence, as is often the case with any such thing, were only as strong as their weakest member. In almost every instance, several names of accused heretics would be put forward. They would be read from the pulpit of the parish church on three consecutive Sundays.

Nothing was done to stop the accused from fleeing. It was half encouraged, because it would be taken as a confession, the process of excommunication would begin, and that would give the Church the right to seize the property and possibly sell it. Much of this procedure was funded in this way, and it was the very beginning of what would be a large-scale property transfer to the Church and its adherents in Occitania. Those who did not flee were put on trial in a secret procedure in which the clerics were the prosecutors, judges, and jury. Only three years after this informal process of inquisition, it would become a permanent Church institution, lasting over three hundred years, and its use would be expanded beyond the Christian heresies of what was about to become southern France. It would terrorize other Christian sects, as well as Jews, Muslims, and many Catholics.

Several priest inquisitors had been killed in the years between 1209 and this year, 1228. Father Alain himself had once been attacked. He was the son of a noble Norman family and was trained to use the sword he had worn under his cassock, so he was able to fend off his attackers. It was how he had received that scar he now wore as an icon on his left cheek. It reminded him daily of the importance, danger, and necessity of his holy task. It was why he now traveled with an armed guard.

Father Alain had been convinced early on of the success of his techniques. He knew that his inquisition would become an office of the Roman Church. He looked forward to that day for many reasons. One was deeply personal.

He had long ruminated over the facts he had gathered but could not remember from that evening three years earlier. His investigation had given him some reliable evidence. The Hound of God knew he had rooted out a nest of heretic women and had tortured one of them to death to gather information about the locations of other schools and other heretics. He later captured another of them. She was young, tall, dark in hair and features. But she had been rescued by a Christian knight. What he could learn about this knight was that he had easily disarmed and disabled the two guards outside his rooms, so he was a considerable fighter and was of noble bearing. He showed the compassion of not killing those guards and not killing Alain. Guy Alain had spoken to many lower-ranking knights and many soldiers, had inquired about their whereabouts and of the movements of others. One fact kept sticking to his mind so that it soon became as attached to him as the scar that would never leave his face.

Simon de Montfort had left his post that night. The implication of this had stood at first as too unlikely to believe. This young knight's father had long been the greatest and most zealous Christian leader, serving the Pope as few others had. As improbable as it was for Simon the Younger to have been the offending knight, he was equally out of Guy Alain's reach. The de Montfort family was of far more noble blood than most, and particularly more than the Alain family. Simon's family had held a hereditary county, de Montfort, in the Île-de-France, since before anyone could remember. Whether or not Simon the Younger had knocked Guy Alain unconscious and freed that girl was really of no matter. Guy could do nothing about it, not against such a powerful family.

This did not sit well with him. He began an effort to infiltrate the de Montfort household and to find out all that he could about who was inside that estate. He instructed his agents to tease information out of the household staff whenever they went into town. At every turn, he was thwarted by one of Simon's guards, a strange-looking Venetian of Byzantine dress who seemed to anticipate his every step. This guard kept remarkably close to all the household retinue, particularly when they left the house on regular errands. He warned them all of Guy Alain's likely questions. The priest finally moved on and decided that if he could not directly question the noble guests of the de Montfort household because of his lower rank, he would employ a local noble who could. It was then that he had learned of a tall, handsome young woman with dark hair and eyes, who worked as a cook for Simon de Montfort. She was about eighteen years of age and Simon apparently favored her with his company.

Guy Alain knew that the day would come when there would be an official Inquisition, and then he would not be merely a priest cleaning up heretic nests. He would have more than just God on his side. He would have the offices of the Pope behind him. He vowed it would give him more of a chance to take down Simon de Montfort and "bring him and his Cathar witch to justice."

This particular Cathar witch had known what Guy Alain had been doing and that her master was not quite equipped or prepared to counter it. Simon was still beginning to grapple with his choices and his future. He was effectively just an ordinary knight in the army of the king now. His brother was no longer the crusade's commander. Amaury was carving out a place for himself in the French court.

50

There was a rumor that he would be appointed the constable of France, one of the five most powerful officers of the king. If the Comte de Toulouse title would be returned to the family, it would go to Amaury. The same would likely be true of the Leicester earldom, and of the title in Brittany if it ever became a part of France again. Amaury had both a significant duty and considerable privilege. Those two things determined his path. Simon had the right to be a soldier or a priest. But as Pauline consistently reminded him, he really had infinite choice and a wide-open future. Once Simon had nursed Pauline out of her gloom, her preternatural confidence in her intellect returned and she settled easily into the role of Simon's confidant. His own feeling was the companion of her manner. He had grown to welcome and value her frank counsel.

"There is nothing you cannot do or be," she told him over a chess game one night that summer.

"That is not the way the world works," he said. "Everyone has his role. Everything has its place. All is according to God's plan."

"Is that why you crowned Guy Alain with the side of your sword?"

"I still do not know why I did that."

"You made a choice, Simon. And you were able to survive its rashness because you were born into circumstances that present you with many choices and protect you from many of the outcomes."

"I am not the firstborn. I will never rule."

"It is likely you will not, as long as you maintain that attitude. You are not a chess-piece knight. You are no less a leader than your elder brother, or your father. I would say you are a better man than either." She moved one of her knights into a forward position.

Simon was stung by this remark. He felt remorse for what had been his family's role in the crusade. He had seen and felt what it had done to Pauline. But he loved his father. He hurriedly made his next chess move.

"You might want to be careful. My father was the Comte de Montfort, and one of the great men of his generation. He always saw himself as a humble servant to the king and to God."

"And if burning cities and people is the path to your Heaven, that is surely where he is," she said.

There was silence. Pauline felt she had stepped too far. She felt flush. They quietly each took one chess move. Bringing a bishop forward.

"Perhaps I should have left you with that priest. I would not have to bear your insolent tongue," he said.

She was relieved he had said something.

"You would not have done that, nor would you have made the decision to destroy those towns and villages. We both know that it is innate in you to think for yourself. I have seen that you are good. And you have more than your fair share of the de Montfort family bearing, courage, intelligence, honor, and piety. You face another situation much like you did that night when a clear decision must be made, and a great deal is at stake."

"What do you mean, woman? What is at stake?"

"You can wander into your role, or the way of the world, or what you will call it. Or you can make your own way, make the most out of the fact that you are a great man. The first path will leave you wondering, questioning your choice for years. The second will challenge all that you are, and you will rise to the occasion and be fulfilled. I know you have a fire that burns inside you. It will either burn you up or you will use it to light the way."

"For a woman who does not believe in the world, you certainly pay very close attention to it," he said.

"I do not see the world as most do. That is the point. I see it as corrupt. I see your spirit most clearly. You can make headway against the corruption. And you can find a place in the world that suits the greatness of your soul." She brought her queen out.

"I understand your faith is only in the human spirit. But let us treat men and women as if they are real; perhaps they are."

Simon turned to face Rocco, who had been standing quietly at the door to Simon's quarters.

"What do you think of all this, Venetian?"

"She is right," he said, "more than she is saying."

"What does that mean?" he asked Pauline.

"It means that Guy Alain knows everything," she said, "and I fear that when his inquisition becomes the official doctrine and practice of the Church, he will come after you."

"I have more standing in the Church than Guy Alain will ever have."

"But I do not," she said. Her face showed that she expected him to plumb the true import of what she had said.

"I do not see what that means. You are under my protection."

"That is exactly what I mean. He will watch and wait for an opportunity to seize me at some point. He knows you will then act against him. And this time it will not be in secret. It will be an open attack on the Church. That will be what he will use against you."

Simon could only sit back for an instant, to think. Then he was compelled to smile at what was either the impertinence of this woman or her self-assuredness and her perfectly accurate assessment of his character. She was correct. He would take steps to save her and it is unlikely that he would consider the consequences before he took action. He glanced at the guard to know what his opinion might be. And for the first time ever, he thought he saw the slight echo of a smile on his broad face. This only made Simon smile more widely. He noticed then his king was in a precarious position.

"I see," he said. "My health and well-being are aligned with what you think is a future for me that might disrupt the very order of the way in which the world has worked for generations. I cannot guess what the next step might be that I must take," he said.

"Oh, that," she said, suddenly smiling broadly, as if she had been waiting for this moment. "That is simple. We are going to England."

"I certainly could not have guessed that. It is preposterous. England is an inhospitable rock in the middle of a cold sea. It is a peasant kingdom, full of Saxons who only speak German."

"Yes, but it has been ruled by the Norman French for more than one hundred and fifty years. The clergy, the nobles, the magistrates, and everyone who matters speaks French," she said.

"All we would ever do is complain about the weather and the food. What kind of future is for me there?"

"I will explain it to you on the way to Paris, which is where we are going first," she said. "One other thing," she said. "Check and mate."

SIX

Whenever a person makes a small change that is part of a larger undertaking, such as leaving for war, engaging in a courtship, or buying a property, he or she may or may not be struck by the deeper solemnity of that smaller event. The soldier may not profoundly consider that he may never return to his home or to any home again. The young man or woman may not pay attention to the important signs on what is a path to the permanence of marriage. The buyer may not attempt to fully understand the import of setting down roots at the selected place. In many cases, the deeper reflection only comes later, perhaps too late. Simon was in effect doing all three. He was moving. He was undertaking what might be a hazardous act. And he was establishing a kind of partnership that might not be simple to sunder later.

He began considering Pauline herself. She was a commoner, a heretic, a woman. And even though she could speak French, in almost every intangible manner they did not speak the same language. He did not always understand her. He knew that she often surprised him and that her unusual insights were many times quite useful. He decided upon one thing that he had to do about her. He had conferred with Rocco on the matter and the two men agreed. She would have to become a boy.

"It is my turn, Pauline," he said one evening, "to speak of your future and of your safety."

"I do not like the look on your face," she said. "You seem to be enjoying yourself too well to be honestly discussing such a serious topic."

"Please forgive me. I am quite earnest. I find no enjoyment in this."

"I am grateful that you are such a terrible liar, so please, out with it."

"We are about to embark from Languedoc and begin a journey of over five hundred miles for more than three months. Guy Alain will surely be aware of our departure. We will not be traveling with my full retinue, many of whom are locals who will stay behind. You will be obvious in our traveling party and therefore particularly vulnerable. So, Rocco and I have devised a plan."

She glanced at the guard and he did not share Simon's amusement at the discussion. In fact, he looked quite a bit more earnest than usual. She knew then that Simon was serious and that he only found the situation slightly amusing. Rocco signaled two porters to bring a trunk into the room. Simon thanked them, dismissed them, and then he turned to her.

"You are a handsome woman, Pauline, tall and healthy, with strong facial bone structure, dark brows, eyes, and hair," he said. "It would be a simple and elegant solution to our problem for you to become my squire, to dress as a lad your age, to cut your hair, and carry yourself as a young man."

Simon hesitated, tried to read her reaction. She remained quiet and still, so he continued.

"A squire must come from a good family, and you can easily give that appearance. You can read and write. You carry yourself with grace and poise. You speak French and Occitan as well as any noble and are learning Latin. You are loyal and are on speaking terms with me. You also have a dusky voice, almost as deep as a young man. It would not be hard for you to fill the role and to pass for my squire at first or even at second or third glance. In that trunk are sets of squire's clothes and shoes for you to wear. Perhaps most importantly, no French man would ever suspect that any cultured young French woman from a respectable family would think to dress as a man."

Simon let this be his last remark, and he stood, watching her with some unease. Rocco looked away from them both but was very attentive to what her response might be. Pauline opened the trunk, stirred her hand among the contents, closed it with a slam, looked at Simon with a bit of defiant pride, and spoke.

"Where is my sword?"

Simon was taken aback. Rocco turned away even more and obscured his reaction.

"I must have a sword if I am to be your squire," she said. "And you will have to give me some training in its use. Teach me how to use it."

"Perhaps I might teach you some manners as well."

"If I had the manners of which you speak, this idea would never have occurred to you. It is because I do not think nor act as one of your little fawning French girls that permitted you to arrive at this plan in the first place. For that reason, I believe it is a brilliant plan. You may find me impertinent, brash, opinionated, and too independent. But I would say that is the same as being frank, confident, intelligent, and strong, which would describe you as well."

"We are agreed, then. It shall be done," he said. "What may you add, Rocco?"

And with this, the man who had been born in the Middle Kingdom turned around. He had undone his sword belt, with his scabbard and sword. He bowed slightly and handed them toward her with both hands.

"I don't think I can take your sword from you, my friend."

"You must," he said. "This sword is lighter, a bit shorter, and stronger than any French blade; made for a smaller man. Forged in Byzantium from Damascus steel, it has been pledged to protect you since that day on the road to Maillane. It has always been yours, you know, really. Now you must have it, my lady."

"You mean 'my lord,' I think," she smiled.

"And yes," Simon added, "you are now of a noble family. And in public, we shall call you Paul."

"Paul it is, then," she said, parrying her sword in Simon's general direction, then poking him with it, gently on the shoulder.

Pauline's idea to go to England had struck him with its simplicity and elegance, but there was quite a bit more to it than she might know or imagine. She told Simon that she had read the chronicle of the de Montfort family, and that it had a claim to the English title of the Earl of Leicester. She had several times discussed it with him, though he had no idea what direction she might take with it. She had given it some thought in the context of Simon's untitled position in France. She felt deeply that his destiny demanded more than that. So, she decided that he should seek the English title and make use of that elevation in status.

She knew that would require a discussion with his brother, Amaury, in Paris. Simon had inherently understood the kernel of what she was suggesting. If he were to become the Earl of Leicester, he would have a land hold, a title, and an income. It would all be in forsaken Britain, but the royal family and other nobles were Norman French in origin. That had been another one of her points. She had told him that he would stand out, not only for his courage, his wit, his virtue, his military experience, and his noble bearing, but for the fact that he would be the genuine object. He would come to them fresh from the land of their culture, their old country. He would speak the language more accurately. He would stand above.

There was more to it than that. She did not say it, nor did she have to tell Simon. He understood this part on his own as he considered what she had suggested. Pauline would be safer if she left Languedoc and France. That would make it safer for him too since he would not let her out of his care and would always protect her. And he knew that it would be better for her heart and mind to relocate from this place in which she felt responsible for the sorrow she had seen and had escaped by happenstance.

The initial obstacle for Simon was to overcome the idea of having to renounce his loyalty to the French crown and to essentially agree to an allegiance to the English one. This was exactly as he, or his brother, or any noble would see it. They had no sense of nation, only of fealty. Their allegiance was to their king just as their serfs and other people were loyal only to them as their lords. It would be relinquishing all that was French culture, but it would still be just vassalage to another lord. He would have to become an Englishman, without ever having visited the island. But that part was surprisingly easy for him. He loved his homeland, but his future here was limited. Allegiance to one king was not much different than to another. Simon's ancestor, the original Simon de Montfort, had been the father of the great-grandmother to Henry II of England, making the King of England his distant cousin. The de Montfort family had also descended from Henry I, son of William the Conqueror.

The current Earl of Leicester had been appointed by King John of England, and that man was Simon's older cousin, more accurately his father's cousin, Ranulf de Blondeville. Not only was he childless, his ancestral title, original estate, lands, and income were in the county of Chester. He was first and most the Earl of Chester. Leicester could not mean a great deal to him. Simon might have a chance to persuade the old earl to convey to him that additional title. But before Simon could even get to that point, he had to obtain certain agreements from three people: his brother Amaury, King Louis IX, the new King of France, and King Henry III of England.

Amaury held the title of Comte de Montfort, with a claim to a title in Brittany, this one in England, and perhaps one in Occitania. What Amaury had to consider was that if any one of these potential titles were to become available, the King of France might choose to give it to Simon rather than concentrate too much power in the hands of Amaury. Or at least he might give Amaury a choice of one title and let Simon take the other. Simon planned to renounce any and all claims to all of the three titles, in France, in Brittany, and at Toulouse, if Amaury would agree to grant him the claim to Leicester. Amaury's heart and future were in France, where he was already a noble and in the court of the king. Getting him to renounce a mere possibility of a title in England might not be difficult. And then the King of France would have to set his seal on the grant and send it to England for Henry to approve. For France, it would mean losing a native son but placing a friend perhaps in a position of power in England.

All this lay ahead, in Paris. A journey of five hundred miles across France could take almost a year if one had to rely solely on the dirt paths that were the roads from village to village. But there were still several vestiges of the glory that was Rome, or at least Roman engineering, in the form of about a dozen paved Roman roads. The path from Avignon to Paris would not entirely be an interminable slog through dirt and mud. The party in question would partly travel the old roads once named for Agrippa, Domitian, and Julia Augusta. They occasionally would stay in lodges and roadhouses, and travel with relative speed. Everyone who might make such a journey from Avignon would take this route and would depart on the same road. The de Montfort party would pass through the town from the occupied estate to the south and would take that road. Guy Alain knew this.

He stationed himself there, along the side of the road where it leaves the town, where Simon's retinue was necessarily traveling. He was on the bridge at Avignon. It had been built on the site of an original and fallen Roman bridge and had been completed forty-four years before, in 1185. Two spans of it had been destroyed in the siege of that town that King Louis VIII had laid in 1226, only one year after Pauline had met Simon very near the same spot, and three years before they began this journey. Those gaps in the bridge were now spanned by a temporary wooden structure over which all must pass to begin the journey north. Guy Alain watched the company very closely. With de Montfort was his guard from the Orient, his scribes, his squires, and several other guards. There were no maids, no servants, no nurses, and no cook. The priest knew that they must have assumed he would see them on the way and that they had either sent the Cathar woman ahead, where they would meet her, or they had left her behind and she would come along later. He ordered two of his men to follow the party discreetly and watch them. He and the others immediately turned to go back to the estate house and search it. Whomever de Montfort had left behind would not be able to stop Alain. All the while, he was unaware that two eyes were never off him. And one hand never left the hilt of its sword.

When he got to the estate, he was surprised to see that the original local owners were already there and were moving in. They must have been nearby during the occupation by the knight from the north and had been poised to return and reclaim their property. Or a servant of theirs had remained behind when they were forced out and had been keeping them informed. Alain did not stop for permission but went with his men straight into the house and searched for the cook. The local family knew the importance of the Hound of God and his men, and they stayed out of his way. The priest found no cook, no trace of the woman he was certain Simon de Montfort had taken from him three years before. They must have sent her on ahead.

GERALD WEAVER

The de Montfort party began their journey on what remained of the Via Agrippa, but the farther north they traveled, the less likely that the Roman roads would still be usable. Over a thousand winters, they had become worn out, eroded, and overgrown. Had they been going the other direction, south, they could have taken a boat down the Rhône and covered much of the trip to the sea in two weeks. Going north on the river against the current would take as long as it would to ride. They were eight riders with four spare riding horses, with a wagon drawn by two draft horses. It was unlikely that most of the common robbers and highwaymen would accost eight armed men. As this was a well-traveled road, they would be able to find an inn or other accommodation perhaps every third or fourth night. On the other nights, they would sleep on the ground. On a very good day and on a paved part of an old Roman road, they might make twenty-five miles in a day, traveling only when the sun was up. On a less fortunate day, if conditions were wet and they were on any of the unpaved roads, they would be relieved to cover five miles.

Even traveling into the summer, it took them six long weeks to journey north along the Rhône to Dijon, with the mountains of the Massif Central to their left and the Alps to their right. Then they followed the remnants of the Via Agrippa northwest over some passes in the hills of Burgundy to reach the valley of the Seine at its source. The Seine was only a stream at this point, so they moved heavily along the dirt road beside it. They traveled another three weeks until they reached Auxerre, and there the Seine became navigable by two boats large enough to carry their party more rapidly downstream. This boat trip was the first chance they had to rest, to eat, and to wash themselves regularly, and for Rocco to begin Pauline's training in swordplay. It was also the first time Rocco felt like he did not have to keep watch for some possible attack by Guy Alain or his soldiers. Pauline was also satisfying her curiosity about the north. There were no warm, dry breezes, fewer flowering plants, less of a scent in the air, less color in the houses and in the dress of the people. But there were more people, and more at every turn in the river. Soon, she looked up the river and saw that most of the fields contained a farmhouse and there were more villages. Off in the distance, there was one thing that stood out, tall on the horizon. She knew they must be nearing Paris.

SEVEN

Construction had begun seventy years earlier and stone had been laid on stone until the Cathedral of Notre-Dame, still not fully completed, rose more than two hundred feet over the plain. Surrounded by one-story and two-story buildings, it commanded everyone's attention. It stood almost complete except for one of its two towers above its west-façade entrance. Even with some scaffolding on it, there was something about the cathedral that was uncanny, and that mysterious element made it as commanding as its towering height. It was unnaturally light and slender for a tall, stone structure. Pauline knew what any child also did: that you can only pile stone on stone for so long before it falls over, or before you must widen the base and stack more stones sideways. All tall structures must resemble a pyramid. This cathedral did not. It stood erect and slender like a strong young woman. Pauline could barely take her eyes off it for the remaining two days of the trip. It was also less of a wonder to her why these people let their lives be commanded by the Church rather than by the spirit of Christ. This building was a miracle.

From a distance, the edge of the city appeared as a line, and as they drew closer, Pauline saw that this was really a wall. With dozens of towers and several gates, and an opening for the river, it was apparently a recently built structure. In fact, much of Paris, including the wall and the cathedral, gave the impression of new growth. Once inside the wall, she could see that houses were being built on the farmland on the outer edges near the inside of the wall, that a few of the inner buildings were adding a third and fourth story, and that there was the hum and bustle of development and commerce. She had never seen so many people in one place. It was a hive of humanity. Most of the streets were narrow and crowded, some only as wide as two people. The roads were mostly unpaved, and the few larger ones that were paved had a trough in the middle that took waste and moved it down to the river. It was almost exactly like any village, only much larger, and with that soaring cathedral.

Most of the city was on the left bank, on the inside of the curve of the river, which sat on a low bluff. They disembarked at the docks, which were on the lower right bank. Pauline was still stunned by the size of the city and by the cathedral, which now loomed directly over them. Simon was pleased to have returned to Paris, which he warmly remembered from his youth. But he wore the more resolute look of a man with a task on his mind.

As they began to make progress to the bridge that would take them to the Île de la Cité, Pauline noticed something she had also seen on the boat and on the road. Here in the city, it was more remarkable. People did not ignore her or overlook her. She had been accustomed to not being seen or heard for her whole lifetime before she had become a noble's squire. The boatmen and those they met on the road had given her a short bow, to show her respect. Here in the city, it was impossible to miss. Everyone nodded at her. One short incident made it even clearer to her. She saw a shopkeeper roughly handling his son, who was his assistant. She quietly said something to him: "As we deal with the least among us is also how we deal with Christ, because He is in them."

The man was deeply ashamed. Among her own people, her words had been heard and understood. As a woman among the Catholic Christians, what she said was of little consequence. But now, as a male squire, she had an impact. She was at once pleased and frightened by this. She liked the respect, but she understood that she could be quite a bit too evident now. There was some virtue to going unnoticed. She knew she must not be outspoken but be quiet and take Rocco as her example.

They made their way to the Palais de la Cité, which lay on the western end of the Île de la Cité, the opposite end of the grand cathedral. That island was the center of the world for Simon, and Pauline could feel why Rocco remained visibly unmoved. It was a crowded, noisome muddle. Their party announced itself at the gate and was soon ushered in and given rooms in the palace's outer buildings. They cleaned up, changed clothes, and had something to eat. Simon was called to meet his brother and he took his scribe and his squire with him. They entered a large hall with a long table in the middle and they sat on one side at an end of it and waited. It was not long before Amaury rushed in to greet his brother with a hug and a slap on the shoulder. Pauline noticed that Amaury was shorter than Simon and stouter. He had Simon's dark handsome looks, but he was more rounded in features. He was also far more expressive, outward, and full of himself. He showed only good will toward his brother and his party. He was followed by a small retinue of scribes, guards, and advisors. The two brothers talked a long while about their late father, the crusade, the trip Simon had made, and about their mother, who had finally retired to their estate.

Nothing these brothers discussed was of greater interest to Pauline than what they said and what she had previously heard about their indomitable mother. Alix de Montmorency descended from a long, wealthy, noble line that was more illustrious than the de Montforts. Her grandfather had been the 4th Count of Hainaut, a county that spanned parts of France, Flanders, and Germany. Her mother had descended from counts of Luxembourg and Flanders. Alix de Montmorency had carried her confidence into her marriage to Simon's and Amaury's father and was never one for shrinking into the traditional role of a noble wife. She had been committed to be his equal partner. She had accompanied him on his campaigns in the Middle East and in France. She took part in the councils and recruited reinforcements for the Albigensian Crusade. She had been nearby when her husband was killed at Toulouse and had stayed on to counsel Amaury when he took over. After a few years, she returned to her family's estates near Paris. Pauline listened raptly and she wondered if Simon reflected during this conversation that his mother's strengths had set the table for Pauline's entrance into his life.

At all times, Amaury was expansive, warm, and open. Simon was respectful of his elder brother, who had been his commander and who was still his liege. After they had shared their recent experiences, Amaury spoke more pointedly to Simon, asking what brought him to Paris.

"I will not take up too much more of your valuable time, my lord. I have come here to strike a bargain with you, my brother."

"What could that be?"

"I would be willing to renounce all my properties and claims in France, Toulouse, and Brittany in exchange for receiving your claim to the title of the Earl of Leicester in England."

"Why, that is trading almost nothing for almost nothing," Amaury said. "Your claims in France are contingent, and the title in England has been taken from me. But wait, I see what you really mean. That would leave me the only de Montfort under allegiance to our king. And you might get something out of that English claim. Our old cousin who holds title in Leicester is childless and already has two other titles and lands. And King John, who took the title from our family, is dead. His son Henry III is now the king. You might have a chance."

"That is my thinking, sir."

"Then think no more of it. I agree. I cannot possibly take a title in England that would place me under the English king. My place is here. England and France are not always on good terms."

No sooner had he spoken than the door swung open. Standing in the doorway was a slender youth of fifteen, medium height with light brown hair and sensitive green eyes. He had about him a shy and gentle air, almost humble, and at all moments seemed to be taking in his surroundings and contemplating them. The youth was Louis IX, King of France. Amaury stood and quickly bowed deeply. Simon and all the others did the same. Behind the king were his guards and retainers, and most notably a woman of almost forty years who was confident, serene, and of regal bearing. She looked like a darker version of the young man and was his mother, Blanche of Castile, the queen regent, widow of Louis VIII, who had taken over the Albigensian Crusade at Amaury's request.

Pauline was struck by the presence of this woman. She had just been listening to the stories of the independent Alix de Montmorency, mother to Simon and Amaury. And now Pauline was in the presence of another strong woman she inherently admired, one who had commanded the Kingdom of France.

The young king approached Simon directly and spoke to him.

"You must be Simon de Montfort. We have heard a great deal about you. You are welcome here always."

Simon just bowed more deeply. Pauline kept her face down but watched it all intently.

The queen regent walked over to Amaury and put her hand on his shoulder.

"So, Comte de Montfort, this is your younger brother. He looks well. We appreciate his service to God and to his king."

Simon bowed again. And the royal party turned and exited the room.

"That was quite unexpected," Amaury said. "You should consider yourself favored."

"If so, my lord, it is as your brother and it is a reflected honor."

"That may or may not be. It looks as if I am to be appointed constable of France, commander of the army, first among the court, second only to the king. It is expected within a few months."

"I congratulate you, my lord. It only makes sense—with the death of the king's father, you are the most experienced soldier in France."

"And that means my place is here," Amaury said. "I can have no use for a title in cold, dank England. I have no doubt that King Louis will place his seal upon my renunciation of the claim to Leicester and will send it to King Henry in England. You should prepare to leave within a few days." Then he hugged his brother, looked at Pauline and the scribe, smiled, and left the room.

"I thought that went better than expected," Simon said.

Pauline waited to answer and looked at the scribe, who was no longer needed now that the substance of the meeting had occurred. Simon dismissed him; then she spoke.

"I would say so," Pauline said, "but I think there is more to it than meets the eye. The queen regent is a fit older woman and not more than a few years senior of your brother. He may want his handsome younger brother out of the country and out of the palace far more than the interested queen regent does."

"You could not be more impertinent. The queen regent is one of the most observant Christians in all of Europe. She has raised her son to be saintly. You can see that about them both."

"Perhaps I do. What matters is that the plan for your future is still in place. But I will make two simple points before we close this discussion. Though one of your Christians, she is still a woman, and a widow at that."

"And what else?"

"You cut a much more dashing figure than your shorter, older brother."

They retired to their quarters to prepare for supper, and again Pauline was almost too aware of the deference she was being shown by the palace servants. She did her utmost to pretend as if she were used to it. It soon became clear to the valets who were assigned to Simon's squire that Paul was one of the kinder and more grateful nobles they had encountered. She was wary of their familiarity and decided that she would spend more time outside of the palace and exploring the city. She particularly wanted to see the cathedral. Their party of eight attended the large communal midday dinner at the palace. There were forty or fifty people seated at the table, and Simon's party was seated far away from the king and queen regent and Amaury. When Simon heard of Pauline's plan to visit the city, he was relieved to know that Rocco always accompanied her.

Pauline and Rocco wandered through twenty blocks of the island that were not either cathedral or palace. Most of those were between the two structures, but some were beside the cathedral. From there, the two friends could get a view of the side of the remarkable structure. Not only was it tall and incredibly light and narrow for its great height, but there were also windows in its sides, long and narrow vertical windows, each topped with a round one. It was a miracle that the building stood at all. The secret seemed to be in the light support columns that stuck out from the sides like ribs, or ribbons, of equally tall and thin design, but which seemed to buttress the structure and supply the horizontal support that permitted the building to be so tall yet light. The cathedral would be complete when the second tower on the west-façade entrance was built. The structure was painted a grayish blue, but the columns and waterspouts, carved as statues of people or saints, and fantastical creatures, chimeras and grotesques, were painted different individual colors.

Upon entering it, they found it no less spectacular. If, as Pauline thought, the Catholic Christian faith was too worldly and too dependent on icons and symbols and rituals, then this cathedral at least surpassed all notions she might have of the pinnacle of all that worldly grandeur. It was magnificent.

After she had been looking up for some time, she felt Rocco's hand on her elbow, gently pulling her back behind one of the columns and into the shadow there. She became quiet and watchful but did not see anything unusual. She looked at her companion's face and followed his eyes to the entrance of the cathedral. A small party of clerics and soldiers had just entered. She looked more closely. There in the middle of this group was the tall man with the aquiline nose and the scar on his left cheek. The Hound of God was in Paris and in the Cathedral of Notre-Dame. He and his entourage had gathered inside the entrance and were waiting for something.

Pauline could feel Rocco withdrawing slowly further into the shadows behind the column. She smiled inwardly, knowing that he was perhaps more recognizable than she was. They had seen some different people from different places in their short time in Paris, but he was the only man of the Chin people in Venetian and Byzantine garb. She appeared to be just another young noble squire. She felt herself behaving perhaps a bit more like Simon than she would have previously. Despite the stricken look Rocco had given her at her first step, she continued to walk toward the group. She moved down the side of the church in their direction, then turned into the last pew and moved quietly until she was right beside them. Then she sat and bowed her head, then kneeled and prayed. No one took notice of the devout young squire.

EIGHT

Simon spent most of that day with his brother. It was a remarkable time for Simon. His elder brother, Amaury, was ten years older than he and had spent little time with Simon when he was a child. By the time Simon was eighteen and had met Pauline, four years earlier in 1225, Amaury had been in command of the crusade for several years and had become too busy for fraternal relations, even before he had left for Paris. He dealt with his brother as one of his lieutenants. But here at court, he was more relaxed and at ease, and seemed genuinely interested in the younger man's affairs. He was among other things surprised at his brother's ambition and his openness to all the possibilities of his future. Amaury truly had no interest in the Leicester title and knew he could not possibly swear fealty to the English king and remain at the French court and possibly become the constable of France one day. He also had family here: his wife, Beatrix, one son and four daughters. He felt that Simon's decision to seek the title in England was a bold and intelligent move. In fact, several years earlier, after the reversion of Toulouse to Raymond, he had petitioned his father's cousin for the English title and had been rebuffed. Amaury told Simon he might have a better chance now, simply because the English king who had taken the title from the de Montforts had been succeeded by his son.

Amaury had then brought his renunciation of the title to Simon, under the seal of King Louis IX, for Simon to carry to London. It had only taken one day to obtain. Amaury was clearly quite significant at court. He told Simon that he was welcome to stay in Paris for as long as he wished. Simon wanted to take some time, to relax, and to shake off the mud from the long journey from Avignon. There was much to see and do in the capital. It had become the center of French life and the French Catholic Church since Hugh Capet had been elected King of the Franks, over two hundred years earlier. Since then, the city had developed considerably. Even in the twenty-two years of Simon's life it had changed and grown a great deal. He wanted to confer with Pauline and tell her the news. He was in the main room of their quarters with his guards when he saw Rocco return without her. He was alarmed, but he did not show it.

"Where is my squire?" he asked.

"Still at the cathedral, my lord. I have no doubt that she will be along shortly. I could not stay. I did not want to risk being seen by an old acquaintance of ours who, to our surprise, walked into the cathedral."

Simon thought about this for a while, and still maintaining his calm demeanor, said that he would go for a walk, intending to go straight to the cathedral. He had not gone more than a few steps from the palace when he saw his squire, moving in his direction, with a sly smile on her face.

"It was Guy Alain," she said, "and wait. Were you just now planning to crown him again with your sword?"

"I would not let him have you again, by my word. Will you favor me with an explanation for all of this?"

"Like all the rest, he and his party remain convinced of their eyes' first report, and I was able to stay close to them without suspicion as they discussed their plans. It seems they have traveled here on some mission, perhaps in pursuit of us. I do not know. Father Alain made Notre-Dame his first stop, to pay his respects to the Archbishop of Paris and perhaps to explain his mission and seek support for it. But then there was some message from the archbishop that caused them all to hurry away and disappear into the city, on the left bank."

"This is not at all to my liking. I will seek my brother's counsel."

They went back to the palace and prepared for supper. When they dined again in the great hall with the court and the king and were once again among that crowd of forty or fifty souls, Simon was able to sit alone with Amaury for several minutes after the dinner. Pauline and the rest of his party returned from the dinner and sat in the main room of their quarters, waiting for him to return. When he did, it was with the news that the Hound of God had been called back to Rome.

"There are two reasons for this," he said. "The first is that there was a strike and a riot at the University of Paris just a few months ago. Apparently, the queen regent was not pleased with the leniency of the Ecclesiastical Courts in handling the students on strike. She summoned the palace guards, and some students were killed. They rioted again, then went away to their respective homes. The university is a papal institution, and the students come from all over Europe, so this is not a situation that Pope Gregory wants to see continue. He has asked Guy Alain to give him a report. He has gone to the university to investigate and will be here in two days to meet with my brother. The university is of great importance to the city and to the reputation of the king, so a solution must be reached."

"Then we must leave tomorrow," Pauline said.

"That has already been arranged."

"What is the second reason that Guy Alain must go to Rome?"

"It is because there is to be a general and official Inquisition. The Vatican will create several offices to formally take the work of the Hound of God and make it a general program in Languedoc and in Spain."

Pauline felt her heart sink. She had felt remorse for having survived and for not having acted to save her friends sooner. Now she felt guilt for not being with her fellow believers who were to be persecuted by this formal Inquisition and for being in the company of a man whose family had been associated with their persecution. The comforts of the last four years had begun to be colored with sorrows. There was nothing that would save the Good Men and Good Women now. They had been punished by twenty years of armed oppression and that had ended. What hope they had was in the spirit of the people, in their faith, in quietly believing and secretly practicing their religion. Their focus was not here, in the world, anyway. The loss of the towns and lords and armies that incidentally had protected them while they also defended their own independence could have been managed. But now there would be many priests like Guy Alain, who would ferret out and destroy the essence of the Cathar faith, using techniques he had begun to use on her. She had only saved her body. Perhaps what powered her sense of having betrayed her faith was that she had been saved by, and was inextricably linked to, the man whose father had played the largest role in the Albigensian Crusade.

She felt her soul would forever be without spiritual companionship.

Her mood did not improve the next day when they embarked on the Seine for the boat trip to Le Havre. Simon's mind was on his plan for approaching the King of England and his cousin who was the current Earl of Leicester, but he could not help but notice the despondency of his squire. He also watched for some clue to this in the behavior of the man he called the Venetian, particularly to see if that man felt the need to comfort her. Had Simon been more a student of character, he would have known that Rocco's makeup was not nurturing or comforting. He only knew to protect. A more perceptive eye than Simon's would have seen that he was always close enough to Pauline to be able to protect her even if he had to protect her from herself.

Simon was also concerned with one important fact. Ever since the time of William the Conqueror, the office of lord high steward of the king had been invested in the earls of Leicester. The first had been his mother's ancestor, Robert de Beaumont, who had been known as Robert de Meulan when he was a powerful nobleman in Normandy and a friend of William the Conqueror. In fact, there had been no Leicester title until William had granted significant lands in the English Midlands to Robert and made him the 1st Earl of Leicester. Were Ranulf and King Henry to grant Simon that title, he would automatically become one of the most important officers in the court, and the one closest to the king. It was true that these major offices at court had since become largely ceremonial, but still he would vault to a foremost position among all English nobles. It did seem unlikely that the king and his advisors, or Ranulf de Blondeville, would agree to that. But as Pauline had said, Simon often took the bold step.

It took only a few days to travel down the Seine to Le Havre in a nar, a square-rigged, oared cargo boat, much like a larger version of a Viking longboat. There, they switched to a cog, a larger flat-bottomed boat that was also square-rigged but had no oars, which they took to Calais, where they resupplied before crossing the Channel to Dover. Then they sailed around the point of Kent to enter the River Thames and ride the rising tide to London. The sight that dominated the city from this angle was London Bridge, a low stone bridge with thick piers and narrow arches, with so many buildings on the bridge, some several stories high, that it looked like a city street suspended over the river. The Thames was not really a river at this low point but a tidal pool that rose and fell with the tide, which determined that a boat could only leave town on an ebb tide and arrive on a rising one. This tidal effect was nowhere greater than under the bridge, in the narrow arches, which ran like rapids in alternating directions according to the tides. No large boat would attempt passage under it, and the de Montfort party disembarked before it, right next to the Tower of London, which William had built.

The city, perhaps a quarter the size of Paris, was only on one side, the north side, of the river and was walled, so it formed a half-circle. On the south side of the bridge were two churches, a couple of inns, and a large swamp. The largest church in the city proper was built mostly of stone, was a mix of architecture, and seemed much less certain to last as long as the great cathedral of Paris. It was called St. Paul's and was the seat of the Diocese of London and its bishop. The town was not the equal of Paris, and what made matters even stranger for the travelers was that apparently no one spoke French. They had to rely on one of the French sailors who knew the Saxon tongue, and even he was having a difficult time communicating. It was only when they arrived at the tower that they found someone with whom they could speak French. There was a good deal of new construction occurring around the Tower of London. It seemed that King Henry was expanding it and improving its defenses. He had also whitewashed it, so that it now stood out even more. One of the foremen directed them to the office of the current lord high steward, who was not there at the time. The acting steward was a member of the king's household.

This gentleman saw to it that the party was given a chance to wash before they would dine, and then they were immediately brought in to meet King Henry. Pauline was struck by how much it was a less severe and dignified setting than they had found in Paris. It seemed almost informal or relaxed by comparison. There were several members of the court present in the king's reception room, and the king himself was moving among them. He seemed light-hearted and extravagant in his speech. He was demonstrably pleased to meet Simon and said so. He was almost the same age as Simon. But he was shorter, strongly built, with a narrow face. One of his eyes, the left, must have been damaged at birth, because the lid was always partly closed, and one could not see all his pupil. It did not seem to check the impulses of the king.

"My God," he said, "we finally have someone who speaks true French. And a very striking person, at that. You are quite the specimen. We are cousins, is that not so?"

"We are not quite cousins, Your Majesty. If you go back five generations, you will find we have a common ancestor. I am curious about your saying I speak true French. That is all I hear spoken in your court."

"Oh, you are being kind to us. As Normans, we never spoke it as well as you who are from the Île de France. And now our French is tainted by the various Saxon words that have crept into it, and we have lost much of the proper grammar. I think the scholars are calling what we speak Anglo-Norman. I desperately want you here at court, if not alone for your excellent French."

"So, may I ask if you have read the message that I handed over from King Louis?" Simon asked.

"Oh, no, no, no. Of course not. I have people read for me. And I have been expecting something like this for some time. My father gave that title to one of his loyal vassals, who has little need for it and has not managed that county well."

"I am sorry, Your Majesty. You must think me impertinent."

"Not at all. I think you are just what we need here. Unfortunately, I cannot accept your homage and make you the earl, not without the agreement of the Earl of Chester and Leicester. And he is not here now."

"Then I am at your command, Your Majesty."

"Not quite yet, sir. But I will grant you a retainer of four hundred pounds per year for the maintenance of you and your men until this matter is decided. And I will agree to meet with you and Ranulf de Blondeville and see what he says. That may not be for a while, perhaps not for several months. He is making plans for our trip to Brittany. I suppose it is not a secret that we design to invade Brittany next year. I hope that does not change your plans."

"I am grateful for your assistance and your honesty. Please let me know how I may be of service."

"You can teach some of these people the mother tongue. In all earnestness, you may do as you choose. Just be prepared. It has been wonderful to meet you. We have enjoyed it."

Simon understood that all that mattered in his world was that one pledged one's fealty to one's lord. Loyalties could be honorably changed. This pledge to the King of England would be like any other. All nobles understood this. Simon's situation was not unique. But he felt uncomfortable now that the possibility of a conflict with France and with his brother seemed quite real.

Simon was also not sure what exactly had happened, nor what exactly he had heard, nor did he know how to consider it. He had never witnessed any sovereign or any lord who behaved so impulsively and who spoke so freely. It led him to wonder if any of it could be something upon which he could rely. He knew that his only loyalty would be to his lord and king, whoever that king may be. But it struck him painfully that he might be giving his fealty to a volatile king who would be attacking France, and facing an army perhaps led by his brother.

There was a lot to consider. And this made him think of Pauline. He had looked at her from time to time during the audience with the English king, and he studied her after they had left. Her countenance was still, her eyes vacant. She gave no indication of any of the keen insights he had come to rely upon. She showed not even a flicker of her unusual perspectives that had so often illuminated his deeper reasoning. In fact, she exhibited no interest in him and did not note that he was looking at her and seeking her contribution to his understanding of recent events.

At first, he was disappointed and perhaps a little angry at her. But in his heart, there was too much of a connection. He could not long line up in opposition to her and soon he began to venture his own opinions on her condition and its causes. This speculation would take more than a few moments. Maybe it would even be years before it would ever really settle into his being. But it did eventually begin to take shape. This very process had been in fact something she had taught him. He had always lived his life as if he were a cart on a path. There was not even a thought that left the track. From her, he had learned to have second and third thoughts. He had entertained doubts, and all that had taught him to reconsider. He now saw alternative paths. This new way of being and thinking, and she, had all led him to this new possible future. He had learned to have second thoughts about his unseeing allegiance to the Catholic Church. He had been able to think more deeply about his fealty to the French king. Now that she had internalized the last and worst blow against her people and faith with the news of the official Inquisition, he began to reconsider his opinion of the one person he had only ever worshipped and admired. He began to question his feelings toward his father, and his father's prominent role in the Albigensian Crusade.

NINE

The English king had meant what he said in at least one important element. He had given Simon and his retainers an income, more than they required to sustain themselves in a large house just outside London. It was in an old town west of the city, down a road called the Strand, near the great Westminster Hall, which was used for trials and other official procedures. It was the largest roofed great hall in all of Europe. William II had begun to build a palace there, which had been added to over the years. There was the abbey church of St. Peter. And all around them, there were various new great structures going up that strove not to disappoint that great hall. All this was beginning to transform the old town of Westminster into the location of many of London's governmental functions. The de Montfort household wintered there and awaited the next directive from young King Henry. Simon did his best to learn about London and its inhabitants, and to put his house in order. Pauline did not change and stayed largely within herself. Sometimes she would leave and be gone for days, during which times Simon did not worry too much for her safety. Rocco would follow her. Simon knew that no ill would befall her. He only worried about her emotional well-being, and whether she and Rocco would return. They always did.

In much of that time, Simon considered what he could sense might be Pauline's opinion of the crusade against her people. He took it to heart, and he began to see his father in a different and unflattering light. The Languedoc had long been home to a brilliant, diverse civilization that had been violently suppressed. The Occitan way of life would perhaps survive, but only as a faint echo and as it had been subsumed into the greater France. Feudal rule would supplant Roman law. Inheritance would be constrained by primogeniture. Diversity of religious faith would disappear. Many groups would lose the independent standing they had previously held. Among these would be Jews, Saracens, Cathars, and particularly women. The culture that had generated Pauline and other women like her would soon be gone, perhaps never to return.

The process had not been peaceful. It would now devolve into the practices and procedures of the Inquisition, as Simon had witnessed it applied by Guy Alain. But it had begun in war, siege, military coercion, and oppression. Young Simon had not seen the massacres of the populations of the towns of Béziers and Carcassonne that had occurred before his father had been elected to command the crusade. He had witnessed that Simon the Elder had ruthlessly taken almost every other remaining town in Languedoc and had subjected the inhabitants to dispossession, persecution, and destruction. He had seen that then as a holy war sanctioned by the Pope. Thousands had died, and many more had fled to the mountains, the woods, and to Spain. At every step, the Cathars had been forcibly converted or simply killed. In many places, this devastation had not spared the Jews, Saracens, or even some other Catholics. Young Simon had only known that all of it had been done in the name of God and with the blessing and assistance of the Roman Church. But he had also seen that it had been a bloody and brutal affair.

He knew that the finality of it now must be impossible for Pauline to manage. Simon was beginning to have a difficult time reconciling all of it with the love he had felt for his father. Eventually, many of these feelings began to resolve inside of him as a nascent sensitivity to guilt, and he began to feel it simply as a manner of being a part of his renowned and noble family.

✳ ✳ ✳

Normandy and Brittany had long been independent of France. Three hundred years before this, Brittany had belonged to a kingdom that included part of northern Spain and all of Wales and Cornwall. Brittany was still an independent duchy, with its strongest ties being to the King of England. For almost two hundred years after the Normans had sailed from Normandy and conquered England, those two lands had been the same kingdom, ruled from London by English kings of Norman blood. It was not until 1204 that the French took Normandy from the English. And for a very brief time, a French king had ruled England. The English king would not soon forget these historical facts, and in 1230, Henry III landed in Brittany with his vassals, including Ranulf de Blondeville, Earl of Chester, Lincoln and Leicester, with the intent of taking back Normandy. It was to Brittany that Simon was summoned in April of 1230 to meet with the king and then Ranulf, his father's cousin.

Ranulf was aged sixty, an ancient man by all standards. He was the last of the great breed of Norman warrior nobles. He had been married twice, once to the Duchess of Brittany, had fought in two crusades, and had served four English kings prior to Henry III. He had played an important role in the management of the kingdom and in the succession of those kings and had been rumored at more than one time to be a possible English monarch. He was one of the few nobles present when King John had signed the Great Charter, and he had remained loyal to the king in the civil war, commanding his armies. He had been instrumental in bringing young Henry back to the throne when he obtained Henry's support for the Great Charter and used that to rally the nobles to oust the French. He held lands in England, Normandy, and Brittany. He was now overseeing Henry's expedition against France. The young king was beholden to him, but Ranulf stood near the end of his road and had few remaining ambitions. When Simon was brought in to meet with Ranulf, it had not been lost on the old man that the king was behind the meeting. The king told Simon to be careful with the man he called "that old Visigoth."

When Simon entered the room, he saw a short but stout white-haired gentleman who appeared to have eaten something that disagreed with him. He was not to lose that look when he began to speak, or after.

"So, you are my young cousin," he said.

"Yes, my lord, I believe that your mother and my grandfather were siblings, making you and my father cousins."

"And now you have come to England to poach one of my titles."

"I was hoping, my lord, that I might be able to do you some favor that would allow you to return the title to my family," Simon said.

"That's all well and good. I knew your father when we were young men. He was a born soldier, the kind of man one does not see anymore. All I see now are boys playing at being soldier. You are right. The title had been his when King John granted it to me. So, it is your elder brother who has the claim, not you."

"He has renounced it, in favor of me. He deems that his future is in France, and he has other titles."

And here the old man laughed raucously and drank mead from a pewter mug.

"Don't I know it, boy," he said. "I have more damn titles than I can count. I am practically the Duke of Brittany. I have claims here and in Normandy. I am the Earl of Chester and of Leicester, and the king just made me the 1st Earl of Lincoln. I have little or no use for Leicester anyway, and no one to whom to leave it. It was without any lord for several years and has fallen to seed."

"I only wish to make you pleased with the agreement."

"Don't fawn at me, boy. King Henry seems to want this. And I will get some recompense from him. The true value of it, I am sure you know, is that the Earl of Leicester is the lord high steward of the king. I am too damn busy for that job, and it is one better suited to your fawning and bowing. Be careful what you wish for, little cousin," he said. "You will have to do something for me before you get to be the king's top vassal."

"I will do what you would like."

"I want you to get rid of the Jews," the old man said. "I am sick of them and their usury. And I had my fill of them in Jerusalem. They should be converted or eliminated."

Simon could only think of Pauline, of his father, of the persecutions in Languedoc. The Jews may not have been Christians, but he could no longer see himself becoming a scourge to another people simply because they had a different faith. He also knew that in Leicester, or any town, they made contributions to commerce and to taxes. Most importantly, he knew how Pauline would see yet another oppression of a separate religion. He felt her in his heart, as if her feelings were his own. He decided on a plan that would allow him to do what his conscience now dictated but might placate the old Visigoth. He would agree to move them to an area just outside of his control and allow them to continue in their faith and businesses. He would allow them to settle just outside the town walls in the precinct of Leicestershire under the control of his Great-aunt Margaret.

"There will be no more where and when I am lord," he said.

"Then there you have it. I will tell the king that I agree. And if I see your elder brother on the field of battle, I will be sure to give him your best."

Simon did not know if he was more shaken by this last statement or with his own agreement to move an innocent people. The former only alarmed him. The latter touched upon that feeling of guilt that had been growing in him. This was not how he had imagined he might begin his new life, his long-sought title, and his quest to repair the name of de Montfort, at least in his own heart.

Mercurial King Henry was quite pleased. He told Simon as much. He smiled during the short ceremony in which Simon pledged him his service, his sword, and his life. There was only one technicality: at some point, Amaury would have to renounce the title in person before him. But no one expected that even to be possible for several more years. The king invested Simon with the provisional title and bade him a safe trip to Leicester. Henry also told him to make sure that he reported back to London once the king had returned, and only after all had been put in order at Leicester. Then the king would invest him as the lord high steward of the king.

Simon told his entourage of the news, and they prepared to leave for London and then for Leicester. It was not for a few months after they had been in London that they were prepared and had been given word that he was ready to be received in Leicester. They would make their way from London to Leicester along Watling Street and the Fosse Way. These were among the few hardened gravel roads in England and they had long since lost the look and the names they had when they were Roman roads. The trip would take ten days and would cover over one hundred and twenty miles. During the trip and for the months before they left, Simon had made some unsuccessful attempts to bring Pauline out of her languor. He had not ever prodded her or pushed her. He simply spoke to her at length about all that he had seen and been told.

They installed themselves in Leicester Castle, and Simon began to take visits and pledges from the burgesses, knights, merchants, and priests. It was an exciting and confusing time. There was much to learn, perhaps too much. At last he sat down with Pauline after dinner one evening, and he told her the one thing he had been wanting to tell her but had held back.

"I want you to know, Pauline, that as we begin this new venture I am pledging my life to begin a new way of seeing the world, and to do what I can to expiate this feeling I have of family responsibility for what has happened to your land and to your people. I am not going to let that manner of thing happen again. I will bend myself to the task of doing the opposite. I hope to strive to be generous in my new roles and to work to make life easier for those who might otherwise be burdened. I have felt your pain almost as if it were my own. My life from this point will be dedicated to these new goals."

He sat quietly and watched her. He felt he had lifted a weight from his own chest. And that felt good. So did the fact that for the first time in a year and a half, he thought he saw something stir in her, something like her original spirit.

"English," she said.

"What?" he asked.

"English; I think we must call it English, the language these people speak. It is no longer Saxon German. And it is not that Anglo-Norman French that the nobles speak. It is a smoother, softer version of Old German, and it is spoken only here and nowhere else. It seems to have evolved on its own and in response to the French spoken by the nobles, clerics, and mostly the magistrates."

"All right, then," Simon smiled, "we shall call it English and we had better begin to learn how to speak it."

"And he is going to be trouble, you know, that King Henry of yours. Have you ever wondered why he might be so quick to embrace you as his vassal, his relation, the lord high steward of his household, when he hardly knows you and you are a Frenchman?"

"I have not thought about it, exactly. No. I do know that I am grateful for it. And the title has been in my family. I have given him my fealty, and I am an addition to his support. I am a new vassal, new support for him. The last Earl of Leicester held other titles and roles."

"And the king likes you," she said, "for the obvious reasons that anyone likes you. But you are still unknown to him. And that is not a good sign."

"How might that be?"

"If he prefers the support of aliens and strangers over those lords who already have vested interests in the kingdom, that means he might not be able to manage people who have more than their own welfare to consider. He may prefer those who only owe loyalty to him, those who flatter him, those who only have an active interest in getting something from him."

"I believe the Earl of Chester may have hinted at something like that," he said.

"But King Henry has given you an outside interest, the town and county of Leicester, whose people now depend on you. You are no longer just the handsome French nobleman who owes him everything."

"I am beginning to understand what you are saying. And my feeling about the king does not contradict your insight."

"Add to that," she said, "the role of lord high steward, which you will now hold. I am sure that might pose some type of conflict. What does the steward do?"

"He was the master of the household and the court, but that has evolved to become the position of supervisor of the king's other counselors and overseer of the ministers of the king's justice."

"So, you will be placed between King Henry and his counselors, and you will be tasked to serve the interests of the king and those of England itself."

"But the king is England," he said.

"Only if this lovely and verdant island is an impulsive and uncertain twenty-three-year-old young man."

"I am beginning to see why my old cousin warned me to be careful what I wished for."

"He may also have been speaking of this mess that the whole of Leicestershire is. One of the advantages I had as a member of your party who did not talk was that the retainers of Ranulf de Blondeville spoke quite freely in front of me. Your old cousin was not around very much, and for over a dozen years before that, the county was run by the merchants, the churchmen, and the burgesses. There is no king's sheriff in Leicester, which in the end will be a good thing for you, but for now, it means that no one has been collecting the fees due to the earl, nor is it even certain what those fees are and who owes them. You cannot simply rely on people to come forward. A great deal of researching must be done, and then the real work begins."

"You have been doing a lot of thinking, I see."

"Yes, I have, Simon. You face a number of great challenges and I have taken to heart your promise to do good. Thank you."

Simon was at first surprised by all this information; then he was alarmed and even perhaps a bit fearful. But mostly this was overcome by the comfort and warmth and joy of being spoken to in such a manner once again. It was as if some horribly wounded limb of his had finally healed. He hid his joy and did not smile, but he had an idea.

"The king is not the only one who must have a steward. I must have one, too. Someone must help me manage the county and my household and all the others who must serve me. I think the term of your service as my squire may have completed. If you wish, I would like you to be the steward of Leicestershire and its castle."

Pauline stood up. She walked a few steps toward Simon. He thought he saw the hint of her smile. He definitely saw a spark in her eye, a flicker of recognition of what they had always shared.

She said, "I think that is an excellent idea."

TEN

Simon and Pauline had agreed that as soon as they had settled in to Leicester Castle he would begin to travel about the county in order to learn about its geography, its people, and to meet with the leading citizens of Leicestershire. She would make it her duty to gather what she could about how the household and the county had been run. She kept mostly to herself in those first days and was waiting for Simon to embark on his survey and journey. At the times when she saw him, she reminded him of her gratitude for the pledge he had made to improve the lives of as many people as he could and to do what he could to recompense for his family's role in the crusade against her people and her land, which resulted in the Inquisition that was now being turned against them. He was very solicitous of her and realized that she needed some time on her own to continue to climb out of her dour stillness. She intended to do just that, and she had plans as to how to go about it.

She would not remain passive. She would not simply remind him. Nor would she expect him to know what to do on his own. As always, she knew she would choose the path of guiding him and of giving his inclinations a practical and constructive operation. While he was away, she would be moving about in the town of Leicester, learning about its people, and developing ways in which she could help Simon to help those most in need. He did not tarry. He embarked soon after they had set themselves and his household in order. She immediately slipped outside the castle and began to walk around the town, taking it all in as much as she could.

The first thing she noticed was that the town showed little practical change beyond its original status as a Roman fortified camp that had been converted by the Saxons. It still had its four Roman walls, fortified by the Saxons with stone. The streets retained the grid pattern that had been customary of the Roman camps. And the four gates had also been fortified. This was a time of population growth in Leicester as in other towns of its size. It contained just under two thousand residents. Pauline began her walk up High Street because it was the main commercial street in the town. She noticed that for a while it went along a walled space that must have been an old Roman forum. There were stalls in that open field, but the main activity was in the shops along the street. And the more numerous of these enterprises appeared to be the production of wool. There were shops with spinning wheels and looms. There were also fullers, who cleaned and thickened the wool by pounding it with hammers in a mixture of water and clay.

She would occasionally catch the almost sweet scent of the clay as she walked along, but it was soon overpowered by the smell of leather tanneries down High Street. They were the second industry of the town. The shops she passed had the semi-finished leather that was being cut, colored, shaped, and sewn. It had a dark, sharp, powerful smell. Her reaction to it must have been obvious because one of the apprentices stacking the raw leather in the front of one of the shops commented to her.

"You must be a city man," he said. "Your looks are dressy, I say. If you think this is a foul smell, you should go down Gallowtree

Street toward East Gate. That's where the odiferous work is done. Hope you don't mind piss."

Pauline's English was proficient enough to answer him. But she chose not to, only to acknowledge that she understood. She thanked the young man, nodded to him, and moved further down High Street, but she marked his suggestion and decided she would make that trip later.

She turned back and walked to the stalls in what had been the old forum. Mostly, these sold vegetables, poultry, eggs, along with foraged nuts, fruits, fish and some wild game. There were also some stalls that sold bread and articles of woolen clothing. She lingered quite long there and listened to the conversations. She learned that this square held a regional market once a week when the number of these stalls would be augmented by those who came from outside of town to sell their wares as well as household and farm tools, furniture, and goods. She also heard from among the bread sellers that there were many bakers in Leicester. She decided she would head west down Cank Street to the well there, which was at the center of the baker sector. Then she would go in search of her main objective, to find the best place from which to work with poor people, the ones she would hope to assist Simon to help.

Her nose told her she was approaching the bakeries and when she got to that area, she could see that this was also a thriving industry in the town and that this neighborhood was one of the more prominent ones. The houses were fairly large and more closely resembled what she had seen of homes in London. Many of them had wooden roofs instead of thatch. One of the things that struck her was that some of these homes appeared to be empty. She made a mental note of this. This neighborhood was typical of nicer areas in other towns in that it sat on a small rise. From this vantage point, Pauline could see at least half a dozen steeples. There had to be fewer than five hundred homes within the walls of Leicester.

She considered the number of churches to be quite extraordinary. She had composed a list of some of them before she left the castle because that is where she knew she would find the people most in need. There was St. Peter's, St. Mary's, St. Clement's, St. Margaret's, St. Martin's, St. Nicholas', and a few others not on her list. Most of them were arranged in a circle around the center of town. Over the next three weeks, she would walk this circle and she would also visit the odiferous section of town in the east.

These walks also took her through most of residential Leicester, which consisted of small, thatched homes that seemed to subsist on home-raised livestock, poultry, and crops. Some of the homes had large plots. Others did not. It seemed that almost all the families in them survived only on what they could grow or raise. Most of them were poor. Pauline realized that scratching out a living in this way in England was much more difficult than it was in warm and fertile Languedoc. There had been a growth in the merchant class and the craftsmen over the last few generations. Some of the men in these houses worked in the bakeries, tanneries, woolen shops, and other small industries. These were the class of people who supported the churches. The churches did what little they could to support the poor. There were beggars in every part of the town, and they were mostly the old or the disabled.

As she expected, on her first visit to the first parish, St. Clement's, she witnessed what little the church could do to feed the impoverished, and to care for the sick. It was itself not an affluent institution. The clergy were as poorly fed and clothed as the people they tried to serve. Pauline watched this church for a few days and picked out the one monk she felt was the most compassionate and who spent the most time working with the poor who came to the church for help. The next time she went there, she brought him a few pounds from the treasury she maintained in the castle.

"God be praised," he said. "This is more than we receive in a year. I will see that good use is made of it. What is your name, good sir? I will pray for you."

Pauline tried her English on him and hoped she was telling him that her name was not important, that she was not from around here, and that she only hoped she could do more. He told her his name was Elbert. She took his hand and looked him in the eye and tried to convey to him her intention to help as best she could. She felt he had a good heart.

She thought she knew what she would do from this point. She would observe each church and she would try to find a cleric like Elbert in each. In some of them, she did not find anyone. But in four of them, she was able to establish a contact with a clergyman. She was deeply impressed with these lesser clergymen of the Roman faith and found them to be closer to the people of her own faith and quite different from many of the churchmen she had met and seen. These Leicester monks had given up their own worldly comforts for the life of helping others. Her plan was to set up a small distribution of funds to these specific men later, to feed the hungry and care for the sick. They would have to agree that none of the money would go to the church itself. She knew this would take time, but it was her goal.

Not long before she knew Simon would return, she made her way down Gallowtree Street toward the stench of the tanneries. Much of the smell emanated from the refuse piles outside each tannery. They kept the skins and did what they could to make use of the outer parts of the horns, and some of the other animal parts that came with the hides. The dried skins were soaked in a mixture of water and urine and bark from trees, which would soften them and allow the hair, dirt, fat, and flesh to be scraped off. The tanners discarded the inner horns, the hooves, the hair, and the fat and flesh they had scraped from the inside of the hides. They then pounded the hides with dung and animal brains, to bate the skins. They finished the process by stretching the skins and applying cedar oil or alum or vegetable oil, before they sent them to the leather shops on High Street.

Pauline hurried through this part of town and through the East Gate to the one parish outside the walls, St. Margaret's, which was in the part of the county that was under the control of Simon's Great-aunt Margaret, the Countess of Winchester. Pauline watched this church as carefully as the others. It was more prosperous and was part of a larger religious complex. Pauline sat at the edge of the cemetery to observe how the church handled the poor who went to it for help. It was not long before she realized that she was being observed as closely and as discreetly as she was watching the church. There was a small girl, perhaps eight years of age, playing nearby. She had brown eyes and dark brown hair and a fair complexion. She would look away when Pauline looked at her. This happened several times over two days. When she realized Pauline was not a threat, she came up to her and she spoke in French.

"You are not a boy," she said. "You are a lady."

"You are mistaken, little girl."

"You look like a boy and you dress like a boy. But you are too quiet to be a boy. And you watch things carefully. Boys do not do that."

"Maybe that is because I am a man," Pauline said.

"You are nicer than a man."

"What is your name?"

"Rachel."

"Have men been unkind to you, Rachel?"

"We used to live in a big house on Cank Street, but men came and moved us out. They did not listen to my father. They were not quiet. They took our money. The men at the church won't help us."

At this, Pauline began to cry. She had lived through this sort of thing and so had her people, and for much the same reason. They prayed to God in a different way. Rachel saw Pauline cry and put her hand on Pauline's arm.

"Please don't cry, lady. It will be all right."

Pauline wiped her face.

"You speak French," she said.

"My family is from Rouen."

Pauline said good-bye to the girl and returned to the castle, where she questioned the priest who ran the chapel about the Jewish people of Leicester. He told her that before they had been expelled from the town, the Pope had ruled that they could no longer collect interest on debts. They had been invited to England from Rouen and other towns in Normandy by William the Conqueror because they could loan money at interest, as no Catholic was permitted.

For the next few days, she went back to the neighborhood around St. Margaret's and talked to Rachel. She asked her to tell her where she lived and what her father's name was. Pauline knew well enough that the girl's parents would be deeply skeptical of her approaching them. Rachel confirmed this and told Pauline her parents would not even want her to talk to a Christian. Pauline did not approach the girl's parents. She also did not want them to know exactly who she was. And this was especially true since this girl had seen through her disguise.

She felt a similarity between the fate of the people of her faith and that of the dispossessed Jewish people of Leicester. There were about eight families. She thought about how she might help them as well as the poor. She would have to wait until she and Simon were able to turn the county around and get it running well. She would need to establish a steady income for the county, and she had an idea how to help the churches assist the poor. It would be more complicated to help Rachel's people. She knew that the Pope had banned interest lending and that many had also lost their shops. She also understood that Rachel's family and friends would not accept charity. She thought she might hire some of them to help administer the matters outside of the town as counters and messengers and teachers.

Pauline had accepted Simon's statement of contrition and she knew he was sincere. But it had not eliminated her feeling of remorse for what had happened to her people but not to her. And even though she trusted Simon's compassion, she still felt empty because she had not known of any way in which this could be converted to good works and deeds. She could not feel right or good until she had a plan and was able to put in place a program to help the poor, the sick, the old, the dispossessed, and the disabled. There was not a great deal that could be done but she would see that it was done. She felt better now that she had some idea what she might do. It would be part of her destiny with Simon, to help him do the most good for people. She felt it was why she chose him in the first place, and why he chose her.

BOOK TWO

ELEVEN

The first thing they noticed was the smoke. Gliding up the Thames, the members of the papal delegation began to speak to each other about how much smoke was in the air. Almost all of them were from southern climes: Spain, France, and mostly from Italy. They were not used to seeing the result of so many home fires burning for warmth and to dry out the air of the interiors. Smoke hung over London Bridge and around the Tower of London as they disembarked on their mission to meet with the English king. One of their number was also on a separate mission of his own. Guy Alain had arrived back in England in the summer of 1231.

Simon de Montfort, Earl of Leicester, was returning currently from his long review of all of Leicestershire, roughly eight hundred square miles of low rolling hills and pastureland, with the town of Leicester and its castle in the center. He had ridden many miles and met with the local knights, burgesses, merchants, bailiffs, and priests as much as he could. At each turn, these individuals were surprised and honored to have the earl visit them. None could remember even the report of such a thing having occurred before. Most of them felt more bound to their lord by it, and word soon spread that the new earl had the common touch. In the latter half of his visits, he had found that he would be anticipated, and he was often greeted by small crowds. The trip had taken over a month and had been Pauline's idea. She had also suggested that he require that all collections for the county be recorded in a written roll. She stayed in the castle and tried to make the most out of the old descriptions and tales from the previous earl's retainers. Simon was anxious to meet with his steward, to report of his travels and to receive her reports.

Arriving at Leicester Castle, he left his horse with his groom. The castle was located on the southwest corner of the town and served as that portion of the walled defenses. Simon also noted that the town showed its origins as a Roman fort in both its name and form. It had once been called *Ligora Caster*, blending the Saxon word for those who dwell on the banks of the River Legra and the Latin word for "camp" or "fort". The river was now called the Soar. The Romans had built the camp on the east bank, in the traditional square formation, with the routes laid out in a grid, and the square surrounded by an earthen wall with a moat on the outside. As the Saxons had settled there, the paths became streets, and the earthen wall was replaced by a stone one. Shortly after the Norman Conquest, the castle had been built right on the river at the end of the southern wall.

Simon cleaned the mud off his boots, and went to his chamber to wash and to change out of his riding clothes. He put on clothes more suited to the lord of the castle and hastened to the workplace of his steward. He was pleased to see Pauline, at her table with scrolls, charts, maps, several dozens of books, and many candles. It took a moment for him to realize he was surprised.

"You are a woman," he said.

"So good of you to notice," she smiled.

"Yes. No. I mean you have shed the boyish disguise you have donned for the last two years."

"You really are showing your powers of observation now."

"That is not what I intend to convey, as you surely must know. I merely hope to express that it might not be wise to do such a thing. And I am not even sure if it is only unwise. Perhaps it is impossible to act as my steward if you are a woman."

"It does not seem to have held me back so far. I can read English and what French is here. I even grasp some of the Saxon and I am rapidly mastering Latin. I can add and subtract probably better than you can."

"I can see this is not going at all according to my meaning."

"Perhaps you should sit down," she said. "I do know what you mean."

He sat down.

"You are wondering how this all might be taken, whether or not the servants and the important citizens of the shire might accept that the earl's steward is a woman."

"Thank you," he said.

"That has not impeded me all that much either. Remember Blanche of Castile, or your mother for that matter. I have found that by treating people with deference and by dealing squarely with them, I have earned what respect might have been withheld at the start."

"But is it wise to shed your cover?"

"I have thought of that. I can still go in disguise if I must do so. If I were to remain in the clothes of a man and my identity was discovered, reverting to feminine dress would be of no help. But now I may revert to my boyish ways if I need to hide. In fact, I have been looking around the town in my squire clothes to remain anonymous. But I have been doing my steward work as Pauline."

"I see," he said. "But I will still worry for your safety. And I think that your flouting of convention may draw unwanted attention."

"That might have been the case in London, but I do not think the locals will care to inquire after my identity. And you certainly must know that we would not be sitting here as earl and steward if I had not been as unconventional as I am."

"I have finished questioning you, and you are correct. I am interested in what you have been able to discover about the administration of the county of Leicester."

"The problem is that Ranulf de Blondeville was not regularly present. And in the time before his appointment and after King John had taken the title from your family, no one was in charge. There has been no effective administration."

"I have gathered as much from my travels. I have invited one knight from each district of the shire to return with me to the castle. And I have brought each bailiff or his representative. I want to impress on them the difference between how things have been administered and how they will be from this point forward, particularly with the importance of written records."

"These English are different," she said.

"I have noticed that they are simpler and more rough-hewn, and perhaps less decorative in their dress."

"I have noticed the same, but there is more to it than that. One interesting irony is that I can explain my position, even though I am a woman, by saying we are French. But that seems mostly to be effective because I think that women have more freedom here. The English are pragmatic."

"I have not made quite the study of it that you have," he said. "What do you suspect is at the bottom of all these differences?"

"I have been reading their chronicles and histories and I think there are two reasons. The first is that they are on an island. The Normans conquered this island more than one hundred and sixty years ago and rule it still. But there was never a massive Norman migration. The commoners look at the rulers as separate and are less obedient to them. The reach of Rome is not quite as strong as it crosses the English Channel, so the churches are more independent.

There have been many different migrations, and there has never been one continuous strong authority. They have more of a tradition of working it out on their own. I think all of this has implications on what you might do and how you might approach your life here."

"I presume we can get to that. What is your second reason for all these differences?"

"I think they are a bit slow to move," she said. "That also may be because, unlike in France, no one has really cracked the whip over them. They have been fighting for themselves since the times of the Romans, then the Saxons and the Danes. But it is difficult to believe how long it takes to get something done in this land. A good example is the complete disrepair into which the administration of this county has fallen. It has been hard to sort it out, and it will be more difficult to get these people to do anything about it. And for a start, I think our push to put all these accounts in writing will not be easy."

Simon sat back. For the seven years they had known one another, Simon had always appreciated the way that Pauline would easily glide into relatively long periods of time with him when neither of them were speaking, particularly because she was normally so expressive and had so many insights and opinions. There was a confidence and comfort in her approach to him that was singular. There was much to think about but first he was taking in the sight before him. He had been quite sincere when he had told her that he preferred to see her in feminine dress, but he had not really taken a good look, nor had he given it any significant thought. He had met her when she was a girl and had noted the gradual changes in her. But for the past two years, she had dressed as a boy. Though he knew she was a woman at that time, the power of suggestion is strong. It served all their purposes not to think of her as a woman. He had not noticed all the ways in which she had grown into full womanhood until now, at the age of twenty-one.

At five-and-a-half-feet tall, she was taller than almost all women, slightly taller than most men, but perhaps only six inches shorter than he. She wore a fine, light blue wool dress that draped over her loosely but closely, especially at her shoulders, on her long sleeves, and where the thin leather belt circled her narrow waist. The dress was lined with a gray cloth, which showed around the draping folds at her lower legs when she walked or sat. Though this dress was made well and of very fine wool cloth and showed her to be a woman of the castle, she did not wear a mantle, or cape, over her shoulders, nor a round hat held in place by a cloth strap under her chin, nor the crispinette to hold her hair in a netting, all of which a noblewoman might wear. She let her dark hair fall to her shoulders as a commoner might and in a way he had never seen before. Her frame was slender but durable, and her arms, shoulders, and back all exhibited a sleek and feminine strength.

Now that he was studying her, he had to catch his breath. She was literally striking. He had to step back for a few moments and realize that she had changed from a girl to a woman during the time she had been masquerading as a young man. The change he most noticed was that some of the facial roundness of her childhood had faded to reveal a superb jawline, high cheekbones, and a strong chin. She was beautiful but in a way that was also handsome. Her face and her form had the superior kind of bone structure that would carry her bodily charms through most of her life. Her skin seemed light against the darkness of her brows, eyes, and hair. It had lost some of the olive hue that it had held in the south. But it still had a cream tone that made her seem exceptionally fit among the pale people of the local population. Her lips were thin but were healthy. All in all, if she had to, and properly disguised, she could still pass for an attractive young man. But as a woman, it took some effort not to notice her. It took him a while to overcome the impact of her appearance in order to process what she had been saying.

She had spurred his own insight and observation about their situation. She was correct. The English were more pragmatic and independent. The concept of absolute suzerainty that was inherent to French commoner and noble alike did not fit so well here. He noticed that in the way that the burgesses, merchants, and knights of Leicestershire had been both flattered by his attention and rather familiar with his person. The major nobles of England had forced the Great Charter on the previous monarch, King John, and had betrayed him to support the invading French prince when John tried to negate the charter. Even at this moment Hubert de Burgh, Earl of Kent, and Peter des Roches, Bishop of Winchester, exercised extraordinary power at court and an influence over the adult King Henry in a way that would be unlikely to occur to a French noble. The king had spent the last year pursuing his personal, costly, and fruitless war in France, to attempt to reclaim Normandy, leaving England to be ruled by a small handful of nobles. Simon had not paid close attention to clerical matters, but he did recall that the Bishop of Lincoln had advocated for the Church a relative independence not only from the crown but also from Rome. He now turned back to Pauline.

"Where does all this leave us, lady steward?" he asked.

"I think that every problem contains within it the seed of opportunity. And we have a few problems, which present some opportunities. The relative independence of the Church and the nobles in England seems as if it might create a situation that would reward merit and work and intelligence more than it might otherwise do in France. You are now the Lord High Steward to the king, and the Earl of Leicester, a very appealing young noble figure who speaks perfect French and has an outstanding military record. There does not seem to be too much, or too many others who might stand in your way if you seek to become a close friend to the king when he soon returns from France."

"Is that what you recommend?"

"You alone can decide what it is you will do with your talents. But I do recommend that you make a stronger friend of the king. Leicestershire will not stand alone if it is to make do with what funds it raises on its own. And your household will surely not stand either. It is almost imperative that the king restore his level of yearly support and that he also increases it. You alone can make that happen."

"May we not rectify the situation here in Leicestershire independently?"

"We may not," she said. "That is one of the things that the reports from the county tell me."

"What else do they convey to you?"

"Oh, that is so simple. You should even know it."

"And what is that? Pray, tell me."

"We have to find you a wife, and a rich one at that."

TWELVE

The King of England was not in his best spirits. Henry had gained his cultured and capricious personality from both his colorful background and his unique upbringing. Now, at age twenty-four, he could be quite volatile, swiftly moving between ambitious and fearful, from confident to petulant, and from the bearing and temperament of a man to that of a child. He had been robbed of much of his childhood. He was nine years old when his father, King John, died, and at that moment, the French and rebel barons held much of southern England, including London. The boy Henry was made king at Gloucester with a makeshift crown. William Marshal, Earl of Pembroke, took over the regency, which Henry's mother had abandoned for France.

Henry III had grown up under the regency and had not really assumed full control when he turned eighteen; he knew no other way and even six years later he was struggling with leadership. King John had also had an unstable reign, one that began with a short civil war against his brother, Arthur, and was marked by the Barons' War, French invasion, and being forced to sign Magna Carta. England had also lost territory on the Continent, which Henry was unable to reclaim. Henry's mother, John's wife, the stunning Isabella of Angoulême, then fled England for France, with her daughter, Henry's sister Joan.

Now, in 1231, Henry III was to meet a papal delegation that had arrived to negotiate peace between France and England, stemming from Henry's failed invasion, and relating to the return of his sister Joan. There were other matters between England and Rome as well. There had long been a struggle over whether there would be a permanent papal legate in England, and over the question of whether the king or the Pope would appoint the Archbishop of Canterbury. King John had not contested the papal appointment of the archbishop, and in return, there would be no papal legate in England. Also, John had sworn himself as a vassal of the previous Pope, to remove his excommunication and gain the Pope's assistance in the Barons' War.

Now, Cardinal Fieschi, the head of the delegation from the Church in Rome, was essentially representing Henry's feudal lord, the Pope. Henry had many reasons to be compliant to the wishes of the Pope. The customary robe and rounded cape of a cardinal at this time were of a purple silk. This was a color only the king wore at court, so the cardinal stood out. In only a dozen or so years, this man, Cardinal Fieschi, would become Pope Innocent, and he would order the cardinals to wear red, the color of the blood Christ shed for all mankind.

"The Holy Father sends his love and his felicitations," the cardinal said.

"And we affirm our allegiance to His Holiness," the king said.

"I also bring greetings from the Queen Dowager of England, your mother."

"And I do not forget that she has long been a personal friend of the Holy Father since he was the Bishop of Ostia."

"His Holiness loves all his flock equally. And he hopes to resolve this matter between mother and son."

"That is unfair to us, good cardinal. The Queen Dowager fled from England with my sister Joan at a very delicate time, when the French and the English barons were conspiring against us. She left a letter of false pretense that she was taking Joan to marry the younger Hugh de Lusignan, but she married him herself and has stated she will not send my sister home until she is granted a yearly stipend from England."

"The Holy Father would like England to grant this request," the cardinal said.

"People have told me, virtually everybody agrees, that my mother has forfeited her title and her right. Still, we will accede to the wishes of the Holy See. We can do no less than that."

"There is also the matter of your invasion of France."

"That was not our idea," Henry said. "That whole costly fiasco was the idea of my regent, Hubert de Burgh. You may be speaking to the wrong person."

"I had hoped I was speaking to England," the cardinal said.

"We don't take responsibility for that war."

"Still, France must have some assurance that England will cease its aggressive actions."

"This is extremely unfair. Those French provinces are ours. We are Normans. We are from Normandy, so Normandy is ours. My grandfather, Henry II, created the Angevin Empire. Anjou is ours. Through my grandmother, Eleanor of Aquitaine, we are the Duke of Aquitaine. It is ours. Brittany has long been the vassalage of England. What can be simpler than these things?"

"Your father lost Normandy, and its accession to France was part of the peace negotiated by Rome," Cardinal Fieschi said.

"We will do something. We promise. It will make everyone happy. You will see," the king said.

Guy Alain was in the background as part of the papal delegation. He had recently been made a monsignor by the Pope, a step up in prestige. He watched the entire proceedings with interest. He knew this last statement by King Henry was an evasion. It had been untrue that Hubert de Burgh was responsible for the invasion of France. It was one of the few things that had been done on the king's initiative. He had confessed as much when he had just stated his claims to those provinces. Monsignor Alain had also been to the court of Louis IX of France, a king a few years younger than Henry. But Louis was reserved and pious and serious, much like his mother, the French queen regent, Blanche of Castile. This English king was a bit too mercurial. Alain knew that this last promise, though strongly stated, was an empty one. Guy Alain asked to approach the cardinal. He conferred with him for a few moments. The cardinal turned back to speak to the king.

"Perhaps, Your Majesty, England might agree to stay out of the affairs of the Continent for a period of time, perhaps ten years."

"We shall agree upon four years," Henry said. "We are pleased to have reached an agreement."

"There remains the matter of the recent death of the Archbishop of Canterbury. His Holiness the Pope shall be sending his choice of a replacement soon. And until such time as that matter is settled, we will leave behind our representative, Monsignor Guy Alain. I present him to you now."

Guy Alain stepped forward and bowed. King Henry acknowledged him. The papal delegation departed.

Guy Alain took up residence at the quarters at St. Paul's Cathedral. It was his intention to begin his investigation of the Earl of Leicester as soon as the matter of the Archbishop of Canterbury had been resolved. But he was to learn that King Henry was more than merely mercurial. The struggle between the crown and Rome involving the archbishop had been a contentious one for seventy years, since the reign of Henry's grandfather, Henry II, who had appointed Thomas Becket, his chancellor and friend, to be archbishop. After long contentions with Henry II, mainly over the balance between Church authority and secular authority, the archbishop was found hacked to death in front of his altar. Henry II never found or prosecuted the killers, who were assumed to have been acting on his behalf. The matter of the Archbishop of Canterbury had been no less contentious ever since.

Guy Alain did not think over his plans all that often. He did not consider making use of the people he met for his own interest. He did not always scheme how to turn circumstances to his personal advantage. He was merely a very worldly man and these things that others deliberated or planned were for him simply a matter of habit. Various strategies and calculations still brewed in his mind, often arising from the situations in which he found himself, from the people in his surroundings, and even from what imagination he had. But he never contemplated them as such. They simply made up the entirety of his life. He did not have one or two such designs and plans. He had dozens of them in the field at the same time, some of them beginning to form, some of them gaining power, others coming to fruition, and yet others that never were to be implemented. He had a knack for cultivating men of power, for exploiting individual weakness, for understanding the vectors and currents of relationships. All his plans, from the personal matter of Simon de Montfort to the grander Inquisition, were simply part of his nature.

Guy Alain then found that these faculties of his were to be occupied for the next three or four years, getting to the bottom of certain facts, delving into associations, and ferreting out the king's motivations. It would keep him from investigating Simon de Montfort much longer than he would have liked. King Henry had been quite impulsive in agreeing to a four-year cessation of hostilities with France when the cardinal had offered a ten-year peace. Henry went beyond that capriciousness with his nominal agreement to allow the Pope to appoint the next Archbishop of Canterbury. He did not want to do either of those things. He concocted a plan of convening the monks of Canterbury and he asked them to elect the next archbishop. He assumed this would assuage the Pope while also hiding his own hand in the selection process. Monsignor Alain would then be kept very busy by Henry's sometimes clumsy machinations.

In September of that year, 1231, the monks of Canterbury elected Ralph de Neville to be archbishop. Guy Alain did not have to investigate very deeply to learn that Neville was more courtier than priest. He was, in fact, chancellor for the life of Henry III and it was an open secret that he had been directed by the king to reduce the English Church's feudal ties and payments to Rome once he became the next archbishop. With the advice of Guy Alain, Pope Gregory quashed the election. The next election found the monks selecting one of their own, a mere monk, John of Sittingbourne, to be archbishop. Guy Alain searched mightily but could not find any hidden motivations Henry might have had for selecting this humble monk. He sensed that John of Sittingbourne might be a puppet that would allow Henry to control the Church in England. Alain decided that the monk was not one stout enough to maintain his masquerade. Alain counseled the Pope to question him directly and intently. When in Rome and upon questioning, the monk John could not maintain his charade. He resigned his position as Archbishop of Canterbury.

Next to be elected by the monks was John Blund, a scholastic at Oxford. His great patron was Peter des Roches, one of Henry's chief court advisors, whose only equal at the court was Hubert de Burgh. Monsignor Alain had to do the significant personal research that would give the Pope a reason to quash Blund's election. It appeared that the Oxford don believed in diversity and pluralism and planned to conduct himself with respect for all faiths, which on paper was even more inexcusable than being too closely aligned with the interests of King Henry.

Henry III had turned the archbishopric into something of a potter's wheel, spinning off his appointments like bits of clay. It had become almost a laughing stock, a governing by impulse, to the point that with the guidance of Guy Alain, the Pope was able to appoint the next Archbishop of Canterbury in 1234, Edmund of Abingdon, an ascetic priest and papal loyalist who had served Rome in the Sixth Crusade. He was temperamentally the opposite of Henry III. Monsignor Alain had done his job and he had done it well. He was now able to think about his next mission, to find a specific heretic in England and to prosecute her protector.

The monsignor had been thwarted by Simon de Montfort and this had festered in Guy Alain for seven years. His family was a minor noble one in a provincial town. His elder brother took the lands of their father. Guy Alain could have chosen military service, but he was not particularly brave, and he was quite intelligent. He decided a career in the clergy suited him. Once he had established himself there, he found it to be a good way for a clever man to manipulate circumstances to his advantage.

Throughout his stay in London, the Hound of God had moved in a wide circle of the clergy, the minor nobility, the members of the guilds and crafts, and the local civic leaders of London. He came to know the city and to set aside his prejudice against its cool, damp weather and its rough populace. He would have felt at home entirely, except that there were moments when it seemed to him that he heard an additional echo of his footsteps on the stones. And there were times in the fog that rose from the river when he seemed half-certain that he cast an extra shadow away from the lights. A suspicious man might have considered from these strange feelings that he was being followed. Guy Alain simply knew that he was.

Guy Alain had heard reports of Simon de Montfort's travels to London on several occasions during this time. He had known of de Montfort's visits to the king and of his position at court. During those times, Alain was certain that his own presence in London had been noted by the Earl of Leicester or by one of his retainers. The priest had not forgotten how de Montfort and his retinue had slipped out of Avignon without his noticing the Cathar girl. It was apparent that there was some cunning or intelligence within the earl's entourage that was an effective counterpoint to Alain's efforts. He was not sure how that was, or who it was, but he was on alert now. He knew that whatever approach he must now take had to be indirect. His native worldly instinct was now attuned to the echoes and shadows.

THIRTEEN

By 1236, while Guy Alain had spent four years intriguing with King Henry and the Pope over the installation of the Archbishop of Canterbury, Simon de Montfort had spent that same time traveling between Leicester and London, and visiting France, where he had explored his matrimonial prospects. In London, he continued to enjoy the favor of the king and to avoid the criticism of his other advisors. He had also obtained the yearly subsidy for Leicester that his lady steward had said was required. At Leicester, he allowed Pauline to have free rein to set the county and the household on an even keel, and he made sure his household and the county knew that he stood behind her on any disputes that had arisen in his absence. And in France, he wooed not one but two wealthy women. Perhaps because he had ranged too far afield, he had not been successful. Maybe he failed because he had not had Pauline's direct assistance.

When she was not administering the county of Leicester for Simon, Pauline had spent this time working to address herself personally and individually to examining and reinforcing her faith. Like all the other Good Men and Good Women, she had always kept a copy of the Lord's Prayer and the Gospel of St. John, which was different from the other, synoptic gospels in that it placed more importance on the individual's relation to Christ and gave less standing to the sacraments. She also understood it to mean that Christians were supposed to find salvation through knowledge and wisdom, not faith alone. Good works were also required. She was happiest when she was able to give a few pounds to select monks at the churches to help the poor and when she had hired Rachel's father to transport goods purchased for the castle.

Pauline remembered what she had been taught in her school by Esclarmonde de Foix, that Jesus had said that the world is a bridge and that a believer should pass over it and build no house upon it. She knew that all men and women were vessels for spirits that were neither male nor female and that the spirits mattered but the bodies did not. She fed her spirit relentlessly with reading. She was reconciled to the fact that she was building a house in the world so that she could improve the spirit within Simon and in turn help all those whom he was more capable of reaching than she would ever be. Still, this balance between her ascetic and spiritual focus and her actions on behalf of her rescuer and friend, and indirectly on those he knew, was always in her mind. Never more so than when Simon was in her presence. She had been raised to believe and had always believed that only spiritual love is Christian. She had long lived with that in her heart.

It was a hot summer day when Simon returned from his trip to France in pursuit of his second candidate for the role of his wife. He quickly washed and put on a loose shirt and hurried to give his report to Pauline. He walked into her workroom and leaned over her table, his hair still wet, and his shirt clinging to the dampness of his torso. He made a jesting remark about how this second trip to France to find a wife had also been unsuccessful.

He was quite close to her at that moment. She could feel the warmth that emanated from him. She was suddenly conscious of his movements. She caught a slight scent of him, the lure of his masculine charm. She saw him as a man, a tall, confident, courageous man, made strong by his active life and his time in the saddle. And from then on, she could not fail to see this. It was as if a person on the road in a fog sees what she thinks is a house in the distance and upon approaching it, discovers it is a fallen tree. She can no longer bring herself to see it as a house. Pauline knew at that moment there existed between them several barriers. There was his noble standing, which was in direct contrast to her common birth. And a still larger barrier, for her, was her faith and her will to maintain it. But she would now forever see him as an attractive man. Her mind and her heart felt charged by an unknown expectation. She felt a quickening in her chest and a curious ache. It was a bit of a struggle to bring herself to speak.

"So, Joan, the Countess of Flanders, was able to resist your charms," she smiled.

"That may have been true of Mahaut, Countess of Boulogne, on the previous trip. But with Joan, things seem to have progressed a bit further," he said.

"As I remember, Mahaut appeared to have her sights set on a gentleman of a more Mediterranean temperament. She resisted your northern respectability."

"Yes, the lovely widow Mahaut of Boulogne seems to have preferred a gentleman of Portugal. I conclude that I was late to the table with her. But Joan of Flanders was the widow of the Prince of Portugal and I believe was no longer so enamored of those southern ways. She and I got along quite well, and I was convinced I might soon have had Flanders within my authority."

"I am pleased to see that our strategy may have been correct in at least one instance."

"Do you mean that you suggested I should approach widows and not maids?"

"Yes," she said.

"I believe you said that a woman who had already been married would be no stranger to the relative merits of men, and that a widow would therefore be more attentive to me as a man, rather than merely as a fit alliance for her noble house. I think you said that I had more to offer as a man than as a diplomatic match."

"I may have been wrong, then, since your arrow as a man seems to have failed to find the mark a second time."

"I see. I believe Joan did see my merit. At least, she indicated that much to me. In fact, I believe we had an implicit agreement. Then it suddenly evaporated. I did not discover the certainty until I had later visited my brother in Paris."

"What did Amaury tell you?"

"He had several things to say. The first, apparently, was that the late husband of Joan of Flanders had been an ally and a favorite of the queen regent of France, Blanche of Castile. She was not happy with the idea of Flanders going over to the Earl of Leicester, whose allegiance is to the English king. She put an end to the prospect and made Joan swear there had never been an understanding between us. In fact, Amaury chided me for not speaking to him first about our plans. King Henry is looked upon with greater suspicion now, more than when we left France."

"That is understandable, given that he invaded the continent."

"Amaury said that King Henry failed with that invasion as well and that he never had to take the field against him because Henry never actually moved on Normandy. He marched south from Brittany and did little more than reinforce his hold on Aquitaine."

Pauline and Simon settled into one of their comfortable silences, in which they did not need to speak in order to understand one another. Simon knew his report would cause Pauline to consider what might be done next. He believed he saw that in her quiet look. She enjoyed that he was so relaxed in her presence and she was considering the future, but only after she mulled over the possible scenes that were indicated in Simon's report from France.

One day, only a month later, Rocco returned from London and sought an audience with the earl to bring him some news. Simon sent for Pauline. Rocco soon joined them. He had long since abandoned his foreign garb and dressed very much like any London craftsman or guild member. He wore a tunic over a linen shirt, with a square coat over them. The coat had a hood, which was down and behind his neck. He wore hose of a dark wool, with leggings to below the knee, and shoes with a slight point. His hair was cut to look like a page. The only thing notable about his appearance was his face, and mostly his eyes, which were unlike many to be found in England or Europe. But everything about him—his movements, his expression, his attitude—was so colored by an extraordinary quiet that he struck the eye at somewhere between plain and almost invisible. But with Simon and Pauline, he was direct and open. Over several years, he had studied and had learned the language. He spoke more fluently and confidently now.

"There have been changes at court," he said. "King Henry has dismissed the large council that has acted as a regency for the last eighteen years. Hubert de Burgh was the first to go, and now Peter des Roches has gone. Henry has taken control and now he will have a small council that acts only in an advisory capacity. He is effectively in complete control of the kingdom."

"Do we know the reason?"

"The sons of William Marshal, Henry's original regent, had a dispute with Peter des Roches that became a minor war. The new Archbishop of Canterbury, Edmund of Abingdon, persuaded Henry to again swear to rule by the precepts of the Great Charter. The peace was negotiated, and the senior ministers were all dismissed in favor of that smaller council of advisors. The departure of Peter des Roches had been something the Pope wanted. Henry was also unhappy with the military leadership of his ministers because the moment the peace he negotiated with France had ended, the Duke of Brittany yielded to Louis IX and changed his allegiance from England to France."

"What is your other news?" Simon asked.

"Henry has called for the lord high steward to return to London. Your position has improved."

"What do you think, Pauline?" Simon asked.

"I have seen the way the king treats you. He views you quite favorably. He certainly admires you for your military experience, your superior French, your bearing, and the fact that you come from France, the land of his Norman forebears. It is also appealing that you have never fawned over him nor curried his favor. He views you with none of the suspicions of self-interest with which he sees the hereditary English nobles," she said. "I also think that we have always benefitted from the assistance and advice of our friend, Rocco, and should heed it."

"I have always accepted your service, Rocco, without question or inquiry," Simon said. "What more do you have?"

"I have been following Guy Alain in London. He has worked very diligently to thwart King Henry's efforts to make one of his own men the Archbishop of Canterbury, and now that the Pope has his own man in Canterbury, the monsignor's work is done. I fear he has his eyes on Leicester and I believe he knows that Pauline is here and that you have kept her in your retinue. I do not think he will move on us himself. I believe he will send spies. He has successfully recruited ambitious young monks who are anxious to gain favor with one of the Pope's men."

"We must be careful, then," Simon said. "But I do not know how much he can do here in England. There is no Inquisition here. And no English king would take kindly to it. From what else you have been saying, I am about to be elevated in the court. That seems to make it even less likely that the priest can pose too great a danger."

"You are too bold, my lord," Pauline said. "Your inclination is, as always, to plunge your horse in to ford the stream without checking the depth. We are in even greater danger, and for the reason that you state."

"I seek your correction, as always," Simon said. "Please, go on."

"Being in the king's favor is far more dangerous than to be far from it. It is safer to view a bear from a distance than it is to be in the cage with it. And Henry III is a temperamental sovereign. You are to be fording the wider river now, and there will be larger risks. Guy Alain, or anything or anyone for that matter, can be a small key that might turn Henry against you or give him a rationale if he decides to go against you for another reason."

"There is one other rather important matter," Rocco added. "King Henry III has asked the Earl of Leicester to London to install you officially as his lord high steward. You will also be responsible for all the arrangements, protocols, and the implementation of the royal wedding."

Pauline said, "It is another way that I think the king has decided to emulate you, Simon. He knows why you have been traveling to France. And he has decided to take himself a wife."

"It seems I will be crossing the bigger river now, as you say, Pauline. Nor do I want to approach that on my own, without the two of you. Prepare yourselves. We are going once again to London."

With that, Simon left them. Rocco turned and spoke to Pauline.

"This royal wedding," he said, "will be a matter that will occupy the earl and it will be an inescapable example of that world of royalty and nobility that you and I may never enter."

That was all he said, but she had understood him even before he spoke. She admitted to herself that she loved Simon. This was for who and what he was, and not what she could receive from him. She loved him for the feeling she had when she added to his life and helped him toward what she always felt was his destiny. This love was served by doing all that she could do for him. It would have been less of a love if it were dependent on caresses. She looked at Rocco for a long time then and his eyes searched hers for this understanding that she was now feeling. He saw she knew what he meant when he spoke of a world beyond their reach. More importantly, he saw that she knew she had always had everything she ever really needed, which was a chance to serve her compelling desire to do all that she could for Simon de Montfort.

Rocco and Simon had entered Pauline's life at the same time, and it was also the same time that worldly considerations had begun to compete with her faith. All these were in a kind of competitive balance at times. But at this point, they all seemed to align with the same conclusion. She knew she did not want to have a life without Simon, without what she could help him do in the world, without the respect of Rocco, and without relying on the strength of her beliefs. It was simple. Simon could never marry her. The world called upon him to do great things. Her faith dictated that she love him without expectation of return. It was in fact the courtly love that was made famous by Cathar troubadours who traveled all over Europe. And Rocco was Pauline's best example of that kind of devotion.

FOURTEEN

Eleanor of Provence was widely considered to be one of the most stunningly and classically beautiful girls in Europe. She was slim and of medium height, with dark brown hair and sparkling, gentle, dark brown eyes. She had a straight, slender, prominent but delicate nose and a long, perfectly symmetrical face. Its length was more than offset by her high cheekbones, elegant jawline, lovely rounded forehead, compact chin, and full lips. She looked every bit a queen. She had been well educated, was fond of reading, and was known to dabble in poetry. She was also considered to be highly fashionable, often exploring new styles and materials. Her mother, Beatrice of Savoy, was also famously beautiful, almost as notably so as her own mother, Eleanor's grandmother, Margaret of Geneva. Margaret had been betrothed to King Philip II of France, but when she left Geneva to travel across Savoy on her way to Paris, Eleanor's grandfather, Thomas of Savoy, fell in love with her on sight and carried her off to marry her himself. Eleanor was known to have a romantic temperament too and to be fond of music. In fact, there were always troubadours in her father's household. She would make an excellent wife for Henry.

Henry III had never seen her but as was the royal custom he had seen a painting of her. He relied more upon reports of her beauty and the romantic tales of her stunning mother and grandmother. There were other reasons she might be a good match. Provence was a wealthy kingdom, not yet within the realm of France. Eleanor's father could provide a good dowry. Her older sister, Margaret, who was as renowned for her piety as for her beauty, had just married Louis IX of France. A match between Henry and Eleanor would create a competing interest for England in Provence, and it would make Henry III of England and Louis IX of France brothers-in-law. The many conflicts and disputes between the two kingdoms might more easily find a peaceful resolution. France had taken the independent Languedoc and had wrested Brittany and Normandy from England. France's territory was growing. Of its many lands on the European continent, England at this time only held on to Aquitaine, and within it, Gascony, Anjou, and Poitou. The new relationship between the two kings might help to preserve these English holdings.

Simon had become a confidant of the king. His original idea had been that Henry should marry the powerful Joan of Flanders, who ruled her kingdom alone, thus bringing Flanders into the English realm and flanking France. He knew the widow Joan well. She had been the subject of his second attempt at obtaining a bride for himself. She possessed an expansive heart and would be an excellent companion for the mercurial king. But someone had told Henry of the beauty of the daughters of the Provençal court. Henry then set his heart on marrying the stunning Eleanor. Simon approved of the match for the stated more practical reasons and told King Henry of his approval. The king was pleased.

Henry looked at Simon much differently than he had seen the other, older, native English nobles who had essentially served as a collective regency in the form of his larger council. It was largely as Pauline had said. Together, they made an unusual pairing. King

Henry was shorter, strongly built, with a narrow face. The lid of his left eye was always partially closed. He often spoke and acted without considering first. Simon was reserved, tall, well-formed, and handsome. One example of their differences was evident when Simon had negotiated a considerable dowry to be paid by Eleanor's father, Ramon Berenguer IV, Count of Provence, but when the count later balked at paying it, Henry simply capitulated.

Simon knew that the royal wedding would be a massive undertaking. It was almost entirely a diplomatic affair, but he would also have to keep a weather eye on the king. Every important English noble had to be invited, as did many of London's important citizens. There would be a delegation from Paris and the King of France, and one from the Pope in Rome. Eleanor's relatives would be arriving from Provence and Savoy. The king's relatives and vassals from Aquitaine, Poitou, and Anjou would attend, as would his mother and her second husband. The most important and ranking Church leaders would attend. Everyone's rank had to be respected and noted. There had to be a wedding, a banquet, and a coronation of the queen. Everybody had to be housed and fed. The young bride would be leaving her family surroundings and arriving from a rich and storied kingdom on the Mediterranean Sea to travel to a cool and damp, relatively provincial kingdom in the North Sea, to marry a man twice her age. Steps would have to be taken to make her more comfortable.

The lord high steward had the reins of the king's household and the king's support in organizing the nobles. He received plenty of advice and he had Pauline to help him sift through it all. Her own advice had been to recognize everyone's desire to attend the wedding and to harness that desire into assistance. The visiting foreign dignitaries were asked to house themselves on their boats. The leaders of London were asked to open their homes to visitors. The merchants were asked to cut their prices for the honor of providing for the royal wedding. The churches were asked to house visitors. And the English nobles were asked to make public contributions to the ceremonies. Since all wanted to be involved and recognized, this help was forthcoming. The wedding was to be at Canterbury Cathedral, the coronation at Westminster Abbey, and the banquet at Westminster Hall. All the royal residences were upgraded in preparation for Eleanor. Pauline recommended that Eleanor be greeted in France and escorted to England by the only two English nobles she had ever met, who had been envoys to her father's court. Pauline managed the communications that Simon would have to send, and Rocco kept a watchful eye on everything going on around them.

Pauline had begun her life as a commoner in Languedoc and a member of a loosely organized Christian sect that rested on the individual's relationship to God and not on the institution of the Church. Since then she had learned to live among northerners, nobles, Roman Catholics, and had made the move to England. But her humble roots gave her the scope for wonder, and she found that this wedding was commensurate with that capacity. She observed it with a fascination and an attention to detail that would be of use to Simon later.

The Provençal and Savoyard contingents were greater than expected and arrived on large vessels, appointed with banners and ribbons, and lit up with braziers on the decks. They floated up the Thames as if they had been Cleopatra's barge. The churchmen alone were a veritable parade. Archbishops, bishops, and cardinals wore their full ecclesiastic vestments. The bishops in their green cassocks and capes and miters carried their staffs. The cardinals were all in purple. Since no occasion was more extraordinary than this, these clerical robes were exceptional. Many were embroidered in gold silk that ran along the robe's borders and sleeves and covered the clasps. Silk had to be imported from Paris or Venice. The embroidery contained images of Christ, Mary, or the cross. Pauline was dazzled by the richness of these robes worn by the servants of Christ in this rural kingdom.

Each English noble tried to appear wealthier and more well-appointed than the next. The robes were seen most and first, so they wore the finest woolen robes lined and collared with fur. The most common furs were deerskin, rabbit, or lambskin, but the richest men had their robes lined and collared with the short, fine gray fur of squirrels. These men also wore the finest wool, which was called scarlet, for its color, and was made only in Lincoln. Some of the robes also bore silk embroidery, and the jeweled clasps were made of silver or gold. The sleeves of these robes widened as they approached the wrist, and the large cuffs were embroidered or furred. Pauline noticed that many of these great robes appeared to be quite old. She remembered that in Leicester Castle there had been mention of robes being left as part of inheritances. She knew they must have been valuable enough that they were passed on for generations.

Nothing spoke of a noble person's wealth more than color. Pauline had lived in a noble household and even there the commonly worn clothes were generally linen and the colors were muted. The fine wool and silk of these noble robes were dyed and colored bright reds, blues, greens, golds, whites, and yellows. Above all they were patterned with stripes, panels, crosses, animals, and abstract designs. Every hem was a color different from the cloth and most often embroidered or tipped with fur. The most common item of jewelry was the brooch and almost all wore them. Some men wore thick gold chain necklaces that had been imported from northern Italy.

Men's robes were ankle-length, and they wore their finest pointed leather shoes. Pauline could not see the shoes of the women under their full-length robes. Their entire wedding wardrobe was more involved. She could also not see the women's hair. Many wore a colorful and ornamented version of the cap that was worn for more general occasions, often just a round or cylindrical cloth covering, only these were made of silk and fine wool. The more impressive noble women wore a combination of an elaborate barbette, wimple, or crespine, which to Pauline looked like varying versions of the same headdress. They all wrapped under the chin and over the side of the head and ears, with the barbette being a cylinder sometimes shaped like a crown, the wimple was a beautiful cloth veil fully covering the neck, and the sides and back of the head, while the crespine would hold the hair in a net, often of gold or lace, on the sides of the head like two clouds beside the face, and its veil would also be lace.

Unlike the men, the sleeves of the ladies' robes were form-fitting and fastened with buttons made of fine metal or coral. The robes were layered and often ribbed and gave the impression of being more than one item of clothing, appearing to have vests, or tunics, or more elaborate designs woven into the garments. They were even more colorful than the men's robes and presented a more formidable front. The robes were lined with the same furs as the men. Over these considerable robes, the women wore a mantle or a cape of a different color, and all had a cowl or a hood that was rarely worn on the head. Pauline did not have to wonder how these women managed to move around in such magnificent garb, because she too was clad in a more modest version of these clothes and she found her movements had to be contained and reserved in a way that was forcibly elegant. Her robe was several shades of blue and her hair was in a tan cylindrical barbette with the length of her hair in the back wrapped in cloth. She was taller than almost all the women and many of the men and her headdress added some inches.

All of London was bedecked with banners and lanterns. It was January, so warming fires blazed everywhere: in the streets, at the docks, and along the roads out of town to Canterbury. All this great assemblage turned out and awaited the bride near the dock. Simon was in the forefront, to officially greet the bride and her party. Pauline watched with wonder. When Pauline had been Eleanor's age, she had run in the woods and read as many books as she could and played with the boys. She was curious to see this girl who was from a land right next to hers, who also spoke Occitan and who loved the music of troubadours but was in every other way so different.

Pauline had to concentrate her efforts to be able to remove her gaze from Simon. He had not outfitted himself from the closets of Leicester but had been dressed by the king's dressers from the king's wardrobe, as the lord high steward and master of the events over which the king, as bridegroom, could not preside. His long rich robe was of the darkest scarlet, patterned with gold silk lions. The cuffs, the edges, and the hem were lined with white ermine and the sleeves lined with subtle blue silk stripes. He was also the only noble permitted to wear his sword. His mantle was a fine slate gray wool, also trimmed in ermine. It was held to his upper body by a thick jeweled chain that ran from shoulder to shoulder and across his chest. The links alternated between gold and lapis lazuli. Simon commanded the landscape with his bearing, his dress, and his charisma. Only the king was more elegantly dressed, in purple instead of scarlet, with fine white silk lions, more ermine, a chain of gold and sapphires, and his jeweled crown.

The Provençal ship disembarked last. The retainers came off first, followed by the English envoys, all of whom were greeted by Simon, and they then bowed to King Henry. The family came last, Ramon Berenguer IV, Count of Provence, and his wife, the beautiful Beatrice of Savoy, accompanied by their daughter. The lovely girl was dressed in a shimmering golden gown that fit tightly at the waist and flared out to wide pleats at her feet. The sleeves were long and lined with ermine. It was a much sparer and more elegant look than the ladies of the court, as was befitting her status as the bride. She was a magnificent-looking girl. Pauline noticed that her glance stayed for a long time on Simon as he waited to greet them. He bowed and introduced himself. She smiled brightly at him. Then he took the family to the king. They bowed to him and extended their hands in greeting. Henry had long since convinced himself that he was enamored. And now it was love at first sight. It would later grow into a deeper love that would fatefully become quite indulgent.

Pauline had never seen any weddings. They simply were not sanctioned by the Cathar faith and when they had occurred, they were discreet events. She also felt and thought along spiritual lines, and to her, Simon and Rocco and even the people of Leicester were now linked to her in spirit, without the need of any ceremony. She also felt something of a pang, a recognition that she was not part of this society. This ceremony was a stunning spectacle. The wedding procession alone was a dignified festival of pomp and color. To a woman who had been brought up to abjure all forms of oaths as being too possibly lies, the exchange of marriage vows was a great peculiarity, especially as it was set in the ostentatious splendor of Canterbury Cathedral. The unreal aspect of it all was emphasized by the sight of this burly, slightly misshapen man of twenty-eight years with one damaged eye facing a delicately beautiful much younger girl. Most notable of all to Pauline was that Eleanor seemed to be the only one who was not completely enthralled by the spectacle. It was a stunning display of Catholic ritual. Priests preceded the bride waving smoking censers that filled the air with fragrance. The cathedral was filled with all the nobility of Provence and England. Henry seemed smitten and almost distracted by his bride and by the ceremony. Young Eleanor was calm. She had been raised for this moment. She kept a reserved expression through the chanting of the priests, the wedding procession, the Latin Mass, and the exchange of vows. Only after the Archbishop of Canterbury pronounced them man and wife did she break into a sweet smile.

The next day, Pauline wondered what could have been going through the young girl's mind when she was made Queen of England at the coronation in Westminster Abbey. Eleanor again handled the entire matter with stunning grace for one so young. And Henry was beside himself with pride and adoration. It was even more magnificent than the wedding. The Latin chants of the priests at the wedding were replaced by minstrels' music. Psalteries and citoles played their stringed songs in melody with the dulcimers. Trumpets, pipes, and flutes rose to a crescendo until the ceremony began. The clergy and the noblemen added to their robes the badges, garters, sashes, headdresses, and mantles of their high offices. Both events had been affairs of state, but the coronation was more completely an official state ceremony. There was even more color in the women's robes.

Henry and Eleanor sat facing the crowd in Westminster Abbey and he was dressed much the same. But she was now no longer wearing her own slender and elegant gown. The royal wardrobe had dressed her in the purple wool and silk ermine-trimmed robe that had been worn at all state occasions by King Henry's mother, the enchanting Isabella of Angoulême. Pauline felt for the first time that Eleanor seemed smaller. This feeling was enhanced by the fact that Eleanor was the only woman in the vast hall whose hair was visible, who was not wearing a large headdress. Henry and Eleanor sat on thrones while the Archbishop of Canterbury performed his ceremony in Latin. This culminated in the crowd rising to its feet as the crown of the Queen of England was placed on her head. At this point the entire assembly bowed and curtseyed while Henry held his queen's hand aloft.

The banquet was also like nothing Pauline had ever seen. Among the English lords alone were men who had been in great disputes, even wars, with one another. All were in the convivial spirit of the joyous match. She wondered at the ability of these men to act as if their greatest passions and strongest interests did not exist. All this applied in greater meaning to the mix of foreigners and English. Bloody wars and internecine struggles were set aside as if they had never happened, and more, as if they would not soon boil to the surface again after the ceremonies were over. Among the guests were

Henry's mother, Isabella, who had abandoned her son and land to marry Hugh de Lusignan, who had warred with Blanche of Castile, who was there representing the King of France, which had twice lately been at war with England.

Pauline thought she had grown accustomed to life within a noble household. She believed she and Simon had made a study of the nobility of England to better understand the landscape in which they had chosen to operate. Here they were all in one room. It was impossible to keep track of the operation of the alliances, grievances, and ancestral connections. The banquet itself was like a show or a battle or a parade. The most important nobles and clergy of England and Provence sat on benches at tables that ran the length of the room while observing the most stringent etiquette, chatting quietly while cutting their food with their knives and delicately eating with their fingers. All the cups, knives, plates, and dishes were made of metal, the finest of them of silver. There were more servants than guests and they scurried through the room, keeping cups filled with wine, ale, the wine/water mixture, and making sure all the towels on the tables were clean ones. Each course was brought out in display. The bread was piled in formations on large wooden trenchers. The crusts of the meat pies were designed with lions and crosses. The soup was a thick pottage of cabbage, carrots, nuts, onions, and garlic, served in the finest pewter bowls. The venison and boar were carried out on a spit and carved beside the tables. The main course was a flock of pea fowl. Although they had been cleaned, stuffed, and baked, they were presented with their tail feathers fanned out behind them. This was followed by the fruit and the sweet pastries.

Pauline's eyes at most times were on Simon as he moved from his seat at the end of the head table of the royal couple that faced the rest of the hall, and circulated about the room, making sure that all went well. She saw clearly how well he managed this world, excelled in it. He was called by the king to return to the head table on several occasions, where the new queen looked at him with interest. Nor were she and Pauline the only ones who were closely watching the Earl of Leicester.

The men of the Church, to Pauline, were just as much a part of the social and political mixture as any other of the worldlier groups. She could not see them as the representatives of Christ on Earth, so her eyes were keen to recognize their actions taken in their own interest for material and worldly gain. The new Archbishop of Canterbury had played a role in the sudden departure of many of these nobles from the court of King Henry. He was the Pope's man and therefore was in the way of the high-ranking English clerics, such as the estimable Bishop of Lincoln, Robert Grosseteste. As with the Bishop of Lincoln, many of the English bishops had been appointed by the King of England or elected by the local clergy, and just as many had not risen through the clerical ranks but had been religious scholars, such as the Bishop of Lincoln. All of them had a strong interest in secular affairs, and to Pauline's eyes alone were cloaked merely in the cant of Christian faith.

All was well in the Kingdom of England on that day, or so it seemed. And on the following days, there was much visiting and revelry. It was not until several days later that Simon was able to relax and bask in the king's approval for how well all of it had gone. He was feeling rather well when he finally had a chance to discuss the events with Pauline.

"I think the king is quite pleased with how all of it turned out," Simon said.

"I believe that may be true, but he may not have noticed if it had all been a disorganized nightmare," she said. "His greater happiness is in the person of his beautiful young queen. He could have married her in a barn, and he would be happy."

"I know what you mean. I think the queen approves of it all as well."

"The queen approves of you, although that may not be a strong enough word. I saw the way she was looking at you."

"I knew you might have seen it that way. She is our queen, and I cannot think of her in any other way."

"I was not talking about how you think of her," she said. "But I do believe that the queen is already quite fond of Henry and that she is just as enamored of being queen. I doubt that her obvious attraction to you will amount to anything more than her approval and affection. That will be important to remember. But you do know that in this game you are playing, all the stakes were just raised significantly. You are the favored noble of both the king and queen now. The potential benefit is equal to the possible dangers. There is also an even greater peril."

"Then I will need some help."

"Yes. I think you should make use of the Church. I know—you are going to say the Church is whatever holy emblem you think it is, and no one can make use of it. I have studied it and I have watched the clerics. Those Church officials are the true courtiers, and they work the court under the cover of religion, which gives them a measure of protection. You are the scion of a particularly important family in your religion. You can speak and write in Latin. They will also see you as you are now, a favorite of the king and a young noble with a bright future. They will be interested in making you an ally, while you will be smart to do the same with them."

"I see how you reason. Henry is deeply devout. He wants to rebuild Westminster Abbey. He idolizes Edward the Confessor. He attends Mass every day, at least once. The Church could provide some protection against the vagaries of the king."

"And on the other side, it can give you leverage to do some good for the people of the county of Leicester and the people of England."

"And what is this even greater peril you mention?" he asked.

"It is also an opportunity, if not one that is fraught with possible pitfalls."

"Do advise," he said.

"Eleanor."

"The queen? We have already discussed her."

"I am beginning to see exactly how you can be such an appealing man and of noble blood, and still have failed twice to convince a woman to marry you. I do not mean Eleanor the queen. I am talking about the other Eleanor, the Countess of Pembroke."

"That Eleanor can have no role in this matter. She is the king's sister."

"That is exactly why she is dangerous, and why she also presents an opportunity."

"She swore a vow of chastity upon her husband's death and has lived a chaste life ever since."

"And how exactly is that supposed to make her somehow less susceptible to your obvious appeal? At the risk of ranging farther into the library of your ignorance about women, the looks she was giving you were not exactly chaste. She was married at an early age and widowed at sixteen. She knows what men are. She instinctively feels exactly the ways in which you are different from all other men, and she also understands that on a basis that is informed by her marriage. And living without a man for the last three years has only sharpened her interest. She knows you are favored by her brother. I saw how she looked at you. Her heart has kindled. If you thought the approval of the queen has amplified your dangers, you are going to have to sit down for a good long while and contemplate the effect of Eleanor of Pembroke's considerable affection for you."

Simon and Pauline again transitioned into one of their long, relaxed silences. Simon was considering all that Pauline had brought to his attention and was warmly grateful for her observations, her care, and her frankness. He would occasionally look at her warmly. Pauline was considering how this intelligent and good man could be so unaware of feelings of the women in his life, not only Eleanor but herself.

FIFTEEN

One of the strengths of Pauline's upbringing in her faith was that she was not easily persuaded by the trappings of nobility or of the clergy. In many ways, she did not even distinguish between men and women, and she tried to see each as a vessel for an immortal spirit that was neither male nor female. She had been taught that if each individual spirit had its independent relation to God, then each of them were equal. This may have been one of the ideas that made the Cathars dangerous to the Roman Catholic Church and to the prevailing social order. For Pauline, it was the way she saw all of humanity. All this had been ingrained in her from birth and reinforced by the Cathar tradition in which girls were raised in a school only for girls that was run by women. At this point in her life, in 1236, having lived eleven years in the de Montfort household, she had changed. She was more susceptible to the world, more vulnerable to its charms and risks. Some of those risks could cause pain.

She had not been overawed by Simon's nobility nor by his status as a man when she observed him that first time, when she had decided to find a savior among the men who had invaded her land. It had enabled her to look at him frankly and openly, and to gain a sense of what it was that made him different, more thoughtful, or sensitive. And since then something else had happened and it had changed her. In her heart, she was always bound to him, but for the first time in her life now, she was vulnerable to his attentions and distractions. Some part of her was lost to herself and now belonged to him. She was also more drawn to him personally. She had not and could not say anything about this to him. And she believed he might not have confronted any similar feelings he had for her. He certainly did not seem to consider what might be her own feelings when they discussed the king's sister. Pauline decided then that it would be her sacred mission to work to live more in her faith and less in her passion, while she continued to think about it.

She had never been blind to his unique appeal as a man. She had commented on it many times and had calculated it into her considerations as to how he might succeed in various endeavors. It had been clear to her that he had a natural appeal to other men and particularly to women, due to his bearing, his attractive appearance, his height, his courage, and his honest integrity. But this was the first time she had felt it personally. Maybe that was not entirely correct. Perhaps she had only lately begun to admit to herself that she had always felt it in some way. And once that had happened, she could not soon stop feeling it. It made the discussion she and Simon had about Eleanor of Pembroke, the king's sister, more than a little uncomfortable. And for the first time, Pauline began to examine her faith and what it meant to love generously and spiritually. She knew she would have to apply herself to that more diligently.

Pauline turned her contemplation toward what she thought might be Simon's thoughts and feelings. He had revealed to her that he was swayed by her feminine appeal. She determined that he must see the obligations of his status and the wisdom of not giving up on his destiny. She began to focus on the way in which he had saved her, more than once, and particularly the way he had nursed her from the guilt and remorse she felt for not having acted sooner to save her friends at the school and for being its only survivor. Later, he made his solemn promise to her to do only good for as many people as possible, after she had learned that the Inquisition would ferret out and persecute the remaining members of her faith. Simon was noble in more than the social sense. His heart wanted to do what was right and good. She would live in that idea and guide him to do so as well.

She had changed him, and he had changed her. They understood one another. And they were each improved by the other's friendship. And she now could not hide it from herself that it was more than friendship, deeply so. But she would have to hide it from him and from the world.

He had proclaimed it his duty to personally repent for what she had considered the crimes of his father against her people. This was an incredibly significant spiritual development, but she also knew that it had to spring from some specific feeling that he must have had for her. He had saved her life, even when he had hardly known her or could not have known her value as a person, or what she would later bring to his life. She understood that this too almost had to spring from something close to a deep affection. He also readily accepted her advice, even when it had been critical of his actions or assessments. She knew that there had never been another woman in his life, not even his charismatic mother, the formidable Alix de Montmorency, who spoke to him quite the way she did. He had told her as much, in one or another of those conversations, which only lately had become uncomfortable.

It was the tenor and context of those conversations that left her mostly convinced that Simon might have always been romantically inclined toward her, but that he had a way of not being aware of that. She knew enough now to know this was a thing that a man could do more easily than a woman. But she also knew that Simon could hew closely to the noble and chivalrous path. She hid her discomfort when she encouraged him to be exceptionally open and forthcoming when he spoke to her of his growing involvement with Eleanor of Pembroke, King Henry's sister. He may have had reservations about whatever discomfort Pauline might feel, but she labored effectively to get him to put those aside. She encouraged him to speak to her as he always had, as a friend, and to never consider how she might be hurt. It was one of the more difficult tasks she ever managed. She felt she had succeeded when one day he congratulated Pauline on how she had very accurately gauged Eleanor's reaction to him as a man.

The vow of chastity Eleanor had taken upon the death of her husband was in keeping with the Church doctrine that two souls united in the Church by the holy sacrament of marriage remained together for eternity. Eleanor had lived a noticeably quiet, private, and chaste life from that point forward, until the wedding of her brother, the king, which she had attended as a matter of course.

Before she had become Eleanor of Pembroke, the countess, she had been Eleanor of England, the princess, the daughter and the sister of a king. She had not been raised to be shy. After the king's wedding, she began to venture out to more of the events at court and to occasionally cross the path of the lord high steward, Simon de Montfort. By her glances and gestures, she made it apparent that she had not made these changes in a vacuum, but that she had bent like a flower to the sun, and that light had been emanating from the Earl of Leicester. Simon told Pauline that he would not have noticed Eleanor's changes had it not been for the way in which Pauline had shown him to be aware of such things. He had more self-awareness now and was able to observe more closely his effect on Eleanor. In fact, he had even been able to pay attention to the way in which Queen Eleanor saw him and he told Pauline that he believed that the queen was silently encouraging the excursions of the other Eleanor, her sister-in-law, into the orbit of Simon.

He told Pauline that there had been occasions when he had the opportunity to speak to the widow Eleanor but that she had not responded to him. She had remained withdrawn and reserved. He had been speaking to her in the manner of the court, in the same fashion that he had courted Mahaut of Boulogne and Joan of Flanders. At that time, Pauline had simply kept her own counsel, but then finally had asked him, "And how has that been working for you?"

He stopped speaking, looked at her and smiled. She continued.

"Can you not think of a better example of how to speak to her?"

He then confessed to Pauline that he understood the idea implicit in her question. He had been going about it incorrectly in the past. He had not revealed his warmth, his humor, or his lively approach to life. He had not shown that he was any different than other nobles, other than in his appearance and bearing. So, he told her that suddenly he was struck with the idea that she had just implied. He should speak to Eleanor in the way that he had always spoken to Pauline. This suggestion struck Pauline in more than one way. She was proud of herself and perhaps more so for bearing such discussion without revealing her pain.

He found later that the widow responded to that. She had never had a man actually listen to her, weigh her comments, seek her advice, and be sensitive to all the possible meanings she might have. And she had never had any conversation that had been so engaging. Simon spoke to her as an equal, with warmth and without judgment or distance. Eleanor's reserve began to lift like a summer-morning fog. She began to entertain ideas she had not previously considered. Her marriage had taught her about men, but in large part, she had learned the way in which men could be dismissive, inattentive, and self-regarding. Simon made her feel as if a man could see her, or really know her. Most importantly, she felt as if Simon saw the woman who she had always really been on the inside, but who had never been given the room and encouragement to grow. Pauline knew all this because Simon had told her, and he knew it because Eleanor had told him. Eleanor had become forward and direct with Simon. Pauline also knew it because it was the way Simon had returned to their former way, that he and she could be open with one another. That openness was Pauline's recompense for her decision and for her resolve.

This all had occurred over the period of several months since the wedding of the king and Eleanor of Provence, now Queen of England. It had happened in the court of Henry III without his notice. Simon found the young widow to be attractive. The chaste widow had fallen in love with the Earl of Leicester. That he had made no secret of this to Pauline was something to which she also devoted some rumination. It seemed that he and Pauline had begun their relationship with remarkable candor and that it would always be their hallmark, no matter what. He could not consider changing it for whatever reason. He did not seem to be sensitive to the fact that his relationship with Pauline had also been the guiding star to his courting of Eleanor. And in that courtship, he did not see Pauline as someone to be kept uninformed or to be protected from its meaning. He chose to see the greater openness that he and Pauline had always shared.

Pauline considered all this and wondered if Simon had told Eleanor about her, or what he might have told Eleanor about her. She concluded that he must not have told her the length and depth of their friendship, or Eleanor would not have entered a liaison with him so easily. But maybe he had told her something. Pauline was for the first time in all this somewhat confused. She had a strong notion that Simon did not really or fully know his own heart. Pauline always considered that he had not expressed that he loved Eleanor. And there was always present the fact that she could be a fit, rich, and noble match for the Earl of Leicester.

Pauline strived to balance her personal feelings with what she had learned in her faith. She knew she desired Simon's presence, that she wanted to engage him, but she had always believed from her youth that she should love only in spirit. In this she was aided by the fact that well beyond his appeal as a man, there was a great deal about him that called for spiritual devotion. His heart was open and compassionate. He was curious about people and their differences. He was bold in his desire to do right. Her faith helped her to see that. But there was something more. Simon was entering some very deep water and he would need her. Her love for him must be largely protective. It was one thing to be a favored member of court, and another to have the love of the king's widowed sister. His prominence would expose him.

Pauline needed to get away. It had taken her several months to get all this clear in her own mind. Now that she knew what to think and what her own feelings were, she wanted to be alone and feel the fresh breeze on her face. She slipped into her quarters and changed into her complete squire outfit, pinning her hair up into her hat. She went out her second-floor window and climbed down the trellis. Her primary goal was to evade the notice of Rocco, who was always watching out for her. She could avoid the other guards easily enough. She entered the stable alone and saddled her horse. Rocco had not detected her departure. Only one groom was in the stable, the youngest one, and he did not feel free to speak to her and was not even sure who she was. He only saw a noble squire in the earl's retinue and that the squire knew his way around the grounds. She saddled her horse and set out. But she had not been unseen by all.

She decided to ride south along the River Soar and chose to take the road on the eastern bank, opposite the more heavily traveled Leicester Road. The river valley here was quite level, and the river itself meandered and opened into two or more channels. The surrounding meadows were often soggy. There were stands of trees and forest on either side of the road. Pauline stayed on the road and began to feel the joy of the sun and the wind, and the freedom of moving on her own. This added to the emotional strength she had gained from the long months of contemplation and examination and the conclusions she had reached. She felt that whatever she could do for Simon would be amplified by what he would do for the people of his realm and of England. She had always felt that he had a unique and important destiny. She was newly interested in what her own might be, separate from his.

She understood immediately that he would have to go to King Henry and confess his courtship of Eleanor. There should be no more keeping it a secret. That could only create a greater problem, worse than the one they faced now. She would advise that. And that would reinforce her position as his closest advisor, even in matters of the heart, which in Simon's case would also always be matters of the kingdom. She would support him in all things.

With calm resolve and a feeling of grace that often arises when one has just passed through mental or emotional commotion and has mastered it, she took her horse off the road at one of her favorite spots, where the river turned from flowing west to flowing north toward Leicester. There was a rise in the bend of the river here, and the ground was solid. The trees had long since been removed, to add to the higher ground's view up and down the valley. She dismounted and walked her horse toward the vantage point and stood to look at this part of southern Leicestershire.

She had not been there more than a few minutes when she noticed a man walking toward her from the upriver stretch of the road. He was not dressed as any of the farmers or burgesses or guildsmen of the area, many of whom in this region she knew by sight. He wore the garb of a soldier, but not one from Simon's realm or the neighboring counties. There was something about him that was slightly foreign. And his gait was noticeably purposeful. Hers was a clear head. This man had left his horse on the road and was striding across the ground with one purpose in mind. His look was dark, his hand on his sword hilt. He made no greeting. She had lately felt alone and frightened and that temperament served her when she caught a flash of malice in his eye. It seemed to her that he meant to kill her.

She made no sudden move but pretended to be attending to her horse. She spoke to the animal in gentle tones as she gradually moved it around so that it was between her and the stranger. As he drew close, she addressed him with a friendly greeting. He did not answer but looked over her shoulder in a manner that told her of the need for precipitous action. With her hand on the hilt of her sword, she dropped below the horse and simultaneously drew the weapon from its sheath. She saw the soldier reach for his own sword at the same moment that she stuck the point of hers into the inside of his upper thigh. She would long remember that disconcerting feeling, of how easily the steel point punctured and cut the flesh. As he fell to the ground, bleeding freely, she rolled under the horse and over the top of the man and stood up. She caught sight of the second soldier just as she did so. He had been behind her and was now striding around the horse toward her from the opposite direction and was only ten feet away.

She had maneuvered her way to victory over the first assailant, but she knew now she would be in a sword fight. Neither she nor her sword would be stout enough to parry this man's blows, with his heavier sword and frame. If she were to have any chance to survive, she would have to rely on quickness and guile, and on the training that Rocco had given her. The first thing she would do would be to discourage him from taking exploratory thrusts. He could reach farther and would recover more quickly. She wanted him to swing his sword in a broad arc, knowing that she could not block it with her smaller blade and her weaker arm: such a swing would be easier to dodge. She feinted at him with a flurry of her sword, and he swung at her, which gave her enough time to retreat. And retreat is what she did, gradually and resolutely, step by step, backing herself toward the river. He smiled because he knew he had her cornered against the riverbank. He advanced with confidence, knowing it was only a matter of time before she could no longer retreat.

Pauline thought about what Simon had told her, and she knew she could apply that lesson to this terrain. She kept yielding ground rapidly, backing up toward the river. He continued to advance, swinging his sword more wildly. As she reached the river's edge, her foot felt where the land began to slope. She made a few more demonstrative thrusts and swings with her sword and waited for him to deliver what he expected to be her deathblow. He reached back, and just as he began to swing his sword, she hopped down onto the ledge she knew was there, three feet below. Simon had told her that a man on a horse holds his sword in the air well over the head of a man on the ground, while the man on the ground holds his weapon at the horseman's waist. He swung over her. She drove her sword into the soldier's lower abdomen, well up into his chest, killing him instantly.

She could not believe she had done this. Some part of her had acted on instinct yet had also made use of the training Rocco and Simon had given her. She had not been given an instant to consider that she had killed the first man. Now, there was time to consider that she had slain two. Her hands were shaking, and she was almost sobbing. But she had acted with resolve in her own defense and some part of her knew that this was still a dire situation and there was no time for an emotional reaction. She thought about what she should do in the few moments before she knew she would have to quickly get away from there. She would try to find out as much as she could about these attackers.

She then set about to search each man's body. The first man had bled to death by this point. Her suspicion was that these men had been in the employ of Guy Alain, but as she found no sign of this in her search, she reconsidered. Monsignor Alain would want her alive anyway, so he could use her to prosecute Simon. She was confronting something more along the lines of a genuine mystery. The only sign of anything of note that she found was that one man had a small fish symbol embroidered on his cloak, and the other man had that same fish on the hilt of his sword. It was not the stylized fish symbol that the Church used to signify Christ. It was simply a realistic symbol of a green fish.

SIXTEEN

Pauline returned to the castle and was stunned by what she had done. She was in shock and quietly slipped into her quarters where she sat shaking for several long minutes before she became quite sick. She tried to slow her mind down and become calm. She tried to think of Simon. But she kept returning to the idea that someone was trying to kill her and that she had just slain two men. She sipped some water and sat quietly. She was only sure of one thing and that was that she was in no condition to leave her room.

Rocco was castigating himself for allowing Pauline to have escaped his protection. His every instinct had told him that this was a dangerous moment for her. He was certain of it when he saw her return. She seemed rattled and distant and preoccupied. And she was a bit disheveled in her dress and appearance. Her face was a little flush. He knew better than to approach her. He placed a guard on her door and told him he wanted her to remain in her room until he returned. He went to the stable and mounted his horse and set off down the road from which she had returned, his ever-watchful eyes trained on her tracks and the surrounding land. It did not take him long to find the bodies, strip them, and slip them into the river.

Then he bundled up their clothes and tied them to their swords and dropped them into the water at a point a few miles away. He logged his observations and considered what his next steps might be.

He knew that he had to get back to Pauline before she tried to leave her room to speak to Simon. He hurried back. Pauline took a few hours to gather herself well enough to go and speak to Simon at dinner. Before that could happen, Rocco showed up at her room. He looked to her like he did that first moment that she had met him on the road from Avignon. He was calm but resolute and it meant to her that she would be doing what he suggested next, whether or not she agreed. And he suggested that they take a walk into town and he told her that he had told Simon and the staff not to expect them for dinner. They would be taking dinner somewhere in town.

They walked into Leicester and turned onto Cank Street and into the bakery district where the nicer houses were surrounded by the more pleasant aromas. They stopped in front of a medium-size home and before they could knock on the door, it opened to them. A nice-looking, brown-haired woman of about thirty years of age, with brown eyes and a pleasant build, opened the door and said, "You must be Pauline."

"This is Emily," Rocco said. "She has kindly arranged for us to have dinner here."

There was a table set for two, even though there appeared to be two children in the house with Emily. She gathered those children, patted Rocco on the shoulder and turned to walk with them out of the front door. Before she left, she turned to speak to Pauline.

"I have heard many good things about you."

"Thank you," Pauline said.

The two of them did not speak. Rocco got some soup out of a pot and put a bowl in front of each of them and he watched Pauline intently and kindly. For many minutes, she did not speak or eat. She stirred her soup with a spoon, looked at Rocco.

"Two men tried to kill me."

"I assumed that must have been the case. I followed your tracks to the bluff over the river, saw the tracks there, and disposed of the bodies. I only wonder who helped to defend you."

"No one did. I defended myself."

"That is surprising and perhaps it is not surprising. You are resourceful."

"It was your training, and what I learned from Simon." Here she began to choke in her speech. "Who would want to kill me? What have I done?"

"It is not worth speculating at this point. I will look into it. There were some clues that I can examine. There is just one important thing right now that we must both understand."

"What is that?"

"You cannot tell Simon."

"He deserves to know, and I need to tell him."

She started to cry. He stood up and moved his chair around the side of the table to her and sat next to her. Pauline was slowly pulling herself together and after she had unloaded her heart, had told the story of the attack, and expressed her fear and was grateful for her friend's sympathy and compassion, the sense of his point began to take hold with her. She knew the truth of what Rocco had said. Simon would react too strongly. And Rocco won her over because he had promised that she could eventually tell Simon about it once he discovered the underlying facts and motives and told her.

He knew she had begun to recover when she sat up and said, "Wait a minute. Who is Emily?"

Rocco stood up and moved his chair around to his side of the table again. He told her that Emily was a widow of a baker who now had to do much of that work herself. He had come upon her two children in the street, one eight, a boy, and the other a six-year-old girl. He undertook to watch them and make sure nothing happened

155

to them. They began to ask him questions. It was not very long before they were talking to him and enjoying his company, when their mother came out of the shop and found them. She asked him no questions but simply invited him home for dinner. He told Pauline he and Emily had secretly married. She was not startled by that news because her capacity for surprise had been exhausted this day.

Pauline then took some food. She ate some of the soup and had a few bites of bread and Rocco suggested afterward that she seemed to be ready to return to the castle and get a night's sleep, to begin the new day tomorrow.

"When you wake up tomorrow," Rocco said on the way back, "you will have to be with Simon and not let on that anything has happened."

"I think I can do that now," she said, "thanks to you. I will think about what happened. But you have helped me through the worst of it."

"I am happiest when I can help you. And I owe it to you for having let you face those men alone."

"It was not your fault. I did everything I could to slip away from you."

Pauline spent much of the next day actively involved in her charts and reading. She felt well enough to be with Simon, so long as she could keep the conversation impersonal and on the important matters. She was sustained by the fact that she had a subject she wanted to discuss with him. After dinner, she spoke to him.

"Do you remember how we had discussed that you should use the Church?" she asked.

"Yes, of course I do," he said. "You know that I have been following your counsel, although I see it as being devout and engaging and honoring the leaders of the clergy. I have built a promising relationship with Robert Grosseteste, the Bishop of Lincoln, who has assumed the role of my mentor. He has said he notes great things in me, and he has been very obliging to me in his conversations with King Henry. I know he is a great supporter of mine."

"You told me that he has assigned his young protégé, the Franciscan Adam Marsh, to be your liaison with his office because the bishop is busy with his teaching at Oxford as well as with his business in the diocese," she said. "I understand that Adam Marsh is the confessor and advisor to each of the two Eleanors, the queen and the king's sister. I believe that he and the bishop should be consulted first about anything you might want to tell King Henry about you and his sister Eleanor. I also believe the queen likes you and can be convinced that your marriage to the king's sister would be a good thing."

"That makes remarkable sense. Adam is a wise man and a good friend. I trust him implicitly. And now that I think about it, I also think he might support the idea of the Countess of Pembroke and I marrying."

At this, Pauline had to pause. "It is also in the interest of the bishop, if what you say is true about his beliefs regarding secular politics," she said.

"There is going to be an issue with the Church, more importantly with Rome itself," he said. "Eleanor must be released from her vow of chastity."

"That seems like a long process and I am not sure Eleanor can wait. But you are correct. You can approach the bishop through Marsh, and you can go to them, seeking their counsel. I think it will turn out as you hope."

"I am grateful, as ever, for your counsel, Pauline. I am always surprised at how I am no longer surprised by how much you know and how insightful you are," he said.

"Thank you, my lord."

He looked confused at her use of his honorific, but he let her continue.

"Much of the information I receive comes to me from Rocco, who seems like he has an ear to the ground and hears all the rumblings of England. Much of it comes from what I hear in your own household, and the rest from all the reading I have never ceased to do. Only the thinking is my own. And I think you need to write to Adam Marsh and to the bishop," she said.

"I will do that. What will you be doing?"

"I will be figuring out ways to save and to raise some money. I have a feeling this may get expensive."

Simon smiled. Pauline was able to make her exit without having lost any of her composure. The next time, it would be easier.

Pauline was also making an excuse. She would indeed apply herself to increasing Simon's income from Leicestershire, but it would also be her way to get her heart away from the subject of its discomfort. There was much she could do and more she could learn. There were also people with whom to meet, knights, reeves, tenant farmers, bailiffs, and members of the seignorial council. The work she could do, the new things she could learn, and the people with whom she would work would occupy her, or they could help to occupy her. She also felt the need to continue her work with the poor and the dispossessed. She recognized that she could address her duty as steward and augment it into an opportunity.

Robert Grosseteste had been the Archdeacon of Leicester prior to his appointment as the Bishop of Lincoln, the diocese that included Leicester. He took a natural interest in anyone who might be the Earl of Leicester. He had also been an innovator among churchmen in the study of the natural world, science, and secular law. It was unusual that he had written treatises on these subjects in addition to his theological discourses. Now well into his fifties, he had also taught at the Franciscan school at Oxford and had been elevated to be the first master at that university. He was exceptionally adept at managing the interplay between the Church in Rome and the

Kingdom of England, mustering the authority of the king in efforts to obtain some independence from Rome for the English Church, and asserting the power of the Pope in dealing with the king. He was a vanguard figure in England. No cleric up to this point had been so openly intellectually curious and active, nor had any been so active in so many spheres of society.

His best friend and his acolyte, was Adam Marsh, more than twenty years his junior and a theologian and scholar who also taught at Oxford. He was nominally a priest of one of the abbeys of northern England, but he was most notably the Bishop of Lincoln's plenipotentiary. Wherever he went and to whomever he spoke, it was assumed he stood in the place of Robert Grosseteste. He had eschewed any further advancement in the Church and had always been charged with the bishop's most responsible commissions, including being the confessor and advisor to Queen Eleanor, and to the king's sister, Eleanor, Countess of Pembroke. He was a quiet and unassuming man in his early thirties, with very dark hair and eyes, and his tone of skin was not as pale as his countrymen. He was below medium height and was exceptionally charming, with a knowing sparkle in his dark eyes. He had a good deal more brain than tongue in his head. He arrived at Leicester shortly after he and the bishop had received Simon's letters. He met with Simon.

"Your letters present a very interesting situation," he said.

"I am afraid I had not really thought of it that way," Simon said. "I simply became fond of Eleanor's company and she has some feelings for me. I have always intended to marry for the service of my king and my county, to choose a bride whose family and connections would be of benefit. This seems to have confused the matter and now Eleanor seems quite attached to me."

"The king's widowed sister, you mean."

"Yes."

"The same woman who has taken a vow of chastity, which is almost the equivalent of becoming a sister in the Church, a bride of Christ?"

"I confess I had not given that as much thought as I ought to have. Or perhaps I did at first, but soon I was caught up in the way in which she simply engages me."

"You have stepped right into the thorn bushes, then?"

"I feel I must go to King Henry and confess everything to him. I owe him that much. He is my liege lord, and he is Eleanor's guardian. And, I imagine, he is as much a friend of mine as a king may be."

"Which may not be much," Marsh said. "You have certainly placed yourself at odds with both his interest as king and as the guardian of the countess. You have also called into question his relationship with the Church."

"What should I do?"

"Do you not think you have done enough already?"

Adam Marsh sat back and looked carefully at Simon. Then he looked around the room as if he were looking for someone else. He rested his head in his hand for a while. Then he spoke.

"There is nothing for you to do. The queen knows all that has happened, or at least she knows so much as her sister-in-law, the countess, has confided in her. The queen loves the countess, whom she sees as an older sister, and she likes you. That is a great boon. The king may take an authoritarian stance toward his sister, but he is very indulgent of his young queen. I also believe that the countess has expressed the degree of her passion to the queen, who has already set in motion much of what will need to be done in order for you to marry Eleanor of Pembroke."

"I cannot express the burden that you have lifted from my heart," Simon said. He was struck at how much of what Adam Marsh had told him was along the lines of what Pauline had told him she had observed.

"You need not be so quick," Adam Marsh said. "I believe that the king will allow his sister to marry you. But you know the king. He is impulsive and not circumspect. He will not want to wait, not once he has given his word to the queen and to his sister. He will revel in making them both happy. It is not likely that there will be time to do what else must be done."

"Do you mean to get Rome to accede to the marriage?"

"Yes, but that will only be half of it. The Bishop of Lincoln is the ecclesiastic representative among the nobles whom the king is supposed to consult. You are on that council as well, but the bishop has been there longer and knows its ways more personally. He knows intimately that the ranking nobles of the kingdom will rightly consider the marriage of the king's sister a matter of state, not one of love. They will feel they should have been consulted."

This time it was Simon who sat back and looked at the man before him, and who then looked around the room before he spoke.

"And I suppose that those same nobles will not take kindly to one of their own being elevated over them, especially since I am already the lord high steward."

"And a foreigner," the priest said.

"Yes. But I do not feel like a Frenchman anymore. I love England. I love Leicester. But I do know that I landed on these shores only several years ago."

"Yes. And it is not entirely a bad thing. The English barons are all connected by blood or separated by blood feuds, and these issues have been in place for generations. Coming from the outside, you are free of such intrigues. With respect to each other, none of them gain or lose from your elevation. Perhaps that may be what God had in mind for you."

"How do you mean that?" Simon asked.

"The bishop has always seen you as the honest, upright, and good Christian nobleman who will marshal the other lords and magnates to serve as a check on the caprices and impulsiveness of King Henry."

"I am honored. Please tell the bishop."

"I will. And before I leave, there is one other thing."

"What would that be?"

"I would like a private audience with your lady steward."

SEVENTEEN

Simon was in good spirits at Christmas of 1237. The king had promised to have his sister Eleanor married to the earl in a ceremony at Westminster, to be presided over by the king's chaplain, on the following January 7. The king had also promised to write a letter of state to the Pope that Simon could carry to Rome, stating that "our dear brother, and faithful subject, Simon de Montfort" is charged with matters important to both the kingdom and to the king personally.

Henry had spent many pleasant days over the holidays with his queen, his sister, and her intended. They were excited at the prospect of being of one family and of raising children who would be loving cousins. Henry made no secret that Simon was his favorite and Simon remained genuinely humble. Pauline was inevitably drawn into the modest contentment of her best friend. When he asked her what had been the outcome of her private audience with Adam Marsh, she gave him her most affectionate and devoted answer, which was her honest one: "Be careful what you wish for."

The wedding was a private and essentially secret event, and to Pauline it was even more remarkable than the lavish ceremony for the marriage of the king to Eleanor of Provence. Eleanor of

Pembroke and Simon de Montfort were not married in St. Paul's Cathedral, as might be fit for the sister of the king. The Archbishop of Canterbury did not preside. Eleanor had made her vow of chastity to him and she was now about to break it. There were no guests of state. It was January of 1238 and the wedding was as austere as the weather. It was held in the king's own private chapel in Westminster and the officiant was Henry's court priest. It was striking in its intimacy. The royal couple were not dressed in the ceremonial robes of state but in their formal court dress. The king and queen did not stand at a ceremonial distance but were a part of the ceremony. The king spoke for his sister and commended her choice of a husband. The queen beamed with genuine happiness for her sister-in-law and with the satisfaction of knowing she had been the one most responsible for allowing this match to occur. Eleanor, the bride, wore a simple long pale blue silk dress that was suited to a second wedding. Simon wore his full symbols of office as Earl of Leicester.

Perhaps most noticeable and even painful to Pauline was that Simon and his Eleanor did not seem to be playing the roles of a marrying couple, as had the king and queen at their wedding. Pauline knew little of weddings and in her Cathar faith they were private if they happened at all, but this wedding struck her as more of what she might have expected in her homeland. There was truly little ceremony at all. It was informal and it was about the people. Eleanor of Pembroke was not the child bride she had once been, or as the queen had been. She had all the presence and command of a twenty-three-old princess who had once been married for several years. She seemed more in command than her thirty-year-old groom, who was a man of two kingdoms and many battles. She had also been a widow for another several years. The knowing way she looked at Simon unnerved Pauline because it contained elements of the way Pauline saw Simon and added some others.

The king also unnerved Pauline. He was almost too happy, too ebullient, too full of praise and warmth. Henry was always expressive. He was also capricious and given to statements that were different or the opposite of what he had most recently proclaimed. This was never truer than when he was his most effusive and demonstrative, as he was on this day. His praise of the match was overwrought in the way that always seemed worrisome to the hearer.

When the marriage became known, most of the barons were surprised. Many of them liked Simon. The Bishop of Lincoln had also smoothed the waters a great deal. Some of the few nobles who were complaining were in a quandary as to what to do or to say. In most such cases, the first person to whom they would take such a concern would have been the lord high steward of the king, who in this case was the Earl of Leicester himself. They might also appeal to the clerical leaders, who were in support of the earl. The primary complaint therefore was to the person of Richard of Cornwall, the king's younger brother. He took it as a personal affront that he had not been consulted on his sister's marriage, so he became the leader who took the apprehensions of the nobles to the king, that they and he had not been consulted on a matter of state. Pauline's solution was that Simon proffer an emolument of five hundred pounds to Richard. The minor storm quickly subsided.

There soon was another small tempest with which to contend, and it was a blue-eyed blonde one: Eleanor, Simon's bride, who was cast very much in the mold of her mother, the captivating Isabella of Angoulême. Pauline noticed that in a crowded room, almost all male eyes would fall upon the pretty Eleanor, now the Countess of Leicester, and they would remain on her. She had inherited her mother's dynamic temperament. Pauline knew the stories of Isabella, how she had enchanted King John and how when he died, she had married the man intended for her daughter Joan. Eleanor was lavish in her praises and it struck Pauline that she felt she was charming when she expressed her opinions. She was gracefully confident in receiving attention. It had long been her natural state. She had been born Princess Eleanor of England, and she had been raised among the same small council of nobles who had formed the child King Henry's regency. They had fawned over her, while in Henry they had struggled to instill the solemnity of his office. At a little over five feet tall, she still carried the innocent charms of her youth.

Pauline could see that Eleanor knew several ways to manage her husband that may not have occurred to him. Pauline had never tried to handle Simon as Eleanor now did. Eleanor understood the power of appealing to his male vanity. She swept into his castle with her retinue of ladies-in-waiting, many of whom came from the other noble families of England. She immediately began to take over the household and set things according to her own tastes, which were no less than extravagant. It seemed only a matter of moments before she calculated to turn her attention to Pauline. When she spoke to Simon on the topic, she did not choose a private moment but addressed him in the presence of most of his household and Pauline.

"Simon, I can't believe you have a young woman in an important position in your household," she said. "That is rather odd and hardly in keeping with custom. There will no longer be any need for a woman's touch around here, so perhaps you might find a more suitable place for her employ."

"Though Pauline is indeed a young woman," Simon said, "she has been in my service and has been my friend for greater than twelve years. She left behind all that her home in Occitania held for her to serve me in England. The value of her assistance and friendship has been incalculable to me and to Leicestershire. We found this county in impoverished disarray and now it functions smoothly and provides a reasonable income. She has also run the household impeccably. I do not think you would want to assume such a common set of duties yourself, nor would I be able to find as competent a steward or one in whom I would have the same level of confidence."

This may have been the answer that Eleanor had expected because her response came swiftly and decisively and not without some irony.

"You are so adorably loyal, my love. I must honor you for that. And I respect your judgment. We will not remove your loyal servant from this household or from her duties to the county. It will be best that she remains anyway. My brother has promised me that you and I shall have Kenilworth Castle, not far from here. We shall need your capable friend to stay here in Leicester to take care of it all, while we move on to Kenilworth."

Simon moved across the floor to his wife and took both her hands in his. He smiled and held her in his gaze. Kenilworth Castle was just across the southwest boundary of Leicestershire, in Warwickshire. It was not the main residence of the county. That castle was in the town of Warwick. Kenilworth had been a separate and royal castle under King John, who had expanded upon the original Norman-tower stronghold. He had built a stunning and capacious walled structure around the tower and he had dammed two local streams to create the Great Mere, which was more than a simple moat. It was a lake defense that combined with the walls to make Kenilworth one of the most strategic castles in the kingdom. When the king granted it to Simon, he would be in command of the most magnificent castle in all of England not in possession of the king himself. In fact, it was better than some of the lesser royal castles.

Had Pauline been almost any other woman, she might have been appalled at Eleanor and what she was doing. But she also saw this young woman's spirit and she had to credit her vibrant strength and obvious passion. She also had to feel impressed at Eleanor's cunning. Still, something in her felt a terrible pang at the likelihood of being separated from Simon. It was a pain that was additional to the larger one she felt at having lost him to Eleanor.

Simon, at that moment, had not considered that his marriage to Eleanor had not yet been sanctified by the Church in Rome. And, just as importantly, he did not reflect that he had not yet been officially invested with the title of Earl of Leicester and would not until his brother could come to England and renounce his rights in person before Henry III. These first few months of his marriage were spent joyfully, and only after it was discovered that Eleanor was with child did he hurry to leave for Rome, intending to stop by Paris on his return, to meet with his brother, Amaury.

In early 1238, Simon made his way to Rome and to Pope Gregory IX. He took with him the king's letter, a letter from the Bishop of Lincoln, and such funds as might be necessary to appease the Vatican. He found the Pope to be the astute politician that he and Pauline, and he and the Bishop of Lincoln, had discussed he was to expect. Gregory had instituted the formal Inquisition. He had also promoted the causes of the Franciscans and the Dominicans as a potent arm to combat the worldly excesses of the rest of the Catholic Church. He had known both Saint Francis and Saint Dominic in his youth and he appreciated the commitment that each had toward serving the poor and needy, and eschewing the rich trappings of the other clergy. And he was now in a struggle with the Holy Roman Emperor, who was neither Roman nor holy but was a Hohenstaufen king who had subjected many of the other German kingdoms, as well as those of northern Italy, to his rule. Pope Gregory welcomed any help from Henry III. And he recognized the legacy that resided in the person of Simon de Montfort, whose father and brother had "taken the cross" to serve in the crusade against the Cathars.

The Pope kept Simon at the Vatican and promised him that he would consult with his cardinals and consider the request of the King of England on his behalf. In those next few months, Simon was able to spread around many of the funds he had brought with him and to purchase a great deal of good will. The Pope had also called him into a private audience on several occasions. In the first of these, he enlisted Simon's able assistance in a small military exercise in Brescia, Lombardy. And in the others, he elicited Simon's promise that he would at some point also take the cross and serve in a crusade.

Simon was fascinated by the machinations and the splendor at Rome. He had seen some few ancient Roman ruins in France, particularly in the south, but the conglomeration of these symbols of ruined empire in Rome was stunning and humbling. Still, he began to be anxious to make his return, to stop to see Amaury, and to be at Kenilworth before his first child was born.

After a few months, the Pope handed Simon a letter to his wife, absolving her of any sin, and a letter to the king, pronouncing a solemn decision in the earl's favor. Simon suspected that much of this was part of the labyrinthine series of disputes and negotiations between the Pope and various leaders in France, Spain, and England. It was all quite subtle for Simon, but he understood much of it. He was glad to have been successful in Rome and to be on his way to visit his brother in Paris.

Amaury was preparing to take the cross again and join the so-called Barons' Crusade. He was to lead the large force that France would be sending. Richard of Cornwall, the brother of King Henry III, was supposedly preparing an English contingent. Amaury was not too busy to warmly greet his brother.

"You have done well, Simon," he said. "You have exceeded all expectation. Father is in Heaven and smiling down on you. You are a great credit to the family name."

"It is wonderful to see you, brother. Yes, it has been an interesting several years in England."

"I am sure you will continue to prosper over there. That kingdom is a bit backward and you must seem like a towering sophisticate to them."

"If I were to tell you all of it, you might not believe me. I hardly believe it myself."

"I do believe it and I know about it. I receive regular reports from our envoys in London, who pay special attention to you. Congratulations on your felicitous marriage and on your elevation to be first among nobles there. I must tell you. I have received an invitation from your king. He plans to confer upon you the official investiture as the Earl of Leicester, and he wants it to be something of a present to you and your wife on the anniversary of your first year of marriage. I will be seeing you in England at the start of next year."

"I will compensate you for your renunciation, Amaury. I can do that now."

"Forget about it, Simon. Your love is compensation enough, as is my understanding of your good and strong heart. If there were more I could do for you, I would."

If Simon thought he could not have been happier, he would have been mistaken. When he arrived at Kenilworth in October of that year, his wife was about one month from giving birth. The queen herself had come from London to be in her attendance. With her, she had brought little Edward, her own firstborn, only four months old. When Simon's wife was about to go into labor, the king arrived from London. At the end of November, slightly more than eleven months after they were married, the Earl of Leicester and his wife had a baby boy. They approached the queen with a special request, and she brought it to the king, who gleefully granted it. He permitted the child to be named Henry, and the king happily stood as his godfather at his christening.

The royal couple was quick to put the two boys together, Prince Edward and the infant Henry de Montfort. The king ordered the Leicester couple to London, where he planned to officially invest Simon with the earldom. Characteristic of the impulsive king, he could not wait for Amaury, who could not arrive until April. The newly officially married Simon, also newly a father to the king's godson, officially became the Earl of Leicester in February. When Amaury arrived, Simon's happiness was complete. Or at least it felt that way. Only in the quiet moments did he feel that something was lacking. He had so much reason to rejoice. But he was not now sharing any of it with the one person who had played the largest role in securing his happiness. His thoughts turned to Pauline.

She had once suggested that he come to England. She had advised him at every step of the way, even to the point of assisting with his courtships, all three of them. She had begun to put the county of Leicester back in order. And she had practically anticipated every possible contingency and had prepared him. She had never asked anything in return. She respected him, but figuratively she never let him get on his horse without his sword. She never let him wander too long in his own mistaken notions. She believed in the greatness of his destined future. She never sought anything from him. She spoke to him directly and critically, but always with his best interest on her tongue and in her mind and heart. He realized all of this with the arrival and then departure of Amaury. He loved his brother and admired him, and there was not much he would not do for him. And he reveled in the opportunity to share his happiness with him. Once Amaury had left to return to France and to begin his journey to the Holy Land, Simon realized that he also felt the same way about Pauline, only much more so. He could not wait to see her. He wrote her a letter to tell her that he wished to see her and asked her to come to London.

Pauline read the letter with some sadness; she knew much of the reason for it was that she wanted to see him also but was too wise to intrude upon his life at this point, and certainly would not do it in London, at the palace of his wife's brother, the king. She knew the dangers that might await her there, and she suspected that they might be greater than she could assess. But she also knew that the dangers to Simon posed by her presence there would be even greater. In fact, she was more fearful for him than anything. So, she answered his letter.

My lord, I remain your humble servant and am honored that you might also consider me your friend. I owe you nothing less than my life and have hoped to repay some small fraction of that debt with my service. That you might attribute some of your happy success to my efforts is a kind mistake on your part. You are ever too generous. The flame that lights your inner self is brighter than any other, and it is purer. Any achievement that you have made has been by your own effort and by the limited but certain ability that other men possess to see that flame in you. Whatever you might attribute to me also springs from that same phenomenon. I am not deserving of your gratitude, as I am more grateful for the chance to be in that light to some small degree.

I rejoice in your happiness, and in the rewards you have received for your strength and goodness. But my service to you would not be true if I did not remind you that it is always better to view the bear from outside the cage than from inside of it. Though you have reached a great height, you are now inside that cage. And the bear is impulsive if not frivolous, and I fear that your success, if not your safety, may be more ephemeral than you might ever be able to see, as it is not in your character to know the ways of bears. Please take care.

Your servant,

P.

It was not more than a few months later, in August, when Pauline's warning was to prove prophetic. When the king was happy, as he had been, he was ecstatic. At such a time, his behavior became erratic, disjointed, perhaps even ludicrous. There were always whispers of ridicule at court, but on this occasion, the king heard them. Or perhaps he always heard them and ignored them, but he did not in this instance. He connected this mockery to his sister and to her husband, who were innocently the source of his mirth and, therefore in his mind, of the laughter aimed at him. When Simon then approached him with a request to officiate over the matter of an alleged debt claimed of him by the Count of Flanders, the king flew into a rage against Simon and against his own sister Eleanor. It was dramatic and startling and frightening. The couple had no way of dealing with such a baseless ill temper, so they swiftly and quietly returned to Kenilworth.

EIGHTEEN

For the next several months, Eleanor and Simon darkened the bright garden and grounds of Kenilworth with their despondency. Simon had known the volatility of the king before, but the effect of falling from the pinnacle of Henry's regard to suffer such public ridicule was as puzzling as it had been abrupt and painful. Eleanor may have suffered more. She had spent more time in the sunlight of her brother's favor and had grown up in it, never knowing anything else. He had been more lavish and demonstrative in his affection toward his sister than he had been with anyone. The fact that it might have been the product of an overly effusive heart could not have ever occurred to her. She simply felt suddenly and terrifyingly cast off. Her pain was then doubled because the king's tirade had placed her in the position of an outcast alongside her husband. There was a flickering of the idea that she was now placed between the two of them and would have to decide which to support. She loved Simon and he had given her life, and family, and meaning, all things that she had relinquished before. Though she could not see any kind of a real choice between the two of them, Henry was not only her brother, but he was also the King of England.

Pauline arrived at Kenilworth one day in the spring of 1240 and met with Simon. This did not occur absent the notice or comment of Countess Eleanor.

"Why do you need to see her?" Eleanor asked. "What business does she have here?"

"Pauline would not be here if there were not some valid purpose."

"Then I suppose you have to find out what is happening."

"I intend to do that."

Simon had not told his wife that he had sent for Pauline. He was deeply at a loss for what to do. And he had been in the habit his entire adult life of relying upon her and had benefitted from it. She had taught him to be more circumspect, to consider the motives of others, to examine what their interests were and how various interests competed or aligned. She had never shirked from telling him when he was wrong or when he was overly proud or rash. From her, he had learned a great deal and he had internalized her viewpoints and instincts to some extent, and now that was part of his strength. For the first time in a long while, he was in a genuine quandary. But it was more than that. All the rapid and precipitous changes of the last two years, both good and bad, had unmoored him. At every dark turn and every empty road in his mind, he remembered the value and the meaning that Pauline brought to his life.

When she came in, he was also touched by a different feeling. He was a husband now. And though his heart belonged to his wife, his first instinct upon seeing Pauline was to embrace her. He checked himself and blushed.

"Are you going to be all right?" she asked.

"I think that is the pertinent question."

"I mean, do you need to sit down? Should I send for someone to bring you something to drink?"

"I will be all right, but we should both sit down," he said.

"It is good to see you," she said.

"This is going to sound rather peculiar, but I have a question for you. This inquiry has always been at the center of the friendship you and I have had for the last fifteen years. Before I get to other specific queries, I will ask you this central question. Is that all right?"

"Is that the question?" she asked. "If so, yes, it is all right."

"I appreciate your jesting. I always have."

"I am sorry," she said. "I know you are serious. What do you want to know?"

"Who am I, Pauline?"

Tears came to her eyes and she cried freely for a moment. Then she dried them with her kerchief, aware that he was watching her intently and that he had not moved to comfort her. He was earnest. That is what moved her so. She realized that their story, the account of Simon and Pauline, had always boiled down to this question. She helped him to know himself. He was expressing that need for her now. The intimacy of that opened her up. She felt honored and loved, and it all made her quite afraid. It was a new place in which to find herself. And it was a powerful responsibility, one that she had always known was hers, but the weight of which she had never confronted. She was afraid to answer this question, but she had always known the answer. In fact, he was right. Every question he had ever asked her was appurtenant to this one, and all her answers had been some version of what she knew she would say now.

"You are the noble man who always does the right thing, the good thing," she said.

Now it was his turn to feel overwhelmed. She was like a looking glass, but one that was far more accurate and detailed than any ever made. She was more than that, too. She was a guiding star. He had saved her that one day in 1225 for this very reason. If he was dedicated to the good and to the right, he sensed even then that she amplified that in him. When he was young, he had once thought of this as doing what the Church would dictate was holy. But from her, he had learned to find the good in his own heart and to follow those inner rules. Suddenly, he was less despondent and less uncertain.

"Then I must do something positive and not remain in this castle any longer," he said.

"I agree. You should join the Barons' Crusade, go to the Holy Land to assist the king's brother, Richard, and your brother Amaury."

"Exactly as I had this instant thought, thanks to your simple answer. In the bargain, I will fulfill my promise to the Pope."

At this moment, the door opened, and Eleanor walked into the room. She looked confused, and her expression moved between haughty and hurt. She momentarily glared at Pauline, and then at her husband. Then she sat near them, quietly. She studied them now and thought about what she saw. After some time, she thought she understood it a little better. She could see that Simon had been seeking and receiving Pauline's advice and realized that Simon had sent for Pauline and had not admitted that. And Eleanor knew it was because he had always trusted and relied upon Pauline's advice. And Eleanor realized she had spent far too many long gray months in a deep sadness over her brother's behavior and had too long felt lost. There was little room in her for anger or jealousy. She looked at Simon now and asked him a question, ignoring Pauline.

"I know that your friend is here for a reason and it is likely that you are again seeking her counsel. What does she advise that you do?" Eleanor asked.

"Pauline and I agree that I should go to the Holy Land to aid the Pope in the Barons' Crusade, to offer my services to your brother, Richard of Cornwall, and fight alongside my brother."

Eleanor turned now to Pauline and her look softened a little. Still, she held on to a fragment of her proud detachment. She was largely and genuinely seeking an answer to her next question, but it carried a hint of negative expectation.

"What do you think I should do?" she asked.

"You must go with your husband," Pauline said. "It will be in the tradition of his family; Simon's mother accompanied his father on his campaigns. You will have a much easier time in his company than you would here, all terribly alone in Kenilworth. But the main reason is that I believe it is time for each of you to get away from England and from the king. His displeasure is most likely to fade once you are both away and on the crusade with Richard. Take your son, Henry, too. And since you are with child, I recommend that you only go so far as Italy or Sicily and await your husband there. In any event, you should not want to be here without him."

"Thank you," she said.

They sat quietly for several moments. It was an awkward situation in so many ways. But Pauline's wisdom was of value to Simon, and to each of them as a married couple. Eleanor felt this on her own and she felt it in sympathy with her husband's profound feelings to that effect. Then a servant arrived and announced a messenger from Leicester Castle. It was Rocco. He had a letter for Simon, and he handed it to him. Simon unsealed it and read it and explained its meaning to them all. Amaury had been captured in Palestine.

There was now a great deal of discussion among all four of them about preparations and how they should move in some haste. They discussed the arrangements to travel through France and Italy, to pay homage to the Pope, and then to procure a place for the family to remain, while Simon went on to the Holy Land. Simon suggested that the Pope would organize for them to stay in an estate in the port of Brindisi, in the southern part of the Italian peninsula that was part of the Kingdom of Sicily. Rocco knew that castle and its grounds and felt it would be comfortable. Pauline agreed to muster the resources of Leicester to support them in their journey. Simon would take his own small force of Leicestershire knights with him. After a few hours, all had been decided and only Rocco and Pauline were left in the room.

"It seems you are getting along well with the Countess of Leicester, my lady. I assume it was not always that way," he said.

"You know it was not always that way. She would like to see me out of the way."

"I was not going to say this now, though I believe it is true. I have not talked to you about it because I did not want to complicate matters. But I believe that she may have been behind that attack on you on that fateful day."

"I have noticed you increased my guard recently. I had thought it might have been the Hound of God, but Guy Alain would want to take me alive. That demented soul would have tortured me to the edge of death before he then would have used me against Simon. During Simon's courtship of Eleanor, he surely must have told her about me, not knowing what effect it could have had. In fact, it was I who had told him to speak frankly with her. And she seemed to know in advance how he would defend me to her."

"Pembroke," he said, "is that portion of Wales that is a peninsula. There are many fishing villages on its coast. One of the minor houses that was pledged to her when she was the Countess of Pembroke has as its symbol a green fish, the same one that was on those two men you dispatched next to the River Soar."

"I had thought she might have been behind those men, but I could not bring myself to believe it," she said.

"It is a good thing I had disposed of their bodies and all the evidence. I think their failure to report back may have stayed Eleanor's hand for a while. She may have thought Simon had saved you and she was worried about what he might know. Now it seems she has accepted you somewhat and we can pretend as if such a thing never happened, which may be for the best. It is only unfortunate that such a story may never be known. They would sing songs of the mighty lady warrior who skewered the two knights who had pinned her between them."

"I am surprised to learn after all these years that you know how to make a jest. They will never sing songs of women warriors, only of women's beauty," she said. "Where have you been?"

"I was in London, where I finally discovered what happened to Monsignor Alain."

"That is important news," she said.

"Apparently, once the matter of the Archbishop of Canterbury was settled, he was charged by the Pope to discuss with King Henry the possibility of bringing an office of the Inquisition here."

"Well, since that hasn't happened, I can only imagine that our mercurial, childlike, and improvident king must have had an interesting reaction to that. The English are different, as I have always said. I can't see them tolerating an Inquisition here."

"It is even more interesting than that. Apparently, the king was not paying all that much attention when Guy Alain spoke, as might be expected. So, the monsignor decided that he would make it more specific and he brought up the Earl of Leicester and stated that our earl might be harboring a heretic. That finally got the king's attention."

"Did he happen to mention who the heretic was?"

"No. He did not. Your identity was not his point. He wanted the king to know there was a problem with one of his nobles. But when Henry heard what he had to say, he immediately had the Hound of God put in chains and taken to a prison in Yorkshire, about as far away as possible."

"It is fortunate indeed that he tried that when Simon was the king's pet and favorite. Had he showed up last month, we might all be in some torture chamber now," she said. "Although, it does seem unlikely that the king would allow his sister to be subjected to widowhood a second time. Her son is his namesake and godson. As volatile as the king may be, he is unlikely to lose sight of that for very long."

"I don't have the insight you do," he said. "I simply know the facts. Those men with the fish symbols came from a house pledged to Eleanor of Pembroke. And Guy Alain is wasting away in some Yorkshire dungeon. I also think that King Henry assumed that making Guy Alain disappear would put an end to the discussion of bringing the Inquisition to England."

"I don't imagine he will be let out anytime soon either, because he would then likely report his mistreatment to the Roman Church," she said. "But still, the Hound of God and the Countess of Leicester have shown mortal intent. Each may be stayed for now, but it could be temporary in either case."

They found quarters for themselves in Kenilworth, awoke the next morning, and made some more arrangements with Simon and Eleanor. Rocco, without being noticed, studied Eleanor very closely. He was curious about what such a person looked like and acted like, one who could coldly plot the murder of someone she had never met. He also studied them all, to see if any danger might persist. He did not see any for the time being. But in the same manner that Guy Alain could be released from prison at any time, Rocco agreed with what Pauline had said and felt that Eleanor might release her mortal intent again, if ever some new reason should occur to her.

Pauline wandered the splendid Kenilworth Castle that evening, taking the time to gather her thoughts. When she came into the great room, she found Simon there alone. She had known that this had been a likelihood. She did not want him to leave to take the cross without having a moment with him. He apparently felt the same because he smiled and was relieved to see her. So much of the way they each thought about the world was tied up in the other person. And this time there was more, there was a feeling that was shared and which they would not discuss, even with each other. They reiterated some of their plans and urged each other to be careful. Then they sat at length before the fire together. Then she spoke.

"You have been my entire world, you know," she said.

"You may be overstating. The world is something I did not fully see until you showed me. I do not and cannot move anywhere in it, even to Jerusalem, without you being in my heart and mind."

He stood up to leave the room and he took her hand and held it gently in his own.

"I promise to return," he said, "not so much for Leicester or for England, but for you."

And he left the room.

On the thirty-mile ride back to Leicester the next morning, Pauline told Rocco of her plans to withdraw from Simon's life for a while and to find something of her own. There was simply the case that being part of Simon's life had put her own in danger. And there was also another emotional toll on her from being too close. She told Rocco she was informed by the way he had found his own life in Leicester town and that perhaps she should do the same. He looked at her with affection and some skepticism.

"I do not easily imagine you finding a way out of the earl's life. I believe if you were to try to do so, his problems and his needs would draw you back. He has a great destiny and so do you. He is the larger part of it, the part that everyone sees. But you have done great things too, through him and on your own."

"I am thinking of that latter part more now. I will move out more into the world on my own. I have Leicestershire to run, and there is much to do and learn. And there are people outside of the household of the earl."

Rocco smiled. Then he changed the subject. He and Pauline discussed what Simon might do on the crusade. They expressed their shared certainty that he would succeed, in any event. They could not have known what would actually happen. Simon would distinguish himself on the field of battle. But more importantly, his integrity, his ingenuity, and his strength of character would be recognized by the

European barons, knights, burgesses, and citizens of the Kingdom of Jerusalem, who would petition for Simon to be the regent of the kingdom until such time as their young king Conrad came of age. If Rocco and Pauline were to have known that, it would not have surprised them.

NINETEEN

Pauline had resolved to make a life of her own and knew that would be simpler in Simon's absence. When she returned to Leicester, Pauline opened the rolls. The county rolls had been her original idea, a straightforward invention. A roll was the simple account, a list, the record of the business of Leicestershire. Before she had taken over as steward, accounts were managed as a matter of custom, of memory, and of oral record. There had been only occasional written reports of what had been said or done. Under the chaos of the previous earl and the royal agents, so much of this had been forgotten, and the county had never fully recovered from the disarray and mismanagement that had characterized it during that period. Pauline had attempted to recreate it and then to make it a matter of written record from that point forward. As steward, Pauline had charge of the administration of the county, and the management of the earl's household or estate. Managing the Leicester household was a simpler matter now that the family lived in Kenilworth. Pauline would merely do what she could to find savings and to cut costs at the estate. She could discuss those costs and accounts with Rachel's father, who had also been managing the transport of goods. Pauline saw the large amount of work that needed to be done as her opportunity to carve some life for herself out of the business of Leicestershire. Rocco had little or no interest in accounts. But he knew the county well and he was her friend.

"Will you bring in all the sheriffs, the bailiffs, the magistrates, the clergy, and the knights from each one of the four of Leicestershire's districts?" he asked.

"That would be unwieldy. Such a convocation would discourage openness. Besides, I need to get out of this castle. It would do me good. I want to learn more about each of the four districts in the county. And I want to see the land and meet the people."

"Then, we can ride north to Goscote, and swing around to the east to visit Framland, then south to Gartree, and finish up in the west at Guthlaxton."

"Let's start at Framland," she said, "and save Goscote for last since it is the largest hundred in the county."

A "hundred" was the administrative unit that was smaller than the county but larger than the several parishes in each hundred. Each such district had a magistrate who served as a judge, justice of the peace, and officiant. There was a sheriff who managed the feudal obligations and a few bailiffs who served as officers of the court. There were also several knights in each hundred. These were all part of the local council and the rest of the association comprised the clerical leaders of each parish of the hundred and some burghers who were usually merchants. In the very first visits that Simon had made to the districts, Pauline had made sure that he ordered each to establish a practice of keeping the rolls, of listing the accounts. Under this new regime, each hundred had a clerk, called the treasurer or receiver, who worked for the sheriff and was responsible for the roll and for getting the funds to Leicester Castle. She decided she would meet with each council and go over the rolls with the receiver for each hundred.

As they approached the meeting of the council in Framland, Rocco spoke to her about the business of the county.

"What is the largest income producer in the county?" he asked.

"That is an interesting point," she answered. "Eleanor, the Countess of Leicester, is the largest producer of income. She receives a yearly payment from Pembroke as the widow of the count there. And she receives an equally large payment from the royal court as a settlement of her claim to some of the dowry property that was seized by her brother Richard. The county could manage to get by on this income alone. But we obviously need more."

"I understand these noble marriages a little better now."

"More is collected from all the various rents, from the fiefdoms granted to knights and the lands granted to farmers. But as you might imagine, these amounts vary and managing them all within the county is a difficult matter. We also charge a fee for merchants who participate in markets on market days. We are heading to Melton Mowbray, the market town of Framland. I think that the market collection is rather cut and dried. The collection of rents is where we will focus our efforts," she said.

"And the churches collect a tithe, correct? And does some of that come to the county?"

"Only a small part of the tithe is taxed. That tax on the churches goes to the king. The same is true for the payment for the rights to hunt in the king's forests. One penny out of three stays here for the earl to use in Leicestershire. But the income from one other source stays here entirely."

"I assume that is the money that is collected as fines in the courts. This strikes me as an encouragement for too much justice."

"Indeed, it is. But the funds do not stay in the hands of the magistrate or the bailiffs. They have less incentive to engage in the harsh collection of fines because what they collect goes to the county. Of course, they may want to impress the earl. All of this structure means that much of the collection is done as a matter of trust, depending on the honor of the individuals involved."

"You have your work cut out for you."

The meeting for Framland was held in the great hall of the largest manor in Melton Mowbray, which was located near the largest parish church of St. Mary's. Pauline asked the magistrate about the number of fines and their collection. He began a long and involved discussion of the many malfeasances and trespasses of the people of the hundred, and implied that they may have had a difficult time following the Christian tenets taught by the clergy. If Pauline had been only thinking of the business of the county, she would have gently led him to come to the point. But part of her purpose was to learn more about this land and to get to know its people. It was not long before the several parish priests weighed in and there was a spirited debate. Pauline allowed this to continue.

The sheriff reported on the market fees. Market day was Tuesday in Melton Mowbray, which was one of the oldest market towns in the kingdom. Perhaps sensing that she was open to permitting debate, several of the merchants began to raise gentle complaints about the fees, at first. Then they complained about the conditions of the market. They protested most sharply the fines they had to pay. Finally, Pauline closed the discussion.

Through all of this, these men referred to her as "my lady," not knowing the conditions of her birth. They knew she spoke French very well, could read Latin, that she was the steward of Leicestershire, and was of the earl's household. Many must have assumed that she was a relative, perhaps a distant de Montfort cousin from France. They also knew that the improvements and the requirement of a written record had been instituted under Simon's rule and her stewardship.

Father Paul, the head of St. Mary's parish, one of the priests who had sparred with the magistrate over the righteousness of his parishioners, gave his accounting of the tithes collected from all the parishes and the share that was set aside for the king and the county. Perhaps he was the man who had the most difficulty in managing the fact that he was reporting to a woman. Pauline knew that the Catholic Church had begun to discourage priests from marrying about a hundred years earlier, but many still had wives. Celibacy was more likely at the higher levels of the Church. She assumed though that Father Paul did not have a wife. And unlike those churchmen of higher rank whom Pauline had known, this priest was humble. He gave a complete explanation for the tithes and taxes of his parish and the other parishes in the district. This accounting had been consistent with what had been known for many years. Perhaps the one source of income that had been regular and well reported within the county during that time before Simon de Montfort took over was the tax paid by the church. Pauline enjoyed listening to this humble man and found his respectful demeanor to be close to those Christians of her own faith.

The sheriff and the receiver brought out their rolls and began to go over the list of the collection of rents on the various properties. Pauline also allowed this conversation to flow on its own and she watched the participants with interest. Since she had encouraged participation, various landowners and a few knights offered their opinions and complaints. It soon became rather tedious and somewhat confusing. She was struggling to maintain her interest and suspected that she would be better served by looking over the rolls and speaking again with the sheriff and the receiver later. Then, a noteworthy thing finally happened.

One of the knights stood up, the youngest of them all. He could not have been much more than the age Simon was when Pauline had first met him. Maybe he was as old as twenty, ten or twelve years younger than Pauline. He reminded her of Simon at that age in the way that he seemed gentle and poised. He was slender and above medium height for a man, which meant he was as tall as Pauline. His hair was a dark auburn. He had fair skin and blue eyes. By standing up, he brought the room gradually to a silence as he waited patiently to speak.

"It has been a considerable development in the administration of this county to now have a written roll, a record of accounts. So, it might surprise the lady steward to learn that I believe this practice has been so well received that I think there are two sets of rolls being kept here, one of them quite in secret."

Pauline was surprised. She looked at this young knight. She studied him. He had no official position beyond being a knight with a grant of land and the duty to supply himself and men for the king's army and to pay his rent. She did not observe the slight movement that had occurred in the room. She had only sensed it. But Rocco had seen it. He stood up, looked at the knight and then at Pauline. He walked to the side of the hall, pulled a chair next to the tall cabinet against the wall, climbed on top of the chair, and pulled a pack of papers from the top of the cabinet. Then, looking only at Pauline, he approached the sheriff and the receiver.

"The two of you looked to the top of the cabinet when this young knight made his remarkable statement," he said.

There was a loaded silence in the room. Men shifted in their chairs. Several of the merchants and farmers began to clear their throats. Some of the knights spoke quietly to one another. Then, the receiver started talking.

"Those are the second set of rolls," he said, "the accurate ones."

The sheriff stood up and denounced the man, claiming that he knew nothing about it but clearly expressing a knowledge of what was in the papers. Pauline merely nodded to Rocco. He and the bailiffs took the sheriff and the receiver and ushered them out of the room. The other participants began to speak almost all at once, expressing what had been their suspicions and adding details. Pauline waved them to be silent and she ordered them to leave and to return at the same time tomorrow. She decided she would look over both sets of rolls this night. The men filed out the door. The young auburn-haired knight was last. He turned to look at Pauline before he left.

"Not you," she said. "You are to go get Master Tzu and return with him here to me."

Pauline was certainly learning the ways of the outlying areas of Leicestershire. She was getting to know the people. She smiled to herself and was still doing so when Rocco and the young knight returned. She spoke to the young man.

"What, good sir, may I call you?"

"You may call me anything that pleases you, my lady."

Pauline laughed. She looked at Rocco. He smiled back.

"He is called Richard de Havering," Rocco said.

"Where is Havering?" she asked the young knight. "It is somewhere in the south, I believe?"

"It is fifteen miles east of London."

"Yes. I seem to recall that Havering has a royal connection," she said, "going back to Edward the Confessor, one of the last kings of the Saxons. I believe our current king, Henry III, has visited Havering Palace and there is some Christian relic there. Am I correct?"

"Yes, Havering Palace is a royal manor, and the relic is a ring of Saint John. It is at the chapel there."

"What is a sophisticated young man like you doing in the hinterlands of Leicestershire?"

"My family holds some lands in Havering and my ancestors were Normans who came to England in the army of William the Conqueror. My father purchased my fiefdom here and I have managed it for the last two years. I like it here. I am pleased to pledge my loyalty to the earl, and I have long been an admirer of his lady steward."

"You will find that I am offended by flattery, Sir Richard. But I am impressed by honesty and intelligence. How did you know that there had been some embezzlement here in Framland?"

"I apologize, my lady. I truly have admired you. I do not think of it as flattery," he said. "I try to be a student of people. I felt that the level of complaints I had been hearing in the district required that collections must have been quite severe. I am new here and my observations of the sheriff were that he liked the old way of doing things without any records. I must confess that my suspicion was only more fully filled out as I watched this meeting. I took a chance with my remark."

"You will be staying here with us tonight and you will help us with examining the rolls. I want your commentary on the men involved. You will also be traveling with us on the remainder of our travels to Gartree, Guthlaxton, and Goscote, and you will help us with our audits in those districts. You may go to your estate now and get what you need. And please stop by St. Mary's and bring Father Paul here tonight."

"Yes, my lady, I will do as you…"

"Do not tarry," she said.

He left the room.

"That was a little sharp," Rocco said. "You cut him short."

"I did not want to hear any more fawning."

"I think you like him. You did not want to let him say anything more that might make you like him less."

"You might be right."

"This seems to be your calling."

"What is that?"

"Teaching men."

"Richard de Havering did the earl and us a favor. He showed great insight, understanding, and bold initiative. I believe he will be useful and helpful and that is why I think we should keep him around. In fact, I have often thought that Goscote has grown too large. We may divide it into two districts, I may put our young friend in charge of one of them. I do not think that the young knight is yet a man though. I will also say that teaching men is not a task that has fallen alone on this one woman's shoulders."

"Yes, but you may be the one woman who is offended by flattery."

Pauline smiled and looked at Rocco very carefully. He was a man of few words and fewer expressions. She tried to assess what he was thinking. She was not sure what she thought she saw, but she had a feeling that he had decided to keep an eye on Richard de Havering. Pauline smiled at this and fondly considered Rocco's protectiveness.

TWENTY

It was 1242 and Pauline now found herself often visiting East Goscote, merely eight miles northeast of Leicester Castle. She had asked Simon to divide the district of Goscote into two new districts, or hundreds, East and West Goscote. The relatively large town of Loughborough had been the administrative center of the original, larger district of Goscote and it remained the hub of West Goscote. The portion of the former hundred that lay to the east of the River Wreake became the new district of East Goscote and was centered in the village of the same name. To its east was the district of Framland. It had been a simple move for Richard de Havering to become the sheriff of East Goscote and still easily manage his estate in Framland.

There had been some moments over the course of her long relationship with Simon that Pauline had felt distracted or lost or very tired for no discernible reason. These had occurred much more often in the recent years. In those spells, she would often not be able to attend her duties easily or effectively manage her affairs. It sometimes seemed her heart was like an open wound. Rocco would become solicitous in these moments and would make her aware that she was not alone and that he stood by her. She was buoyed by what she knew was his devotion. She was also happy for him because she knew how good it made him feel now that he had to look after his new wife and her children and to feel their love in return. In a way, Rocco and Pauline had each been perhaps too selfless, too devoted to another person. In her case, she had lived much of her life through Simon and spent herself toward what she saw was his greater purpose or destiny. Rocco was the same in his devotion to her and also to the earl. But Rocco and Emily had married. He had found another life for himself, and she saw how that had made him more whole. Part of her knew she needed to find something, or perhaps someone, that was not so closely related to Simon.

The understanding that she and Rocco had long shared was so strong that he played a role in the beginning of the matter that followed. When they had traveled with Richard de Havering around the county and had installed new people in the important positions and instituted many important reforms, young Richard had curtailed his verbal expressions of his admiration of the lady steward but he made that feeling known with his attentions and his eyes. The stoical Rocco kept a weather eye on this development. Pauline could see he was trying to gauge Richard's character and intent.

Rocco must have found him worthy because it was Rocco who first suggested that she might visit the new sheriff of East Goscote. It was again a matter of the way in which what was important between Rocco and Pauline was always unspoken. He never said so much to her, but in his suggestion, he seemed to be saying that sometimes the most restorative place to be is where the only thing required of a person is that she allow herself to be admired. Rocco knew that Pauline enjoyed Richard and his keen intelligence. She knew she admired his forthright nature and honesty. He was nice looking. The larger room in her heart was reserved for Simon, but she was drawn to the younger knight.

To Richard, she was nearly a figure out of myth or legend, the tall, beautiful, and exotic woman from Occitania who had been to the French and English courts, was the trusted lady steward of the greatest nobleman in England, and who was as wise and as good as she was striking. She was also in many ways something like his liege lord. He owed his new position to her and he was devoted to her. When she arrived at his manor, his servants treated her as if she were the earl or the countess, and they did this not so much out of deference to her position as the earl's steward but because they were happy to serve the warm and gentle young knight and they sensed his admiration for Pauline. It took some time for her to condition him against flattery, though Rocco had been correct in assuming that she was not entirely offended by it. She encouraged him to apply his native intellect and honesty to speaking with her as a friend and as an equal.

This brought several consequences. Richard settled into himself more and found the confidence that he had always had but which had been unearthed and nurtured by the attentions of this exceptional woman. He was always inclined to listen to her, and he soon became skilled in understanding the way she thought. He took to their conversations the way a child learns to walk. Soon his admiration grew into something more complex and profound. Pauline for her part began to measure the importance of how much she loved Simon de Montfort with the comfort of how well she was loved by Richard de Havering.

She knew that the time had come for her to convey something important to her young knight. She wanted to find some way to warn him, to let him know she had priorities more significant than he could ever be. She had to make clear her commitment to Simon and his destiny and she had to impress upon him that it was more a matter of fact than a choice she had made. Before she could involve herself with him, she had to let him know where he stood. And what may have been more important to her, she wanted him to support her in the destiny she shared with Simon. She decided to tell him what she had not told anyone and that was what Adam Marsh had told her about her role in Simon's life. It would show Richard where he stood but it would also reveal an intimate confidence that she wanted to share with him. She did not know if the warning would discourage him entirely, or if he would see that she was warning him so that he might be honestly informed before he take the next step. She knew she had to be honest with him and take that chance.

"Do you know who Adam Marsh is?" she asked.

"I think all of England knows him," Richard said.

"Did you know that he is secretly a Cathar, or that he at least accepts them as Christians?"

At this, Richard became silent and gently stared at Pauline.

"Then you must know that I am one too," she said.

"I have heard some rumors, though I am not certain what the nature of your faith is, other than that it is a heresy." Here he stopped himself. "Please do not think that matters to me."

"I might have expected that it would not matter to you. But that is not why I bring this up now. It merely explains one reason that Adam Marsh sought a special audience with me in 1237 and told me several confidences that he and the Bishop of Lincoln had discussed, and which I will now relate to you."

"I am honored," he said as he lowered his eyes.

"You will be the first and only person to whom I will tell this."

Now he looked up and into her eyes.

"Adam Marsh and the bishop have always taken a special interest in the earl," she said. "From the beginning, they have seen something in him that is destined to change England to serve the greater good of the people. They have made a study of him, which means that they have also examined my life very closely. Adam understands my faith and my history better than any man in England."

"Even better than the earl?"

"Perhaps the earl is too close to fully see me. I am also certain that no one sees Simon de Montfort as clearly as the bishop and Adam Marsh. Nor does anyone understand the two of us as they do. They have made a study of us and our intertwined destiny."

"Again, I am honored that you share this with me," he said quietly. "If Adam Marsh told you the bishop said this in 1237, then he told you on the year of the earl's marriage to the countess."

"In part, that may be why they told me. They are aware of the influence of Eleanor and that her role as the king's sister will present obstacles, and that she herself will also be a complicated matter for Simon, one that will require my help."

"That may be the strangest thing I have ever heard," he said. "And you want me to know all this?" he asked.

"Yes."

"And only me?"

"Yes."

"It seems then that you want me to know my place."

At this, Pauline looked down. When she looked up, she had tears in her eyes. She feared she had hurt him and might lose him. His eyes were welling too, but his feeling was not sadness.

"Then I have one thing I must say to you."

"What is that?" she asked nervously.

"It seems my own destiny is to consort with a heretic."

"That is rather a strong word."

"Heretic?" he asked.

"No, consort." She smiled.

"I do not know what else it is that we are discussing. I love you. I have loved the idea of you since well before I met you. And at every instance since I have known you, that love has grown and has taken root and has flowered. There is little else that matters to me, other than loving you. I have noted that you did not prevent this from happening. And you certainly must have been aware of it. You have been a regular visitor to East Goscote."

"Then, I am sorry," she said.

"I do not believe that you are, but I am honored again that you would say that, and that you would tell me I can never be first in your heart. I appreciate that you are now giving me a way out. And what you have just said did certainly put me in my place. I think you want me to know where I stand because you do not want me to love you with false hopes or with misunderstanding. But I believe that means that you do want me to love you."

"You speak rather frankly, Richard."

"I could say that I have learned that from you. But it is also in my nature. You have encouraged it. I understand how it is I must love you, and from what position. It has never been foreign for me. I have always believed in your superiority and I think that it is my own great blessing to be able to be any part of your life at all. It would be more than I could ever hope just to sit in this room and look at you and talk to you."

"I see you have reverted to flattery," she said. "And I do not want you to merely look."

At this, Richard broke into a shy smile, stood up, and crossed the room. He took her by the hand, and he felt it trembling as much as his own. He pulled her hand up to help her to rise. She stood.

Pauline had a confidence with Richard that she had never felt before. She had always stood in awe of Simon and she was never entirely certain where she stood with him. She always projected confidence with him largely because he encouraged and rewarded it. And it was always just part of the way they had always been. The attraction she felt for Simon had continually unnerved her, as had his considerable appeal. And her sense of his greatness was almost as much of a barrier to her as was his noble standing, or her faith, or his inability to see the passion she felt for him. She had met Simon at a young age, when she was still very much in the life of her faith. She had not fully outgrown that. Her love had been spiritual at first, and she never felt quite right about the feelings she had let develop beyond that. Simon had always been just out of reach. Richard was not. He was standing right in front of her. He had told her he loved her. She wanted him to love her. She had wanted him to know that he could only ever have a part of her. She was pleased that he understood, and he still loved her.

It was what she had wanted. She may not have known that in the beginning, but she knew now that it had been there since she first met him. She was afraid and eager at the same moment. She did not think about how she had been in the company of kings and queens, how she had killed two assassins sent to murder her, or how she had played a major role in the life of the most important nobleman in England. These things were simply within her and they were what enabled her to proceed beyond the fear that she was now facing, something that was completely new, a man who loved her and whom she wanted. She felt flush and was unable to move.

He stepped closer to her. Still holding onto her left hand with his right, he put his left arm around her waist and pulled her closer to him. She was surprised and glad at the same moment. In his early twenties, he was roughly ten years junior to her thirty-two. His worldly experiences had not been nearly the equal to her own, yet in this matter he seemed to have confidence and control.

"So, there is more to it than the fact that you are a heretic," he said as he smiled.

"Now you are jesting with me," she said, also smiling.

"Not entirely, Pauline," he said. "You will never belong to me. But then again, I never thought I would be standing here with my arm around you. I have tried to, but I cannot have imagined such a magnificent moment. Nor could I have ever hoped for it. And here we are."

"I am glad we are here, Richard."

He slowly turned to her and canted his head to the side and gently kissed her on the left side of her neck. She felt the perfect gentle touch of his lips. She let go of his hand and placed her own behind his head, cradling it gently. He was very gentle by nature and admiring in his affection. It had been the way he had always looked at her and talked to her. She was warm and she felt elevated. He was loving and honoring her with his touch. At every point, she was a little afraid. She was crossing some barrier. She was hesitant. But he gently took her to each next step and rewarded her for overcoming her concern in every instance.

She had always made another man the center of her efforts and attention. This was pent up in her and was now finally releasing. She was letting herself be the one who was being served. She felt far away from the overarching concerns and apprehensions that had long occupied her. She was flooded with the feeling of liberty, of freedom to be loved. It was what she had been seeking. The lack of it was what had wounded her heart. This was all very magical and beautiful, but she was not entirely swept away by it. She did not lose sight completely of what she was escaping. This consideration gave her some added boldness. This wave of delightful relief was what she had sought when she had told Richard the single most important fact of her life.

When Richard began to kiss her gently on the lips, she let him. And then she pressed herself against him more eagerly. They stood like this for some long minutes, just living in this moment. He was in the passion of being with the woman he loved and had never hoped might let him love her. And she was in the moment of discovering something new and vibrant about herself. In the arms of this English knight, she was as far from England as she could get, if for a few moments.

"I think you should take me to your room and make good on your promise," she said.

"I will do my best," he said. "But what promise is that?"

"All of them," she said, "every promise that was in every look, in every word, in these kisses, and especially in that comment about consorting with a heretic."

Pauline had never been a Catholic and she had wandered for some time outside the bounds of her Cathar Christian faith. She contemplated what she was doing with Richard de Havering and she decided that where love is, there can only be good. He made her feel better than good. He was as gentle and admiring with her in their intimacy as he had always been in his demeanor. She began to return his passion, but she always remained true to her warning to him. And they each gently kept it in their conversation, in their loving.

She made several visits over many months. On those occasions, they lived a quiet life of warm companionship. Those months would become years. She never lost sight of his worth as a man. And she remained discreet in order to protect his role as an important person in the county and her own position within it. They shared ideas as much as they shared affection. He was instrumental in all her work as steward and came to know Leicestershire as well as she did. They had a working relationship and a profound friendship. In their secret world, she was his queen and she never did anything to discredit that honor he paid her.

She was also buoyed by his acceptance and enthusiasm for her program of helping the poor and the Jewish people of Leicester. His own work in his district reflected her commitment to good works in the county. He understood this part of her and he found it in himself to reflect it in his own management. In the public realm, his attention was courtly and spiritual.

The warmth of the intimate companionship Richard and Pauline shared was made more poignant by their mutual realization that they remained in England, that the concerns of the kingdom were always just outside the door. They knew there was much yet to be determined in the destiny that the Bishop of Lincoln had sent Adam Marsh to discuss with Pauline. Richard knew well that at some point Pauline would be called away. He cherished their time together very delicately.

TWENTY-ONE

Henry III could not be circumspect in any matter that pertained to pleasing his wife, whose Savoyard relatives remained in England after the wedding. Nor was he prudent or cautious when it came to his mother, who also installed a permanent contingent of her Poitevin in-laws, of the Lusignan family. To these noble relatives of Queen Eleanor and King Henry, the Kingdom of England was an opportunity. England was no longer governed by the large council that had acted as Henry's regent. It was governed by Henry, who loved his Provençal queen. He had found the involvement of the English barons too nettlesome and he resented that he had been subject to them for so long into his adulthood. He disliked the Great Charter, which was designed to give the nobles a voice in his kingdom. He preferred the company of these French nobles who did not represent vested English interests, which were often competing, and which often had ambitions upon his power as monarch. And he had no aversion to their fawning. He liked these new French faces, for much the same reason that he had once liked Simon de Montfort, who had seemed to be a foreigner with no English interests. Henry could not discern that, unlike Simon, these French nobles had ambitions that had nothing to do with the interests of any of the English people, nor did he realize that by this point Simon was quite English.

These members of Henry's court were not competent in any other respect than that they had no interest but to agree with him and to curry personal favor with him. They never spoke to him of the interests of the people of their lands because they did not hail from English counties, nor did they care much for them. They never pointed to the provisions of the Great Charter that Henry's father had signed, and that Henry had reaffirmed at least once, and which had guaranteed certain rights to the English lords. They certainly were not qualified to speak on matters of English justice or the army of the kingdom or of the management of the king's lands. Their primary interests in matters of the treasury were only that they sought to tap into it for their own benefit. They expressed none of the concerns for the good government of the kingdom, nor even of the interests of the various fiefdoms within it. They treated their positions at the court of Henry III as personal estates. And they never failed to express their superficial loyalty to the king's person, above what may have been the king's duty to his kingdom and people.

The resultant resentment and antipathy they caused among the indigenous English barons is not difficult to imagine. This was particularly true, given that the English lords were responsible for the levies of funds and men for the army. And it was their interests and those of their subjects that were to be protected by the Great Charter and by the king. Simon de Montfort was the Earl of Leicester and had once spoken for their interests and those of the kingdom. As the lord high steward, he could again up the cause of all the other barons. Henry may have first favored Simon because he had come from France, but for the English lords, he had long since become one of them and largely because he stood in contrast to the Poitevin and Savoyard relatives of the king, whose disdain for them and for England was barely concealed.

This was the setting at the English court, which Simon and Pauline had predicted would fester noble resentment against the king's relatives and the king, and might raise the call for Simon's return.

✳ ✳ ✳

Simon and his family departed to join the Barons' Crusade in the fall of 1239. Eleanor, expecting their second child, stayed in the castle at Brindisi with their son. Had she not been expectant, she would not have followed Simon to the war. She was not as confident nor as seasoned as Simon's intense mother had been when she accompanied his father on his campaigns, nor was she as integrated into the public aspects of Simon's life as Pauline was. Simon went on to the town of Acre, on the coast of Palestine, which at that point was almost the full extent of the Kingdom of Jerusalem, which had once included all of Palestine. There, Simon and his men met with Richard of Cornwall. Simon suggested that Richard could capitalize on the division within the forces of the Moors. Richard then began negotiating a treaty with As-Salih Ismail, the Sultan of Damascus, who had broken with the Sultan of Egypt. As-Salih Ismail was eager to protect and preserve his own position against the Egyptians, so Richard was able to make a great deal of headway without resorting to armed conflict. He had preserved the territorial gains made by the earlier crusaders, including the restoration of the city of Jerusalem to Christian control for the first time since the end of the Third Crusade in 1192, and had also greatly added to the other Christian-controlled territory in the Holy Land. They then began negotiating with the Sultan of Egypt, As-Salih Ayyub, offering peace in exchange for more territory, and to establish greater Christian control over even more of the Holy Land. The leaders of the Christian Kingdom of Jerusalem were elated to have their city restored and to have their lands reach such a large extent, the size of which it had not known in over fifty years.

Simon also distinguished himself in a series of battles against the divided forces of the Moors. His men stood out among the armies of the other English lords for their bravery and their cohesiveness. They took their lead from their earl, who always fought at their forefront. By the time Simon arrived in Jerusalem with Richard, he was welcomed and greeted as a hero. The leaders of that kingdom were also impressed by his humility, his compassion, his calm reserve, and his courageous bearing.

His own great joy was not in this honor but in the fact that he would be meeting his brother, Amaury, who had been released from a dungeon in Cairo as part of a prisoner exchange with that city's sultan. That joy was to turn to grave concern as soon as he saw his brother. Amaury was weak and sick and seemed broken.

"I am pleased to see you free again, brother," Simon said.

"Were I so pleased, Simon, I would join you in your efforts here, but I am afraid I am unable," Amaury said.

"I can see that you have been treated roughly, Amaury."

"I spent eighteen months in the sultan's prison with six hundred other Christian prisoners taken after our dreadful defeat in Gaza. I received especially harsh treatment because I refused to divulge the identities of the other knights among the prisoners."

This heroism was one of the reasons that Simon had always admired his elder brother. It was a great heartbreak to see him in this condition.

"You must rest. And then you must go home. There you will recover."

Little else was said and Simon saw to it that his brother was given the greatest of care. Amaury was attended to night and day. Simon arranged for his transportation to Italy and from there to France. The noble men of the Kingdom of Jerusalem then petitioned

Simon to become the regent of their boy king, Conrad II, the son of the Holy Roman Emperor Frederick II, under whose rule the Kingdom of Jerusalem was established. Frederick would not need to answer their request because Simon declined the offer. He had served the crusade well and it had been a stunning success. Simon wanted to see his family. His wife had given birth to his second child. She had taken it upon herself to name the boy Simon. He was also concerned about his brother and intended to visit him in Paris. Simon had spent almost two years in the Holy Land. He departed the Kingdom of Jerusalem.

Upon reaching Brindisi, in the "heel" of the Italian peninsula, he was greeted by his wife, Eleanor.

"I want to see our son, Simon the Younger," he said.

He was surprised that this remark was not met with complete joy by his wife, over whose face a shadow had crept.

"Tell me, Eleanor, nothing is wrong with our child?"

"No," she said. "It is simply that the mention of family saddens me. I must tell you that your brother has passed away. He died in Otranto, not fifty miles from here, soon after he arrived."

"I am terribly grieved that I have been too late to save him," he said. "Let us go see both our sons and let us go back to England as quickly as we possibly can."

Much was happening in England at this time. King Henry had been swayed by the twin influences of his vanity and the urging of his mother, Isabella, to undertake another expedition against France. He had been opposed by the English lords in this. They remembered too well the ill-advised military misadventure of his attack on France in 1230. Henry III remembered it differently and considered the unsuccessful foray as something he had to remedy. The king's forces had reached the Gascon port of Royan in the spring of 1242. Simon received his royal summons to Royan when he reached Burgundy.

Simon sent his family on to England and made his way to Royan with his men. The king was overly demonstrative in his greeting of Simon. This reminded him that the king had indeed not forgotten the slights he had leveled at his sister and her husband. Henry was simply attempting to will it all away with the excessiveness of his own fabrications.

Simon's greeting from the English lords was entirely sincere. They were all relieved to see him. Roger Bigod, the Earl of Norfolk, was the scion of an old Norman family. William Longespée, son of the Countess of Salisbury, was essentially the king's cousin since he was the son of the illegitimate half-brother of King John. The young Richard de Clare, the Earl of Gloucester, was effectively a relative of the king, as he too had been under the guardianship of Hubert de Burgh when that noble had been the king's regent. They recognized Simon's great military prowess and looked up to him in that regard, particularly Richard de Clare, who was only nineteen years of age.

But by this time, it was already almost too late to prevent a catastrophe. Even before Simon had arrived, the king had ordered his forces to move from Royan toward Poitou to the east and north. Simon had no choice but to muster his men and to serve his king. Three days later, they reached the town of Saintes, twenty-five miles east-northeast. The king ordered that they stay there. Simon was anxious, and the nobles took their cue from him. His late brother was no longer the constable of France, no longer in command of the French army. But Amaury had commanded them for nearly a dozen years. Simon knew that they would fight as his brother would have, as his father would have, as he would. This army, trained by a de Montfort, was about to meet the remaining de Montfort in the tangled vineyards and forests just outside the town of Saintes. The French had boldly and effectively stolen a march on King Henry and were awaiting him in ambush. It was only an advance guard of the

French army, but they outnumbered the English and the Gascons, who might well have known what had been about to happen.

The fighting was fierce, and on the English side, it was desperate. The English forces, which had hitherto been disorganized and dispirited, rallied behind the fierce valor of their captain, the Earl of Leicester. Each one of the other English lords responded to his leadership. No man among them could stand back while they watched him, ever at the front, directing his knights and engaging in personal combat. Simon knew the French and how they fought. Just as in Occitania, under his father and brother, these French soldiers were fighting far from home and their hearts were not in the battle, which they expected to easily win by dint of their superior numbers. The English, Simon knew, were fighting for their lives. And he exhorted them to do so. He also ordered them back into the town, using his men to fight a rearguard action during their retreat.

That evening, the king called them to council.

"We finally fought them valiantly this day," he said. "They will not last through the day tomorrow. We shall crush them."

The English lords were silent, almost shocked, and Simon could feel their eyes turn toward him. It was a pivotal moment. Men were about to die, men who were relying on him. He looked around the room at them. The king's own life was in danger. Simon was deeply moved when he rose to speak. He looked to the stricken faces of the English captains first, and then to the king.

"With respect, Your Majesty, we are terribly outnumbered. We have no hope of reinforcement, and this is merely the front end of the French force. They will only grow in numbers, and very soon," he said.

"I hate Wednesdays," the king said. "I should have known that it would not be a good day to attack. Tomorrow will be better."

The king seemed distracted, even whimsical. The eyes of the nobles, which had been trained on Simon, became mournful and plaintive. Some of them looked down, acknowledging that the king's intentions would likely lead to their deaths. Simon felt their deep concern as if it were his own equally profound responsibility.

"There will be no good day to attack, Your Majesty. We will be fortunate indeed if on the morrow, we are able to withdraw from here and fight to cover our retreat to the boats."

There was silence for a while. The king did not speak. The English lords looked at one another and some showed a spark of hope. The Earl of Leicester had already saved them this day. Perhaps he would keep them from dying tomorrow.

"Am I surrounded by cowards?" the king asked. "Surely you are not siding with your French brethren, de Montfort."

"You stupid fool," Simon said, "we will soon be surrounded and no escape will be possible at that point. Do you want to be like the infamous King Charles the Simple, who was surrounded and captured in France in 923, and who died in a French dungeon? That is the fate that awaits you. I am simply telling you what your only chance of survival is, and our only chance."

There was no moment of prolonged silence, no burst of royal outrage, no kingly rebuke. The English nobles and Simon had been awaiting such a response to Simon's heated outburst, one they would remember and of which they would speak for years to come, if they were fortunate to escape the deadly trap in which they found themselves. It did not come. They looked anxiously among themselves with great unease. Then they turned their eyes to Simon and the king.

"I don't like this at all," the king said. "This was supposed to be a tremendous victory, really amazing. I have been sorely served by you, de Montfort. I don't like the looks on any of your faces. I also don't like the way you are dressed. You look like peasants. I am leaving this country now and returning to England. The rest of you can work it out."

And he departed, taking with him his retinue of trembling relatives, and his personal force. The king had simply left Simon and his lieutenants to decide what to do, and then to do it. The stunned gathering slowly turned to Simon and he gave them their orders. They received them with an overwhelming relief, which was only evident beneath their stunned astonishment. It took a while for them to actively participate in the planning. But they did, knowing that trusting the Earl of Leicester was their only chance.

The fighting the next day was equally fierce. Simon knew that the main French force would arrive from the north, so he sent the bulk of the English south, and he only held the French at bay in the town of Saintes until he was certain the king had embarked from Royan. Then he fled south with his own men, knowing that the French soldiers would be relieved to have taken the town of Saintes and would stop there to rest, eat, and regroup. He had ordered the other nobles southwest to the town of Blaye, and to put all their effort into fortifying that port town. His own men marched there only two or three days ahead of the French. Upon reaching the town and the fortifications raised by Longespée of Salisbury, Norfolk, and Gloucester, they began their plan for gathering the ships to sail away. Simon had again calculated correctly. The French army was overextended. They sensed the English were leaving. And they did not have the heart to risk death in attacking the defenses. The English sailed away.

BOOK THREE

TWENTY-TWO

Simon felt consistently at unease after he returned to England from the Continent. For some strange reason, he was not concerned about what might be the king's reaction to what he had done or said. In fact, Henry showed no anger and made no hint at retribution, nor had he made any overtures in that direction. Queen Eleanor's mother had arrived in England at the end of 1243 with her second youngest daughter, Sanchia, Eleanor's sister, who was the intended bride of Henry's younger brother, Richard of Cornwall. The king, at this time, extended several acts of generosity to his sister Eleanor and to her husband, the Earl of Leicester. Simon knew well enough not to take this to mean that the king had forgotten and forgiven all. He simply knew that the king continued to show that Simon was in his good graces. Simon's persistent and irritating sense of error stemmed only from his assessment of his own behavior. He had again been rash, and it troubled him. He knew as well that this self-questioning faculty of his had been developed as a consequence of his feelings for Pauline and for all that she had given him, all that she had refined in his way of thinking.

They spoke of it the first moment they were alone in each other's company.

"I feel that I am never quite home until I have seen you," he said.

"I am honored. I feel what you mean to me and that my purpose is as you say, to help you find and serve your destiny. I have been working to make Leicestershire more prosperous and less corrupt while also following matters in London. I have been busier than is usually the case when you are not around," she said. "I have heard that you made great gains in the Holy Land and largely without too much bloodshed, and that the Kingdom of Jerusalem offered you the regency. I am sorry to have heard you lost your brother. He was a great man."

He was moved to see her again, to be talking to her. And yet, he also felt there was some new distance between them. It was unsettling and he did not know why. But he chastised himself quietly for letting this bother him. This time, it was she who approached him, and she rested her hand on his shoulder.

"I have long felt quite poorly, Pauline. I have yet to learn to keep your counsel and to think things over several times before I act."

"Do you mean you should not have called the king a stupid fool, or that you should not have saved him?"

"That is an interesting point you raise. In each case, I simply followed my heart."

"Then I suppose that is not a bad thing and it is perhaps the very best thing. Your heart is good, Simon. And it is stout. I do not think that it is in your nature to question your feelings, nor do I think you should do so. I am beginning to get a sense now for what your position here is. Perhaps you may call it your destiny."

"I am not certain of your meaning."

"From the very first moment you and I met, you have had it in your heart to do the greatest good for those who need it. I do not know where that comes from, and I do not sense it in any of these other nobles. It is the reason you saved me that day in Avignon. And it is why you spoke up the way you did and why you fought the way you had. If you hadn't been so direct with the king, he would have continued in his folly of engaging the French in battle. The other nobles and all those men and the king would have died. You fought hard to prevent that from happening, and your frank speech was just a part of that effort."

"Perhaps the difficulty with that is I see how it contradicts all that I have been, all that I have been raised to be, and all that I see around me. No other noble would have spoken so rashly. The king is our liege lord, and he is England."

"We both know that you do not really see it that way. It is also how you now know to find God and what is right and good, in your own heart, rather than receive it from the Church. No other noble would have saved the day as you had. I think the barons all recognize that in you. They see you as their leader, their check against the vagaries and caprices of the king. To put it plainly, you have more of England's interest at heart than Henry does. The way to greater influence may once have been through the favor of the king. Now the noblemen of England need you and will support you. The king also needs you, and though that may be something he resents, it is still very real."

"I am beginning to understand what you say. He has even now made it clear to me that he is in need of my services to help negotiate a peace, to help finance the war debt, to serve as liaison with the clergy, and to negotiate with the other barons who bear some anger at having had to accept the expense of the war in men and in gold."

"So that is exactly what you are going to do, then?" she asked.

"You make me smile. I must do what is best for England. You know I plan to advocate on the other side, to take the concerns of the nobles to the king. I hope to win more concessions from him and to check his current intent to fund and to mount another invasion of France. But I feel this deeper obligation, Pauline, to do more. The shame and remorse for what my family had inflicted upon your land and people is a weight I still bear."

"I remember," she said, "and I was moved by your pledge to do some penitence for that. And do not forget you made an ignoble bargain that expelled a people from Leicester."

"Here I now renew that pledge to do only good," he said, with a bow. "Now I am in a greater position to do much more for those who need it most. For this conversation and for all that you are and have been to me, I am forever obliged."

Pauline was silent at that. Her instinct had been to make another jest, but she too had internalized much of Simon. She knew that this was not a statement that needed her comment. Still, she spoke.

"I will always stand ready to help you and understand that I am part of your destiny. I will attempt to focus on the good you promise to do, and on that same understanding, which was the reason I first approached you. While you have been away, I have worked in your name to help the poor and those people you dispossessed."

England had a long tradition of advisory councils to the king. The Anglo-Saxon kings had the witenagemot, or "meeting of wise men." The Norman kings since William the Conqueror had a *Curia Regis*, or a "king's council." In each case, this assembly of nobles and high clergy served at the call of the king and was simply an advisory body. The Great Charter, signed by King John in 1215, established more power in this body, granting that the king could not levy new taxes, beyond the customary feudal fees, without the consent of the council. It also limited royal incursion into Church affairs and prohibited the summary imprisonment of nobles without a trial by the council. In 1225, the noble regents of King Henry III established themselves as the primary part of the council that sat on a more permanent basis in that early part of young Henry's reign, before he began to assert personal control in 1232.

By 1244, there would be no doubt as to the leadership of this body being in the person of the Earl of Leicester, the lord high steward of the king. In Simon, the nobles each saw a just and fair representative whose interests were England's and their own. They also knew that the king respected and feared him, that the king was bound to him by marriage, and that the king recognized in Simon the value that he had to the crown.

Simon and the noble council, now called a parliament, demanded of the king that he curb the power of his foreign relatives and depose them from important positions. They necessitated that he swear to the provisions of the Great Charter once more. And they proposed that he must accept their appointments of a new justiciar and new chancellor, two of the five highest offices in the kingdom, another one of which, the steward, was held by Simon de Montfort. The king quickly put the parliament in recess and began to attempt to suborn some of the individuals on the commission. He failed at turning them around. At the meeting Simon was later to have with the Bishop of Lincoln and the other clergy on the commission, Henry surprised them by appearing at the assembly and making his case for reopening the ecclesiastical accounts for his greater use, essentially to increase their taxes. He was told that they would consider it and they adjourned without granting his request.

Simon then met alone with the Bishop of Lincoln, who advised him to negotiate with Henry and do it gently, pointing out that Henry came to be king as a child and in many ways was consistently in need of approval and guidance.

Simon spoke with Pauline.

"What does the hair shirt you wear tell you?" she asked.

"You touch upon the issue with a needle," he said, "though not too delicately. In all humility, I feel for Henry. He is lost in the question of how to deal with grown men, though he is now thirty-seven years of age. I wish to deal with him gently, as the bishop instructed."

"We came to England with nothing but your uncertain claim to a title. You needed the support and assistance of the king. You advanced with his backing. You see him as your liege. Yet when you saved him in Gascony, you let your true feelings show. He has not turned on you for that. It seems likely that even though you are exactly his age, he is now reacting to you the way you once related to Amaury. Though he is king and may resent you, he instinctively recognizes your strengths, your skill in battle, the respect you have rightly earned from the nobles and the clergy, and your honest goodness and virtue."

"Then how shall I keep some change from interfering and triggering his resentment?"

"I think you know how to be gentle. I have seen you with your sons. I know how you have always been with me."

Simon went to the king as his steward and as his brother-in-law. He told the king that he wanted to help him get what he wished. Henry was surprisingly modest and wanted to know how Simon could help him. Simon explained that what the king wanted was something very concrete and very real: funds to repair the kingdom's debts. What he had to give up to the nobles was nothing so material or real. He simply had to accede to the principles of the Great Charter, as he had done a number of times before. He had to put a few nobles of English blood into high positions and let them replace his foreign relatives, who would still need him and had no place else to go. Agreeing to the demands of the English Lords would garner their support of the king for what he wanted. It was as simple as that. And he would still be king, after all. Henry was practically relieved. He assented to the demands of the commission.

Simon was almost stunned. The demands of the commission had been imperious. The appointment of the chancellor and justiciar had ever been royal prerogatives. The parliament had only ever been an advisory council. These concessions would never have been made by a French king, nor did Simon imagine any other English king doing the same. He thought a great deal about this and about King Henry. He had long discussions with Pauline on this matter.

Henry had often lied or gone back on his word. Among other things, he had turned on Simon and Eleanor after having lavished them with affection. He had consistently violated his oaths to the nobles to honor the Great Charter. He had vacillated in his military decisions in France. He had tried to deceive the papal delegation in the matter of appointing the Archbishop of Canterbury.

Simon used to believe that this meant the king was foolish or duplicitous. But he came to believe something quite different. He decided that Henry did not keep much in his mind that was not already in front of him. He only ever addressed the situation at hand. He was not technically lying or going back on his word. He simply was not always aware of what he had previously done or said. This had been a classic instance of that. Henry only saw what he wanted, and he quickly grasped Simon's solution for getting that. He did not see the implications. The concern Simon then had was that it meant Henry was not bound by much of anything, except what he had most recently seen or heard.

The following few years were marked by Simon's favor with the king and among the nobles and clergy. He assisted the king in matters in Wales and in France, and in ecclesiastical issues. The new Pope, Innocent IV, none other than the former Cardinal Fieschi, who had come to London in 1231 to settle with Henry the matters of the peace treaty with France and the payments to Henry's mother, had been in the papal office only two years and was embroiled in a dispute with Frederick II, and had fled from Rome to Lyon.

Henry had also sent Simon to the court of Louis IX in Paris several times as his personal emissary. He returned from one such meeting in 1247 and the king was excited to learn Simon's story of how King Louis had agreed to take the cross and was about to lead

French forces on a crusade. The new Pope had decided to renew his authority by issuing a papal bull calling for a new crusade. Devout King Louis was eager to oblige.

Simon insisted that England not stand by while France sought this glory. Henry decided that Simon should command the English contingent and made plans for funds to be raised in England. Simon, the minor nobles of Leicester, and most of his knights took the oath to take the cross. The Pope expressly recalled the services Simon and his ancestors had provided to the Church and asked the English clergy to assist him with additional funds. Simon gave instructions to Pauline to take control of Kenilworth Castle and to continue management of Leicestershire.

Pauline agreed but told Simon that she was uneasy about the family leaving England and being away from the wandering attention of the king. She could not have known, though she had suspected such a thing, that the king had already changed the focus of his consideration. He had decided there was a more important matter. And as such, the only person he could imagine attending to that concern was his brother-in-law, Simon de Montfort.

TWENTY-THREE

It is often the case that in a failing enterprise, one cannot accept the inevitability of loss. It is simply not in human nature to easily yield to defeat, and there are certainly times when that should never happen, such as in defense of life and home and family. But the essential critical faculty is often suspended even in cases where the outcome is predetermined and when the loss is not dangerous. Gamblers call this throwing good money after bad. English kings would long be in the habit of doing this very thing in the case of their claims on the European continent. King John, the father of Henry III, came to power in 1199, when England held twice as much land on the Continent as was contained in France. English lands then included the duchies of Normandy, Brittany, Gascony, and Aquitaine, which itself contained seven counties, in addition to the separate counties of Anjou, Maine, and Touraine. At that time, the county of Toulouse, roughly equivalent to Occitania, was still independent of France.

These disparate lands, all separated from England by the Channel, were connected to France by roads, family connections, and a roughly common language. They were also coveted by a series of increasingly wealthy French kings. John almost lost England itself when his rebellious barons sided with the French. He did lose Normandy and Anjou. Henry's failed invasions of France cost him Poitou, Maine, and Brittany. Despite two failed military excursions on the Continent, Henry III remained obsessed with "reclaiming his inheritance", "restoring his rights", and "defending his legal claims" regarding his lands across the Channel. But as a practical matter, these lands were already lost.

His remaining large holding was in southern Aquitaine, in Gascony. The Gascons were inherently independent and had consistently threatened to throw off their English overlords. The Poitevin and Savoyard relatives of Henry had devised a plan even before the king had told Simon that he supported Simon's leading the English contingent on a crusade to the Holy Land. The plan was that Henry would order Simon to bring Gascony under stricter control. No other noble was so well equipped for the task. Simon had fought in nearby Toulouse and Languedoc and he knew the area. He had also saved the king and the English forces in Royan. His victories in the Holy Land were from a combination of military and diplomatic skill. He was a great military leader and was England's most important noble.

Simon had stopped on his way to the crusade, returned to Kenilworth and sent word to Pauline to come from Leicester. He wanted to talk to her. She had been expecting this message for some time. She went to Kenilworth without anxiety and without any nervousness. She would see Simon with more self-confidence and with a greater understanding. She also knew that he truly needed her. Simon had to make a decision and Pauline wanted to ensure he made the correct one.

"You can't do this," she said. "You have told me as much. You know the king has shown you his hand when he went back on his word, and again when he asked you to go to Gascony. He is extremely focused on his claims on the Continent and he will not let you operate there without seriously interfering with you. It will be a disaster."

"I cannot very well refuse the king," he said.

"That is interesting, coming from the man who survived telling him he is a stupid fool."

"I did that in the service of the king and of England. You are the one who pointed that out to me."

"You and I know the Gascons. Gascony overlaps with Occitania. I grew up among them. You fought them. We both know they all have larceny in their hearts. They are basically brigands. The corruption and highway robbery they engage in is in their blood. They are constantly offering to sell their allegiance alternately to England, Castile, France, Aragon, and Navarre. And the Gascons are natural fighters."

"Those problems are also their weaknesses. You have consistently shown me how to think more deeply about such matters. I believe I can turn those issues to my advantage."

"Then there is the problem of the Pope. You swore an oath to take the cross. And the Pope is in need of this crusade. He is still in Lyon and has yet to consolidate his authority. I do not think it is worth it to go back on your word to him just to placate a whim of Henry's."

"I think the Pope needs England and needs me too much to do anything about it. He will do as Henry desires."

"But it is more serious than just disappointing the Pope. The Gascon clergy is as likely to work against you as are their barons. They want to be free of England. You will be there as England's governor. There will be no limit to how they will stab you in the back. You may be assured that some high cleric in Gascony will excommunicate you the moment that you upset some of the lords who are patrons of the local church."

"I do not contest your points. I see each of them. I think that the English nobles will support me in what I must do, which is to negotiate a solid understanding with the king. He will need to join me in seeking protection from excommunication from the Pope. He will have to supply me with funds and with men. And most importantly, he will have to grant me full authority for a specific time, with a promise not to interfere."

"We both know the value of Henry's promises," she said. "I am finally getting comfortable here in England. I have a lot to keep me here, but I sense you will be in real danger in Gascony, so I will come with you. It may be good to be close to my old home. Gascony is just west of the Languedoc. I sincerely believe you may need my help."

"I would like that for one thing as well," he said. "I plan to do no harm and to do as much good as is possible. I know that is in your heart also because you have inspired that in me."

He overheard his own words and it was as if it had been something said to him by someone else. He looked at Pauline for several long moments. She felt quite balanced and settled as she simply just smiled at him.

"I have missed you," he said, "and I sense that you have changed."

"Perhaps change is constant, and you are the one who has changed by not changing."

"I will do what I can to catch up to you then."

Simon drove what he thought was a hard bargain with King Henry. He pointed out that the two previous attempts to quell unrest in Gascony had failed. The first was when the king himself had been unsuccessful four years earlier and the second was when his chosen commissioner, Richard de Grey, had not been up to the task. The Earl of Leicester correctly averred that the duchy was on the verge of being lost forever to the king and his heirs. Simon was to have absolute authority over Gascony for a fixed period of seven years, and that would be to include disposition of all income from the duchy. Henry III signed a royal patent granting Simon everything he had requested in May of 1248. He also joined Simon in sending a letter to the Pope, who agreed to its provisions that no Gascon churchman or other cleric could excommunicate Simon de Montfort.

With Pauline to advise him, he made straightaway for the court of King Louis IX of France. They arrived in Paris just before the king was to depart. Pauline was struck by how much different this meeting was from the one that had occurred twenty years earlier. Louis had attained a regal and religious authority that put the earl and her in awe. The French king had gained the confidence and authority that had come from France's growth and its ascendance to become the wealthiest kingdom in Europe. The king's mother was in that meeting because Blanche of Castile was again about to assume the role of regent, once Louis departed on the crusade.

It was a simple matter to get France to extend its truce with England. King Louis wanted peace before he was to leave his kingdom. And his mother wanted no part in a war while the king was away. It had been just five years previous that Louis had defeated Henry in battle and had gained Maine and Poitou. It was the truce that came from this battle that was about to expire. That war had been urged upon Henry by his mother and her second husband, Hugh de Lusignan, who lost their Poitevin castles and possessions, and which caused an influx of Lusignan half-brothers into the court of Henry III. Between Louis and Blanche and Simon, there was a great deal of mutual respect. Pauline noted that it was in stark contrast to any appearance Simon had ever made in the court of Henry III. She also noted that after the agreement, Blanche took Simon aside for a short conference.

"That is one formidable lady," Pauline said afterward. "She is always an inspiration to me. She basically managed her husband's invasion of England in 1215. She took over as Regent of France eight years later and then ended the French crusade against my people diplomatically, by taking the county of Toulouse from your family and giving it back to the original count, who then agreed to cease defending my people. She required that his only child, a daughter, marry her second son, the brother of King Louis. So, Toulouse will soon go quietly into the control of France. She managed several armies in several battles, including some against the English. And she has used marriage like a weapon, several times thwarting the Lusignans, the English, the Castilians, the Flemish, and even yourself in your attempt with Joan of Flanders. It is a shame there will be no histories written of her."

"She is more remarkable than you know," Simon said.

"How is that?"

"She told me that she will canvass the French nobles when Louis leaves for the Holy Land. She said she believes that there must be a provision for someone to replace her as regent in case she dies while Louis is on the crusade. She knows Louis will not hear any discussion of her possibly passing, so she has said nothing to him about it. But she believes that the French nobles of the king's council here will surely agree with her that I am the best possible candidate to succeed her as regent."

"She really is impressive. There is a certain genius in that idea, and it is typical of her. And it is refreshing to see that at least one royal house recognizes your great worth and does so without a hint of resentment."

From Paris, Simon and Pauline set out for Gascony to meet his forces there. They boarded a riverboat and moved down the Seine to Le Havre, where they boarded a seagoing craft and sailed along the coasts of Normandy, Brittany, and Aquitaine to Bordeaux. They spent much of the time on deck, going over their reports and making plans. Simon's family was not on this trip, and there were moments when Pauline was alone with him and took the time to discreetly look at him, forty-two years of age, still strong and perhaps even more attractive for the seasons he had passed. It had been about thirteen years since she had been deeply stirred by her first profound notice of his masculine presence, when he had returned from France and his two failed excursions to make a sound marital match. And it had been twelve years since Adam Marsh had told her of her role in Simon's destiny. Perhaps most importantly, it had been eight years since she had begun to more fully understand the ways of men and women. Richard de Havering had filled her with comfort and confidence. And that gave her more insight into Simon.

When she looked at him now, her mind would often wander, and she would contemplate how it might have been different with them, how she might have come to mean more to him. She could see that more clearly now and she could feel the echoes of that moment thirteen years before when she admitted to herself her personal feelings for him. Because of her newfound understanding and strength, the heat and pith and tension of these moments would cool and settle into the deeper realization of the fact and wisdom of Adam Marsh's words. She and Simon had been inseparable in spirit for two dozen years, had grown up together in a way, and had grown into one another in other ways. Her feelings for Simon would no longer jangle and gust. Passion was not a stranger in her heart. But she was also aware of how Simon touched that deeper part of her in a way no other man could. She could calm herself in that understanding and she let her heart settle into the long-worn serenity created by the power of their sacred bond. She would often reinforce her strength by remembering East Goscote.

The sea voyage took only about ten days. They had devised a plan to march Simon's army into each of the four main feudal centers of Gascony: Bordeaux, Bazas, Dax, and Saint-Sever, all on a hundred-mile arc and largely connected by old Roman roads. At each point, Simon demanded that the nobles of the area come to him and swear their fealty to the King of England and to him, as Henry's representative. He, in turn, guaranteed that he would govern them according to the laws and customs of Gascony. He and Pauline had assembled a report on each of the nobles and Simon dealt with them accordingly. At Dax, he seized some lesser nobles, whose brigandage had halted all local trade with seizures of the goods of merchants and travelers. He made them release their strongholds to him and required that they pay a heavy ransom, while also forbidding them to carry arms. He did the same thing at Bazas and at Bordeaux. By the time they reached Saint-Sever, many of the petty nobles had heard of this. Some of them appeared, and those who had taken part in the disruptions were dealt with similarly. Others did not appear, and Simon marched his army to their fortresses and forced them to capitulate.

One noble held out against all the pressure that Simon had applied. Gaston, the Viscount of Béarn, was Queen Eleanor's uncle. Though many merchants, burgesses, and other nobles had lodged complaints against him, and he had been guilty of some of the same thefts as the others Simon had punished, Gaston de Béarn knew that Simon would not risk open war with him. Keeping his pledge to Pauline to do no harm, and working with her advice, he did all he could to isolate Gaston. Simon negotiated rents and assumed control of castles surrounding Béarn. Soon Gaston was hemmed in and rendered ineffective.

Pauline advised Simon to make treaties with the King of Navarre, who had often made excursions into southern Gascony, and with Raymond, the ailing Count of Toulouse, who had been returned to that title which had once belonged to Simon's father.

"You have to eliminate the outside threats to your efforts in Gascony. Navarre has long had designs on this land," she said.

"And Raymond would like to get out of his agreement to cede Toulouse to France. I think I can convince him not to risk battle with me. And I will grant Navarre's requests in its disputes with Gascony."

In the space of only several months, Simon had eliminated threats from outside of Gascony, put a stop to the rebelliousness of the Gascon lords, rallied the king's supporters, and brought several outliers into allegiance to the king. He had done all this without spilling a drop of blood. Pauline had one more suggestion for him, to set up his own transport boat and connection to bring Bordeaux wine to Leicester. It would cut the county's costs and fund her other efforts.

He and Pauline returned to England. She went to Leicester and then paid a visit to East Goscote. Simon went to London for Christmas with the king and both their families. Pauline was happy and relieved to see Richard and live again in his love, where nothing was expected of her other than she be herself. She felt that remarkable blend of excitement and comfort that attends the emotions upon one's return home from a trip. Richard was thrilled to see her. He did all that he could not to let his love for her engulf him or overwhelm her. He also hid whatever pain he had felt from her trip to Gascony with the earl. And she was tenderly solicitous of him.

Later, she met Simon at Kenilworth. He told her of his reception at Westminster.

"It was an event both glorious and heart-warming," he said. "I was greeted kindly by the nobles of the council, who all hastened to congratulate me. The king was effusive in his praise and greeted Eleanor with just as much commendation for having such an outstanding husband. He showered us and the children with gifts and made many toasts to our health."

"And that did not strike fear into the marrow of your bone?" she asked.

"I understand what you are saying and felt that in small measure at the time. I am not a novice when it comes to the king's mania. I was just trying to stay in the spirit of the season and the event. But hearing you now, I realize again how insightful you are. I will even tell you what else indicates what you say. He showered more than as much praise on his half-brother Guy de Lusignan."

"So, the king equated you roughly to a ferret. That is what Guy de Lusignan is. He never did a single thing in Gascony. He oversaw a troupe of knights, but they were never put to the test. He spent most of his time drinking and bragging incessantly."

"His uncle was a great knight and was King of Jerusalem."

"That is another thing about you nobles. You are all interrelated. Blanche of Castile and Henry III are cousins, and both are grandchildren of Henry II and Eleanor of Aquitaine. The Queen of England, Eleanor of Provence, is the sister of the Queen of France, Margaret of Provence. Your wife is the sister of the King of England and is also the cousin of Blanche of Castile, who is something like your cousin-in-law. No wonder she likes you so much. The whole of the nobility of both kingdoms is like one small village. And all these wars are like bad family arguments that get thousands of other people killed."

"Don't forget," he said, "the King of England is half-brother to a ferret."

At this point, they both laughed, and Pauline felt a slight pang. She was happy to have had this time with Simon. And she was glad she would be able to see Richard again soon. Her happiness was not unalloyed though. She would miss Simon even more, and would do so when she was at East Goscote. She resolved that there was something else she must do for herself, something that was also related to what Adam Marsh had told her, something about Cathars in England.

"I do know," she said, "that you must part from me when you return to Gascony. I believe our work is done there. The Gascons are sure to cause some more trouble, but I hope the situation is well in hand. You should take your family now that so much is settled, and you still have six and a half years of your rule in Gascony. My trip to the Continent proved to me that I really am as you say. I am English at heart now. Things are a bit more solid here and more practical, and the people are more independent. To be even more to the point, they seem less Catholic than on the Continent. I will see that matters in Leicestershire and at Kenilworth are in order. I have begun to find a life for myself here. And soon, I will set out to do something I have been wanting to do for some time."

"And what might that be?"

"Perhaps I might tell you one day. It depends on how things work out."

TWENTY-FOUR

Pauline set out from Leicester with Rocco early one late-summer morning in 1249. They each rode a horse and towed two more, carrying baggage and supplies. They had planned a ninety-mile trip southeast to Hertfordshire. They would first travel southwest twenty-five miles to Coventry on the old Roman road known as the Fosse Way; then they would turn southeast on another old Roman road called Watling Street, the main road to London. They would travel sixty-five miles on that road to stop short of London in the small village of Piccotts End. That busy road would have many inns at which they could overnight. For the first leg of the journey, they planned to make it to Coventry by nightfall.

"You are rather quiet today," Pauline said, "as much so as you used to be when you were unfamiliar with the language. I could use more of your terse conversation."

"My interest is more in giving you the use of my watchfulness and protection. I do not like being on the road."

The Coventry in which they arrived that afternoon was one of the most bustling towns in England. One of the earls of Chester, an ancestor of Ranulf de Blondeville, who had ceded Leicester to Simon, had been granted charters by Henry II to allow Coventry to hold markets and not to be required to charge the merchants the royal fee. It had then become a major commercial center and promoted local goods such as wood, soap, metal, leather, and above all, wool. Guilds had begun to form, and perhaps the most important was that of the dyers, who could color wool and other fabrics a "Coventry blue", which was coveted in England and in the rest of Europe. Several thousand inhabitants made it the fourth largest town in England.

They had a good look around this town on the River Sherbourne before retiring to an inn and setting out the next day on Watling Street. Rocco was even quieter than before, his eyes scanning the roadside and every traveler they saw on the busy road. Pauline knew better than to interrupt him. In four days, they had reached the small hamlet of Piccotts End, which was too small to have an inn. They found one in nearby St. Albans. The next day, Pauline began her investigation of Piccotts End, with Rocco ever on the watch.

The village was much too small for them to remain for more than a few moments without drawing attention. It was part of a group of small villages west of St. Albans, the furthest one to the northwest edge of this group, bordering the Chilterns, a set of wooded hills on a chalk escarpment rising out of the plains. Long before the Saxons or the Romans, the early Celts had considered those hills to be spiritually meaningful. They would often excavate the grass and trees to make designs and symbols out of the chalk beneath. There was something remote and dark about the Chilterns, but they were also accessible and not too forbidding. Adam Marsh had once told Pauline about a location in Ashridge, so she knew it was somewhere in those hills. She and Rocco set up their watch in the trees just off the road into the Chilterns from Piccotts End. There were occasional travelers who stayed on the road, but in the late afternoon, some small groups of villagers passed them, and turned to go into the woods. Rocco quietly followed them at a distance from off the road, while Pauline stayed at her station. A few hours later, those same villagers passed her on return to the village, and several minutes after that, Rocco arrived.

He told her that the villagers had all turned left off the road, four miles in, heading southwest. He had not followed them far into the woods and had remained hidden. But he had marked the path where they had turned off the road. The next morning, they went there and took the path only about a mile into the woods before it seemed to end at a short, fairly steep drop where the exposed chalk had turned gray. They could see light scrapes where people had clambered down, and they followed these markings. At the bottom, the path resumed into the woods to a few small stone benches and some crude wood structures that blended into the forest. There were signs of fire and there were simple cabinets. All surrounded a small stone house-like structure that was open on all sides and was able to hold a couple of dozen people under its roof. Pauline and Rocco went deeper into the woods opposite from the way they had come, ate, and rested.

In the early evening, they heard the villagers arrive, about twenty of them. They lit a fire and stood around it silently. One of them, an older man, sat on one of the stone benches while each of the others came up to him and said something. He placed his hands on them and said something in return. They went before the fire and stood quietly. After each one of them had made their exchange with the man, he came to them at the fire and led them into the stone house where Pauline could tell that he was praying aloud. Then they left the structure, passed by the fire, and went back up the path at different times. They had arrived and left not as the group they clearly were during the ceremony. Rocco and Pauline walked in the twilight to the stone house, and she placed two loaves of bread in one of the chests inside the building. The next morning, they left for St. Albans, Coventry, and Leicester.

On the road, they both grew silent again. She thought of Simon. He had returned to Gascony, this time with his family. His royal charter was to stay there another six years, though King Henry could always change his mind. She wondered if she would ever see Simon again. She knew that her life with Richard would comfort her and she began to be less certain that the destiny she shared with Simon would bring him back to her.

She imagined he felt that more surely than she did at that moment. She understood him as a man more clearly now. She knew she would miss him. She decided this was her test and that finding these Cathars in England would be her chance to revisit her faith. She was interested in what might be her reaction and she felt that something might be drawing her back to the life of the spirit.

She had left that bread at the Ashridge house for a reason. Rocco had objected. But she had a plan and it involved making several return trips. It would take some time to be able to approach those people of that persecuted faith and to gain their confidence.

They stopped overnight a handful of times on the way from St. Albans to Coventry. Aside from that conversation she and Rocco had, and a few others, they remained quiet and spoke very little. They were quite happy. After a while, he began to speak, mostly of his life with Emily and the children.

"I suppose the fact that you are now speaking means we are no longer being followed," she said.

"Not since we left Coventry. Whoever it was that was tailing us turned back when we entered that town."

When they arrived, there was a letter there for Pauline from Adam Marsh. Several priests among Simon's military detachment in Gascony had been tasked to report to the Bishop of Lincoln. Adam Marsh had distilled these reports into one letter and had sent it to Leicester. Several of the Gascon houses had risen against Simon and sent armed men to kill him in his sleep. Simon awoke when he heard a great number of men attacking his guards. He grabbed his sword and rallied his knights and staunchly cut his way through the attacking men. The Gascons had anticipated the earl's personal valor and skill and had a hidden force that emerged and surrounded the English. Simon's men united around their leader and were prepared to fight to the death. The Gascon ambushers hesitated in the face of this formidable defense and the fight slowed long enough for some of Simon's other men to return with a contingent from the Mayor of Bordeaux. The attackers fled.

Simon noted the identity of the rebels and demanded hostages from each offending house and took ransom from them. He also selected a small number of houses that he required to disarm completely and permanently, to set an example to the rest and not to require them all to deactivate. Several of the petty nobles fled their houses with their retainers before he arrived, so Simon ordered them to come before him and be judged. They feared this, so he took possession of their properties in default of judgment. He also confiscated livestock and food and supplies that the rebels brought with them and which had been supplied by their local clergy, who were in league with them. These clerics then sent a delegation to Pope Innocent in Lyon to begin excommunication of the earl.

Adam Marsh's letter left no doubt that the Pope would not accede to the requests of the Gascon clergy to excommunicate Simon, but he also related that the insurgents had sent two delegates to King Henry in London to complain of alleged rough treatment by the earl. By the dictates of his own written patent agreement, the king should have sent those complainants directly back to Simon in Gascony, who had been given full charge of the duchy, but the king listened sympathetically to the delegates. He consulted his Poitevin and Savoyard relatives as advisors and signed an order that Simon return all the property he had taken from his attackers. Simon had not been unaware of this intended effort and had dispatched the Mayor of Bordeaux to London. His truthful testimony put a stop to the king's action, and the English barons urged that his story about the earl be the one the king should believe.

They also convinced the king to issue an official pronouncement to be sent back to his governor in Gascony, along with the delegates under guard, again giving Simon grant to do with them and with the duchy as he saw fit. The king did this and also mentioned several other matters in Gascony and again left the final disposition of them to the Earl of Leicester. The king stated at the end of the declaration that Simon should not be so indulgent with the rebels as to encourage further rebellion nor to punish them excessively, lest such judgment reflect poorly on the judge.

This was classic Henry III, Pauline realized as she set aside the letter. He restates his grant of full power to Simon, which he should not have had to restate in the first place. Then with the other hand, he retains the right to judge what the earl might do. He yielded to the English nobles who supported Simon, perhaps because he feared them or more likely because they were the last ones to speak to him. And he sent back the complainants while also opening the door to further grievances. From these events described in the letter, she also knew several other things. She knew this rebellion would have significant consequences. She knew the Gascons well enough to believe that they had lied about taking allegiance and swearing off brigandage. And she had no doubt at all that the uprising had been planned a long time before and that it likely involved the entire duchy. Simon's skillful exercise of authority had done no more than clarify to them how much they all really wished to throw off the English yoke. Simon had become their focal point. He had been an effective representative of his liege lord, King Henry, who did not fully support him. Simon faced a daunting task ahead of him in the form of a coalescing crowd of bandits and insurgents whom he had to defeat in order to protect the interests of the King of England. Yet this same king was poised to undermine him. And the worst part of this was that now the Gascons knew it. Simon was also going to face pressure from the Pope, who was waiting for the great soldier to satisfy his oath to take the cross. There was one other thing that struck Pauline now as even more dire.

She knew Simon missed having her with him.

TWENTY-FIVE

Simon felt that he had to struggle simply to keep up with the rapid development of events. He no sooner received the declaration from the king than he learned of an internecine struggle that had broken out between two houses around Bordeaux that had resulted in many deaths. Then the same thing happened in Bazas. He set forth to settle both matters and then learned of the death of Raymond, the Count of Toulouse, which meant that Alphonse, the brother of King Louis, would take over that county. France would now take the land directly to the east of Gascony, establishing the first border between the Kingdom of France and the Duchy of Gascony. Simon hastened to meet Alphonse and successfully extended the peace treaty with France for another five years. Then he had to sail for England in the summer of 1250 to make sure that King Henry supplied him with the money and men he had been promised. The king had withheld both. He then gave both to the earl, saying he recognized his bravery and effectiveness, and then, again opened the door to Gascon complaints about his leadership.

There were many times Simon tried to talk to Eleanor, his wife, about all the matters he was facing. But she simply had never been exposed to any understanding other than that she would need to do nothing more than be a wife and a mother. It was not in her background or comprehension to carefully listen to topics of war or statecraft. Even as a member of the royal family, she had not been admitted to these types of discussions. Simon also had the matter of not being able to discuss with her his perhaps most significant problem, which was the king, her brother. It got to the point where she did not try to listen to him when he did approach her. And he did not try to engage her. He wrote and received letters from Gascony to and from Adam Marsh and Pauline, but the delay in communication was significant. He had days to make decisions, and those responses would take weeks. He felt confident in his judgment. And he was committed to doing the most good with the least harm and he always intended to err on the side of caution and calmness. Most of his lieutenants were unable or unwilling to venture any opinions. And those who did so were usually Henry's subordinates and relatives, who spoke out of self-interest.

In early 1251, many of the disparate rebels, malcontents, and highwaymen had banded together in a league to oppose the earl. Simon, again confronted by a disastrous state of roiling and armed unrest, had dispatched with the many and complex problems in Gascony and had put the land at peace. He also skillfully suggested to the king that all was complete now and that the king himself should resume government of the Duchy of Gascony. The king again returned to his original promise to fund the efforts of his governor on his behalf but did not take over the direct rule of Gascony. The queen invited Simon to York for the marriage of their daughter, Princess Margaret, to Alexander III, the King of Scotland, at the end of the year.

No sooner had this happened than another delegation arrived from Gascony to accuse the Earl of Leicester of being a brutal tyrant. Another league had also been formed to oppose him. Simon prepared to return to Gascony, to suppress this insurrection, but

Henry held him back and said he wanted to hear the complaints. He then ordered his clerk to Gascony and invited those barons to send as many complaints as they might have and guaranteed their safety. Simon was disturbed by this turn of events and made his feelings known at court.

"What?" Simon asked. "Will you open your ear and heart to traitors? Do you not know that they speak against England, against you, when they impugn your representative? Will you really assist them in their rebellions? Will you believe them rather than the English lord who has served you and England?"

"If you are innocent, you should welcome the inquiry," the king said.

The king's council and the other English lords reminded the king of his original duty and that those Gascons making complaint were the selfsame ones who had made war against England. The assembly of nobles at court could often become quite raucous and not more so than they were in this instance. Henry again gave way, but this time he set up an arbitrator to determine what the war should cost, and that the earl should pay the remainder. Simon then set forth for Bordeaux, from where he intended to deal with the latest rebellion. As soon as he arrived, in March of 1252, he learned that the king had again asked for a Gascon delegation to come to him in London and detail their complaints against the earl. Simon returned to London as quickly as possible. This time, the king did not give way. He ordered a public trial to begin in May.

During these few years of Simon's travails in Gascony and with the king, Pauline had been in touch with him by letter. She had thought she might have been called to meet him in London or even to travel to Gascony. But he had been knocked back and forth like a pin in the commoner game of skittles, with no opportunity to know where or when he would be for very long. And when he had been in Gascony, he was fully occupied in responding to the uprisings and disputes that arose every day. He had advised her to stay busy in England until he knew he might be there for any length of time.

Pauline was occupied with the undertakings of Leicestershire and the castles at Leicester and Kenilworth. She had pressed Richard de Havering into service beside her. They worked well as a team and profited from each other's counsel. Her duties became opportunities and she enjoyed them. She and Richard knew to expect interruption, and they felt the time they spent together to be more precious for that reason.

The duration of Simon's trial had not been determined, but it was clear that the king intended to hear many complainants from Gascony. It was equally certain that he would attempt to set up a small council of his relatives to sit in judgment. The Bishop of Lincoln, the Earl of Gloucester, other key English nobles, and Simon himself would muster a larger group, a parliament of English barons, to intercede on behalf of the Earl of Leicester. Simon was to be in London for at least several weeks. Simon wrote to Pauline and asked her to make herself ready for that time when he would need her counsel.

Pauline was now compelled to find a new Leicestershire steward. Before she could give it a minute's thought, Richard volunteered to take over.

"You are far too good to me," she said.

"You act as if this were not in fact a promotion," he said.

"It might be that. But it is a considerable set of responsibilities. I have been aided these months by your assistance. You will be alone."

"But I will be helping you. I can think of nothing I would like to do more."

"I am afraid it will put you right into the thick of it. You will become more directly part of the de Montfort estate and the official second only to the earl. You will also be in contact with the countess."

"You seem to be saying that it will change the way you will look at me, and it will mean that I will no longer be separate from your world, or from the destiny that you and the earl share."

"I am afraid so."

"I believe you know me well enough to know that I only see you and can only attend to your needs and feel I must assuage your worries. I love you. I can accept what happens."

Pauline had hoped she would have more time with Richard, but she was immediately confronted by problems with Simon's estate at Kenilworth. Eleanor had just returned with her family to Kenilworth and had now taken over the management of the castle. Eleanor had become extravagant in her expenses and in the mistreatment of her retinue and the household staff. They lodged their concerns with Pauline. Eleanor had grown more resigned to Pauline's role in the county in the life of her husband, and even her family. But Pauline knew she would always have to treat the countess with politesse. So, Pauline obtained a letter from Adam Marsh that reminded the countess that her duty to God and to her husband counseled restraint and serenity. This way, Pauline would not be required to confront her. Pauline then brought Richard to Kenilworth and told Eleanor of her plans to put him in charge of the castles and the county. Eleanor acceded to these suggestions. She was immediately fond of the calm and sensitive young knight. She let him take over and she waited patiently for her husband's return.

Pauline was waiting to hear from Simon. But for the time being, she was now free to make several trips to Piccotts End with Rocco. It had become important to her. She continued to leave tokens at the Ashridge house site, and she began to be seen in the town. It was several visits before the old man who was the leader of the group realized that she had been their secret benefactor and he approached her. At that point, she and Rocco began to take part in some of the ceremonies, and Pauline delivered goods and funds to the group and put them under her protection. It was well after this, one day not long before Simon's trial, that she and Rocco were set upon by attackers on the road back to Coventry. They had not been surprised, since they had noticed that on some occasions they were being followed by a small, ragged band of soldiers led by a gaunt, fearsome older man. He was tall, with a long nose and a scar on his left cheek.

When Guy Alain had been released from the prison in Yorkshire, he had been reduced to an unbalanced and dissolute version of his previous person. He immediately went to the nearest cathedral and tried to relate his story and to make his claim of being a special envoy of the Vatican. His appearance and his disjointed speech and story were at odds with this. He was too deranged to approach his predicament sensibly. He did not quietly seek to return to France or travel to the Vatican. He clung only to his animosity and to his destructive impulses and recruited some few former clerics and dissolute soldiers he had convinced would be rewarded by the Church for helping him root out heretics. He told them he had discovered, by accident, what he had thought to be a community of heretics outside of St. Albans and had maintained a presence there. Some instinctive memory had informed him that he might one day discover Pauline there. She had become a focus of his obsession, and he had long since lost sight of being able to do damage to Simon de Montfort. Had he returned to Rome and taken his time, he might have been more effective, but the immediate possibility of catching his long-sought quarry occupied his distracted mind. He had only waited to be certain that he had found the woman he sought. He had witnessed Pauline's attention to the people of Piccotts End and that had convinced him.

Rocco had been watchful and had made his preparations. He had ordered two guards to always be within calling distance and to move ahead of them. When Guy Alain and his band attacked from behind, he drew his sword, smacked Pauline's horse on the flank and sent her forward. His call brought his men, who passed Pauline on the way, to the fight. Rocco knew that Alain had only one goal, to capture or to kill Pauline. He quickly told her that and she knew immediately that she would be in peril if she remained, and that her presence would make it more difficult for Rocco and his men to defend her. She understood Rocco's plan immediately. He could only defend her if she fled, and if he and his men would block the path behind her.

She was reluctant to leave and turned back only to hear Rocco tell her to ride on and to preserve herself for the earl, for the people of their faith, and for him. She last saw him with the two guards, fighting with Guy Alain and his ragged band of about six soldiers and clerics. She feared for Rocco's life but knew he was a great fighter. Still, the entire event was disheartening and she could not take her mind off this predicament, even as she rode with speed to put distance between herself and the fighting, all the time thinking of what she must do for her friend.

She rode on alone, making her few stops on the way back to Leicester. When she arrived, there was a letter from Eleanor, asking her to come to Kenilworth and stating it was an emergency. It was the only matter that could have called Pauline away from her desire to ride back with help for Rocco. She turned immediately and rode to speak with the Countess of Leicester.

"I have come as soon as I could, my lady," she said.

"I am glad," Eleanor said.

"I take it that you have news of the earl."

"And not good news it is, I am afraid. My brother has decided to hold a trial. He has decided to hear the very traitors he sent my husband to contain. I do not understand his motive. We have made significant sacrifices on his behalf. Simon has achieved great results in quelling the rebellions in Gascony. I and our children have had to suffer his absence and the fear of what might become of him."

"I cannot speak to the king's motives, my lady."

"I know that. I certainly cannot understand them. But my husband has long been able to depend upon your advice, and I know that I and my family have benefitted from your friendship. I would like to know your counsel."

"I think we must set aside any question of why this has happened. And we must set aside the past. Now is the time to address the situation as it is. The earl is not without friends and he is not without resources. And he has done the right thing and with the least damage. The truth is also one of his resources," Pauline said.

"I think that you must come with us to London. We need you. Simon needs you."

"I am honored, my lady. I will do as best I can."

"I know you will," Eleanor said.

Pauline was torn between her duty to Simon and her desire to find out what had happened to Rocco and perhaps to assist him. She remembered that Rocco had urged her on and that he had offered himself for this very purpose, so that she might assist Simon.

Simon greeted his family with gratitude and affection when they arrived. He spent a great deal of time with his eldest, Henry. And he spent many hours alone with his wife. She brought him a letter from the Bishop of Lincoln that pledged the bishop's support. The bishop counseled him to remain true to his faith and to trust in God. He also listed the nobles whom Simon could trust, as well as those who were more cautious but who resented the incursions of the king's relatives and who hoped for some check on them and on the king's caprices. In the presence of his family, Simon finally relaxed. And he began to plan what he must do. It was then that his wife told him that Pauline was nearby and that he should consult her. He called her to his rooms, and they dined in silence for some time. He was simply relieved that she was there. She watched him carefully. After they ate, he spoke.

"I have been in need of your friendship," he said.

"You are too kind. From all that I have heard and understood, you have conducted yourself with great wisdom and caution, and you have done the greatest good with the least harm. You have served your king and your God with exemplary humility and effectiveness."

"And yet I find myself about to go on trial for those very virtues and accomplishments."

"The wicked flee when none are chasing them," she said. "But the just should never embrace fear. Whatever happens, even if it be an injustice, you have marked yourself for salvation. If destruction will come to you, it will find you have sacrificed yourself for extending the well-being of others. You are surrounded by dangers, but you are nobler and better than those who imperil you. There is nothing to fear. Your only measure is your spirit, and it has been pure."

"I was correct. I have indeed been in need of your friendship. You have removed the shadow that has been over me with just a few words and with your presence. But at this point, you must have some counsel regarding what must be done."

"In a sense, I have just told you that. Be cautious and be reserved. Live in the justness of your actions and your cause. Know that each action you have taken in the past has brought you some peace and recognition but that each has been subject to the king's betrayals. It will be that way from now on. I think you must move the king to the side of your calculations. Continue to concentrate on the salvation of your spirit. You have stood and have sacrificed for the Kingdom of England. Let that always be your guide."

"I hear what you are saying as if they are my own thoughts. I know that the king, the Gascon traitors, and the king's toadying relatives will be on one side. They will seek my downfall. Some of the English nobles and many churchmen will support me because that is what justice demands. Many more will watch to see which way the trial is going but will secretly wish for my acquittal and for some power to remain with the barons. I will be calm, but your words

251

have shown me that I should not shrink from the truth or from what is right."

Pauline looked at this man she had first met when she was a child. She had always been in awe of his spirit from that early age. Time and experience had only made clear his superiority. In the more than two dozen years she had known him, he had grown in wisdom. He was still bold but no longer rash. His great gifts had even made him somewhat humble, and he lived by his promise of service to the people and to his faith. He was a good father. He had been favored by the Pope and the nobles of England, France, and Jerusalem for his strength and for his virtue. She had been his friend and she had played a role in his remarkable life. He had been her life, her whole life until recently. She was humbled by it all, and not least by the fact that his wife now seemed to recognize that without too much pain or jealousy.

"I feel that you are different," he said. "I know, I have noticed this and commented on it before, when you came with me to Gascony. You are stronger. And there is something else. You are strikingly beautiful. You glow. I am overwhelmed by it."

"This is an exceedingly difficult time for you, Simon. You are about to go on trial in the court of King Henry. Your heart may be seeking more than it would in another circumstance."

"Perhaps it is only these troubles that allow me to see clearly. I have always found you to be beautiful in mind and in spirit. I have long noted how remarkable you are. Your personal beauty is no longer hidden behind the veil of youth. I am no longer looking at you through the screen of my own concerns, or in the context of our shared enterprise. I mean, I don't just see you as my greatest friend and helper. I don't know how I can have been so blind. You are perfect, Pauline. You are more than any man could hope to have in his life."

"Still, your words are too bold," she said. "I am sure you will think better of them in some time. And we need these days to concentrate on the matter at hand. You are once again at the mercy of our vain and capricious king."

No more words were spoken. Pauline and Simon disengaged from their previous conversation and sat down. They knew it was an unsafe time and that they had work to do. During this discussion, Pauline told Simon that she had a candidate in mind to replace her as steward of Leicester. And she told him that Eleanor had already met Richard de Havering and that the countess approved of him. Simon signed the appointment and added his seal. He knew more than he said, which was nothing. They discussed the upcoming trial.

As she said this, a messenger knocked on the door and entered the room. He had a report to give. Rocco Tzu had been missing for some time. Pauline had hoped not to have Simon distracted by this and knew that Rocco would not want him to be either. She had hoped to be able to address it on her own.

Simon stood and said, "That is it. There can be no trial. I must take some men and look for our friend. I will send a message to the king."

"You can do no such thing," she said. "Your own life and that of your family hang in the balance now. Henry will try you in your absence and you will lose. You must go to London and stand your ground and let the English nobles see you do it. I have given you my counsel on these matters and this is my last piece of advice, so you may let me go for a while. Give me the order for your men and I will go to your new steward and we will ride to save Rocco."

There was a considerable argument after this. Simon's blood was up. But Pauline continued to remind him that it was not only his life at risk. And she warned him he might be letting his aversion to the trial sway him. It took him a while to begin to realize she was correct. And what may have convinced him most was what he had never told Pauline. He knew of the appointment of Richard de Havering and he liked and respected him. More importantly, he felt the danger faced by their friend Rocco would be well met by the good knight and new steward of Leicester. Of Pauline's feelings, he only knew that she trusted Richard. He made Pauline agree to send him regular reports on their efforts.

She immediately rode to Leicestershire and to Richard de Havering. He was at work at the castle in Leicester and had not expected to see her.

"I had assumed I might have seen the last of you," he said. "I have heard news of the impending trial. It seems the earl is in dire need of your spiritual guidance and will be for some time."

Her answer was to close the distance between them, to hug him tightly, and to whisper to him.

"I need you, Richard. Something has happened."

Richard wasted no time. He mustered five mounted guards and he rode with them and Pauline to the south, to Coventry and beyond. Along the way, he asked her about her faith, about the people at Piccotts End, about what Rocco had meant to her all this time. He did not question her about Simon or London. She was aware of this. At St. Albans, they stayed at an inn and took meals at a separate tavern. It was not long before they learned of the loose band of men that had been on the road between there and Coventry. It then struck Pauline. Guy Alain must have discovered the Cathar colony at Piccotts End.

He must have gone to Leicester and waited to see her and had followed Rocco and her on their trip. His instinct told him she went to see members of her faith, the very people he had spent so much of his life persecuting. He had not pursued her, and his men must have overpowered Rocco. She realized he had been kept there by his discovery of the colony of those who had long been his prey.

They rode there the next day and Pauline knocked on the door of the large hall house in town. She was greeted by the leader of the community whom she had met earlier.

"I believe you are in danger," she said.

"We are no longer in danger, thanks to your strange friend. He rode to us to warn us of a band of brigands who meant us harm. He had escaped them on the road with you. I believe you witnessed that. He believed they rode to follow you after he delayed them, but he was wrong. They followed him here. No sooner had he turned to leave here, but they set upon him again and captured him. He would have not been caught if he had not come to warn us. The rest of us have fled, to hide in other towns. Only I remained here."

"Do you know where these armed men might be?"

"We have not returned to our wooded sanctuary at Ashridge, but I believe that is where they are, waiting for us."

"Or waiting for me," she said, turning to Richard then back to the man she knew was a Perfect. "Bless me, Good Man. Pray to God for me."

"God be prayed that God will make you a good Christian and lead you to a good end," he answered.

There had been many times that Simon had said that he acted while having her voice in his head, that she was very much a part of him. She marveled now at how the reverse was also true. She wheeled her horse onto the road, turned to look at Richard and the men, and rode on. Richard marveled even more at this woman whose wisdom and compassion he had loved. He was seeing something in her that was new to him, something that was bold and strong. She was as much like a noble knight, he knew upon consideration, as Simon de Montfort was. He took his men and soon was alongside of her.

"They will be disordered," she said. "And Rocco is in danger."

She rode her horse off the road at the path and took it all the way to the rocky drop and dismounted. They walked rapidly with her through the woods and came upon the men who were sitting about the stone house and not standing guard. Richard and his men quickly attacked and wounded several of them before they rounded up all of them. Pauline ran into the house and found Rocco tied on the floor. He had not been fed nor did it look like he had been able to sleep for some time. He was worn and tired and had been beaten. Though he was glad to see her, he took her water and her affection with some trepidation. Guy Alain had not been among the men.

They gathered themselves and their prisoners and began to walk back toward the small chalk rise above which they had tied the horses. The men and the prisoners waited while Richard helped Rocco up the incline and Pauline went beside. Rocco was weak, but it did not keep him from flashing his alarm with his eyes as he turned toward Pauline.

"Witch!" Guy Alain shrieked as he flew down the slope at Pauline. He was wild and disheveled and now there was more than one scar on his face. Rocco's warning had allowed Pauline just enough time to parry the thrust of Alain's knife, which fell from his hand as the two of them tumbled to the bottom. They landed in front of the men, who now had to quell an uprising among the prisoners. The scene was a melee. Richard set Rocco on the hill and ran to Pauline. Guy Alain had his hands around her throat and was choking her when she elbowed him in the ribs. He still held her.

"Stay away," shouted the mad priest. "This heretic is mine." Then he began to scratch at her clothes and to bite her.

"No," Richard said, "this heretic is mine." And he thrust his sword into the madman's chest.

They took Rocco back to Piccotts End, to the hall house to wait for the Cathars. They left Rocco in their care because they had to take their prisoners to the Hertfordshire sheriff. Pauline could tell that he would recover. They then left two guards at the house and set out on the road with the rest. Richard spoke.

"I did not mean to say that. I am sorry."

"Do you mean that you did not mean I was yours?" she asked.

"Yes."

"I suppose you say that because you believe that I am the Earl of Leicester's heretic."

"No."

"Then, what is it?"

"I have listened to you and I have watched you. To some extent, I have known you. But I saw something else today."

"What might that be?"

"You are a singular part of this kingdom. You are England's heretic."

TWENTY-SIX

The trial began in May of 1252, in Westminster. The king had tried to place his relatives in judgment as an ad hoc small council. But the Bishop of Lincoln and the Bishop of Worcester and several of the most important officers of the court had successfully impressed upon the king that a trial of the lord high steward who was also the governor he had commissioned to quell the rebellions in Gascony could only be heard before a large council, a parliament of the earl's peers. These assemblies of nobles could be boisterous events and this one was set to be among the most unruly because emotions were already running high and there was a foreign element that was both flamboyant and inimical to the interests of England, and because it seemed that the king was siding with the enemies of the kingdom.

Only Westminster was a large enough hall for this trial. Adam Marsh was appointed to be the earl's intermediary before his accusers. His more important role was to keep up Simon's confidence and to encourage the dignified and moderate attitude that Pauline and he had counseled. Surely his astonishment and that of the English barons and Simon could not have been mitigated by the stunning and unruly way the proceedings began.

The king invited a parade of Gascon nobles, clergy, and commoners to present violent and extreme arguments against the earl, the king's own governor in Gascony, accusing him of theft, brutality, arbitrary confiscation, and sinful conduct. Against the principles of justice, the king had also met with them in private before the trial to hear their complaints and to encourage embellishment.

The Gascons were a colorful crowd amid the English court. They dwelt on the northern slopes of the western Pyrenees Mountains in that corner of Europe that had held onto its ancient Celtic roots against successive invasions. They were Basque and vividly livelier than the English, more dramatic in dress and in speech. At first, they all began to speak at once until Henry quieted them. Then Gaston de Béarn rose to speak. If such a raucous group could have a leader, it would be this man, chosen largely on the strength of his military bravery and resistance to England, and his kinship with its queen.

"As you know, Your Majesty, the Earl of Leicester has oppressed your loyal subjects in Gascony. He has confiscated our lands, forced us to vacate our castles, and desecrated our churches," he said. "Simon de Montfort has attempted to enrich himself at our expense, and to the disfavor of our king."

Before Simon could speak, Richard, the Earl of Cornwall, the king's own brother, spoke.

"This man," he said, "led the rebellion against England, Your Majesty. The Earl of Leicester was only doing your bidding and suppressing the rebellion. This rebellion began long before Simon de Montfort arrived in Gascony and was finally quelled only by his efforts. These men do not complain about anything more or less than being once again brought under the suzerainty of your throne."

"We have not rebelled, Your Majesty, we have always been loyal subjects," Gaston said. "The Earl of Leicester has acted only in his own interests."

"It was Your Majesty himself who ordered Simon de Montfort to 'take measures to repress this scourge.' This is what it says in your own edict," Richard said, reading the document in his hand.

"We know nothing of such a scourge," the king said.

Now it was Richard de Clare, Earl of Gloucester, who rose to speak. He had first met the king and Simon de Montfort on his initial military campaign when Simon had saved the king and the English forces at Royan, in 1241, when he had been only nineteen years of age. The memory of that time was in his mind and encouraged him to speak. He stood and walked among the Gascons with an energetic satisfaction.

"This very man, Gaston de Béarn, was among the Gascon brigands who in all cowardice attempted to kill the Earl of Leicester in his sleep," he said. "I saw him with my own eyes, as well as the men from his house."

Richard de Clare then began to look at the faces among the Gascons. "I saw this man in that craven attack," he said, pointing to one. "And this other one was there. I know. I gave him that scar you see on his face. These other two over here were among that group and were some of the first to run before our swords."

There was a palpable silence now in the great room that had been filled with murmurs and conversations and the movement of men. The boldness of Richard de Clare and the integrity of Richard of Cornwall had impressed the crowd and had silenced what had seemed ready to become an outcry against the Earl of Leicester. Simon and his supporters felt no need to speak further and the Gascons seethed to fight but were checked by a look from Gaston de Béarn, who then turned to look at the king.

"The clergy of Gascony have excommunicated the Earl of Leicester," Henry said. "This cannot be overlooked." The Gascons began to whisper encouragement among themselves.

The Bishop of Worcester rose now and spoke.

"We have all known Simon de Montfort to be steadfast in his devotion to the cross and to the king. The Pope refused to go forward with the actions begun by the Gascon clerics. Only the Pope may excommunicate a nobleman and His Holiness has pointedly not done that. The record of the rebellion will also show that the Earl of Leicester, in great piety, referred all disputes to the ecclesiastic tribunals of Gascony. No man could have been more pious in his duties to God and to his king."

The king was openly angered by all of this and he turned to Simon de Montfort and demanded to know what he had to say for himself. Simon remained dispassionate, according to the plan he and Pauline had formulated.

"I only ask Your Majesty that you live by the agreement by which you made me Governor of Gascony, that you honor your promise to support my efforts and to give me reign of the duchy," the earl said.

The assemblage was astonished by the king's reply.

"No," he said. "I will not keep my promises. They have been rendered meaningless by your betrayal."

"That is not true," Simon said calmly. "I feel your remorse at ever having made such an utterance that is not becoming of your royal dignity. I know you repent your words even as you speak them. I know you to be a good Christian."

The king was enraged, but he looked upon the assemblage of nobles and clergy, and he checked his anger.

"Never," the king said, "have I repented anything as much as the day I allowed you to enter England and possess land, title, and honors here."

Simon looked to Adam Marsh and remembered Pauline's advice. He held his tongue and maintained his dignified allegiance to his sovereign and kept his mature poise before his adversaries. Though he had asserted the king's own directive regarding his rights and duties in Gascony, Simon also then addressed the trial according to the arbitrary rules the king had laid out, and he defended himself against the charges.

He spoke of his accomplishments as governor, his moderation and mercy, the care he had taken to preserve the king's interests, and the safety he had delivered to the Gascons. For every accuser, he brought forth twice that number of Gascon burgesses, knights, and laymen, who all testified to the earl's sacrifice, wisdom, tolerance, fairness, courage, and passion for serving the king. They spoke of how he had restored order, censured the rebels, and had rewarded the king's loyal subjects, all at some expense and danger to himself. Simon proposed that further disputes be settled by a tribunal set up by the king, a fair proposal that the other side rejected. They only wanted the earl's removal. And Simon promised leniency in dealing with his opponents.

Richard, the Earl of Cornwall, the king's brother, rose to speak again.

"Your Majesty, we all recognize the motivation of these Gascon subjects as being eager to escape their duties to you as their liege lord. They seek to do this by undermining the governor you had appointed and empowered to subdue their rebellion. They have dealt falsely, and their just reward will be to return the Earl of Leicester to unrestrained rule of the Duchy of Gascony. I ask my fellow English barons and clergy to stand up and say if we are not all unanimous in this assertion."

The king could see that his brother was correct about the feelings of the court. They were certainly unanimous. Each one of the English nobles and high clergy stood and uttered their support. There was a chorus of approbation.

"We must then agree with you, brother," the king said. "The Earl of Leicester is cleared."

And with that the Bishop of Worcester brought forth a royal proclamation to the effect of what the king's brother had said. Henry signed it and it was read aloud to the assembly.

The next morning, the king awoke to speak a different view. Without consulting his parliament of lords, he made threats and issued recriminations. He summoned Simon and railed at him in front of Gaston de Béarn and a few other Gascons. The earl suggested that he be allowed to return to Gascony and rule it according to the king's proclamation, and if that failed, to mount a military effort to bring the duchy into submission. Henry rejected that. Simon then proposed that he resign his commission to govern Gascony, on the condition that there be no reprisals against his supporters and himself. The king refused that and imperiously dictated that there be a truce for six months, that the prisoners, lands, and fortresses be returned to the complainants, and that the king would later place his son, fourteen-year-old Edward, as the Governor of Gascony. Simon was not the only one who knew that in one stroke the king had set in motion actions that would eventually create disorder in the duchy, erode the king's rule, and weaken the Kingdom of England.

The king yelled at Simon, "You love war and rejoice in it, as did your father. Return to Gascony and do as I say."

Simon simply agreed to go. The Gascons were meant to be pleased by the reference to Simon's father and apparently to his reputation as the man who ruthlessly had crushed their neighbors in the Languedoc. But they were more disconcerted by the fact that they had not dislodged Simon from the governorship and that he would be returning to Gascony. They sensed that Henry had a short attention span, and that Simon knew that and that he had handled the king well and had retained his commission to rule them.

Simon returned to Gascony and immediately consolidated his forces and awaited what he knew would soon march in his direction. The returning Gascon rebels spread the story that soon the king would send his son to govern them and that Simon no longer had the full support of the king. They raised the largest army that had been put in the field in the years of the earl's rule. They quickly seized an outpost of Simon's English forces and made the men prisoners.

Simon's lieutenants counseled that he bide his time and gather his forces, while waiting for the inevitable jealousies and infighting to break up the Gascon ranks.

"I will not allow one Englishman to suffer at the hands of these bandits. I know the craven hearts of these renegades," he said, taking up his sword. "Who is with me?"

They were all with him and despite being well outnumbered they were emboldened by the courage, skill, and reputation of their leader. Simon raged at the Gascons, cut right into their mass, hurling insults at them and exhorting his men. They were as a slender knife cutting into a pie and they were similarly unimpeded. But it seemed that soon they would be surrounded. There were a few moments of confusion. Simon was unhorsed. For several long minutes, he was alone, surrounded by men who hungered for the honor of killing the earl. His bravery as a leader had ever been known, but in this instance, his personal valor was never more evident and many of his knights would tell of it later. His men fought to his side and then they fought onward.

When they reached the English prisoners, Simon had several pages unpack swords and spears for them. The prisoners rose with one unified roar, seized their weapons, and set upon their captors. The English were still outnumbered but the imbalance was now not so great. The surge of energy provided by the release of the prisoners and by the valor of those men themselves frightened the Gascons and turned the tide of battle. Returned to his horse, Simon wheeled his men to pursue the now fleeing enemy. After half a day of battle, he had defeated the confused and dispirited adversary, utterly subduing them, taking many prisoners, and leaving many dead.

After that, there were several random castles and outposts to pacify. Simon did this with moderation and negotiation, and soon there was little chance of a large insurrection in Gascony. When messengers arrived from the king, they bore orders that Simon give up his command and lay down his arms; the earl ignored them and told the messengers he could not do so with the duchy so recently in open and armed revolt. He told them that he would not sacrifice the interests of England to the caprice of the king and reminded them of the original charter that gave him the freedom to govern the duchy as he saw fit. In England, the clergy and the lords of the large council continued to support him. They assumed what Simon had expected, that Henry wanted to declare Simon a traitor and hand over the earl's lands in England, as well as the Gascon lands he had seized from the rebels, to some of his Poitevin or Savoyard relatives.

After all his awkward efforts had failed to remove the earl, and after the support that the English nobles had given Simon could not be cracked, Henry decided to buy out the remainder of Simon's commission. He offered the earl a large sum and promised to pay his debts. Simon agreed to turn over all his confiscated Gascon lands and castles to young Prince Edward. He told the king he would hold his prisoners for ransom. The king balked at this last provision but conceded when the Pope intervened again on Simon's behalf and urged the king accept all the earl proposed. Simon proclaimed that he would obey his liege lord, as he always had, and resigned the charter of the government of Gascony. He left for France and sent for his family to join him in Paris.

No sooner had he departed than the King of Castile claimed rule over the duchy and many of the Gascon lords who had promulgated the rebellion traveled to that land and transferred their allegiance from England to Castile. Once they had done that, small wars among the Gascon nobles resumed. Simon stopped in Rome to learn of how the Pope had received the Gascon clergy, who had thundered for Simon's excommunication. Pope Innocent had, in turn, accused them of encouraging revolt against the earl among Gascon nobles who had sworn holy oaths to support him. With the Duchy of Gascony once again in open revolt, this time supported by a foreign power, the king appealed to his brother, the Earl of Cornwall, to take up arms against the rebels. Richard reminded his brother, the king, that he had given the duchy to his own son, Edward.

In Paris, Simon was greeted warmly by the French nobles. King Louis IX was still in Palestine. He had suffered defeat and had been captured in a major battle. His mother, the regent, had earlier organized to pay his ransom and Louis had decided to stay in the few remaining Christian lands in the Middle East and strengthen their defenses. The absence and the capture of the king had exacted a toll on his mother and the indomitable Blanche of Castile had expired before Simon arrived. The court of the French king preferred that the regency be in the hands of one person. They agreed again that Simon should be that man.

Simon and Eleanor now had six living children. Henry, the eldest, was fifteen years of age. His five younger siblings were young Simon, thirteen, Amaury, eleven, Guy, nine, Richard, two, and the baby, Eleanor. They had lost a daughter, Joanna, during that time when the family had been with Simon in Gascony in 1250. Simon rejoiced to be with his family and to be released from the yoke of governing Gascony and being subject to the whims of King Henry. He put off any decision about the regency in France and simply enjoyed his time with his wife and children. But Eleanor was uneasy. She knew her brother, the king. She had personally felt the loss and the sacrifice that her family had undergone in his service. She had an opinion on the pending decision. And she had a plan.

"We have had a very difficult five years," she told Simon.

"I am sorry for all of that," he said.

"The French recognize you. They see your virtue and your strength. You were born here. Your family has served the French king in the past. We could live calmly here. I could live calmly here." She accented the personal pronoun.

"I assume that you want me to accept the regency and leave England behind."

"I only know that I am in no hurry to return. I am so tired of the intrigues."

"I understand," he said.

"I have ordered our household be brought here," she said. "That friend of yours is here with her friend, your Venetian guard. I have brought them because I think you should speak to her. I will have them come to us."

Pauline quietly entered with Rocco. It was the first time either of them had seen Simon since the night they had last been all together. Rocco watched them both very carefully. He saw that Simon was calm, but that Pauline was anxious. He was as unsettled as Pauline about Eleanor's motivation for bringing the two of them to speak to Simon in front of her. Eleanor spoke first.

"Pauline, thank you for coming," she said. "Your counsel has always been to the benefit of our family and of my husband. Please share your opinion of the offer to be the regent of France. Tell him he must stay here."

"I cannot rightly offer my opinion on that, my lady. Our lord is the most favored man of all the nobles of two separate kingdoms," Pauline said. "I cannot say which he should choose to serve."

"Surely the kindness I and my husband have shown you should lead you to feel free to offer your opinion."

"I am certain, Countess Eleanor," Simon said, "that our friend knows what your decision would be on the matter. And she also likely surmises that I have already made my decision. So, she is simply being tactful. She does not want to favor one of us over the other."

"Oh, Simon, my husband, do not take us back to England," Eleanor said. "I won't like it."

"I cannot serve two masters. I have pledged my fealty to England, to your brother, the king. I have received a title, lands, a castle, and have served him for over twenty years. I have taken you, his sister, as wife. He is godfather to our eldest. Most importantly, I cannot now go back on my oath."

"My brother has gone back on his oaths many times. You would subject us to that."

"No, dear wife, I would have us live by my word. And what would happen here when Louis returns from the crusade? We have nothing here. The de Montfort estate in France is in the hands of my brother's grandson. We will do well in England."

"I am not so sure, my husband."

She was exasperated, tired, and resigned. She also felt that Simon and Pauline understood one another in ways she could not.

"But I guess I must support you, as a good wife. And now, please excuse me," she said, and she left the room. Rocco's eyes had never left her the whole time they were all together.

"I am sorry," Simon said to Pauline and Rocco. "These last five years have been more difficult for her than for me."

"I know that," said Pauline. "We have all had to suffer not knowing whether you were alive or dead and whether you would be branded a traitor unfairly. Given all of that, she has been quite steady."

Simon looked at Pauline more closely and he paused. He knew how well she loved him, and he felt that most clearly now. If Eleanor had been steady, Pauline had been a rock.

"I have just received a message from King Henry. He has been in Gascony, trying to clean up his own muddle, and failing. It seems he needs my help, and he has asked for it."

"Who is surprised by that?" she asked.

"No one in this room," he said. "I will take my small force and go to help him but will do so on my way to England. I am no longer governor of the duchy. I cannot be forced to stay there. I will ask you to escort my family and meet me at Kenilworth. And what of you,

Rocco? I hear you have protected our friend here once again. You will always be saving her, will you not?"

"It was something like that," Rocco said.

Simon looked blankly. Pauline grew still. Rocco continued.

"We had a small contest with Guy Alain."

"I have not thought of him in years," Simon said. "It takes me back to when we all first met, outside Avignon, all those many years ago. How far we have come. You have long since lost your Byzantine garb and your newness with our language, but you still are there when most needed. Tell me about the Hound of God."

"He had descended toward madness, from his many years in a dungeon. He had been scorned most by those most important members of the Church most likely to help him. He had mustered a small band of men and had been following us. He recognized and remembered Pauline, barely, but enough to know only that he hated her and wanted her dead."

"And she is not dead," said Simon, "so I suppose he is, and likely at your hand."

"No. I wanted to take him alive, the poor wretched creature. I believed we owed him some human mercy. I also knew that his band of ragged soldiers were untrained, and I easily held them off with some sword work. Later, we confronted Alain and his men. One of our men, a young knight, was simply too appalled by Guy Alain's raving. He did not know what to do, so he ran him through with his sword. The poor young man was terrified of that mad priest."

"Thank you, old friend," he said. "And, Pauline, I do not have to ask you how you knew my decision on the regency in France had been made. You have always known my thinking."

"Not always, Simon."

Simon left them alone in the room. Rocco reached out and put his hand on Pauline's arm and held it there.

TWENTY-SEVEN

Pauline arrived in England with the seed of an idea growing in her mind. She thought that she might gently remove herself from the matters at Kenilworth Castle, Leicestershire, and England, to quietly take a place among the members of her faith in Piccotts End. She felt that she had helped Simon through his trial and having been so much a part of discussions within his marriage made her uneasy. From the beginning, the presence of Eleanor had disquieted her. Then she had been fearful of Eleanor's profound antipathy. Now, she was made even more anxious by Eleanor's ostensible friendship and trust. There was something threatening about it, as if Eleanor were a cat gathering itself to pounce. There was a great bond of love between Simon and Pauline, and Eleanor's seeming acceptance of that also signaled her awareness of it. Eleanor was Simon's wife and the King of England's sister. Pauline felt in some peril and knew that getting away was her best option. Rocco could only protect her against so much, but not all. She also knew that Richard was no longer her separate friend. He was the steward of Leicestershire, the household steward of Kenilworth and Leicester. Countess Eleanor knew him. He worked for Simon. Rocco knew him. More importantly, she felt it unfair to keep him from a life, and a family, of his own.

For most of her time in England, Pauline had managed to live in the world while staying largely true to the basic tenets of her faith. Now, it was not so much a question of being in the world. There seemed to be more of the world in her. She had a life in Leicester, and she had a man who appreciated and admired her. She had not practiced her faith since she was fifteen. Now, seeing Simon again, being needed by him, having that need recognized by his wife, and now having Richard serve as the steward of Leicester was all rather worrying. At this point, her faith seemed to reoccur to her on a regular basis. Perhaps it might be that it was appearing to her to be a refuge from the demands of her life. The community of Good Men and Women seemed to be a convenient place for her to go. She had mulled over this idea for the past year and had finally settled on it as a plan of action.

Our lives are odd combinations of fate and choice, with one or the other seeming to come to the fore at different points. There is also a playful dialog between the two, where one bears an effect on the other. Careful plans can decide our destiny and fate can overthrow the most careful plan. Pauline now had the clear plan of placing herself into the humble congregation that met at the Ashridge house. Pauline left Simon and his family at Kenilworth in early 1255 and went to Leicester to close out some matters, settle some questions, and to prepare secretly for her planned personal exile. She would also meet with Richard de Havering, new steward of Leicestershire. He seemed to want to speak to her first, before she could tell him of her thorough plans. And he did not wait to give her an affectionate greeting before he gave her his report.

"I don't know what we should do, Pauline. There has been a robbery. No, there have been a series of robberies in the county," he said. "A band of thieves has settled in Leicestershire."

"And what have you done about it?" she asked.

"I have done nothing."

"That does not sound like you, Richard. You are a man of action and know well what to do. You should know to seize the thieves and take them to the king's justiciar, to hold until the scheduled term of the Courts of Justice."

"You may have guessed that I cannot do that," he said.

"Why not?" She now realized there must have been some good reason for Richard's inaction.

"The leader of the band is William de Valence ..."

"The king's Lusignan half-brother."

Throughout the period of his entire reign, Henry had rewarded his Poitevin relatives, and later his Savoyard in-laws, with lands, titles, and funds that had been originally in the hands of his English subjects. The twenty-six-year-old William de Valence, originally Guillaume Lusignan of Poitou, had been given an important post in King Henry's household and had been made the new Earl of Pembroke. Of the five great officers of the English court—the chancellor, the chamberlain, the steward, the treasurer of the exchequer, and the constable—three were held by the king's foreign relatives. The subordinate posts of these officers were staffed largely by other relatives. The lesser office of the justiciar was not only held by a Poitevin relative, but he had also been instructed that no court decision should ever go against the king's other relatives. The keeper of the privy seal was an in-law of the king. Various Savoyards and Poitevins had been appointed to important positions in the Church, including the Bishop of Hereford and the Bishop of Winchester.

"You have wisely restrained yourself," she said.

"I wish now that I had simply met the brigands on the road, precipitated a fight, and killed them."

"That would also not have been like you. You are fair."

"I sense what this means," he said. "I think that you will be drawn more into the role of assisting the earl. In a way, that will have been facilitated by the fact that you have given the duties of the steward to me."

"I do not know if I have ever expressed to you what an exceptional man you are. I am not sure I am able to do so. I want you to know ..."

"You may stop there, Pauline. You have more than expressed it merely with your attention and with your presence in my life. I have never expected anything more from you and you have honored me by being truly clear about that from the beginning. Please just know this. I will honor you here by doing my best at this post that you have convinced the earl to give me. How can I complain about all the ways in which you have elevated me?"

She realized in a sense that he was speaking her own words and feelings to him. Her love for Simon had always been its own reward. It had also rewarded her in more tangible ways, in the life she had gained. She also knew that he was restraining himself from expressing his love for her, so that it would be easier for her to make a break. This thoughtful gentleness on his part had always been something she valued and admired. It was a more profound expression of his love than any other.

"You have always been wise beyond your years," she said. "I have never been able to love you as much as you are so obviously deserving. You move me beyond my own ability to express. You make me want to be with you more than you know. I must take my destined path, we both know. I would love to take the time to show you how much I adore you."

"I do not need you to tell me that, especially not now. We do not need to have this conversation. We have a task before us."

"I know," she said. "And we will not be able speak much from now on. But I want you to think of your own destiny. You are too good a man not to find yourself a woman who will always be yours, a wife. And you are too good a man not to have a family of your own."

Pauline immediately rode out with Rocco, Richard, and the Leicester watchmen. They found the stolen property and seized it. They also arrested the thieves that they found and brought them back. These men confessed to working for William de Valence, who was not present among them. She knew that Richard would return all the money, livestock, and goods to their rightful owners among the people of Leicestershire. Then she and Rocco rode to tell Simon. On the road to Kenilworth, she knew that her plan to live among the members of her faith in Piccotts End would now be indefinitely postponed. She also sensed that her life with Richard de Havering had taken a significant turn. It seemed as if they both knew that the pull of the destiny she shared with Simon was getting stronger.

Simon may have escaped from Gascony alive and with his honor and finances intact, but this event promised to enter the earl into a new set of profoundly menacing difficulties here at home. She would necessarily become an important part of it. She knew the circumstances would only become more complicated and threatening. She had managed the county of Leicestershire. She had established a life in that town. She had established the practice of keeping a household roll for the castle and a county roll for Leicestershire. She had traveled and read and examined the life around her. She had found a life with Richard, who took the time to love and admire her. But she knew the deeper meaning of her life was to guide the actions of this one unique man, perhaps the only powerful man who might also accept the direction of a strong woman. If Rocco had sworn to protect her, she was bound by a powerful bond to protect Simon de Montfort, often from himself. He may have saved her at first, but she had spent the rest of their lives saving him.

There could be no other life for her, and certainly no peaceful life of worship for her, not yet at least. She knew it to be her destiny to be part of Simon's life and all it might come to mean. And there was also another matter that would press on Simon and which would require her advice.

Two years before, in 1253, Pope Innocent IV had consolidated his rule, having been strengthened by the death of Frederick II, the King of Germany, three years before that, who had intrigued and warred against Innocent. Innocent died only a year later and was replaced by Pope Alexander IV. The new Pope quickly moved against the heirs of Frederick, whose infant grandson was the King of Sicily. The Pope had no army, but he could intrigue. He declared the Kingdom of Sicily to be under papal jurisdiction and offered the kingship to Richard of Cornwall, who simply responded that he could not agree to an offer from anyone who might give him the moon and then tell him to go get it. Richard knew it was an empty offer. The Pope could not give away Sicily; it would have to be taken and held. Richard of Cornwall's brother, King Henry, did not see it quite as sensibly. Still stinging from his losses in France, he seized upon the idea of gaining the Kingdom of Sicily for his younger son, Edmund. He had not consulted the larger parliament of English nobles but had relied only on the automatic approval of his small council, comprised almost entirely of his relatives. He accepted the offer when the Pope turned to him and made it.

He raised as much money as he could from his counties and sent it off to the Pope in Rome, and he made a promise to send men as well. This had not technically violated the terms of the Great Charter, which had required the king to get the approval of his council before he could raise taxes or muster more men into the army. But he had violated it in principle. The Pope had also ordered the Church in England to raid its own coffers in support of Henry's efforts. There was now a powerful unrest among the burgesses, merchants, and guildsmen, who bore the brunt of the higher taxes. The clergy of England was deeply disturbed and, in some cases, refused to make payment. The practical matter of the relative independence of the

English Church from Rome and from the king had been evoked, as it had in the time of Thomas Becket and Henry II. The magnates of England were sorely upset at what they saw as a return to the total autocracy that had been somewhat curtailed by the Great Charter, Magna Carta, signed by Henry's father, King John. Henry had also sworn to uphold it on several occasions. The very term "parliament" had only come into general use after the Great Charter.

The Welsh lords, sensing the unrest in England and that the king's attention had been diverted, had moved down from their mountains, and had begun making incursions into the plains of western England. The Scottish barons, too, grew restive and were threatening Yorkshire. Henry had called upon his lords to raise an army to deal with these threats to England, but the barons of England were resisting. They knew that the king would then have no choice but to call them to London. Simon would take the lead among the barons.

Pauline was also afraid because she knew that Simon would not be pleased by the news of William de Valence's predations upon Leicestershire. He would take it personally. She knew that in the larger scope of this situation, the clergy, the barons, and the people of England would look to one man to take up their cause. The events of the last several years, in Gascony and in England, would prove that there was only one man they could possibly seek. They would turn to Simon to be their leader. The William de Valence matter would only complicate the larger issues.

As she knew he would, Simon did not take the news of William de Valence's brigandage in Leicester very calmly. Simon went directly to London to complain to the king. At the court, William de Valence denied the claims against him and went so far as to accuse the Earl of Leicester of being in league with the Welsh and called Simon a traitor. Without responding, Simon drew his sword and moved to kill the new Earl of Pembroke right there in the palace. The king ordered his men to intervene. Simon left, unsatisfied and convinced that the king's unwarranted protection of his relatives had emboldened de Valence to rob his lands and to slander him. He returned to Kenilworth in a fury. Pauline did not wait for this to subside. She went straight to him.

"You have ridden your horse into the stream again without testing its depth or the strength of the current," she said. "We should have long since passed such recklessness. You have learned too much and have gone too far to be reverting now to the ways of your impetuous youth."

"Am I supposed to stand by while villains prey on my people?"

"No. But you are supposed to approach that problem thoughtfully and devise an intelligent solution. To do otherwise does not protect your people or your person. It only endangers both."

Simon looked at her and he saw her clearly in that moment. He sat down and was quiet for several minutes before he spoke.

"What have I done?" he asked.

"You have learned first-hand again what you should have already known. The king cannot ever be trusted. He places his personal interests before the welfare of the kingdom. And he is not at all steadfast or sensible when it comes to serving or even knowing his own interests. His rash and insensitive actions and words are as likely to damage his reign, his authority, and himself, as much as any incursions by a foreign power. He drives the good men out of his service and prefers the company of sycophants. He acts and speaks without thinking. He is a thoughtless creature of the moment."

"You are correct. I should know these things better than anyone."

"That is an understatement," she said. "You must also consider that there are larger issues here than your pride or even the people of your county."

"I am ashamed. I know these things. For years and while I was in Gascony, I carried your voice in my head. I ought to have known better. I have been a fool."

"There will be a time for action, but that time is not now. And when that time comes, you must act according to your well-made plans. And you must not act alone. You have resources other than your sword and your valor. Many of the churchmen and the nobles of this kingdom see what you and I see."

"The people are often lost in this. I feel for them. Too often are they treated like chattel. My father never allowed his concerns to move beyond the nobles and clergy. As a result, many of your countrymen perished."

"The nobles and the clergy are your most effective tools for you to use in helping the common people. They have the power, and they are also oppressed by this king," she said.

"Remember what we have always said, you and I, that the English are different? It was one thing we contemplated before coming here. The Great Charter sprang from this unique history. King Henry is trying to erase that history. It may be time to reassert the historical balance that is one of the many things that makes England different."

"That document required the king to get the approval of the nobles for certain important actions, but it left the power in the king's hands to call the nobles to council and to determine its composition."

"That is exactly one of its problems," he said. "There are others. The council or the parliament has no power of initiative. And it has no authority over the appointment of the high officers of the court."

This should have been a dry conversation, one about principles and processes of governing. But Pauline could tell that with each idea he expressed, Simon was speaking faster and with more passion. She continued to speak.

"Magna Carta does not address the problem of what powers it might have in the event the king is mad or is destroying the kingdom."

"Since the king rules by divine right, the clergy might have a role in that. But I think another major question is the composition of the parliament. It must be regular and established and representative. It

must arise from the counties, and not from the king's appointments."
Simon spoke now from the excitement that comes from new insight.
"And I think there are some roles for the knights and the merchants
and burgesses."

"That is an extreme notion," she said.

"In a way, it is not. The Great Charter does not speak of limiting
the power of the king. It speaks of the inherent rights and liberties of
the noblemen of England."

"I still have never seen that notion expressed in terms beyond the
nobles. You are talking about a kingdom, but one in which the ruler
is bound by the inherent right of his subjects."

"I get this awareness from your life and from the lessons of
the Bishop of Lincoln. You are a commoner. But I know you to be
superior in mind and heart to most of the nobles. You also believe
that we are all equal before God, that nobles or even the clergy are
no different from anyone else. I believe this can exist in the way that
England is governed."

"But not by Henry," she said.

"Perhaps not, but it must start with some ways in which we
reassert the rights of the English lords to place a check on the power
of the king, as in the Great Charter. But it must be more than that.
Henry's rule has shown us that much, that something must be done."

"I don't think you can confront the king directly."

"I have in the past," he said.

He was still excited now but in a calm way, the way that comes
to a person who suddenly sees something that should have been
apparent. All the ideas he had ever had seemed to be settling into
a place of wisdom. Even the promise he had made to Pauline about
doing the most good for the most people fit into what he was thinking.
She sensed this germination in him and was excited by it herself. It
was their own chess game and it played with the throne of England
as one of the many pieces. She continued to prod his thinking.

"I think I mean to say that confronting the king directly may not be the best approach. I think his power over the parliament is his weakness. He uses his relatives as a council that never questions him. I think they are his weak point. Perhaps you should challenge their role. It will be less inherently threatening to the king. And many nobles who might be afraid to antagonize the king directly would be less likely to be concerned about challenging the role of his in-laws and half-siblings."

"I can see the wisdom of that," he said. "And I can see the wisdom in you."

"I am thinking right now of your hair shirt. Surely it must scratch you."

"Not as irritatingly as you did, when you walked in here to upbraid me."

"Is that what you call it? I call it saving you from yourself. I sense that I may have done that several times in the past and will likely be called upon to do it in the future."

"Maybe that is why I saved your life in the first place. I knew I was in desperate need of correction," he said.

"I am not certain that makes us even," she said.

"No, but it might make us what Adam Marsh once told me about the two of us."

"He told you as well?" she asked.

"Of course he did."

TWENTY-EIGHT

For the next couple of years, Simon traveled around England according to the plans he and Pauline had devised. He spent many days in consultation with Adam Marsh and Robert Grosseteste, the Bishop of Lincoln. He met with Richard de Clare, the Earl of Gloucester, and Roger Bigod, the Earl of Norfolk and Marshal of England. He called to Kenilworth many of his closest friends among the minor nobles. After some time and through his efforts, a loose agreement was reached between them all. They would act as a unit with the Earl of Leicester in the lead, to work to influence the other nobles to behave as one when action was necessary. Simon had created a formidable alliance that would strive to bring all the other barons into one unit. No one could know what turn events might take, but they were prepared to face the situation as a single component. They simply awaited the call to parliament that they expected was coming. Henry wanted men to fight the Welsh, and he needed money for that cause and to satisfy the papal request for the Sicilian crown. Henry had not yet overcome the resistance of the English nobles or clergy, so in April of 1258, he had called a parliament in London to make his demands.

William de Valence began the discussion, "We are sure that the successes of the Welsh invaders come from the assistance of the Earl of Leicester."

There were loud exclamations against this, largely led by Richard de Clare, Earl of Gloucester, who said, "These lies are made up out of whole cloth."

Simon's many supporters cheered his remarks. But Simon would not rise to the bait.

"This is a time for unity," he said, looking at the king. "We face incursions against the kingdom from the Welsh in the west and the Scots in the north. It is not the time to be sowing discord. Perhaps he who seeks to divide us gives the most aid to our enemies."

The king looked at his half-brother, de Valence, to silence him.

"The Earl of Leicester is correct. We not only face these problems on the borders of our own kingdom, but we also stand facing an opportunity to expand our influence and acquire rule over the Kingdom of Sicily. I demand that each county put all of its available men into service for England's defense and that we levy a tax on all free men and serfs alike of one-third of their personal belongings to pay for our defense and for our expansion."

There was a general outbreak of shouts and exclamations from the lords. "Unheard of", "Burdensome", "Terrible", many of them cried. When this din generally began to die down, Robert Grosseteste, Bishop of Lincoln, rose to speak. At this the room grew quiet to listen to this man of the Church who was also an academic leader.

"As Sicily is over a thousand miles from us, perhaps our minds cannot reach it from here very quickly. And as for our military needs, I am not capable of that judgment, but I know it is also a weighty matter," he said, looking directly at Simon de Montfort.

Simon knew this was the signal for what he and his allies had been putting in place. The rowdy room had quieted for the bishop, but now it remained calm for the words that many expected from the

Earl of Leicester. Only the king's relatives, a minority faction, began to mumble.

"I believe," Simon de Montfort said, "that Your Majesty has put some momentous decisions before us, ones we might be rash to consider answering at this point. I suggest that we each look to our own counties to see what our capabilities might be and then return here in three days to discuss our options."

This met with general acclaim and an almost unanimous approval. The assembly adjourned. The leaders of the Church and the nobles who were the leaders of his majority faction met in secret during those three days. It was decided during these three days that the clergy could not and would not participate openly in the resistance that the barons had proposed. The churchmen wrote to the king and asked to withdraw, and the king allowed them to not participate.

The discussion upon reconvening began with the king restating his demand for a one-third tax and a complete military levy. One of his Savoyard in-laws seconded that idea. Then Simon's allies each spoke in turn. They were orderly and concise and direct, but the discussion had turned dramatically in the other direction. They inveighed against the power of the king's relatives.

"The Courts of Justice never issue writs against the king's foreign relatives, so they run roughshod over our lands," the Earl of Hereford proclaimed.

Before there could be an answer, the Earl of Norfolk stood and cited William de Valence as principal among these transgressors. This caused the relatives of the king to try to shout him down, when eight of Simon's allies stood at once, and then Richard de Clare, Earl of Gloucester, stepped forward from among them and spoke.

"Your Majesty has used your foreign relatives as a council that would always accede to your wishes and thereby allow you to sidestep the provisions of the Great Charter."

Henry was stunned and it was not in his nature to stand firm in the face of mounting opposition. His relatives complained but looked largely to him to speak for them. Then Simon spoke. He demanded that reparations were due from the plundering of English lands, lords, and their subjects. He looked to the king, whose face was blank. He finally spoke.

"What would you have us do?"

"We have here a declaration for you to sign that will agree to the reforms we hope to propose that will take Magna Carta as their foundation and will expand upon them. These reforms will be determined by a committee of twenty-four noblemen listed in the declaration. These lords will meet in Oxford and the provisions they approve there will constitute a stronger form of governing the kingdom with the participation of the barons who also serve the king."

"I will sign this declaration," the king said, to the panicked murmurs of his in-laws and half-siblings.

This had all happened too easily. Then the king called for another parliament of nobles, this one to meet before the meeting of the nobles at Oxford. Simon had seen too many of Henry's reversals and his faction of nobles had known the king to break his previous oaths, so they formulated a plan.

In early June of 1258, the earls, barons, and knights arrived again at the court of King Henry III, this time in their full battledress, swords at their sides, and with additional retainers. At the entrance of Westminster Hall, they disarmed and laid down their weapons. When the king arrived, they kneeled before him and paid him the reverence due to their sovereign. He was stunned by the appearance of this great body of his noblemen in suits of mail.

"What is this, sirs?" the king asked. "Am I your prisoner?"

"No, Your Majesty," said Roger Bigod, Earl of Norfolk, the Marshal of England, "but the miserable and insufferable Poitevins and all other foreigners must be banished from your presence, and from ours. This is what is best for the honor, dignity, and well-being of your rule."

"And how do you think that I should be made to follow your counsel?"

"Swear on the Holy Gospels," Simon said, "that you and your heir, Edward, will do nothing until you hear the report of the two dozen good barons, bishops, and earls who have been elected by us and will convene at Oxford; that you will in no way drain your subjects with burdens that have never before been placed upon Englishmen, and that you will without delay turn over the highest offices to loyal English subjects elected by this body. We stand unified here before you and ask only that you defend the rights and liberties of England and Englishmen."

The king acquiesced before this consensus and did as was requested. He and the nineteen-year-old Prince Edward swore on the Holy Gospels. Then the meeting adjourned. Simon joined many of the barons who had gathered at Durham House, with the Bishop of Durham, Walter de Kirkham. The king retired to the Tower of London. Several days later, he decided to dine on his boat on the Thames, to escape the summer heat. A great summer thunderstorm broke out. Alarmed by the lightning, the king ordered the boat to be put to shore a mile downriver. This happened to be in front of Durham House, the bishop's palace in London. Simon moved to greet his brother-in-law. He smiled and bowed to his king.

"I believe the storm is passing," Simon said.

"That is good," the king said, "for though I fear the lightning, by God, I am more afraid of you than all the thunder and lightning in the world."

"You should not fear me, for I have ever been the loyal servant of king and country. You should fear more those who flatter you but live on the pillage of England."

Pauline and Simon had discussed what to expect next. He had prepared his alliance for it. The king immediately sought to intrigue and attempted to approach individual barons and undermine the organized effort. Simon had prepared the nobles to arm and equip themselves and muster together to appear to prepare to march on the Welsh. In this way, they remained united and the king's efforts went for naught. This military procession instead made its way to the Dominican convent at Oxford, where they began their deliberations. They would build on the principles of the Great Charter and strengthen them. Within the assembly of twenty-four were two smaller groups, which were set to different tasks. Simon was a member of each of these. His military successes, his independence, his courage in opposing the king had all made him the leader in these councils and of the larger interests of the barons and their subjects. The process would take many months and several meetings. He consulted Pauline from the very first.

"You have been trying to carry water in a basket," she said, "when you think that Henry will be bound by an oath or by his own proclamation and writ. They mean almost nothing to him. He has shown you that much, repeatedly."

"The primary restrictions must be that this parliament will meet three times a year according to a schedule, whether or not the king presides over it or calls for it, and that we will have the power to take the initiative without the king submitting a measure. It will place the king under the tutelage of the parliament."

"That is an amazing precept, and completely new. The king rules by divine right, and by a long tradition," she said. "This parliament of nobles does not rest on any foundation, other than the agreement of the nobles, each of whom may be bought or suborned by the king, or who may come to disagreement among themselves. That is a very tenuous position from which to try to balance against the divine right and two hundred years of Norman–English tradition."

"We will remove the power to appoint the great officers from the king and give the assembly of lords the power to reject the king's selections. The appointments of the steward, the marshal, the chamberlain, the chancellor, the constable will all be subject to our approval. The offices of the treasurer will be returned to English nobles and protected from all incursions from within the royal household. The office of the justiciar will be elevated and he will determine justice within the kingdom without any interference of the king. There will be a rule of law, common to all Englishmen," he said with building excitement. "And the king will not be able to issue any writ, either under the great seal or the privy seal, without the approval of the parliament."

"You still have the problem of the king, whose foundation is far stronger than that of your parliament," she said.

"The officers and the nobles will swear an oath to the parliament and to each other."

"Only men, or boys, would find that sufficient. You men are so enamored of your own honor that you believe the oaths you swear actually mean something. A woman knows that a meal is not made with an oath. It is made with utensils and with food. A Cathar woman knows men's oaths can be lies."

"I am aware," he said, "that the people of your faith never give an oath because they believe that men may lie, that only actions matter. What would you suggest?"

"I speak not only as a member of my faith on this, but as a woman and as a commoner. I am thinking as a person whose people were exterminated by men who swore oaths to king and Church. You are seeking to rein in the excesses of King Henry and the damages that he does, but you cannot do that without creating a new system for the rule of the kingdom. You are really doing something for England, for the rights and liberties of the English people. That should be your foundation."

"I see that clearly now. And it fits with what many of the nobles want. They want to create a standard set of laws to govern other matters, such as cases in the courts, the rights of heirs, the rules of property, and other matters. This must be constituted in writing and distributed widely."

"Yes and no," she said. "Support for it must be sought widely, not just circulated. Take it to the towns, and to London first, and ask the burgesses, knights, merchants, and guildsmen to elect to support it or not. They will support it. They have borne the burden of Henry's heavy taxes and levies of men for war. They will rally to a constitution of laws that will protect them from arbitrary rule. There is something about this that is very English, and it has been in the wind for these past forty-five years since the Great Charter. The men of the towns will be the foundation."

"I think we can make it even more attractive and give it more of a foundation. There should be a provision that gives the landholders of each county the power to elect their own sheriff, who will no longer be selected by the king or the local lord. Each sheriff should serve for only one year. That will ground the new provisions in a solid foundation."

"There is one other thing," she said, "and it should be obvious."

"I do not see it, but I am sure I will once you say it."

"This writing, these Provisions of Oxford, this constitution of laws, must be written in English."

"No official document has ever been written in English. They are only ever written in Latin, and sometimes in French. But you are correct. It must be in English. It is English to the core and it is for the English. That is such a brilliant idea. I am certain I would have thought of it myself."

"I know you are. You are sure of many things. Not the least, you are very sure of yourself." She smiled at him.

"That is not the case, not when it concerns you. Half the time I say something to you, I just know you are going to correct it. The other half of the time, I am not sure that what I think or say is not really your voice in my head." He smiled now too.

"You might want to stop now," she said. "There is no need to say that, and this may not be the time. No other man in England or in France would listen to me the way you always have. No other man would know how to profit from what I say. You have been more open to me and more patient with my criticism than you might ever have been, even with another man."

Then there was a silence that sat as a calm lake surface, one with a storm passing above it.

"We both know that I see you as a woman, even if I have been partially blind to that."

Pauline had been caught up in the excitement of their discussion and she realized that they had always talked like this, sharing ideas, discussion options, being intellectual equals. And while this was spiritual, there had always been an inescapable element, which was that he was a man, and she was a woman. It was their chess game of words, but it was also like a dance. It was almost physical, as if their intellectual back and forth had always been some form of caresses. She waited some time for her composure to return before she responded.

"Perhaps your blindness has always been a good thing. Maybe it served our interests to remain on spiritual terms. I know it has served England and her people well."

Now, he stood and crossed the room to her, stood in front of her. She took one step back and gave him a calm look, one that hid her yearning. He did not come any closer. She remained quiet for a minute. She did not let her discomfort or excitement show. She stayed focused on the larger issues.

"You are more of a man than any of these kings and nobles," she said, "and yet you see these good things in a woman. You are humble enough in your heart to take what I, a woman, have to say and often to value it more than your own ideas."

"I know," he said, "that you speak more of yourself in this. You are unlike any woman among the queens and nobles. You are better. I will always feel that. I suppose I know now that I have always felt it."

He took one more step toward her and was again in front of her. His face was flush. She pulled away several inches. She could see that he had realized what she had always known about them, that he felt it too.

"We are older now, Simon. We have come to terms with these things. We have always been kept apart by faith, by class, by the demands of your destiny, though we are bound together in spirit. Now, we have the wisdom of the years to hold us in place. And we have your destiny, which is something I have also always felt. There are great things in God's plan for you."

"We may be older," he said. "We may have great tasks that are before us. But you always take me back to that time when I was eighteen and you were a disrespectful girl importuning me to do the right thing. In your presence, I am ever that young man."

"There is wisdom in those words too. Because of you, I do not feel older. We must retain our youth now as best we can. I must also declare: you have consistently outdistanced me in the matter of impertinence these last few years. You have stood up against a king."

"Importuning him to do the right thing."

TWENTY-NINE

Isabella, another sister of King Henry and Richard of Cornwall, had married the Holy Roman Emperor, Frederick II. This made Richard of Cornwall, already the brother of one king, related by marriage to two sovereigns, Frederick and Alexander III, King of Scotland, who had married his niece Margaret. In 1256, six years after the death of Frederick, the electoral princes of many of the German kingdoms decided that Richard should be their new ruler. He paid some of them to support him and was duly elected. It was largely an important ceremonial position since Frederick II had been their last strong leader. Richard would largely settle disputes between the kingdoms, which now ruled themselves. But he had made some statements from Germany about being homesick for England, so the English barons sent him a message not to return without their permission, at the risk of forfeiting his English holdings. They did not want the king's strong and respected brother to be in England while they negotiated to subject the king's authority to the rights and privileges inherent in the English people.

At the meeting in the spring of 1258 that Simon held in the London Guildhall with the leading townsmen of the city, William de Valence burst in and swore that he would never yield his title or his holdings in England. Simon replied that he should then give up his life instead. This gave the Londoners cause to cheer Simon and to approve of the Provisions of Oxford by acclamation. They had long suffered the depredations of the Poitevins as well as the levies of the king. It also proved to be the starting point for the English baronage to begin its purge of the king's foreign relatives. Knowing now that all of England, the nobles and the commoners included, were arrayed against them, the Poitevins fled to Winchester. The forces of the barons and the London militia pursued them, and the king had no choice but to pronounce them exiled and guarantee them safe passage to Dover, from where they sailed to Boulogne. The barons then distributed copies of the Provisions of Oxford to the towns and cities of England, where they were approved by each council. The seals of these towns and cities, and that of London, which had also supported the barons against King John in 1215, were affixed to the Provisions. By October of 1258, the king had signed a proclamation in English and in French that declared he would maintain the Provisions and he ordered all his subjects to swear to them as well.

The Provisions of Oxford confirmed the principles of the Great Charter, establishing the baronage's power to act as a check on the king. They went further, establishing that there would be three meetings of parliament every year, whether called by the king or not. They gave the barons the right to select most of the members of the Privy Council and created separate councils to oversee the appointment of the great offices of the royal court, and to govern the operation of the local courts. Simon de Montfort sat on each of these three councils. In addition to controlling the central government, the Provisions sought to address the grievances of the lesser aristocracy, townsmen, merchants, and freemen in the localities by establishing an investigation into abuses by local officials and by reforming local government, giving the townsmen a say in choosing their sheriff and other officials. The common law of England was also elevated and given priority over the arbitrary decisions of the royal appointees. In this way, the Provisions of Oxford limited not only the power of the king but also of the barons. The local people attributed this part to Simon. The Provisions of Oxford were the first written constitution of England or of any European kingdom and the first official government document written in English.

Throughout the remainder of 1258 and most of 1259, the Provisions of Oxford were enhanced by parliament at Westminster, and the constitution was strengthened and expanded by the October of 1259 Provisions of Westminster, which later came to be known as the Provisions of Oxford and Westminster. The Church had not taken part at Oxford, and at Westminster its right to hold lands in perpetuity was made a matter of law and against the custom of only allowing an individual to own property and to leave it by will to an heir. The local legal reforms were made stronger and established the rights of the local townsmen to seek redress even against their lords.

King Henry was absent from England for much of this time. It was notable that Simon was also away in France. The reason was that Henry III wanted to negotiate a new treaty with Louis IX, who had returned from the Holy Land. For part of the negotiations, Henry had acceded to the new ascendancy of the English baronage and he had allowed the Earl of Leicester to act as his ambassador. But in the end, Henry's exiled French relatives had convinced him that there was a trade to be made in France that would strengthen his hand in England. For Simon's part, he and his wife were in Paris to receive a payment for renouncing their individual rights to land in France, Eleanor through her father, King John, and Simon through his family holdings and through his victories in France. King Henry made greater concessions and received even more significant rewards. Henry renounced his rights to Normandy, Anjou, Poitou, and Maine, and retained his rights to Aquitaine, and Gascony within it, but only as a subject of King Louis. Henry received some rights to lesser holdings in France. But he also received a very large payment for the maintenance of five hundred knights over a significant period. King Louis intended that these men serve in another crusade, but they significantly strengthened Henry in England. This Treaty of Paris was signed in December of 1259. Henry took a knee and pledged fealty to Louis as his liege for the holdings in Aquitaine.

Henry had only renounced what he had little hope of ever recovering. The remnants of his holdings on the Continent were protected from further incursions with the aid of the French. And he now could finance a sizeable army of knights. His half a year at the court of Louis IX had also strengthened his relationship with that king and had put the storms and disruptions of the barons' resistance far out of his mind. He now saw England and Simon and the other English nobles from a greater distance. And he saw them with even more animosity. In February of 1260, he failed to appear in England for the scheduled first meeting of parliament for that year. It was the beginning of Henry's counterattack.

The barons, under Simon's direction, held session without the king. They continued to expel the king's foreign relatives, this time the Savoyard relations of the queen. They limited the taxes collected by the king. Young Prince Edward had been convinced by his father's agreement with the barons and his support of the Provisions that Henry had been sincere. Edward had participated in the parliament in the king's absence and had supported all the measures. The king then received his first large payment from France, but he tarried on the Continent, claiming to await favorable winds. At the end of April, he arrived in London with his French relatives and an armed force and ordered the city gates locked behind him and manned by an armed guard. Young Edward was the first to defect from parliament and the Earl of Leicester. Henry requested individual nobles, but not Simon, to visit him at court, where he complained against the earl and condemned the principles of the Provisions of Oxford and Westminster. He flipped his position again in August, when a Welsh incursion required that he assign a leader for the English forces against them and he made the obvious choice of Simon de Montfort, who made short work of the matter. Still, Henry had begun to weaken the barons' coalition.

In April of 1261, Henry obtained from the Pope a papal bull that declared the Provisions of Oxford and Westminster to be null and void, as affronts to the divine right of kings. The Pope saw that a diffusion of power in England would limit his own strength to influence events through the king. Henry immediately recalled the rest of his Savoyard in-laws and Poitevin relatives. He enforced his control over various castles and fortresses. And he replaced the English officers of his court with his returning relatives, also awarding them some of the castles and lands. This show of force, the papal bull, and Henry's cajoling had coerced many of the nobles to his side and they renounced the constitution as represented in the Provisions. The king then offered a pardon to any of the remaining magnates who would do the same, naming several of them by title and name, including Simon de Montfort. Now at Kenilworth, the Earl of Leicester found himself at the head of a collapsed alliance and facing the choice of either agreeing to the king's terms or opposing them virtually on his own.

"I say you take your lead from Henry's own actions," Pauline said.

"What might you mean by that?" Simon asked.

"Leave England for a while."

"That hardly seems sensible."

"Surely it does. You will eliminate having to make that difficult choice. Many of the English lords may have abandoned you before the returning power of the king, but there is massive unrest among the merchants, burgesses, knights, and guildsmen of London and the towns. The nobles will feel this and soon they will also remember their resentment of the king's foreign relatives, who are unlikely to be measured or lenient in their return to power. Henry will also, by his nature, generate resistance. When that happens, the English barons will plead for you to return."

"Then we must go to France and proclaim I intend to go on a crusade," he said.

"We?"

"Yes. It had been my plan to convey to you that we are entering perilous times and that you must go away to protect yourself. But I knew you would interpret that to mean you must remain to help me. Now, that is a discussion we need not have."

Pauline hesitated for a few seconds before she spoke.

"Your family and retainers must accompany us. And I will bring all my disguises. These are indeed hazardous times."

* * *

In Simon's absence in the first part of 1262, Henry wasted no time. He reinstated royal appointment of the sheriffs. He put out a levy for soldiers on the boroughs. He secured another papal bull from the new Pope, Urban IV, releasing him from his oaths. And he published and disseminated a decree formally annulling the Provisions. The only obstacle to complete destruction of the Provisions of Oxford and Westminster and to the baronial alliance that had forced them on him was his failure to subordinate the Earl of Leicester. Henry followed Simon to France. There, he sought the intervention of the French king. Simon then agreed to abide by whatever Louis IX would decide.

Pauline saw a scene at the French court that was unlike any other. Simon took his stand between two kings. King Louis IX of France was tall, slender, soft-spoken, and gentle. His light brown hair had turned gray prematurely, which highlighted his green eyes and the glowing complexion of his clean-shaven face. He reflected quiet strength. King Henry III of England was of medium build and height with some gray in his dark hair and beard. He was kinetic to the degree of being distracted and he had a bump on the middle of his long nose. Pauline always noticed that his upper left eyelid never fully raised, giving her and everyone else of that time the impression of a flaw in his character. Simon was as tall as Louis with a more solid build, and dark-haired with the straight, strong features that had always attracted women and men to him. He stood quietly, particularly so in the company of two kings, though all could see he concealed his great passion.

Henry began with his attack on the Earl of Leicester. His French was colored with some Saxon words and syntax and an accent not heard anywhere in France.

"This man, Simon de Montfort, has attacked the divine rights that God has granted to kings. It is sad. He has made the English barons rise in rebellion against us. He has spread false news about us and has sought at all points to enrich himself at the expense of the realm. He has made my people not love me as much. He has assumed the role of baronial leader and has attempted to commandeer many royal rights to himself. It is terrible, really bad."

Simon's French was Parisian, and he had been several times to the court of Louis, even at the time when Blanche of Castile had been regent, and later when Simon's brother had been constable of France. He spoke with less deference of Henry than he would in London.

"I do not see, Your Majesty, how the testimony of the King of England can be used against me, when he has admitted to having broken his own oath. He put his own hand to the Provisions of Oxford and Westminster, and he did it to protect his rule and to strengthen it. He seeks now to gain your pious assistance in continuing to break that oath."

"I did not break my word. You did. You did," Henry said.

"My oath is to England and therefore to the king and it is the same word we signed when we each put our name to the Provisions."

Louis sat quietly for several moments before he spoke.

"England, you are our brother, as your Queen Eleanor is sister to our Queen Margaret. These strong ties have been tested long, by yourself, in your many incursions into France."

"To reclaim my lands, my lands," Henry said.

"No family has served France as well as the de Montfort family," Louis continued. "We owe many great debts to the family of your Earl of Leicester. His brother was our constable. His father was our good right sword arm. I will not judge either of you at this time."

Henry made a brusque farewell and prepared to return to England.

"Henry will do what he can against you," Pauline told Simon.

"Yes, but your original assumption still holds true. And the failure of Louis to take his side will not aid his cause. We will be better served to wait until the English noblemen seek my return."

The English lords still retained their resentment of the presence and elevation of Henry's foreign relatives and Henry's abrogation of his own sworn oaths. The townsmen, particularly the Londoners, were restless at having lost the local autonomy that they had only briefly enjoyed. The minor nobles and the younger ones, particularly twenty-year-old Gilbert de Clare, who had inherited the title Earl of Gloucester from his fiery father, Richard, were among the most numerous voices now clamoring for Simon to return to England. In April of 1263, he did just that, and resumed leadership of the reform coalition. Things moved swiftly from there. Henry's Savoyard and Lusignan relatives fled London. But they only went so far as Dover and ignored the charter to sail for France. Simon led a force to eject the king's foreign relatives from several castles and cathedrals. He seized the castle at the important port of Dover and severed the king's communication with France.

During this time, Henry did not act. He moped behind the walls of London and the moat at the Tower of London. Queen Eleanor refused to be useless and attempted to take a boat up the Thames to join Prince Edward, who was commanding a small force at Windsor in July. She was immediately confronted by a crowd of furious Londoners, who shouted their anger at the king from the shores. Shaken, she returned to the tower. Henry grew afraid and asked Simon to come to London, where the earl presented his demands. Once again, the facile king swore to uphold the Provisions of Oxford and Westminster and to expel his foreign relatives and the French knights. This was formalized in a royal charter again and approved by parliament in September.

King Henry immediately began to suborn various individual nobles. He particularly focused his efforts on young Gilbert de Clare, whose father had fought beside Simon in Gascony and had been his strongest ally. The king joined his son Edward at Windsor, along with their partisans, and marched on Dover Castle. Simon had left the castle too well defended for them to succeed by assault. Simon then took advantage of the king's absence and attempted to enter London. He was stopped by the king's guards at the gate, but the rising tumult of townsmen in favor of Simon caused the guards to relent. The situation was at a standstill. Simon and his forces held London, and the Strait of Dover to France. But the king had an armed force and was now at large around Oxford. The king sent emissaries to Simon to seek his agreement for the stalemate to be negotiated by the King of France.

Pauline and most of Simon's allies argued against this idea. But Simon felt that he had long been well favored in France and by King Louis. He was also reluctant to allow the confrontation to continue and wanted a way out of finding himself being forced to engage in a battle against King Henry. Henry then prepared to depart for France. Before he left, he circulated a false royal decree stating that the noblemen's claims that he planned to permanently eliminate the local reforms and to appoint his foreign relatives to major offices were not true. He falsely stated that he had intended no such thing. He lied and claimed he would uphold the oath he had sworn to support the constitution of the Provisions, and that the Earl of Leicester was pursuing his own gain. Henry left for France on December 28.

Simon, too, was about to set out for France at the same time, but his horse slipped on some ice at Catesby and rolled over onto Simon's leg, breaking it. Pauline and the countess ordered his staff to prevent him from walking on it. They looked after him for the next month. Each of the women was concerned about his physical condition and about his difficult situation within the Kingdom of England. Pauline worried more about the former and Eleanor more about the latter. Simon seemed not to be too anxious about either and spoke to both of them.

"Nothing will happen in France before I get there," he said. "These things have always gone slowly. King Louis even refused to make a decision at all on the last matter."

"But that was a difficult decision to make," Pauline said. "It was more personal before. It was an abstract argument between a lying king on one side and an upright and noble son of France on the other side. Now, there has been conflict, a siege, forces have been raised. This is a decision regarding a possible armed struggle between two systems of government: a monarch restricted by and subject to a higher law, and a king with unfettered power, such as the King of France has. Louis will not have to balance any merits. He has a stake in the outcome, in preserving the absolute power of kings against the armed nobles."

"Louis will not make a decision until I am present," he said. "And he will try to be just. That is his way."

"I do not know about that," said Pauline.

Rocco walked in with a messenger, who handed Simon a letter, which he handed to Pauline to read. She reported what she read.

King Louis had issued the Settlement of Amiens. His declaration was that the strongholds taken from the king's foreign relations must be returned, that the right to choose the high officers of the court resided in the king alone, that all local reforms and English common law be replaced by whatever the king chose. It declared the Provisions of Oxford and Westminster to be annulled.

"It took only three weeks for these two kings to agree on the absolute power of kings," Pauline said.

"Be that as it may," Simon said. "We now face a terrifying dilemma. Five years of struggle for reform are sadly erased. The Lusignan relatives of the king and the Savoyard relatives of the two queens will not make use of this victory in moderation. King Louis has only made things much worse. We must decide now whether we stand for England or we bow to Henry and his foreign relatives."

"I will stand with you, no matter whatever you choose to do," Eleanor said. "But I hope you work this all out. Please make peace with my brother."

Pauline only looked at Simon. They both knew what he would do.

BOOK FOUR

THIRTY

Pauline had decided to make use of one of the privileges of her position within a noble house. She wanted to prepare for the expected visit from Roger Bacon, the protégé of the late Adam Marsh, who had died in 1259. Simon's leg had healed, and he had been busy mustering his forces around England in anticipation of Henry's return from France. Simon would return to Kenilworth before he moved out with his men, in preparation for whatever the king had planned. Pauline also wanted to do something to mark a change in her for when Simon returned. It was Christmas of 1263 and Simon's time upon his return would be spent with family. In any event, Roger Bacon had said he was coming to speak to her and not to Simon. He had stated that what he had to say had been related to him by Adam Marsh. She wanted to be ready for him, and to make special preparations. She wanted to take a bath. Had she been almost any other person in England, she would have had to travel to London or to Bath in order to make her preparations in a public facility; it had long been the only way a commoner might bathe. But in the castle at Leicester, she would not have to leave. She could stay put, and her bath would be hot. She would also make use of something that had been available in Italy and Spain for over a hundred years, but which had only been made in France and England for the use of nobles in the last generation. She would use soap.

She ordered a large wooden tub to be taken into her room. A linen cloth was placed in it to cover any imperfections in the wood that may cause splinters. Pots and kettles of boiling-hot water were carried from the kitchen. By the time this process had filled the tub, the boiling water in it had cooled down to only being quite hot. Pauline dismissed the servants, undressed, and slipped into the tub. She used a cloth to absorb the soap and began to bathe herself. It was a remarkable, almost unique experience, to feel so warm and clean and relaxed. She remarked to herself that this was her first private, hot bath in the full fifty-three years of her life. She also surmised that it might be her last since the days ahead would be fraught with critical decisions and frantic activity. Her previous meeting with Adam Marsh, though over two dozen years earlier, was still and always fresh in her mind. As she arose to dry herself and to put on a clean dress, she felt how different this next meeting would be, and not only because she would not be meeting with Adam Marsh but with a priest who had been his student. At the earlier meeting, she had been young and tentative. That was no longer the case.

She was entirely within the noble house of de Montfort now. She had helped Simon through many difficult times and had also later done the same for his family. Richard de Havering had taken over the steward's duties and she hoped that his life was beginning to move forward without her. She had administered to the poor and dispossessed of Leicester. Pauline was also gathering herself for the travails she knew were to arrive soon. She spent her days as if she were a noble aunt or cousin. She decided to dress the part and put on a Coventry-blue smock made not of wool but of linen, a finer material that was again available to her as part of a noble house. Over her smock, she put on a light white linen surcoat with a fine leather belt. Under both, she wore delicate wool hose. The surcoat had a light hood, which she decided to put up. She valued substance over style, but she recognized the power that style had over others. And she understood that her clothes would influence her bearing, and she wanted to appear as she felt. She also understood it might be one of the last times she would be able to wear a dress.

Roger Bacon was already quite renowned. He had been a master at Oxford, where he had taught his students the philosophy of Aristotle. Years before, he had met his mentor in France, where he had accepted a teaching position at the University of Paris. It was at that meeting that he decided to become a Franciscan friar and where Adam Marsh had taken him under his tutelage. He was very much in the mold of Adam Marsh and of Robert Grosseteste, the late Bishop of Lincoln. He was a scholar of secular studies, particularly the sciences, as well as theology. He was fond of ancient philosophy, and his theological studies were aimed at reforming the Church to make more use of rational and secular teachings and opinions. He was skilled at mathematics, astronomy, optics, and other sciences. He could read and speak several languages. At this time, he was not attached to any university and had served quietly at the Diocese of Lincoln. He was forty-eight years old.

"Thank you for receiving me, my lady," he said when Pauline joined him.

"We all miss Adam Marsh," she said. "Anyone who was close to him is more than welcome in Leicestershire and at Kenilworth. He was a great man and a good friend."

"He thought very highly of you, my lady, and of the Earl of Leicester."

"You need only call me Pauline, and though I am of this house, my beginnings were quite humble."

"I think that only makes you more remarkable," he said.

"I am also aware of your own accomplishments, father. You might be careful, lest you appear condescending."

"I am only a brother friar and not a priest, though I know from what I have been told that you are indifferent to the mysteries of the Church. I have also been told of your direct way of speaking."

"Then you may directly tell me of your mission. Why have you come here?"

"When Adam Marsh was on his deathbed, he spoke of little else but you and the earl, and what he and the Bishop of Lincoln had long seen on the horizon. In fact, much of what he said and believed were opinions and insights the Bishop of Lincoln had shared and discussed with him. It seems that they had foreseen much of what is now happening."

"Go on," she said. "I am interested in what they thought and what you see happening."

"You may remember that the bishop and Adam Marsh had long believed that you and the earl were inextricably linked and that you were that part of his destiny that simply would not come into effect, absent the part you play in his life."

"I remember that as if it were yesterday. It surprised me at the time Adam told me. And I have since believed it to be the truth."

"Your counsel to the earl will never be more important and critical than it is right now or will be in the near future."

"I sense that as well," she said. "I recall Adam telling me that the bishop had said that Simon was benevolent and righteous, and that he would die a martyr to these virtues."

"The bishop and Adam believed that Simon's spirit is one of those singular ones that never bends to pressure, to inducements, or to vanity. They believed that this would do great good for the people of England, but that it would stand out as a terrifying obstacle to the whims and tempers of the King of England. This has been happening now for many years. They also predicted the current state of affairs, that the nobles and indeed the common people of England would see the earl for what he has always been, and that he would grow in renown and in power, and that someday this would all come to a head."

"The king has an armed force in the field," she said. "All his vacillations settled into a resolve when he was in France with his resentful and exiled relatives. He has been removed from the concerns voiced by his parliament. He feels emboldened by the whisperings of those relatives, and by the actions of the King of France and by your Pope, to violate his many oaths to uphold the Provisions of Oxford and Westminster and his more numerous oaths to live by the principles of the Great Charter."

"That is one way to look at it. It may be more reasonable to say that he simply has realized that the Kingdom of England is not wide enough to hold both him and the upright, honorable, and respected earl, who will always stand up for the subjects of the king who has forsaken them," he said.

"I see that you speak quite directly as well. What is your message then?"

"You must never leave his side. The earl and you are as one. He will not be what he must if you are not with him."

"If you are saying that I should help lead him to his martyrdom, I do not see it that way."

"Maybe not," he said. "Everything you are and everything you have been to the earl advises you to do what I have said that Adam Marsh and the Bishop of Lincoln would urge you to do."

"I too have sensed that this is the crucial time. I could not possibly leave him now. That much is certain. I am contented somewhat to learn that this is what Adam and the bishop have seen and have wanted. Is there something more?"

"Do you remember the part of the conversation you had with Adam that touched on the matter of blood and the family?"

"I could never forget. He charged me with an even greater duty to Simon because he was about to be married and would have children. Nothing could have surprised me more."

"I believe that Adam told you about the sons that Simon would have and the sons the king would have. The king's son, Prince Edward, has his father's blood in his veins, which is the blood of the late King John and of the volatile Isabella of Angoulême. For that reason, Edward is tempestuous. But he also has the Savoyard blood of his mother, the queen, so he is equally strong and smart and brave. The balance has tipped him in favor of his Savoyard blood because he was raised by his mother. She enforced those traits, and he has had her for an example."

"I see," she said. "If it is the blood of the woman, the mother, that makes the difference, then we must see Simon's Henry and his other sons the same way. They have Simon's blood and his boldness and strength. But they also have the blood of Henry's sister, the blood of King John and Queen Isabella. And in Henry and his brothers, the balance will be tipped toward that side and they will be vacillating and unsure. That is terrifying news, though what I have seen seems to reinforce that."

"You need only look at Simon, who has his father's bravery. He also was raised by his mother, Alix de Montmorency. She was strong and good and a veritable soldier for Christ, helping her husband on all of his quests, not unlike you, I might add."

"You are telling me, then, that Simon's sons will be a problem."

"Yes. And you know it is your destiny to protect Simon from all quarters."

"Simon loves his sons," she said. "I cannot very well stand between his sons and him."

"Of course you cannot do that. But you must always take them into account as you assist your friend and lord."

"When will you priests stop placing impossible burdens on me?"

"It is good that you can jest," he said. "You have grace. I can see that clearly, as good Adam and the bishop have seen it in you. You must retain that grace in all situations. I believe your grace comes from above and that you are like Simon in that way. You must certainly know that this world will not always provide justice, but that it will come in the next world. You know that the two of you must stand up for charity, for those who are the least among us, for justice, and for what is right, in the spirit of Christ."

"I can tell you have more for me."

"Adam Marsh told me that now would be the time that I should take Rocco Tzu and his family someplace safe. He is quite old now, and it is likely that he would meet an unfortunate end in the coming struggle. Neither you nor the earl would want that. He will live out the rest of his days with his English family."

"We are all rather old, sir."

"You do not look old. You are in your early fifties, but you look many years younger, even though few women live to be your age. Your lord is also still very fit and strong at only three years older than you. Rocco is at least eight years older than the earl, and he is near his end. I suggest that you have some moments with him before he leaves with me. I know you also bear a great love for him as he does for you."

"Though it pains me, I again recognize the truth of what you say. I will do as you say. And I will ask no question."

"To any question you might ask about all of this, there is only one answer, and you know it," he said.

She settled into her chair and looked directly at the man, sadly and prudently, before she spoke.

"Love is the answer."

THIRTY-ONE

Pauline still wore her blue dress and had brushed her hair when she went to see Simon at the oak room in the tower of Kenilworth Castle. She also wore a sort of spiritual clothing underneath comprised of her understanding of her role in coming events, as it had been strengthened in her resolve by the words of Adam Marsh as conveyed to her by Roger Bacon. But it was also composed of a stronger substance, the bond of understanding that she and Simon de Montfort had always shared. It would soon no longer be the time for contemplation but for action. She knew no one was more suited for that task than Simon. She also understood that when that happened, he would become a force of nature, and her role as advisor would at once become more difficult and more important.

"If all leave me," he said, "I shall remain loyal to the true cause that I have sworn to defend for the honor of the Church and for the good of the kingdom."

"Have we had other defections?" she asked.

"Roger de Mortimer and Roger de Leybourne have fled. I have sent my son, Henry, west in pursuit of Leybourne with a small force of Welsh archers and some of our English knights."

"Mortimer and Leybourne are marcher lords, tasked with guarding the English lands on the border with Wales. They cannot like that the Welsh have decided to act against King Henry now that there may be a civil war. Do you think it wise to send your son in pursuit?"

"Trust has become a valuable commodity in these times. I trust my sons. I have also sent Simon the Younger with a force to the east in pursuit of Mortimer."

"We both know you can trust your sons, but Henry is twenty-five and Simon is twenty-three. While they are strong adult men, they have not had the military experience you had at those ages, which is to say they have had none."

"That is of little matter. I will remain here with the bulk of our army and will await word from them and will go in support of them if needed," he said.

"No," she said. "We will ride to London with your main force."

Simon stopped, grew quiet, and looked at Pauline for several moments.

"I have always known you to be direct," he said, "but when have you taken an interest in learning the ways of war?"

"I am not sure if you are jesting with me now. I have learned from you, Simon. And you have always been my sole interest. For thirty-eight years I have listened to your tales of war, Lord Hair Shirt. I may know more about it than many other men."

"I do see that going to London makes sense. The king will have to go there eventually, and it may be better to be provisioned and rested, and to wait for him there, where we will be on the defense. The barons who are loyal to me still hold London and the ports. It might be best to strengthen our hold on London."

"The men of London are also in support of your cause, which is the just and right cause, and is in the interest of the commoners. We will also be able to strengthen your force with the militia of London."

"But what of Henry and young Simon?" he asked.

"You have said that you trust them."

Since Pauline had come to England and been part of the de Montfort house, she had been exposed to displays of which she could never have dreamed when she was a common girl in Languedoc. The royal wedding had been one such spectacle. She had seen two royal courts in full regalia, but nothing had prepared her for the ride to London. They moved with five or six thousand men, including carts for weapons, food, and supply. There were a few hundred heavily armored knights on armored draft horses, with their lances, swords, and shields. All were from the noble families and it showed in their colorful garb and in their bearing. There were three or four times as many other horsemen and light cavalry recruited from the wealthy commoners. These men carried lances, javelins, bows, and crossbows. The bulk of the army consisted of soldiers, some mercenary and others recruited from the farmers and workers of the land. They carried maces, pikes, swords, and axes. There were separate sections of them that were armed only with bows, and a few others armed with crossbows. These soldiers ranged from many fit and equipped men to others who were little more than a rabble. There were some women in the supply train and several others who simply followed the force on foot. Pauline had changed out of her dress, had cut her hair to the length of a page, and had donned the garb of a light cavalryman, with her own sword and a small shield across her back. Simon had assigned her a small corps of guards, also of the light cavalry. She finally had a sense of the romance men had seen in going to war. Her every sense was alert, and she felt her heart bend to the music of the procession.

The romance wore off whenever they had to stop for the night. Tents were pitched for many of the knights and for the leaders. But most of the men slept on the ground. It also turned into what may have been expected of any large convocation of men. There were fights and swearing and personal displays she had never imagined or hoped to see. Some of the men visited the women who had been following. There was also some drinking and a good deal of singing. And there was always the smell of men and their leavings.

It all improved when they reached London. The burgesses, merchants, and people of London thronged to welcome Simon. They saw him as the man who stood for the principles of some local self-government, for the uniformity of the rule of law and its enforcement, and for the rights and liberties of all Englishmen against the domination of the king and the nobles. It was not difficult for him to extract food, provisions, and lodging for his men, though most of them still bedded down in the open spaces of the town. It was even reported to Simon that a move had been earlier afoot to take control of the town from his deputation of nobles. He arrived just in time to put a stop to that. He had been correct to follow Pauline's advice. They only needed now to await reports from the country regarding the movements of Simon's sons and of the royal forces.

The reports were not good. Henry de Montfort had pursued Leybourne to Worcester but had been unable to take Worcester Castle. He had turned south to join his father in London when he found the small force with Prince Edward and managed to trap them against the walls of Gloucester. He was confused about what to do. He had been in pursuit of Leybourne. He had not expected to confront the prince, who then called for a meeting. Henry de Montfort granted his cousin a truce and returned to Kenilworth. Edward immediately broke the truce, took the town of Gloucester, left William de Valence to ravage the countryside, and marched to join King Henry, who had arrived at Oxford with his loyal barons and their soldiers. Henry de Montfort was cut off from the Welsh archers of his supporting army, who had retreated into the countryside. Edward had also taken many prisoners from Gloucester, which was sore news for Gilbert de Clare, the young Earl of Gloucester and Simon's ally.

Simon the Younger had fared even less well. He had driven Mortimer and his small force ahead of him and had entered Northampton. King Henry and the royal army had reached the town the following day, in early April of 1264, and promptly besieged it. King Henry's force was repulsed. But one morning soon after, the prior of St. Andrew's guided some royal troops in scaling the walls of the priory, who then entered the town and fought to open the gates and let in the royal army. Young Simon and his men fought valiantly but lost. Simon the Younger was taken prisoner. The royal troops were then able to devastate the lands and country of another area that was loyal to Simon. These royal successes added to the ranks of the king.

Simon immediately rushed to the aid of his sons but was checked at St. Albans by a report that King Henry had reached an agreement with the leaders of the other four towns of the Cinque Ports, while the fifth, Dover, was still in the control of forces loyal to Simon de Montfort. Queen Eleanor was mounting reinforcements in France and there were now ports, other than Dover, where they might land. Simon wheeled east to Rochester, on the road from London to both these ports, and smashed the royal resistance at that town. He pillaged supplies and money from the royalist leaders of that town, left a garrison, and effectively blocked the roads from the other Cinque Ports to Dover. He returned to London. There, he rested his men and resupplied. He also mustered the London militia and conferred with his supporting barons. The army of King Henry and Prince Edward marched south and took Winchelsea, another smaller port town forty miles southwest of Dover, giving the possible French reinforcements of Queen Eleanor a place to disembark if and when they sailed.

Not waiting until those French troops might arrive, Simon took his entire force south on May 6 to meet the royal army. Six days later, they arrived at the small town of Lewes, on the banks of the

River Ouse, where the king had taken refuge in the castle. Under the seal of the two earls, Simon de Montfort of Leicester and Gilbert de Clare of Gloucester, they sent a message of truce to the king, seeking to negotiate a settlement, keeping in place all the reforms of the Provisions of Oxford and Westminster, granting amnesty to all combatants, and allowing the king to rule under the tutelage of parliament. The answer came back in the negative. It also included formal challenges to de Montfort and de Clare from Prince Edward and his uncle Richard, now the King of Germany, who had traveled to join his brother and nephew.

Pauline watched as the preparations were made for battle. She knew that the two armies were roughly the same size, at several thousand men, with the London militia being an additional strength on Simon's side. Simon's forces were rested, while the king's army had fought several battles across the Midlands and southern England. They had also been constantly harassed by the Welsh archers who had withdrawn at Worcester but had then traveled on the periphery of the royal army. The two armies were drawn up in battle order on May 14. Simon had split his own troops in three and had placed two large parts on either side of the London militia, which was posted in the middle on a hill commanding the plain west of the town and river. Simon held his own group in reserve. Pauline was in this reserve.

She had an idea, and she rode to confer with Simon. Then she and her guard grabbed the standards and colors of the Earl of Leicester, rode to the center with them, and planted them on the hill with the London militia. She rode to Gilbert de Clare, on one side of the battle line, and took his standards and colors, and carried them to the militia on the hill in the center. Her surmise had been correct, but too quickly effective. The sight of Simon's standards had been enough for Prince Edward. He was flush from his previous victories and immediately attacked, arriving at the center exactly when Pauline and her guards did. His charge of knights and light cavalry was a fearsome sight. The men of London held, but not for long. Soon Pauline was in the middle of a melee. She rode around and rallied certain segments of the militia, but most of them broke into an unruly retreat. Edward and most of his troops took off after them in an equally disordered pursuit.

Pauline and her men and some portion of the emboldened militia stood and fought. She stayed in the center of her group. Now, she saw the true horror of war. Nothing could have prepared her for it, as she watched men be cut, stabbed, bludgeoned, and shot, men who had served her and men she had known. There was an awful smell of blood in the air, and the sound of clashing steel and neighing horses was accompanied by the shouts of the combatants and the screams of wounded and dying men. She was soaked in perspiration and filled with fear. Still, she soldiered on and soon there were very few of her side remaining. Then a royalist cavalryman rode hard at her. She braced herself, rapidly climbed off her horse, and stabbed him as he rode by. He rode off with her sword in him and fell to the ground. She was now unarmed and on her feet. A royalist soldier approached her with his mace. She held on to her shield with both hands and parried the first blow, but he struck again. This time, she gave way and stumbled backward and fell to one knee. She held up her shield again as the mace came crashing down and the shield struck her head so hard that she lost consciousness.

When she awoke, her head ached, and she was thirsty. She asked for water and some was given to her. Her vision was blurry, and her concentration was lacking. She tried to get up from where she lay but could hardly move. She tried to look around as her vision slowly returned. She was in a large room of an abbey, and there were wounded men all around. Other men were attending them. Then she was not sure, but she thought she saw an old man sitting near her who looked unusual. He appeared to be very weathered. He had straight gray hair, a broad nose, and a wide face with narrow eyes.

He looked worried as he watched her. She thought she saw a hint of a smile on his face, and for an unknown reason, she suddenly felt almost happy. She then made an inventory of all her parts. They registered present. She had blood on her and felt herself to determine it was not her own. Then there was a general commotion as Simon de Montfort entered the room. He crossed the room and kneeled beside her. He had tears in his eyes.

"What took you so long?" she whispered, recalling an earlier, similar meeting.

He smiled.

"I am so glad to find you alive," he said. "I had received reports of how bravely you had fought and that you had fallen. I was filled with remorse for ever letting you join us, and for sending you on that errand."

"I think it must have worked," she said.

"Yes. Prince Edward lost his composure and charged when he thought I was in the center. He took himself and his men out of the battle, chasing the men of the London militia."

"Then we did not lose," she said.

"Edward left his father and his uncle with a fatigued force of then outnumbered men. They were also without their center and were disorganized. We swept down on them and surrounded them. They fought fiercely at first but soon gave way and tried to flee. Many were killed or surrendered. When Edward returned, his men saw what had happened and they fled. We pursued them and many of them were killed or captured."

Pauline cried; then she cried some more, only to stop herself short. Men were surely crying near her, but she realized her sobs were more feminine.

"So much death," she said. "Will I recover?"

"You will," he said. "You are alive, and life has a way of moving forward."

"How did that come to be? How did I survive? I was certain I would not."

"You were saved as you always have been. Here is Rocco Tzu. He arrived at exactly the right moment with some guards he picked up in Leicester."

Here, she began to cry again, this time quietly. Rocco came over and kneeled next to her and took her hand silently.

"You should rest," Simon said. "I will return to get you."

"But the battle, how did it all end?" she asked.

"We captured Richard, the King of Germany, the king's brother, and Prince Edward, and King Henry. We also recovered my son Simon the Younger. Now we must decide what to do with our captives. I am going with our other barons now, to meet with them and reach a settlement that will end all of this. But I had to come here first, to see the brave rider of the center who held ground and fought courageously."

"Then go," she said. "My head is ringing, and mostly from the ludicrous things you say."

"I am not finished yet," he said, leaning down. "I owe it all to you, you know, all of it, from the first day to the last. And so does England."

THIRTY-TWO

For the previous three years, the barons of the reform movement had been divided and had been diminished. The king and his allies had rolled back the hard-won Provisions of Oxford and Westminster. He had restored his foreign relatives to positions of power. He had forged a truce and an alliance with the French. He had obtained the Pope's support for all he had done. In the space of several hours, Simon de Montfort and the allied barons had reversed the events of those three years and had captured the king, his son, and his brother. Now, Henry III was a prisoner with little option other than to agree to the terms that would be dictated by his conqueror.

At the meeting following the Battle of Lewes, the king was distracted and confused. Prince Edward steamed with resentment but also showed great fear of his uncle Simon. Only Richard, King of Germany and Earl of Cornwall, the king's brother, had a grasp of the situation.

"We are at your mercy, good brother Simon," Richard said, "and certainly the love you bear our sister and your loyalty to your king will bring you to deal with us fairly and justly."

"I cannot do otherwise, Your Majesty," Simon said, "and I well remember when you and I fought beside one another in the Holy

Land. I am not your enemy. I stand here in greater love for our brother, our king, than you know. I only fight the enemies of England. And I bring the king a framework by which to make England stronger, and to patch up the strife we have faced for so long, and which has boiled over on the fields of battle today."

"We had the best army ever, the best," King Henry said. "It is all your fault. You have persecuted me, persecuted. Sad. I have done more for England than any king ever has. Everyone will tell you that."

"What my brother means to say, Simon, is that he recognizes the righteousness of your claim and sees that it was reflected in your victory," Richard said.

"He means to kill us," Edward said.

"Be quiet, nephew. You do not know the earl, our brother, as we do," Richard said.

"I only wish to restore the constitution that ensures the rights and liberties of the English people, the nobles, and the Church," Simon said. "I will serve the king once we are in agreement on that."

"Good," Henry said. "I agree. I will sign whatever you want. I will be the best, most loyal, most hard-working king anyone has ever seen. It could be great. It could be better than that. We'll all see."

Richard looked at his brother, paused, and looked at Simon while speaking to Henry.

"I am sure, brother Henry, that the earl has more on his mind than merely having you swear to uphold the Great Charter and the Provisions of Oxford and Westminster. After all, you have sworn to uphold them before."

"Several times," Simon said.

"I believe you will say that there will have to be assurances," Richard said, "and that they will have to be very grave ones at that."

"The barons of the reform party must hold those assurances in hand, in the persons of my nephews, Prince Edward and your son, Prince Henry of Germany."

"We have a deal, then," said Henry. "Let us move on."

"Father," Edward sighed.

"You won the battle, Simon," Richard said. "You already hold us all as assurances. We are here at your sufferance, and I believe you already hold my son prisoner. Will you let my brother and I go?"

"Yes," said Simon. "And when you go, Your Majesty, you will go back to Germany on a pledge never to return under arms. And the king will go under several pledges, and not only to uphold the Great Charter and the Provisions of Oxford and Westminster."

"This much seems reasonable. You are the victor," Richard said.

"The king must release his foreign relatives from any positions of importance in the kingdom or in his household. They may stay in England, but they may bear no arms and they may hold no offices. There must be a general amnesty for all who fought on the side of the barons. The churches and parishes must be restored. Parliament will determine the appointments of all the major and minor offices and will determine revenues and expenditures. Parliament will meet regularly with or without the king's call. The king's person will be supervised by a new small Privy Council of three: the Earl of Gloucester, the Bishop of Chichester, and myself. We will create a larger council of nine, and they will direct the matters of the major offices, including those of chancellor, treasurer, and justiciar, as well as the determination of what is to be done with the castles in the kingdom. Additionally, the Provisions of Oxford and Westminster will be reformed and strengthened. This will all be contained in what will be called the Settlement of Lewes, and it will be issued across the kingdom. The king will also sign the Provisions and they will again be posted in every town."

"Totally absurd," Henry said. "Am I not king? I am king. What is all this? I won't have it. Nonsense."

"This is for your good, Your Majesty," Simon said. "It will heal the divisions that have plagued England. And you may rule a unified kingdom."

"I am England," Henry said.

"So you are, Henry. So you are," Richard said. "And you will still be King of England. If you only look at it closely, you will see our brother Simon is being quite generous. We have lost to him in battle. We would not have been so magnanimous with him, had we won."

"I believe we have settled it here, then," Simon said.

"I believe we have," Richard said. "What do you say to Simon, brother?"

"I agree," Henry said.

"Then I will leave you all," Simon said. "My men will come for Edward later. And before that, the proclamations will be brought here for the king to sign."

"Farewell, then, Simon," Richard said. "And good health to you."

Simon bowed and left the room to meet with his baron allies, to tell them the results of the negotiations, and to take care of the arrangements. After he had left, it was Prince Edward who spoke first.

"We will not be assurances," he said. "We will be hostages."

"You should thank the earl you are still alive," Richard said. "You certainly set out to get yourself and the rest of us killed when you launched your independent charge against the forces of a man who has more military experience than you can imagine. You were thoughtless and selfish, and it is high time that you began to behave differently. This situation may not last. You may one day be king. And you had better have learned from all this."

"I have learned we should have killed him a long time ago," Edward said.

"No good king kills his best man. And if you cannot see that is what the earl, your uncle, is, then I will weep for England for longer than I already have."

"But what he proposes is worse than that. He has made himself king."

"He has most decidedly not done that," Richard said. "William the Conqueror, our ancestor, made himself king when he defeated King Harold in battle. Simon is equally the conqueror here and has left your father to be king."

"I am the king," Henry said.

"That is the point, dear brother. And as king, you will be a rallying point for all the barons who still support you. You have been beaten but not disarmed, not in the least. Were I Simon, I would have taken you and Edward hostage and made myself regent. Another man would have killed you both and made himself king. We have lost to him, but we owe a great deal to Simon de Montfort. Think of what you would have done had we defeated him."

"I would have his head on a pike," Edward said.

"It is so unfair," Henry said.

"It is more than fair," Richard said. "It is so fair as to be almost foolish. As I said, you live."

Edward thought for a second. "I am beginning to see, Uncle. Some of those rebel lords have been on both sides already. Many of them have ancestral grievances against one another. And others are aligned with our supporters by blood and by marriage. We also have my mother, the queen, who is still in France. She is sister to the French queen, and the French may be of assistance to us yet."

"Now you are thinking more sensibly, nephew. You must continue to do that."

"I will, Uncle."

"Good. But also remember now that Simon de Montfort is the best man in all of England. And that may be his weakness. Those squabbling lords may grow envious or resentful. It is one thing for them to maintain their fealty to the king, and another entirely for them to stand by their equal who is also their master."

They walked to a far corner of the room. Richard set his hand on Edward's shoulder.

"I am glad to see you have settled down and have started to think. It all rests on you now," Richard said.

"How do you mean?"

"Your father is not going to like this one bit. He is going to chafe at it. And it will get worse. Writs will be sent in his name, under his seal. Offices will be staffed by men not of his choosing. He will not have full freedom of his person. He has never known anything like this. He will not handle it well."

"He is not managing it well even now, Uncle."

"It is entirely up to you, then. You have grown up in all this. You have seen your father's mistakes. You have known nothing but this struggle for some independence that the barons have been mounting. You will be able to adapt. You can learn, and you can and must be the one who understands what is going on."

"I will do as best I can, Uncle."

"You will need to do as best you can and always think first. Can you promise me that?"

"Yes, Uncle. I promise."

"When the time is right, you will have to make a move. Your father will not know when that may be or what to do. It all depends on you now. We are in a very precarious time. I believe England will never return to the way it was, unless with some of the changes Simon de Montfort seeks. But right now, something can happen, and the king can regain most of his authority. Or this way of being will take hold and Simon de Montfort will grow accustomed to ruling and he will consolidate his authority."

"How will I know, Uncle, when the time is right?"

"You have promised me you will think first. If you are steadfast in your commitment, you will know when that time has come. I want you to know that for all intents and purposes, you are the king now. You have to think like the king I hope you will be one day."

"Thank you, Uncle. I am honored."

"There is one other thing," Richard said.

"What is that?"

"We are in this trouble because you underestimated that man who was in this room with us a few minutes ago. You must swear you will never do that again."

"I do."

"Swear."

"I swear on my mother's life I will never underestimate Simon de Montfort."

THIRTY-THREE

Simon's victory was more complete than he could have imagined. He had been prepared for a long struggle and some difficult negotiations. But now he was effectively the ruler of England. He was the leader of a confederation of nobles who had stood up for their rights and the rights of other Englishmen against a king. They were the embodiment of the principles of the Great Charter and the Provisions of Oxford and Westminster. There would be a parliament and councils, which he would lead. This time, the king could not undo any of what had been done. His son and nephew were hostages. The king himself would be subject to the control of three men, two of Simon's best allies and himself. They would rule in the king's name. There would be local control of local matters. The barons would have a say in all matters. The independence of the Church would be restored. English common law would stand above the whims of the king. Henry had always been weak, and now he would be under control. Simon felt that he was now in a place to do what he had once promised Pauline, that he would do the most good for the most people. It was Pauline who was in his mind now. Specifically, it was something she had said to him and had said more than once. She had always told him to be careful what he wished for.

Pauline had spent the last ten days at Leicester Castle being nursed by Rocco. In truth, she spent more of her time and effort looking after this old friend, now in his sixties, but still honest and loyal and good. Her thoughts often turned to Simon and specifically to the exalted but perilous position in which he now found himself. She was acutely aware that he saw the world through the lens of his own heart and was therefore too good to expect the worst in people. While she loved him for that, she also knew that his view of the world and its inhabitants was a narrow one, and that her duty to him was to open that view to the possibilities that would not occur to him naturally. She also often thought of his pledge to her to do his best for the most people, and she thought a great deal about what she knew Simon had often discussed with her and with Adam Marsh and Robert Grosseteste, who had been Bishop of Lincoln: that there should be a government for the souls and for the bodies of the people of England, a rule of law that would protect the rights and liberties of the people, and give the Church in England a certain and assured independence from Rome.

She also received a visit from Richard de Havering, who was very solicitous of her injury and of her.

"It was not all that much," she said. "My head was not quite right for a while, but I am well."

"Your head, I can tell, is very much where I believe your heart always was, riding at the side of the earl."

"I hope you can forgive me, Richard."

"There is nothing to forgive. You have left me much better than you found me, and in every way. And I would not trade my time with you for anything."

"I am glad you are so generous and gracious. Or perhaps you were always merely being ambitious."

"Please think it is the latter."

"With that statement, you prove it is the former. You will always have my respect and admiration."

"And you will always have my love. You have given me your love too, in a way, from the moment you decided to give me work, all the way through until you kindly let me go, and suggested I start my own family. I believe I will find my way, but you will always be first in my heart."

Before the end of May of 1264, Pauline bade farewell to Rocco but not before she extracted from him a promise that he would return to Roger Bacon and the Diocese of Lincoln and not come running after her again. He so promised, but only on the provision that she would remain out of danger. Despite that, she decided to make the trip to London on her own. The dangers she apprehended were not to be found on the road, and they principally applied to the earl.

Pauline was at that age, and perhaps she also knew that she was at a certain point approaching the destiny she shared with Simon de Montfort, at which she felt a renewed appreciation for the world around her. She had ridden the roads to London, the Fosse Way and Watling Street, which had once been Roman roads, many times in the previous years. It was a four- or five-day ride of a hundred miles that passed through rolling hills of fields and forest for most of the journey until it passed over a higher and more thickly forested rise before descending to the valley of the River Thames and to London at its estuary. She passed through many small towns and even more farms, most of which held sheep. Some old and hidden memory of hers was triggered and she saw the ways in which this landscape was different from the land of her birth. She had felt England to be cold and colorless in comparison to her Mediterranean land when she had arrived. Even now, she knew that the Midlands around Leicester and on the way to London were unprepossessing and nothing about them was dramatic or caught the eye. But now she saw it simply as more pleasing and attractive than Occitania. And above all, it was verdant. There were many shades of overwhelming green, all rich and welcoming. She loved this land now.

Pauline knew that the first and most obvious problem was France. Henry's wife, Queen Eleanor, was still there. Her attempt to land the army she had raised had been thwarted, and the army had disbanded. But she was still a threat, largely because she would urge Louis IX and his queen, her sister, to do what France could to reverse Simon's gains and restore Henry III to absolute power. Pauline had several ideas that might work to stem this preeminent threat. The Pope in Rome was at a greater distance and had no army, but he still had the power to excommunicate and could attempt to rally the English clergy against Simon. There were fewer options to counteract this, but Pauline knew that Simon had many friends in the English churches. There were some things that could be done to draw a line of defense against the Pope. These were the principle foreign pressures that she saw, but Simon had also been too lenient in allowing the king's alien relatives to stay in England and they could become a problem at any moment. There were also imminent threats within the kingdom, and while she believed that Simon saw the foreign problems quite clearly, these were the ones he was more likely to overlook or to underestimate.

The marcher lords on the Welsh border were still at large. The failure of Simon's sons to deal with them had yet to be corrected. They stood as a potential problem, but again this was something with which Simon was equipped to deal. The larger problem was the coalition of barons itself. They had achieved their goal in the victory at Lewes, and that struggle had united them, such as those who had remained loyal. The matter of a battle for their rights, and in fact their survival, was a powerful endeavor that had held them together. Now that they must assist Simon to govern, the old rivalries and machinations would surely arise. Simon would need a plan to hold them united and to broaden and deepen his support. Her primary idea here was that Simon could do well by doing good. If he expanded participation in the government to the burgesses, minor nobles, merchants, and townsmen, he might strengthen his base while also providing the barons with incentive from within their towns and lands to continue their support of the alliance and of Simon.

She was concerned about young Gilbert de Clare, Earl of Gloucester. His father, Richard de Clare, and Simon had had their few differences, but the late earl had been bound to Simon by a bond of blood because they had fought alongside one another at Royan. Richard had been at his first military conflict then, and he had been frightened by King Henry's capricious and irrational leadership of that expedition until the Earl of Leicester had arrived and saved them all. Young Gilbert did not share his father's bond with Simon. He was the same age as Simon's sons. And one of Simon's sons, Henry, the king's godson and namesake, had made the mistake that had led to the sacking of Gloucester, Gilbert de Clare's county seat. There was bound to be some rivalry between the earl and Simon's sons, and some bad feelings for them.

King Henry could never be reliable. Even with his son and nephew as Simon's hostages, and even after his loss at Lewes, he was still volatile and unpredictable. A larger issue was Prince Edward, who now had some experience in war and in statecraft, and who burned with ambition. He also knew that his own future was hanging in the balance. And then there was Simon's blindness to the matter that Adam Marsh had long since identified and which Roger Bacon had conveyed, Simon's sons. In one important way, they bore the same relationship to the earl that the king's foreign relatives had to the king. It had all been a little too easy for them. They were now essentially unofficial princelings, and they may not be measured in their responses to Simon's successes. They had their mother's blood and had been raised by her. They had not been raised as had Simon, in war, and in stern duty to his father, brother, and the Church Simon's mother had ardently supported. They had already demonstrated some of their shortcomings.

Simon was happy to see Pauline when she arrived. He was in a room at Westminster Hall. He had been preoccupied, but he set that aside to welcome her and to express his thanks that she had recovered.

"You look well," he said.

"Well enough to be worried," she said. "What have you done, Simon. Do you know? Have you possibly been able to understand it?"

"I see we are to get right to the pulling and hauling."

"There is more than enough of it to be done. We have landed in a spot where too much work must be done, and I am sure you are capable. I just do not know if you can see all that there is to do."

"I am more buoyed by your impertinence than I am by your apparent health. I can tell you are fully recovered. I am reminded again of how well you look in a dress. But nothing is as pleasing to me as to know I will again have your good counsel," he said.

"What have you done about France?"

"I have sent word to all the castles and towns to be on the ready. I have closed the ports to French woolens and cloth, to avoid France getting a direct payment of money from England. And I have sent a notice, under the seal of King Henry, that France should desist in any plan they may have to interfere in English affairs."

"I am sure they will see through that," she said. "They will know it comes from you. The Settlement of Amiens still hangs over us. In that, the King of France has declared his decision that King Henry must have the absolute power of a king. He is on record opposing everything you have accomplished."

"I am aware of that."

"It is time again, then, to submit ourselves to the decision of the King of France."

"That is foolish," he said, "as that is what led to the Settlement of Amiens in the first place."

"That is exactly correct," she said, "and by agreeing again to mediate this matter, King Louis will necessarily be admitting that he is setting aside the Settlement of Amiens and seeking to generate a new agreement."

"I see it now."

"Only this time, we will not make the same mistake. You will propose some arbiters, a certain number each, from England and France. And Henry will not travel to Paris this time either. We will turn their own lance against them by giving them the sop of pointless negotiation while you maintain the power. You will make sure that the negotiation will drag on, and you will then govern without the Settlement of Amiens hanging over you."

"Perhaps the best part of this idea," he said, "is that it will keep the fractious Henry attending to the possibility that he will be saved by France. We can even send him to Dover with our arbitrators to attend our side of the negotiations, which will proceed very slowly by boat messenger. He will be out of the way there. And since his relatives are there, waiting to depart for France if I should come after them, they will stay put around him and will also stay out of the way."

"I had not thought of that, but it makes perfect sense."

"I am glad that the blow to your head has not made you think any less clearly. I must tell you that having you here makes me feel whole again."

"My original advice was to have been that you take your sword to both King Henry and to Prince Edward and make yourself king."

"You jest again. You would never recommend I take a life."

"Neither of us would want that. So, it is now a much more difficult riddle to solve. With the two of them alive, you will never have any rest. We must always be vigilant."

"But this is an excellent stratagem, one that will be of great assistance. We still have the problem of the Pope in Rome. He is no longer receiving the funds that Henry was sending to purchase the crown of Sicily for his second son, Edmund. That succession is now in disorder. And we have no stratagem that I know that can be used to delay or distract the Pope," he said, turning to her.

"Maybe not, but the English clergy has always been independent."

"Many of the leaders, the bishops, and prelates are tied to Henry by blood and fealty, though many of them are on our side."

"But even those prefer England and Henry to receiving dictates from Rome," she said. "You have many friends among the Church leadership, but as you look down in the ranks, to the younger and the less established clergy, they are almost entirely among your partisans."

"Then we will call a council of the clergy of England. Under the king's seal, we will guarantee them certain rights, to their property and to their ability to determine their own affairs, and to their freedom from oppressive levies from either the crown or from Rome. We will also have them reorganize, to give the lesser clergy more of a say in the matters of the Church and more of an opportunity to advance. This is precisely what the late Bishop of Lincoln and Adam Marsh would have wanted. And it will serve our purpose of expanding the example of involvement in governance to those below the highest level."

"The Pope may still excommunicate you. This new Pope is not like Pope Gregory, the one with whom you had a good friendship."

"He is not even like Pope Innocent, the one who came after Gregory, and whom I had helped when he was in exile in Lyon. The next Pope after Gregory, Pope Alexander, condemned the Provisions of Oxford and Westminster. Pope Urban IV will not be any different than he was."

"You should hear yourself, Simon," she said. "You have had such a life, and you have succeeded and risen by manner of your virtue and your skill. You are all that I thought you were from the beginning."

He took a long look at her.

"I see, Pauline, that you are now diverting from the great deal of work we have here at hand. It was not by me alone."

"What do you plan to do about the marcher lords of the Welsh borderlands, Roger de Mortimer and Roger de Leybourne?"

"Have you not heard me, Pauline?"

"There has always been so much between us that goes without saying. We may want to keep it that way."

Simon had reached that age, and perhaps he also knew that he was at a certain point approaching the destiny he shared with Pauline, at which he felt a renewed appreciation for the world around him, and for the woman who was so much of that world. He only smiled.

THIRTY-FOUR

There was much that remained to be discussed. Simon told Pauline of his actions against Roger de Mortimer and Roger de Leybourne, who had no other resources beyond their lands and men. Simon had dispatched forces that had pursued them and had cornered them in their estates on the Welsh borderlands. In the name of the king, he demanded hostages, which they had supplied. He said he had sent another contingent in pursuit of the king's foreign relatives, principally William de Valence, who had taken Pevensey, a small town on the southern coast. Simon's second son, Simon the Younger, oversaw this contingent and failed to take Pevensey, giving William de Valence and his men an opportunity to sail for France. Simon's eldest, Henry, had been tasked to force the return of French wool to France but had seized that commodity and had put it up for sale himself. Pauline decided to keep her own counsel on these last two matters.

She had always been thoughtful, but at this point in her life and in the face of these momentous events, she found herself in an even more contemplative state. It was almost as if she could overhear her own thinking and she found herself plumbing to the depths of why she thought what she did. Her instinct had been to not challenge

343

Simon on the matter of his family. Obviously, that would be any person's instinct. But she could plainly see the problems that arose from Simon placing too much responsibility in the hands of his sons. And she had been warned of all this when Roger Bacon had reminded her of the conversation that she had with Adam Marsh on the topic of blood. It was also her duty to advise Simon. She wondered then why she had decided to remain uncharacteristically silent. Then it came to her. Her duty was not to Simon's mission to do the best that he could for the most of England. Her duty was to him as a soul. And her duty was to love, to the spiritual love they had long shared. And Simon loved his family. She would never do that harm. She could only serve Simon and the passion that he had for those he loved. But even as she considered all this, she worried that what Roger Bacon had said about Simon becoming a martyr might be brought about by her failure to speak firmly against Simon's sons.

She decided that her approach to the issue of Simon's sons would be to address it through remarks about the young Gilbert de Clare, Earl of Gloucester, who was their peer. She would use him by means of comparison and contrast. She would discuss the earl's ability as a way of shedding light on the sons. And she would stress his worthiness, and indirectly the possibility of his resentment at the favorable treatment of young Henry and Simon. And she had a plan to implement with Eleanor, their mother.

Simon's time was taken up by two recent developments. Richard, the King of Germany, had decided not to leave England but to submit himself as a hostage. He felt his presence in England, even as a hostage, would be more useful to his brother Henry and his nephew Edward. And he was encouraged toward this by Simon's leniency. This was a disconcerting change because it had always been unlikely that he would bring a force from the Continent but his presence and his advice and counsel would be of assistance to his nephew Edward, the royalists, and his brother, the king. Simon had to arrange for Richard's custody. And the marcher lords had stirred again, this time against the Welsh, who had allied themselves with Simon against the king. Simon would lead a large force to the borderlands, and he would expel the lords and give their castles to his partisans among the barons. It was clear that all the provisions Simon had made were built upon an unstable foundation. At every moment, he had to work to shore up all that he had done and take the steps necessary to improve his position.

Simon was also busy with prisoner exchanges, accepting the return of men captured by the royalist army and releasing his own prisoners, taken at Lewes and at various skirmishes. Under the king's seal, he also sent out any number of declarations of amnesty for all participants on either side. Pauline was left in London and took the opportunity to speak to Eleanor.

"How are you, my lady?" she asked respectfully.

Eleanor looked at her quizzically, wondering about this new tone. But then she waved a hand and seemed to Pauline to be a bit too tired to be suspicious.

"It is difficult for me to know," Eleanor said. "I am fearful and afraid sometimes. And other times I am exhilarated. Simon has risen to the highest point. His virtue has been recognized and his skill has been rewarded. But my brother appears to have been humiliated and he is not taking it very well. I just wish we could go back to the way it was."

Pauline recognized the fatigue in her voice, and something else. It was that she was resigned. She was not sure what might happen, but she was no longer the spirited young woman who would bridle against her circumstances.

"But that was never going to remain the state of things," Pauline said. "Too much was going wrong and your husband will never stand idly by when that is happening. His spirit is such that he is not like a man on a path, making choices of which way to go. He is more like a river that will forever flow one way, and in his case, it will always be toward what is right and what is good for the most people."

"I know you have always seen him that way. There are times when I see that as well. But he is also my husband, a man, and the father of our children. I do wish sometimes that he would just be those things. I wish he would think about me."

"I can certainly understand that," Pauline said, recognizing some flicker of the young Eleanor. "But we both know that if that were the case, he would not be the man he is. You might see him differently then."

"You are always so terribly sensible and direct. In any case, I have more concerns that pull me in different ways."

Pauline felt more solicitous now and walked closer and took a seat. Still, she did not lose sight of her purpose for this visit.

"How, then, are your sons?"

"I worry about them. They are still my boys and they have not been forged in the same fires as their father has. And suddenly the risks are so much higher, and they have been thrust into the middle of it all."

"You may be correct to be concerned, especially given that Simon the Younger was captured at Northampton," Pauline said softly.

"I could not sleep that whole time. I have never been so terrified. I have always been afraid, every time my husband went off to war. But he has ever been so capable. He was raised in war and grew up in battles. He knows them. My sons have not had that training. When the army of my brother took young Simon at Northampton, I felt that my worst fears had always been correct."

"You are correct to be afraid for them. Simon has had his efforts bedeviled by the fickleness of his allies, so he places a great value on trust. He knows his sons will never turn against him, so he places them in positions of trust. But you know that these times and these problems call for a vastly different kind of mettle. They require a harder temperament than your sons may have. Young Simon's error at Northampton was just such a mistake. He should have been far more vigilant and distrusting."

Pauline might not have been so direct, but she had been listening and watching. Eleanor was weary and she had admitted that much of that was from worrying about her sons. Pauline was trying to offer her a way to act on her anxiety, by suggesting that she might attempt to remove her boys from the thick of the conflict.

"I know," said Eleanor, "but I am not as you are. I have no concept of what to do about it. I am lost in these matters. I am also between my husband's need for lieutenants he trusts and the desire that my sons have to emulate their father and to play in the great game of war, which we both are old enough to know is no real game."

Pauline leaned forward and spoke softly.

"You must think of their safety. And you will not be able to persuade them that their personal security is paramount, so you must devise excuses to pull them off the front line. You may appeal to your husband for their protection, and perhaps you might impress upon him the need to spread the responsibility and the spoils more among his allies, even those he may not trust as much as he trusts his sons. He simply must see that. And I will make the same argument."

"I will try to remind my husband of that, as you say." And here, Eleanor's look hardened just for a moment, at the possibility that she had just been handled by Pauline. But she recognized the truth of all that had been said, and her look turned more to resolve. Pauline hesitated and then stood up and walked away, before she turned and offered her next comment.

"I think as well that you should take care for the safety of your two daughters and of your youngest son."

"You send a chill through my heart," Eleanor almost gasped. "What could you mean by that? The three of them are safe, here with me."

"I am sure that if you consult your heart, you must know that we are all in some danger. Your third son, Amaury, will be safe in the clergy at York. But the rest of your family is at risk. A great number of people in England and on the Continent do not wish your family well. I say this with regard to whether or not this all goes well or ill. If it goes well, there will still be unrest and division. If it does not, there will be an even greater danger."

"Please do not say such things. You terrify me."

"I am only here to help, and I must help you to see all that is possible so that you may take steps to protect your sons and daughters."

"I simply do not want to think of that. I don't."

Eleanor looked away and stared into the distance. Pauline took her time, walked around the room for a moment and then returned to her chair near Eleanor and spoke softly to her.

"I have thought of it. We all must. Your husband's older sister, Amicie, the Countess of Joigny in France, has built a convent. She has been active in support of the Church in Rome and is close to King Louis. I think that may be the safest place. You would all be welcome there."

"Please excuse me," Eleanor whispered. "I am quite beside myself now."

"That is all very understandable. I am sorry to frighten you. I only want you to be prepared."

Eleanor sat for a while, silently crying. After a few moments, she stood up and walked to the window. She looked out of it for several minutes while Pauline waited patiently. Eleanor then walked around the room for a few moments, her head down. Then she sat down again and spoke to Pauline.

"I guess I know you only want the best for our family. All you have said is what I have needed to hear. I will take what actions I may in this difficult time. I will send a letter to Amicie in Joigny. I will do what I can to remove Henry, Guy, and Simon the Younger from the fray. We both know I cannot change my husband, nor would either of us want to do so. And I know that you have done nothing but help him at every stage. You have done things for him I would never have been able to do. You have made sacrifices of your own in his service. And you have never caused a problem."

"I have done what I have for reasons that are not entirely altruistic, you must know. I have the highest regard for Simon de Montfort. I see that God has conferred upon him a spirit like very few others. He has always been destined for great things and for good works. I have served him and your family, not so much out of choice but because I could not have done otherwise."

"I have not always been as good to you as you have been to us."

"I know," Pauline said. "There is no need to talk about it, about any of it. I understand. And I have no ill feelings toward you." She paused. Eleanor looked at her and she showed a flush of realization and relief. And then her look softened toward Pauline, who continued.

"You were in love with Simon. You were young. You had the power. And you knew I had come over with Simon from France and had been in his household and that he had always shown me favor."

"You love him too, I know. I saw that then, but in a much different light. I have raised six children. I have loved them when they have not always returned my love. I have realized in being a mother that love should be its only reward, and should not be acquisitive or possessive, not if it is pure. I see now that you learned that about love when you were a mere girl."

"It is what I was taught to believe."

"I don't know anything about that. But I do believe you have always been of great assistance to my husband. My family and I have benefitted from that."

THIRTY-FIVE

In August of 1264, the Pope sent a legate to England, but he was denied passage and stayed in France. He ordered the English bishops of Lincoln, London, Worcester, Chichester, and Winchester, who had all been loyal to Simon and the barons' alliance, to come to France and confer with him and with the royalist bishops who had fled England. Simon would not let them depart. The legate then excommunicated Simon de Montfort, Gilbert de Clare, and all the other barons in their alliance. He had carried with him a papal bull that again declared that the Provisions of Oxford and Westminster were void, that the king must be returned to power, and that the hostages be released. He gave this declaration and the excommunication to some of the royalist bishops and sent them to England. They were met at the port by the soldiers of Simon the Younger. Their bags were searched, and the papal bull was shredded and thrown into the harbor.

One of the few royalist prelates remaining in England, the Bishop of Bath, attempted to proclaim the excommunication but was silenced and his property was confiscated. Simon and the bishops who were loyal to the alliance assembled a general church council in Reading and for the first time included the lower clergy. This council forged new rules for appointing bishops and abbots from within the Church and filled the posts that had been held by churchmen who had been opposed to the barons. The English Church, and particularly among the lower and middle ranks, was now solidly in the camp of the revolution. Under Simon's direction, it had established a significant increased independence from both Rome and from the king as well as a more democratic process for choosing its leaders.

This was a template for what Simon was to do next. He conferred with Pauline and related his ideas to her with great satisfaction. In order to expand upon the Provisions of Oxford and Westminster and expand and codify the principles of the Settlement of Lewes, Simon had devised an entirely revolutionary new parliament to undertake the work. Under the seal of the king, the articles of the Settlement of Lewes were dispatched to each county. Then the summons to parliament was sent to the lords and to the Church leaders who would normally attend. But for the first time ever, each county was to send a number of regular knights, and men of no noble birth but of enough property to serve in the army on horseback. Beyond that, again for the first time in history, the towns and boroughs were to elect their own representatives to send to parliament. In the notice of summons, the words declared to be from Henry III called upon these extraordinary measures to abate the unusual discord within the kingdom.

Many of these new representatives could not afford to make the trip to London, but for those who could, it was an exciting and novel experience. Merchants from York, burgesses from Bristol, minor nobles from rural Kent and Devon, mid-level clergymen from Nottingham, and dozens of others prepared themselves to take part in their government for the first time. It had been impossible for them to imagine anything like it before. Abbots and priors and the deans of cathedral congregations received a summons in the king's name asking them to attend parliament. Not only would these newcomers sit with the earls and the bishops, but this parliament was empowered to ratify and expand very real changes. They would be building a system of legal rights and liberties for all Englishmen and expanding on a constitution that would serve as a check on the absolute power of the king. The name of Simon de Montfort was on the lips and minds of all these participants. Perhaps of greater notice, the local people who did not attend but who had played a role in selecting these new representatives all felt for the first time as if they were participating in their government.

Perhaps most importantly, there was a cultural and social element to the membership of this great parliament. Since the time of William the Conqueror, two hundred years before, the king and his court, almost all of the major nobles, and almost all of the bishops, magistrates, and sheriffs had been Norman French. They had been appointed from the victorious forces that William had brought from Normandy. And their descendants had filled all the same roles. They were still the rulers of England. Most of the new participants in this parliament, the townsmen, merchants, burgesses, and the clergy of the lower levels were of Saxon descent. They did not understand French and very few of them would have known Latin. When Simon, seven years before, had the Provisions of Oxford and Westminster sent out across the kingdom in the English language, he had caused more than just a linguistic change. He had opened the operations of government to the understanding of the Saxon majority. Now, they were participating in their government for the first time and they would be doing so in English.

The parliament began its session in January of 1265. Some of the expected participants had yet to arrive, so under the king's name, additional summonses were sent. The parliament convened and then expanded local rule, established for the election of sheriffs by the men of the counties, and expanded the provisions for the English common law to be determinative in legal disputes. The appointment of only native English lords to the positions of officers of the court was ratified, and appointments to those various positions were approved. Full amnesty for all participants in the uprising of the previous year was approved. The Settlement of Lewes was ratified by the full parliament. All the items upon which the king and the alliance of barons had agreed after the defeat of the royalist forces at Lewes were put before this great parliament of commoners and nobles, and they were expanded and approved.

In February, King Henry III stood up before this great parliament. It was a new experience for all involved. It was the first time the king had been made to appear rather than having called a council to meeting. Never before had the parliament been so large or included townsmen and other common people. For most of this new parliament, these sessions almost took on a festive nature. Many of the participants were seen to congratulate each other and to marvel at the proceedings and at their involvement in them. Never more so than on this day, when the king swore before them all to support the general amnesty, to support the expanded Provisions of Oxford and Westminster and the Settlement of Lewes. The king also swore several oaths to never raise any accusations against the earls who had opposed him the year before. He swore by name. He also named the various clergy, the mayors, and citizens of the towns that had supported the alliance of barons, most especially the citizens of London. There was a general roar of approval and for a moment the king was pleased and did not retain his previous sense of humiliation. All of these declarations were to be taken back to the towns and counties, and upon local approval were to be posted with the seals of the local authority.

In the following weeks, Prince Edward came before the parliament and swore the same oaths and made the same declarations. He also proclaimed that he would live by the same restrictions when he became king. Like his father, King Henry, he also declared that if he failed to keep his sworn oaths, the citizens of the kingdom would be permitted to rise in revolt and would be forgiven for doing so. And if any noble or royal kinsman might seek to undermine the new regime, that person should have his lands and goods confiscated. Simon held the king and remained in possession of the king's royal seal, by which he could issue proclamations in the name of the king. Simon's eldest son, Henry, held Prince Edward as a hostage. Richard of Germany and his son, Prince Henry, were held by Simon the Younger. The despondent King Henry put all his hope in France and in his queen, who remained in France. The French continued in the prolonged negotiations with Simon's representatives, as Pauline had planned.

Pauline took additional steps to reduce the participation of Simon's son, Henry. She suggested to Simon that his wife, Eleanor, take over command of the Cinque Ports, on the southeast coast. Eleanor moved there with a considerable guard and her suite of servants. Pauline was among this retinue and had organized the move in advance. She had advised Eleanor's course of action for several reasons. Those ports were of critical importance as the most likely place where help from France might land. Henry de Montfort had stirred up unrest there by making various seizures and taking other harsh actions. Pauline also thought it would be helpful to place Eleanor nearer to the same ports from which she might depart for France if that were required. Eleanor swiftly improved matters for her husband and his allies by inviting the burgesses to the local castle and befriending them over dinners. And she did not seize goods in the ports. She purchased them. She also paid to arm the local militia and spared them that expense. When this had been done, Pauline returned to London.

Simon had yet to return from Wales, where he was meeting with chieftains of that Celtic people. The Welsh had remained separate from England and had never adopted feudal customs. They still lived as tribes, but one chieftain had forced many of the other tribal leaders to pay homage to him. There were only a handful of men with whom Simon would have to make an alliance, and their leader was Llewellyn of Griffith. The Welsh had long wanted control of their border and freedom from English incursions. Simon had promised them that. But what was most important was that he had deposed King Henry. Henry had earlier sent Prince Edward against the Welsh. Edward had seized certain Welsh domains and had attempted to force English institutions upon them, including English taxes. The Welsh had struggled against this up until the time of the Battle of Lewes. There was almost no question then that they would ally themselves with the Earl of Leicester.

Simon returned to London and to Pauline in May of 1265. He was in good spirits. They discussed the proceedings at parliament and the alliance with the Welsh. They talked about the composition of this first parliament with commoners and the restructuring of the English Church. They also discussed Henry and Edward, and how they had each sworn their support for the cause of the allied barons before the great parliament. Pauline was guarded in her remarks. Her primary concern at this point was Simon's spirit, the good he had done for so many, and the part of him that she had always been able to discern, the part that could not be seen with any eyes, perhaps except her own.

"I am most pleased," he said, "that I have been able to begin to live up to the pledge I made to you so many years ago. I have always felt the stain of the de Montfort family for what it had done to the people of Languedoc, done to your people. I promised then to do the most good for the most people. We have begun to give more people in England a voice in their own government. We have begun to establish a rational foundation for limiting the absolute power of the king, and a capricious king at that."

"You have always lived up to your pledge, Simon," she said. "You have lived your life according to those principles. Your soul has always been clean. You are blameless. You have risen to be the protector of the people of England. Whatever has happened in this physical world, you have lived your life well in the eyes of God."

"I know, Pauline, that by this point you would have offered your insights or, indeed, your criticisms. Your reluctance to speak openly is noted."

"I am happy for all the people of England, Simon. You have done them a great service. I don't think we could have ever anticipated any of this. You have exceeded all my greatest imaginings."

"So," he said, "you must certainly have an opinion about what should be done now."

"My opinion is what I have stated. You have done God's work in England."

"I see that you are evading me like a fox. Then allow me to suggest that you ask me some questions."

"I will, then," she said. "What do you propose to do about Gilbert de Clare?"

"He has ever been my ally and supporter in all of this. I could not have done it without him."

"Have you considered his age?"

"Of course I have. He is my sons' age. He is a good young man. He is his father's son. And his father was a great man and my brother-at-arms in more than one battle. Gilbert is as committed as Richard de Clare ever was to the cause for which they have each fought by my side."

"Gilbert is your sons' age, but he is not one of your sons. He is the Earl of Gloucester. Does he have the right to demand the respect that you showed his father?"

"I see what you are saying now."

"I am asking," she said, "not saying."

"Gilbert de Clare is still just a young man," Simon admitted. "And you may be correct. He and my son Henry have almost come to blows once, at a tournament. He may worry that I have given my sons more responsibility than is merited by their inferior positions, while he is the Earl of Gloucester, as you say."

"Do you think he sees himself as your equal?"

"That can't be."

"Is that so?" she asked.

"Of course, the answer is that he must see himself that way. He stepped into his father's title when Richard died. He has been steadfast in his opposition to the king. He is likely to see himself as being equal to his father. I was a young man once. I know how he must feel."

"Then how do you plan to begin to correct this situation?"

"I will have to begin to transfer more authority to him, some of the authority that now rests in my sons. That will make it quite clear to him. Young Simon is again at Pevensey, and Guy and Henry are also on missions. I will talk to them and I will make the changes."

"What would you do now to show the Earl of Gloucester your commitment?"

"I will immediately confer upon him the responsibility for guarding Prince Edward. That will show him my trust in him. And I will let him know of the rest. I will remain in charge of the king and his brother, Richard, and Richard's son, Prince Henry."

"You are a good man, Simon. You are more than that. You are a man of action. You are not satisfied with being good. You do more good works than any man in England or in Europe."

"I will continue to do what I can to make sure you see me that way. I am eternally grateful for your opinion, and today I am grateful for your questions. You have long been more to me than anyone. In your own way, you have done more than anyone I know."

The two of them did then what is only possible between true friends who love one another. They sat quietly together and did not speak. Simon thought of what must be done. And Pauline thought of what must be done. They were not thinking of the same things.

THIRTY-SIX

At this point, several of the foreign relatives of King Henry began to slip back into England. William de Valence had sailed past Dover and around southern England, to land at Pembroke. He began to stir up the old animosities of the English marcher lords on the Welsh borderlands. They were resentful of Simon's alliance with the Welsh. Soon the Welsh found themselves in conflict with Pembroke and the English border counties. They called for Simon's assistance. Gloucester was closest to the problem, so Simon sent word to Gilbert de Clare to ask him to quell this disturbance. No response came from Gloucester. Simon turned to Pauline for her assessment.

"I don't think it is a good sign," she said. "I have read in the Church's historical accounts that when Julius Caesar took power in Rome, he did not make himself the emperor. Instead, he attempted to rule as the first among equals. The greatest danger to him was from those who were closest to him. They resented his power and he acted as if he was still one of them. I believe that you are equally in that dangerous middle position, between being the ruler and attempting to govern among equals. I fear that the Earl of Gloucester may have abandoned you."

"But Gilbert de Clare is opposed to the return of the absolute power of the king."

"That may be true. But there has been some general unrest among the earls and the bishops because you have expanded the parliament to the men of the towns and countryside. The major nobles have fought to preserve their own rights, not to share those rights with the commoners. And the Earl of Gloucester has not been your equal in leadership or in military ability, but he has placed his name on every measure you have taken. He has been your equal in accepting the risk and the possibility of reprisals. He has thus demonstrated his opposition to the king. But he may feel that you have not recognized him properly for that."

"You said something before, about my sons. I think you implied that he resented them."

"I believe that may have been the second injury. The first blow to Gilbert was that you treated him like a young man and did not recognize him as an equal. Then you may have seemed to favor your sons, who are also young men."

"Then above all," he said, "we must deal with Gilbert de Clare. We will take the king and marshal the largest force we can, and then ride for Gloucester."

As they approached Gloucester several days later, it was clear that the Earl of Gloucester had taken up defensive positions. So, they rode around Gloucester, crossed the River Severn, and met with Simon's Welsh allies in the town of Hereford near the Welsh border. From there, Simon sent a messenger to Gloucester to offer to negotiate with Gilbert de Clare. Gilbert responded that he was unwilling to come to any agreement. He listed his grievances. They were as Pauline had predicted.

"It appears that this rift has been a long while in the making," she said. "It seems likely that Gilbert may have even encouraged the return of the king's relatives to this area, and that he may have encouraged his neighbors in the Welsh marches to antagonize your allies."

"I will send messages out under the seal of the king to attempt to pacify the marcher lords, to constrain the movements of the king's foreign relatives, and to raise more troops from England," he said.

The next two events occurred in rapid succession. King Henry, Prince Edward, King Richard of Germany, and his son, Prince Henry, were all essentially prisoners of Simon de Montfort. Simon had offered King Henry and Prince Edward to the Earl of Gloucester to hold as hostages, but they remained in the charge of Simon's eldest son, Henry de Montfort. The young Earl of Gloucester had broken with Simon before the hostages could be conveyed. Simon the Younger held King Richard and his son, Prince Henry. Though they were prisoners, they were still royalty. It could be said again that the de Montforts found themselves operating in what Pauline had called the precarious middle position. The royals were never imprisoned or in irons. They were granted significant freedom of movement and communication. They also had a certain number of retainers, so they always had to be guarded by a sizeable contingent of men.

Then Simon received word from his eldest son, Henry. Prince Edward had escaped. The news of this had no sooner reached Simon in Hereford than the next day he received a message from Gilbert de Clare.

The Earl of Gloucester declared that Prince Edward had now joined him. He also stated that Edward had sworn again to all the declarations of the great parliament of January through March, earlier that year. Gilbert de Clare reported that he had made the prince swear to uphold the Provisions of Oxford and Westminster, to banish the king's foreign relatives, and to subject his actions to the approval of parliament. The young earl proclaimed that he and Prince Edward would hold the king to his word to do the same. Gilbert declared that Simon was no longer needed and that the

Earl of Gloucester and the royals now stood against him together. Gilbert de Clare was twenty-three years old and had been the Earl of Gloucester only three years. Those three years had involved him in the struggle against the king and he felt slighted by Simon.

Pauline and Simon conferred. It was clear to them that the Earl of Gloucester had fallen into the same mistake that Simon had habitually made for many years, which was to believe the sworn oaths of the royals. King Henry had consistently broken those oaths. The only thing that had prevented that happening this one time was the fact that Simon had defeated the king in battle and had taken him, his son, his brother, and his nephew as hostages. Force alone had held the king to his word. Gilbert de Clare had just taken that constraint away and was again relying on the word of a royal, this time Prince Edward. The king would feel no compunction to break Edward's oath or even his own. He had done so many times.

Simon sent for his second son, Simon the Younger, who was in the southeast, and for the allied lords of Surrey, Sussex, and Dorset to come with young Simon to his father's aid. He also sent messages under the king's seal to apprehend Prince Edward. Pauline made certain he was under no delusion that Edward would now provide a rallying point for the dispersed royalist forces. There were already reports that there was a continuous flow of new men into the camps of Prince Edward and Gilbert de Clare. Within the space of just a few days, Simon and his army found themselves in a desperate position.

They were cut off from their supporters and lands in southern England. They were northwest of the Bristol Channel, which separates Cornwall and England from Wales and the western borderlands. The River Severn flows into the Bristol Channel and serves as an additional barrier. Gloucester sits on the river just above its entrance into the Bristol Channel. And the county of Gloucestershire surrounds both sides of the river and for several miles on each side of the channel. Gilbert de Clare held his county, and the growing army of Prince Edward was to the north, protecting the rest of the Severn. Simon knew that it would only be a matter of time before Edward, to his northeast, and Gilbert, to his southeast, would discontinue their defensive posture and would converge on Hereford to trap him between both armies. At this point, all the decisions were a matter of military logistics and Pauline was entirely reliant on Simon's judgment.

Simon's allies held Bristol, which is on the southern bank of the Severn estuary, where the river meets the channel. It was several miles beyond the county of Gloucestershire. Newport was across the water from Bristol, on the northern bank, also beyond the border of Gloucestershire. Simon hoped to preserve his army in whole and convey it back to the counties of southern England and to London, which were still loyal to him. He knew that if he could get to Newport, he could order Bristol to send vessels to convey his men across the channel to Bristol. He also decided that he would turn his back on Prince Edward's army and risk confrontation only with his former ally, Gilbert de Clare. So, they began their march south from Hereford. It was not an easy matter to conceal his travels. The army of Gilbert de Clare shadowed his movements, always staying within Gloucestershire to the east but moving south parallel to Simon's forces.

At Monmouth, on the western edge of Gloucestershire, the forces of the Earl of Gloucester attempted to engage Simon's army. Here they were to witness the distinguished valor and skill of the Earl of Leicester. Simon let the vanguard of opposition come forth from the town. Then he turned his army east to face them, while he personally led his knights and light cavalry around the north and into the town. He cut off a significant portion of the enemy and destroyed them, while the bulk of Gloucester's army withdrew. He then looted Monmouth for as many supplies as his men could find. They moved over hill and valley to arrive in Newport.

Pauline, Simon, and his forces boarded forty ships for Bristol. It was only five miles across the Bristol Channel. She could see the hills on the opposite shore. But they would not be able to see the town of Bristol until they had sailed out of Newport harbor and rounded the point at Goldcliff. Bristol was not directly across from Newport but was three or four miles east, up the southern shore of the channel toward Gloucester. They were almost halfway across to Bristol when they saw three boats rapidly approaching from directly ahead of them, from Gloucester. They were larger crafts with higher sides, and they were armed with archers. Simon ordered all the smaller transport vessels to come about and return to Newport. Several of the slower boats never returned to Newport and were destroyed.

Arriving in Newport, they were informed that the army of Gilbert de Clare was moving down the northwest shore of the Bristol Channel and would be at Newport within a couple of days. Simon decided he could defeat the Earl of Gloucester. But that would leave him with a diminished force, with which he might have to face Prince Edward's troops. His primary goal was still to preserve his numbers. He ordered his men to move back north to Hereford. He hoped there to find that the Welsh had raised more men and that his son Simon and the other allied lords would begin to arrive from the east. At that point, he could maneuver to place either Edward or Gilbert between this arriving army to their east and his men and the Welsh to their west.

It was a dispiriting march to have to return over the same road they had taken on a more hopeful journey. On the way down, they were participating in the bold stroke Simon had attempted in order to extract all his men. On the return, they were tired and worn down from the battle at Monmouth and the clash on the Bristol Channel. They arrived at Hereford, fatigued and hungry. Simon's army was running low on food and had not expected to have to make such an extended march. They sent out agents to buy bread in the surrounding

Welsh towns, only to discover that the Welsh did not know how to bake bread. The local tribal economies were not as productive as feudal England. There was not much hope of remaining in Hereford for long. Another way across the Severn had to be found.

In this the Welsh were helpful. They had spent generations slipping in and out of England and they devised a long route that would take them north of Edward's army and across the River Severn at a secluded ford. Tired and hungry but with renewed hope, Simon's forces marched north. They crossed the Severn again, having not seen any sign of Prince Edward's army. They moved directly east and found the valley of the River Avon, an eastern tributary of the Severn. They followed the river upstream. Pauline knew that Kenilworth, and home, was only forty miles upstream from the confluence of the Avon and the Severn. In the first day, they had moved ten miles upstream to the town of Evesham. It was there at their encampment at Evesham that Pauline saw Rocco arrive with Roger Bacon and some men from Leicestershire. Everything she had long been considering informed her that she should not be happy to see her old friend. Still, her heart leaped to have him with her again. But she had been initially correct. He and his delegation brought ill news.

They brought a report of the actions of Simon the Younger, who had been in command of the men from Dorset, Leicester, Sussex, and Somerset. He had departed from Pevensey, where he had been mounting his third unsuccessful siege, in late June. He headed west toward Cornwall and Wales. For some reason, he stopped at Winchester, drove out the royalist forces there and pillaged the town. Flush from this victory, he turned north to Kenilworth, rather than northwest toward Hereford. He gave his troops a reward for their victory by allowing them a leave in the village of Kenilworth. Tired from their marching, they relaxed and drank to celebrate their accomplishments. The next morning, the combined forces of Prince Edward and Gilbert de Clare attacked the unguarded village. They found the de Montfort men asleep and captured thirteen banners whose bearers were still in their beds. There had been no sentries. Edward and Gilbert de Clare took many horses and supplies. The men they did not kill either fled or were captured.

Simon the Younger heard the noise of the attack and went straight from his bed, mostly unclothed, to a small rowboat on the lake that comprised the massive moat around Kenilworth Castle. He shut himself up in the castle with the household and the limited force that had been kept there to guard the king's brother, Richard, and his son, Henry. Rather than mount a months-long siege of the castle, Edward and Gilbert wheeled around and returned to Worcester, on the Severn, where they intended to block Simon and the Welsh from crossing. This movement to Kenilworth had been why Simon and his men had been able to cross the Severn with no sign of Edward's army. But now there could be no doubt that Edward's scouts knew the location of Simon's army, only sixteen miles to their southeast. They would be there in a day and would be ready to fight on the following day. Simon knew that he could not make a dash to Kenilworth. His army would be cut down in the movement. He had little choice but to stand and fight.

Pauline went to him.

"You do know," she said, "that strategically you are more important than this army. If you were to escape to London and to the south, many of the allied lords and the people of the towns would rally to you. That would be the best chance for this cause to survive."

"When," he said, "have you ever known me to run?"

"I knew you were going to say that."

"You knew a lot of things all along. Now, I am certain you did. I realize that you decided not to speak about some of them lately. And I know why."

THIRTY-SEVEN

Roger Bacon and Rocco came to Pauline, and the priest was the first to speak.

"We are here to take you away," he said.

"I had assumed that is why Rocco came here," she said. "This is an extremely dangerous place. He has never failed to appear when I am in such a situation."

"You clearly know that Rocco long ago pledged himself to your protection, and he has always strived to defend you. Even though he has put up his sword, he is compelled to save you. You may not know that I am here because that too is my solemn pledge, made to Adam Marsh on his deathbed."

"I suppose that is why you took Rocco with you last year, so that you two may join forces."

"You are correct," he said, "as you usually are."

"But you must know that I will not go. I will not leave Simon."

"We know that," Rocco said.

"So, you plan to abduct me then, do you?"

"Only if we must," Rocco said.

"We have discussed this with the Earl of Leicester. He concurs with our plan. You will not remain here through the night," Roger Bacon said. "You should prepare to depart before dawn. And this is your opportunity to speak with the earl."

The priest did not say, "one last time," but Pauline heard that. She also knew that in her life there had been stops in time, moments so vivid that their memories were like paintings hanging in the gallery of her mind and heart. She could always bring herself to see them and be nourished by them in a way that was deeply spiritual. These stops in time were, for her, insights into the divine nature of the spirit itself. And in her life, they were all related to Simon, such as when she met him, when he saved her, when he first took her direction and decided to come to England, when she first felt the stirring of romantic love, and when they discussed their love as a matter of the spirit. Now, she knew she was in one of those moments that she would visit and revisit for many years to come. She knew they would each see this as their ritual farewell, the ceremony of ending a lifelong love. She felt a warm congestion in her chest. Her face was flush.

The camp of Simon's men and the Welsh contingent lay before her like a colorful pageant of all that was beautiful and exciting about this world, as well as all that was fierce and heartless. Men were preparing to go to battle amid the tents and horses and fires and flying colors, and, of all things, singing. She walked her way through the encampment with only one or two fleeting notions of trying to blend in with the men and staying for the fight, a thing she knew she could not accomplish with Rocco also in the camp. She approached the small manor on the edge of town that was Simon's room and headquarters. She saw him when she entered. He stood at the back of the room, looking at a hand-drawn map on a table.

He was still tall and fit and handsome. In his late fifties, he had a share of gray hair mixed with the dark brown he always had. There were some lines around his eyes and mouth. As his face had lost some of its tone, the bone structure that had always been there became more prominent. It made him more handsome in a worldly way, especially as it was also colored by the expression in his eyes and on his mouth, which managed to express wisdom, sadness, joy, intelligence, honor, and an inescapable sweetness all at the same time. He looked at Pauline and she could feel he was making much the same assessment about her look. Her own face had grown more handsome, and her tall and slender frame had maintained its sinewy and graceful strength. At three years younger than he, she had less gray and fewer lines. Many an eye that looked upon them at this time might have informed the viewer that they appeared to be brother and sister, both dark and tall, both strong-featured and of noble bearing, both having an intelligence that was evident in their appearance. In the look they shared, there was said far more than what could be put into words. Still, Pauline spoke.

"You know," she said, "that hair shirt you are wearing will not stop an arrow."

"What makes you certain I am still wearing it?"

"That was a nice attempt at a jest, Simon. We both know at this point you are probably wearing several hair shirts and some hair hose too."

"I am a Christian, which I believe is an answer to the first question you ever asked me. And I am a good Christian soldier. I am at all times penitent."

"Were the rest of the Christian world like you, we would not be in this mess."

"You are not to be in it, Pauline. Rocco and I have conspired against you again. You will be taken away."

"Maybe you could just turn me into a boy, as you did the first time," she said.

"We are well past that, I think. And I thought we have long since established that I prefer you as a woman."

At this, he sat down in the chair at the table. Some of the air had been taken out of him. His face had lost the resolute expression, and he looked at her intently.

"I have always been bold, and I think that has not always been a good thing. But there is a different kind of measured courage that arises from wisdom. What wisdom I may have acquired has in part been taught me by you. But I am wise enough now to recognize that the courageous thing would have been to have loved you all along, from the beginning, as a woman."

Pauline sat down across from him. She kept her eyes on his. The years had taught her a few things as well. She did not lose her upright bearing or her composure.

"The only foolish thing you have ever done, Simon," she said, "was to say what you just said now. It was the way you were then that made me love you. Had you been any different, I would not have been around for you to love. I would never have selected you. And had I been the kind of woman to want you and to take you and hold onto you like that, you would not have loved me as well and as long as you have."

"You are almost always correct, Pauline. Even at this very late point, you are even now teaching me. I suppose I was also foolish not to have known you well enough to know that what you were not saying to me in the last year and a half meant that you had something important to say to me but could not say it."

"I have never been reticent," she said.

"You were when it came to the matter of my sons. You never spoke a word against them. They have not lived up to my hopes for them, and that is what has caused this all to unravel. You love me too well to have spoken any word even remotely ill about my family. I should have known that your silence was speaking to me."

"You may be correct. I am not certain that I ever judged your sons. I do know that in these last two years, I have gained a measure of the same understanding that I was raised to have. Whatever it is that is all becoming unraveled is not all that important. It is of the world. You are not. You touch the spirits of other men by soaring over theirs. You always have and always will. For those reasons, your love is inviolable, especially your love for your family."

"When you say that my reward is not of this world, you know that we are facing a finality."

"Yes. Roger Bacon told me that Adam Marsh and the Bishop of Lincoln and he had all seen that you would become a martyr to the good of the people. I told him I could not see you as a martyr. I said that because I always thought I would step in to save you. But I realize now that they knew I would never speak against your sons, that in an important sense I would bring this day upon you even though I never intended it."

"You have brought all the other days, the grand days upon me as well. You gave me the first light, faith in the way of my own conscience. I have respect and reverence for the Church, but I no longer perceive it as the arbiter between myself and God. I have followed my own sense of what God wants, as is the way of your Cathar faith."

"Was the way, you mean."

"Your words still sting me, you know. The failure to fulfill my purpose wounds me too. This rebellion was meant to do as much good for the most people as possible, to establish a rule of law that is above even a king. It was meant to give more people a voice in how their kingdom was governed. It was meant to put an end to the evil of absolute rule by one man. It was not meant to fail."

"It will not have failed, no matter what happens," she said. "Men will not soon forget what you have done for them. You stood for the people of the Kingdom of England even against their king. The seeds you have planted will grow, and they will grow on English soil."

"It is my fondest hope that this is all true. I suppose I will never know for certain."

"Young Prince Edward has always looked up to you. He has the good sense of his mother, who has also known your worth. You may not have thought of this yet, but you have shown him the way. He is smart enough to know that what you have done cannot really be undone. The practical spirit of the English now will always rise to assert their rights and liberties. He is likely to know that the way to manage this is to do what you have done, to establish a standing parliament that has real power over the king. And he will know that once he brings the nobles and the clergy into a genuine role in government, he will buttress his power and he will legitimize it by sharing it because he will have their support."

Simon sat up now, and much of his color and vitality had returned. He sat thoughtfully for a while, but with a slight smile.

"Perhaps you are right. Maybe you are also correct, that I will find my reward not in this world but in the next one."

"Don't expect to find me there," Pauline said.

"I know. Your spirit will return here in the form of a hawk or a queen or a horse."

"When I was a horse one night, I lost my shoe right around here somewhere. I am sure if we look for it outside, we will find it."

"What?"

"It is an old Cathar saying. It is the story of a man who did just that. He and his friend found a horseshoe exactly where he said he had lost it in another life."

"You never told me that," he said.

"I never told you either that when your father died in the Siege of Toulouse, he was killed by a rock that was hurled by a trebuchet in that town, one that was operated by a crew comprised entirely of Cathar women."

"So, the women of your faith have long been destined to be the bane of de Montfort men."

"I prefer to think of it a little differently. We have long had the talent for straightening out the bad habits and ill-advised actions of the de Montfort men."

"That is one method to describe what you have been doing for forty years."

"I think I knew that when I was fifteen and I picked you to ask the question."

"And I picked you to save."

They sat for a while in silence. It had always been one of the things they could easily do and do comfortably. The time was approaching when they would part and there would never again be that calm and comfortable silence between them. The moment for their farewell was beginning to pass.

That is when Simon stood up. Pauline stood up instinctively. He started around the table. She did not wait, but walked toward him. They stopped before each other. Her face expressed so much in that moment. There was an incipient and repressed smile on her countenance that would never break out. Her eyes were wet, but she was not crying. They were lit by some strange dark light behind their brown surface. It was the last time he would see her; he knew. She looked at his face, which had always had a mild element to it, a calmness that resulted from his assurance of his place in the world. There was also his goodness, his strength, his intelligence. These were always evident. This time there was also something unsure and something a little painful.

Her eyes rested on his, only inches away, as his hand came up and touched her softly on the left side of the curve in her neck, his right thumb moved behind her ear and along her jawline, his fingers gently resting on the back of her neck. She reached her arms around him, putting her left hand on his shoulder and her right hand embracing his neck. His left arm came around her back. He held her close. She remembered the time they had come close to one another before. This felt more alive and more poignant. She was intensely aware of the depth of his passion for her at this moment. Simon's love and desire for her was unveiled and was reflected in Pauline's eyes. Feeling overwhelmed, she inhaled deeply and closed her eyelids. Simon delicately rested his lips on her left cheek. Time seemed to come to a stop for them when all they had felt but never expressed became suddenly present and real.

Pauline would not leave the moment at that. She was in touch with her passion. She knew the poignance of this moment. This man had been more than her love. He had been her life. She took his head in her hands, mingled her fingers with his hair, and kissed him deeply. He responded and returned her kiss and caress. Then he did something that brought her so many deep and powerful feelings that she almost swooned. He took one of her wrists in his hand and lifted it to his face. Then he gently kissed the spots on her forearms where the shadows of old scars barely remained visible, where the spikes of Guy Alain had entered her on the night Simon had saved her. He did the same with her other forearm. She knew that for this moment, they were creating a world in the space between their hearts that was the dream of all they might have been, entwined with what they had actually shared. It was a moment that spanned and changed their entire history together. She ran her hands over the strong form of this man that she had watched and loved for her entire life. She was young again. He was as well.

He was not wearing a hair shirt under the tunic as she wrapped her arms around him, placed her hands on his strong back and pulled him even closer. He was smiling at her while they kissed and tugged at each other's clothes and she knew it was because he was aware that her intimacy was as assertive, honest, and strong as she had always been in their conversations and in all the other ways they related to one another. Her eyes told him something as well, that this was no time or place for sadness or tears. It was their time, their moment, for love and for loving. She would take him as much as he would her. And though it was to be several moments, they did not rush. He had been her world and here and now his person would be hers. She marveled in every element of him.

Simon held her and loved her in a way that condensed all that he had ever felt for her over the years, that touched all those times and ways in which he had admired her strength, wisdom, loyalty, and honesty. Each ever more intimate minute was filled with all those other moments as if he was finding himself inside of Pauline, learning who and what it was they had always been for each other. There was no sorrow over past moments lost or those that would be lost. There was only the two of them loving in a very worldly and intimate manner that was more deeply spiritual than either could imagine. She enveloped him and he lived inside her in ways that could not have happened at another time. Their loving changed that past for them, in their hearts. They could not see all that they had been through since that day in Avignon without it now being painted with the colors of this moment, as if they had always been lovers. And always would be.

THIRTY-EIGHT

Roger Bacon, Rocco, Pauline, and the Leicestershire men rode east, into the roseate sky of dawn coming to the English Midlands. They had originally set out to the northeast, out of the valley of the River Severn and the Vale of Evesham, and had kept the ridge line of the Cotswold Edge to their right. Once they rounded the end of the ridge, they turned directly east toward Lincoln. It was beginning to be a warm fourth day in August of 1265. The pinks and purples of the sky before them began to yield to the brighter light of a rising sun. Everything was then lit by the indirect ambient light of a glowing sky that shone from the reflected light of a sun that was yet to rise above the horizon. The land was glowing and vibrant. And it was all some of the many shades of green. England had never seemed more beautiful to Pauline, nor lonelier. She knew what the rising sun meant to men facing one another in battle array.

Behind them, on the farm fields north of Evesham, inside a bend in the River Avon, Simon de Montfort looked out at the battle lines before him. He turned to his son Henry and told him it was clear that Prince Edward had learned his lesson from having battled their army before. Edward's force was tightly gathered in several groups, to give them discipline and flexibility. Beside Edward was the army of Gilbert de Clare, which appeared to be held back a little, perhaps as a reserve. He turned to Henry and spoke.

"I am proud of you, son."

Then Edward's men moved forward slowly. Simon's force remained calm, with the town and the river to their backs. They had seen many battles in the previous months and years and were not perturbed by the larger approaching force. The Welsh were held in his reserve. When they got close, Edward's men broke ranks and ran toward Simon's men shouting, "Death to the traitor!"

Simon had expected this might happen and had placed a cushion of men before his main line. This advance guard absorbed the first rush and fought a quick retreating action, backing right up to their main line. Then Simon turned to his men and shouted, "We are better soldiers than they! Our souls for God! And our bodies for battle!"

He led his men into Edward's line and began to beat them back. They scattered before his sword and he broke them and drove them ahead of him. In one moment, William de Valence was before him, and Simon cut him down like a weed. At that instant, the army of Gilbert de Clare rushed down the western side of the eastern stretch of the river and crashed into the flank of Simon's army. The Welsh did not hold but broke, and most fled into town and across the river. It had never been their fight and they saw little profit in facing a larger force on English soil.

Simon turned his remaining handful of soldiers to face the army of the Earl of Gloucester. Then Prince Edward's men ceased their flight. They returned to face the de Montfort men, who began to fight for their lives, surrounded now on all sides. Several noblemen fell, among them Henry, Simon's son. Simon was unhorsed and fought on the ground, while the number of men around him diminished. They fought to save their leader, but they were outnumbered.

Simon again displayed that he was not only a great military leader, but also a warrior of exceptional personal valor. His men fought more bravely for his example. He took a blow to his shield arm, so he tucked his wounded left arm into his belt and held the shield at his waist. As each of Simon's few men fell, they would fight to stand over him and protect him. It was a scene that Prince Edward's men would relate in song and in tale for many years. Soon, none of his men were left standing with Simon. There was blood and dirt on his face and his armor. He took another sword thrust, this time to his good right arm. That was it for him. The next blow was to his neck. He was mortally wounded and then he fell dead. To the dishonor of his foes, Simon's death did not stay the blows they rained upon his person.

One chronicler of the times wrote,

So died this illustrious man, Earl Simon de Montfort, who spent not only his property, but his life, to deliver the poor from oppression, to establish justice and liberty. He was well-instructed in letters; he rejoiced in the divine office; he was sober and kept watch at night. His words were measured, his face was austere. He attached great weight to the words of the clergy and showed a great respect toward priests. He was wholly devoted to blessed Robert, called Grosseteste, Bishop of Lincoln. The latter, it is said, commanded him to struggle and to die for the Church and for England. He foretold Simon de Montfort that peace would not be established by the sword, but that the crown of his martyrdom would recompense all who had died.

This same chronicler reported that immediately following the battle a number of English common folk made pilgrimages to Evesham and declared that miracles had happened to them over the spot where Simon de Montfort had fallen. There were many calls within and without the Church for him to be made a saint. And the English clergymen, who had long been favorable to him, especially in the middle and lower ranks, supported the call for the beatification of Simon de Montfort. These calls and claims were opposed by the Pope and by the reinstated Henry III.

King Henry had been hit in the leg by a stray arrow in the Battle of Evesham. He was wounded lightly and forgot it entirely when he was reunited with his son Edward, who was also his deliverer. Henry returned to the Tower of London and was immediately restored as king. He ruthlessly punished all who had opposed him. He repudiated all the Provisions of Oxford and Westminster. He sanctioned an act, known as the Dictum of Kenilworth, which formally reestablished all his absolute powers as king, which directed the Church to forbid that Simon de Montfort ever be considered a saint, and which directed the prosecution and fines for Henry's enemies.

Gilbert de Clare, the Earl of Gloucester, swore an oath to King Henry and began to help him to round up the opposition barons who had not been at Evesham when Simon was defeated. But the earl secretly allowed many of them to escape and he also encouraged them to continue their opposition. Before long, Gilbert de Clare had become the leader of the remaining barons who had complained of Henry's abuses and who advocated for a stronger parliament. It was a mere shadow of the opposition party that Simon de Montfort had formed and led.

Henry de Montfort died at Evesham. His younger brother Guy was wounded but was spared death. Their brother, Simon the Younger, shut himself in at Kenilworth, where he held on to his prisoners, Prince Henry and King Richard of Germany. He held out for a few months, until the end of the year, and then he surrendered and signed a truce. He immediately violated that truce, returned to Kenilworth, and held out for another few months before surrendering again. As part of that surrender, he was banished to the Continent. After his wounds had healed, Guy managed to escape and fled to France, where he joined his brother Simon. They variously pled with the King of France and others for the return of their lands and titles. They later moved to Italy and established themselves there. Several years later, their cousin, Prince Henry of Germany, son of Richard, was at a conclave in Italy, for the determination of who would become the next King of Sicily. When he was praying in a church in Viterbo, Guy and Simon killed him and dragged his body out of the church. The resulting outrage was swift and strong. They spent most of their remaining days in an ecclesiastical prison. Their brother, Amaury, Simon's third son, had been installed as a clergy member in York before the battle at Evesham. He was stripped of that position by King Henry and he moved to France to serve in a church there. He later left the clergy.

Lady Eleanor, Countess of Leicester, fled from Dover, from where Pauline had felt she might make a safe departure. She made her way to France and to the Convent of Saint Dominic, founded by Simon's older sister, Amicie de Joigny. It was where Pauline had suggested she go. Eleanor took her young daughter, Eleanor, and her youngest son, Richard, with her. From the convent, she tried to reestablish her rights to her title and lands in England. And she lived long enough to bear the pain of learning of her two sons' murder of their cousin. At one point, she had a plaque placed in the cemetery at Saint Dominic, denoting it as the burial place of her husband, Simon de Montfort. This also became a site where miracles were proclaimed in Simon's name. In fact, her husband's remains were mostly scattered, although it was believed that part of them were recovered and buried by monks at Evesham. No male de Montfort, neither Simon's sons nor their issue, survived the end of the century.

It was Prince Edward who learned the hard lessons of the time of Simon de Montfort's opposition and rule. Upon the return of King Henry to the throne, Prince Edward immediately took an active role in his father's kingship. He was committed to the principle that the same mistakes would not be made again. His father, King Henry, never really recovered from his humiliation during the protectorate of Simon de Montfort. And it was not lost on anyone that it was not he but his son Edward who had restored the monarchy. Edward ran much of the kingdom as crown prince. In 1267, two years after the Battle of Evesham, Edward forced his father to call a parliament and to enact the Statute of Marlborough, which for the first time set up laws for all England and for the king. It was the first such statute that the king would not later revoke or disavow.

Henry III died in 1272, seven years after the Battle of Evesham. Prince Edward became Edward I, King of England. Edward later declared a model parliament and established the beginnings of an actual constitutional monarchy, following the guidelines set by the great parliament of Simon de Montfort. It was a parliament not only of the nobles but also of the leading townsmen and representatives selected by the counties. Edward was an ambitious king, far more so than many of his predecessors, especially his father. He was dedicated to reforming royal administration and making it a more permanent structure, one subject to the active and meaningful participation of parliament. He restored the rule of English common law in the courts and restricted the arbitrary power of the king's representatives. He examined the tenure of various feudal liberties and codified the precedents of the common law into a series of statutes passed by parliament, creating criminal statutes and the law of property. If Simon de Montfort had been a man of the past, born in feudal France and transplanted to the England of the Great Charter, Edward was the man who recognized that the ideas of the Earl of Leicester belonged to the future. He had observed his father, the king, and had observed the Earl of Leicester. He knew it was from his uncle Simon that he had learned how a leader should comport himself.

Nor was it lost on the nobles and commoners of England that these reforms were the ones originally created temporarily by the Earl of Leicester. Simon de Montfort's powerful and enduring popularity in England was a significant factor in King Edward's decisions. He gained more authority by aligning himself with the image of his uncle.

The new power-sharing arrangement with the nobles, knights, burgesses, and other townsmen in parliament was also a far more effective method of governing than had ever been seen in England. The king faced some restrictions, but Edward had largely co-opted the nobles and leading citizens to his many causes. He did not forget the Welsh, not in how they had fought against England, nor how they had abandoned his uncle at Evesham. Parliament supported his first action against the Welsh, which failed. They also supported his second campaign, which was a full-scale invasion set on conquest. Edward was known as "Longshanks" by the Welsh, due to his height. He conquered Wales and subjected it to English rule. He built several castles in Wales and granted them to the English lords who had been most helpful to him in parliament.

The parliamentary form of government was now permanently established in England. It was the first monarchy in Europe or anywhere that was constrained by written law and by the established power of the nobles and other leading citizens among the commoners. Edward's power was now so consolidated that he turned his attention to Scotland. He was then also known as the "Hammer of the Scots". Edward had also become an experienced military leader, having learned that too from his uncle. Edward conquered Scotland. The essential result of Edward's use of Simon de Montfort's system was that England became more powerful. And even though the king was no longer in absolute control, his slightly limited power was now over a kingdom of united, cooperating lords and commoners.

✡ ✡ ✡

Three years after the battle at Evesham, the scene shifts to Piccotts End, just outside of St. Albans, on the edge of the forests of the Chiltern Hills. Here sits a series of several townhouses that appear separate on the outside but are connected on the inside as a hall. They house a group of families who live as a community. There is a class inside this row of houses, where a dozen students are happily learning their lesson for the day. Their teacher is a handsome, tall, slender woman in her fifties. She has a warm smile on her face as she addresses the class and as she speaks to each individual student. She is sitting on the floor among her students of many ages, from six years old to about sixteen. She is teaching them to read some basic English texts. Sometimes she teaches them a little French. She is tall for a woman, and her frame and face contain an elegant and aging beauty that is also strong and striking. Her hair is mostly gray.

Now she is reading to them from the Gospel of St. John. She is speaking to them of the spirit of Christ and of the spirits of men and women. She teaches them that the world in which they live is not perfect, but that God is perfect. She tells them then that they must find the spirit of God within their own hearts and that they must not live too much in the material world but must work to perfect themselves in their souls. She tells them that a spirit is neither male nor female and that all spirits are equal in the eyes of the Lord. Her way with them is gentle and loving and they respond to her. She is serene and set at a remove from the people and the world around her.

At a table at the side of the room sits an older man with white hair that is straight and lank. Most old men look alike to children, so they cannot see that he is from an exotic land thousands of miles to the east of England. He is cutting fruit and bread for them to eat. The teacher walks to the table and delicately places a hand on the old man's hand. He smiles, and she calls the children over to eat. At the table, she does not give them a lesson, but she speaks to them about the kingdom in which they live. She tells them some things about the recent unrest and a nobleman named Simon de Montfort, who fought and died for the rights and liberties of the English people.

When the lunch is over, the lessons resume. She explains to the students why they do not eat meat. The older children know some of the lessons and help the younger students. After the lessons of the afternoon, the children ask the teacher to pray for them. She begins to pray out loud. It is not so much a prayer as it is a ceremony. Each child is given a blessing before the teacher as she prays individually for them. As they are each given this form of blessing, they gather to one side. She has finished the last prayer for the last child. It is now the time for the students to ask some questions of their own choosing. They begin to question Pauline. She takes her time with each question and gives each child her best answer. And at all moments, she is very encouraging.

All her students are girls.

AUTHOR'S NOTE

The writer of historical fiction is generally entitled to certain liberties with the historical record. The trade-off is that the hopefully vibrant appeal of fiction will bring more minds to the actual history. I have inserted an entirely fictional heroine into this novel, and I feel it is justified by the way in which history has long overlooked strong women. We have little idea how many other women who, unlike Blanche of Castile, or Aethelflaed of Mercia, or Joan of Arc, were left out of historical accounts. I have sought to create and to highlight such a woman. But no amount of historical revision or fictionalization can whitewash Simon de Montfort's expulsion of the Jews from Leicester.

It may only be put in context, and from that I have made an informed conjecture and one I feel fits the narrative. At the beginning of the thirteenth century, Christian oppression of the Jews in England and Europe was growing ever worse. Pope Innocent III had proclaimed interest indebtedness to Jews a nullity and had placed all Jews in the hands of their sovereign. In every borough of England, Jews were the king's chattel. In 1218, the Archbishop of Canterbury required all Jews in England to wear an identifying oblong patch.

There were murderous anti-Semitic riots in London. And as has been the case in modern times, much of this persecution took the form of, and may have been motivated by, the appropriation of Jewish wealth. Perhaps no sovereign had been so proficient at this as King John, the father of Henry III. And in 1255, King Henry III pronounced the death sentence on all ninety-one of the Jews of Lincoln as a reprisal for the likely false allegation of witchcraft and murder against one of their number.

After the period in which this novel is set, King Edward ran up considerable debts subduing the principality of Wales and he also needed funds for his plans to conquer Scotland and to mount another crusade. In 1287, Edward had expelled all the Jews from his Duchy of Gascony and had profited from the confiscation of their property. The debts he owed in England were in part due to Jewish creditors and more largely to Italian bankers, who in turn may have borrowed much of their capital from Jewish lenders. It was in fact the rise of these Italian bankers at the time that in part gave many European rulers the room they needed to cut themselves off from Jewish financiers. In 1290, Edward issued the infamous Edict of Expulsion that ordered all of England's approximately two thousand Jews out of the kingdom. He took their wealth. This black mark on English history is darkened by the murder of an entire boatload of Jews bound for France, and the confiscation of their personal property.

I do not hold with the apologists for American slavery who say that the slavers were only acting within the prevailing moral framework of their time. The abolitionists of the American north and those in England, as well as some American southerners, knew slavery was wrong. The slaves certainly knew it. Though this particular time is deeper into history, and the medieval ethos was driven by utter fealty to the Church, there were still those who opposed the persecution and expulsion of the Jews, and so did the Jewish men and women of England. My reading of the *Iliad* and of the Bible and of countless other ancient texts tells me that the human heart always was and is the human heart. What is wrong now was wrong eight hundred years ago.

Simon de Montfort must be condemned for expelling all of Leicester's few dozen Jews from the town. There is no way around it.

There is some context that I believe allows for my fictional account that he did so not so much from the malignant action of an evil heart but as an expedience that he may have felt was required. There is evidence that he was granted the earldom in an exchange in which the expulsion of the Jews from Leicester was not negotiable. That grant gave him the title and control of the town and only half of the outlying areas. The other half went to his two aunts. Leicester's Jewish community was moved just outside the town walls to this part of the shire not under his control, where the Earl of Leicester permitted them to continue their business. Considering what happened before, what was to happen later, and what was happening in other parts of England at the time, this expulsion does not seem as entirely final in its evil character.

Simon de Montfort's actions are also cast in a darker light than might be true by two extraneous facts. The first is that he was exceptionally prominent in this period. Much was written about him. Even a cursory glance at the history will reveal that this includes his fearful pronouncement that the expulsion was for the good of his soul and that of his ancestors, and that the expulsion would continue to the end of the world. This seems an excessively strong statement to accompany moving the community just outside the walls of Leicester and permitting them to continue to do business. It gives the statement the appearance of being political in nature and in motivation. The second extraneous fact is that the story of Simon de Montfort has been left thus far almost entirely to the English, while I believe we Americans can see him differently and perhaps more truly.

I am reminded of one summer day when I drove around Runnymede, asking the locals where the monument was for the signing of Magna Carta. Most of these lovely folks had not heard of the document and did not know it was of local significance as well. After having been kindly directed several times to the location of the nearby dog show, I found the modest monument sitting humbly in the back of a field, without any signs directing one to it. It had not been erected by the English government nor by any English entity at all, but by the American Bar Association. It seems that the American legal establishment clearly venerates this early-thirteenth-century document as the first, and an extraordinary, expression of human, civil, and individual rights and freedoms that stand above the divine right of kings. It is at the core of our American belief system, elevating the rule of law above any individual, even a monarch. The English seem not to equally venerate it, although it is also at the core of what makes England different from the continent of Europe. I believe that this Atlantic-sized gap in the appreciation for that document is because England still has a monarch, and America has never really cared for one.

The entirely English accounts of Simon de Montfort gloss over what an American sees first and most. He stood up for his fellow barons and for England itself against a tyrannical and capricious king who governed the kingdom as if it were a small family business. Simon de Montfort painstakingly developed the beginnings of the world's first constitution, the Provisions of Oxford and Westminster. He called for the first true parliament and he did not comprise it of lords alone but also included commoners who were burghers or knights or merchants, all of whom were elected. His Provisions established legal principles that were based on rights and duties and were removed from the caprices of the local magistrates and nobles. That he did all this in the middle of the thirteenth century, to the American eye gives him the appearance of being the first post-classical proponent of a democratic republic, and a great hero.

Almost every English account does not see the republican democrat for the dog show that is the traditional British reverence for the monarchy, a sentiment as inexplicable to me as it is to other Americans. The Simon de Montfort I read in the English histories jumps off the pages at me as the most remarkable individual of his century. Almost every one of his legal and governmental reforms was later adopted by his nephew, King Edward, who gets credit for the model parliament and the court reforms. Simon de Montfort was not even English and not a first son and had no title. His singular rise through English society cannot have been on ambition alone, nor was ambition the source of the honors conferred on him by the French and the Kingdom of Jerusalem. Ambitious men are a dime a dozen, particularly in the courts of the English kings. Usurpers were not uncommon in English history either. A purely ambitious man in Simon de Montfort's place would have seized the throne. For that matter, he had two separate blood lines that connected to the English throne.

There must have been something special about the 6th Earl of Leicester, something that even Henry III saw in him when he initially embraced Simon. The French royal court recognized his virtue enough to offer him the regency, as did the Kingdom of Jerusalem. King Henry's widowed sister had sworn a vow of chastity, and she fell in love with the Earl of Leicester. The majority of the other English barons, important and ambitious men in their own right, rallied to the relative newcomer, Simon de Montfort. Robert Grosseteste, Adam Marsh, and several other leaders of the clergy thought most highly of him. Many of the English historical accounts I have read ascribe this to ambition. After all, only an ambitious man would challenge the precious monarchy. The earl's ambition almost goes without saying. But the cavalcade of equally ambitious men and women who admired him, followed him, and loved him seem to indicate a different quality. Simply stated, Simon de Montfort had to have been a good man. I then tend to think that his instincts toward a democratic republic, to my American eyes, spring from that goodness.

ACKNOWLEDGMENTS

My mother, the late Angelina Patricia Blandino Weaver, had forever encouraged me and supported my every effort. She told me from the beginning that I should never shirk from attempting anything. She also had "her story", which like that of so many other remarkable women, has been overshadowed by the history of the man or men in her life, who are merely equally remarkable, at best. My wife, Lily Chu, is the foundation of my life and my work. My son, Simon, is not fully aware that I always write with him in mind. His sister, Harriet, never overtly rejects being repeatedly told the same thing.

Substantial gratitude also goes to this book's best friend, most loyal supporter, initial editor, partial inspiration, and the only first reader I have ever had for any one of my novels. Sheri Lynn Rape is my third cousin, once removed, and we have only met online. But she has read, edited, and commented upon every paragraph of this novel. She has been tireless, loyal, engaged, and nothing short of brilliant.

My friend, John Bond, is funny, wise, helpful, insightful, accommodating, experienced, determined, humbly brilliant, a tousled genius, and indispensable to my writing. To George Edgeller and to Julia Koppitz, his assistants, I owe the same thanks, in only slightly smaller portion. No one has taught me more about deep reading than the late Harold Bloom; I am happy to have been a student and feel blessed to have been a friend. Another teacher, Gordon Lish taught me more about how to approach writing than I will ever be able to remember. I cannot say enough about Susan Leon, the best editor I have ever had. Her grasp of history, narrative, and dialog is perfect for an historical novel. I also owe a debt of contribution and characterization and encouragement to a group of friends who include Carol Fenelon, Rosemary Harris, Rocco Chu, Tom Cassone, Carrie Hatland, Louis Bayard, Eliza Paolucci, Penny McCann, and the inestimable Jonathan Levi. I would be remiss not to single out my dear friend of many years, Polly Draper, who haunts these pages in ways perhaps only we who know her recognize.

The historians to whom I owe an impossible debt are almost too numerous to mention. I list some of them here and I hope that this fictional narrative is at least partly as exciting as the historical accounts they have written about the Cathar faith, the Albigensian Crusade, the histories of England and of France and their sovereigns—Henry III of England and Louis IX of France—and of course the history of the utterly remarkable, heroic, and modern-seeming Simon de Montfort, 6th Earl of Leicester and, for a while, the leader of a proto-democratic Medieval England. These historians include Charles Bémont, J.R. Maddicott, William Holden Hutton, C.H. Knowles, Margaret Wade Labarge, Andrew Phillip Smith, the irrepressible Otto Rahn, and Jonathan Sumption.